# Duology of Postal

FIRST CLASS EDITION

DUOLOGY OF POSTAL
FIRST CLASS EDITION



**Category:** Fiction
**Edition:** Fourth
**Specifications:** Hardcover
**ISBN Number:** 978-0-9856990-7-9
**Date of Publication:** 6/10/2022
**Cover Design by** Charlton "CP the Artist" Palmer

# Duology of Postal

FIRST CLASS EDITION

PETER MCNEIL

# SOMETHING UNSETTLING IS TAKING PLACE AT MIDWAY POSTAL STATION...

With high expectations from her father weighing heavily on her back, the privileged Cadina Wilson enters the postal system as a new employee only to be confronted with immediate drama from her coworkers and management, such as...

...the self-destructing alcoholic Freeman Souls, who must decide to either stay in a troublesome relationship with his fiancée, or start a new and exciting venture with the gorgeous, yet mysterious, Velour Patterns...

…the arrogant Lexington VanGuard and his power-tripping tendencies as he relishes the opportunity to become a career supervisor...

…newly appointed Assistant Manager Denise Tucker, who finds herself being brutally challenged by her manipulative boss, the charming Michael Davenport...

…the devoted father, James Richards, who desperately seeks custody of his daughter Janae while falling in love all at once...

…And it won't be long before Cadina's path takes an unexpected turn when she is plunged inside everyone's unstable world. But when a bitter employee makes a startling discovery, all hell really begins to break loose…

"The language and the characters of *Postal* are not only believable, but they have roots. Therefore, they earn a spot in the readers' hearts. Here, the reader will discover that the *seemingly simple* average American working class is both complex and significant.

*Gladys E. Perez-Bashier,*
*Publisher and Co-Founder of*
*Clique Calm Books,*
*Author of Creepin' Through the Hinge*

"The author's depiction of the melting pot of postal employees was very accurate. He gave another perception of the postal service; a more humanistic side versus us as just 'keepers of the mail'. I thoroughly enjoyed reading it."

*Barbara Parker Reid,*
*U.S.P.S. Window Clerk*

"An extremely entertaining story threaded with life lessons that any person, postal-employed or not, can relate to. I was very impressed...GREAT JOB!"

*Yvonne Mullins, U.S.P.S.*
*Customer Service Manager*

To our Creator, I give thanks for the gift instilled in me to share with the world. An angel was sent to me in the form of my wife, Pamela Smith-McNeil. I thank God every day for her immeasurable love, friendship, never-ending support, words of wisdom, sincere criticism, being the mother and educator of our children, and her culinary skills! (Love ya, honey!) To my children, Justin, Jordan, and Milahn, who have always taken interest in what I was accomplishing and for being my motivation factors, as well; I love y'all. To my mother, Lucille McNeil, thank you for adopting me and my brother Kevin, love you, and may you both rest in peace. My sister Mary-Lee Wright, thank you so much for being that positive nurturer. To the rest of my family, in-laws, and friends, thanks for all the support and encouragement (So many of you, I had to break it down like that!)

Now, for the Dream Team that made it all possible….

Editor Denise Spiller, for recommending that I switch my project from a screenplay to the page-turner it has become. I'm forever grateful for that suggestion. My editors for the book, Gladys

"Poppi" Perez-Bashier, Sandra Kendall, and my wife Pam, thank you for providing my novel the necessary polish it needed. Charlton "CP the Artist" Palmer, thank you for blessing me with eye-popping, attention-grabbing book covers and business logos, I'm forever grateful. To my personal book critics, Yvonne Mullins, Barbara Parker-Reid, and Tashia "Flossie Mae" Smith, for giving me the constructive feedback I needed to ensure the subject matters that I've tackled were properly represented.

Last, but not least, Morgan Postal Processing Station in Midtown Manhattan, Cooper Postal Station in Lower Eastside Manhattan, and Hell Gate Post Office in East Harlem; you were the catalyst for my decision to become a writer. My postal experience provided me the platform to not only give the reader insight into the postal environment but also life experiences and I sincerely thank you.

This was definitely a labor of love and commitment. Hope you will enjoy it.

Pete McNeil

# Dedication

*To the dedicated, hard-working, and colorful postal employees all over the world…*
*I salute you.*

# JANUARY 2016

# WINTER'S HARVEST

# ONE

## VELOUR PATTERNS

Davenport clears his throat and in a booming voice says, "Good morning, ladies and gentlemen of Midway. I don't want to take up too much of your time…we have a lot of mail on the way to our station, so I'll make this as brief as I can. But first, I want to commend you all for last week's performance. The mail volume was exceptionally high and all of you really came through like the professionals that you are. I even tip my hat off to the ones who are not on the overtime list. You really made a difference, especially when our station's roster is short-staffed. Thank you for a job well done."

Letter Carrier Velour Patterns listens while she analyzes Michael Davenport, Midway Station's influential manager. With his shiny dark bald head, charismatic eyes, and pearly-white teeth, Davenport's overwhelming charm cannot be denied. Yet, every employee in the building can see right through those super-tight smiles and exaggerated laughs. He loves the power he has and does not short himself when it comes to using it. The only thing that is as big as his oversized ego is his massive, towering physique, which today, is underneath a dark blue pinstripe suit. This adds to his intimidating stature. Not one person has questioned him regarding his handling of the station's very few inadequate carriers. He has even shown supervisors a thing or two about how to take control of their designated sections, while at the same time, demeaning them right in front of employees, during the process. About the only one who has come close to challenging his aggressive nature is his assistant, Denise Tucker, who vehemently disapproves of his bullying tactics most times. Afterward, she usually backs down and walks away, saving her critical opinions until they are behind closed doors. No one else, however, must be reminded of who oversees Midway Postal Station.

Velour smirks at the manager.

*He wishes he was the only charmer in the building.*

She glances around the postal congregation with eyes probing in search of her primary target.

*Hmmm, he must be still out on the road.*

Instead, her eyes land upon the primary target's nosy little sister, Divine Souls, who is busy thumbing on her cell phone. Probably texting her brother about the morning meeting. Divine loves her brother dearly; it is well known throughout the workplace.

*I would love for your brother to fuck the shit out of me, but that's none of your business, little girl.*

As if she was reading Velour's mind, Divine's head pops up and their eyes connect.

Velour seductively crosses her legs and smiles at the little brat.

Divine shoots her a dark look before resuming to her phone.

Velour snickers to herself and turns her attention back to the manager.

"Now, some of you may have already read about this in the news, but for those who haven't, a letter carrier across town was caught trashing mail inside dumpsters on his temporary assignment over a five-day span last month. A customer recorded the carrier in the act and notified the Postmaster." Davenport pauses to allow his staff to digest that last statement. "This has become a disturbing trend in the past two years. Now, the Inspecting General is taking profound measures to make sure these senseless acts don't become an epidemic. That employee is now charged with Obstruction of Correspondence, which is a federal offense, and will possibly face two years in prison. He may pay fines, as well. The Postal Service will no longer tolerate any displays of reckless behavior that damages the code of ethics which all of you dedicated individuals work extremely hard to preserve."

Divine raises her hand.

"Yes, Divine…"

"Was the carrier a new employee?"

"Yes, he was, and his actions have prompted the Postal Academy to be more critical in their selection of candidates. They're also providing additional training and reinforcing our code of conduct policy."

Velour raises her hand.

Davenport points to Velour. "Yes…"

"Not to switch subjects, but what is being done about the carrier shortage around here? Especially since the other two new hires quit last month. It's getting ridiculous."

"Well, that was to be my concluding discussion. As it so happens, we have a new sub arriving first thing in the morning."

"Just one?"

"You have to crawl before you walk, my dear."

"But that's our problem; we've been crawling for like a whole year now, it's time to take the baton and start running!"

The audience laughs.

Most of the male employees overdo it just because it's her.

Velour smiles, knowing she is the only person in the station that can steal the spotlight from the manager with no effort at all. From the corner of her eye, she catches Divine rolling her eyes.

"We will, I promise you." smiles Davenport. "And she will be assigned to your section, so I expect all of you to be of great support to her. She'll need it. Now, are there any more questions? No? Alright. Everyone, have a safe and pleasant delivery. And again, thank you for last week's effort. It's greatly appreciated."

Carriers snatch up their stools and head back to their assigned sections, privately bickering to themselves or among other carriers about the meeting's topics.

Velour picks up her stool and strolls toward her workstation. A couple of male coworkers vie for her attention. She calmly waves at them as if she was a reigning beauty pageant winner. They eagerly wave back. She gets a kick out of their thirsty expressions.

Velour takes a deep breath as she surveys the mountain of mail that she and her route partner, Dante, have to case up today on their business route. Twenty buckets of magazines, large envelopes, and packages, as well as fifteen letter trays. And more mail is on the way. Most of the bulk mail was left behind yesterday due to her feeling under the weather and leaving to go home early. Dante, on the other hand, was very outspoken about her decision.

*Fuck him, he'll be alright.*

Velour grabs a handful of letters and begins casing. While sorting, one piece of mail catches her eye–an envelope addressed to one of her customers, Ms. Havana Blunt, a wealthy widow who enjoys an international vacation every chance she gets.

She presses her fingers all around the envelope.

Feels like a credit card.

*Hmmm.*

She discreetly glances around her area.

Everyone is tending to their own business.

She purposely drops the envelope on the floor. Next to her feet is her personal shoulder bag, which is already opened. She quickly scans her surroundings before she bends down, scoops up the envelope, and then drops it into the opened bag. She then pushes the bag to the side with her foot.

Again, she looks around to see if anyone is watching.

No one is paying her any attention.

But someone catches *her* eye.

He just arrived on the work floor, taking off his postal jacket, and headed toward her with a small brown bag–probably the oatmeal he said he was going to buy her.

He smiles.

She blushes.

*I wonder if he smiles at his fiancée the same way he smiles at me.*

DIVINE'S TEXT MESSAGE – ***DID YOU FORGET ABOUT THE MANDATORY MEETING? WHERE YOU AT?***

He pockets his phone and quickly screws the cap back on his silver liquor flask. He downs an Aquafina water bottle, followed by four peppermints. He cups his mouth and breathes. *Satisfied.* Finally, he cranks the postal truck and motors down Lafayette Street.

Letter Carrier Freeman Souls could get used to driving the postal truck for the rest of his career. He loves the position so much that he is seriously considering putting his bid in for the truck assignment he is temporarily assigned to. But in his gut, he knows he has a better chance of winning the state's lottery than getting selected over the other bidders who have way more seniority than he. In fact, those same bidding letter carriers, who he often catches peeking in and around his truck, always find the time to go out of their way to inquire about the truck's setup.

*"Freeman! Uh, how long does it take for you to do the early drops? Hey, Freeman! How do you deliver to buildings that usually receive large sums of mail, but no service elevators and only one small passenger elevator? Yo, Free! Did the customers tip you well this past Christmas?"*

These are all the questions he has been hearing for the past month and he will continue to hear those kinds of inquiries until one of those eager carriers is selected for the truck permanently. His sweet, but temporary, assignment is ending real soon and when that fateful day arrives, he is going to be placed right back in his assigned section as a reluctant foot soldier, bouncing from route to route, sometimes cleaning up other letter carriers' messes, and often staying out to deliver mail until the sun settles and the moon pops up. And if that does not irk his nerves, there is always the potential threat of getting transferred to another station. That is what they do to unassigned letter carriers who have been appointed regular status after serving two years as a Part-Time Flexible Substitute, a PTFS, or a sub for short.

The very thought makes him cringe.

It so happens that he does not envision himself going anywhere, anytime soon. The Brooklyn-born-but-now-Bronx-residing letter carrier has feverishly grown fond of the Lower East Side Village area in downtown Manhattan where the station is located. The area is rich with so much ethnic culture and media background, he wonders why he never frequented this section of Manhattan before. From the NYU dormitories which houses students from all walks of life to the swarms of celebrities, who constantly roam the village to tie deals and dine in the finest restaurants –the place is a twenty-four-hour global networking magnet. And on any given day or night, you might find a film crew shooting a scene for a big-budget movie. No, he would not trade this scenery for the world.

And it does not end there. The solid relationships he has built over the past two years at Midway Postal Station, he can't picture duplicating anywhere else. Even the station's manager, Davenport, is making it his business to persuade him into taking the supervisor's exam and joining his elite managerial staff. Freeman, as usual, laughs it off and keeps it moving.

His assistant manager, Tucker, adores him as well. However, lately, she has been constantly reminding him about his recent work performance and attendance, which in her eyes, have both been substandard at best.

Although he is fond of his assistant manager's motherly approach, he does not need another mother figure in his life. The woman who birthed him thirty-three years ago succumbed to a hit and run late last year and the pain of that tragedy is as fresh as if he'd just received the phone call of her death only minutes ago. What he needs is to be on this temporary driving assignment so he can grieve by his lonesome. He also revamped his Hennessy indulgence, which was conquered a few years back when he started going back to his family church. Unfortunately, right after his mother's funeral, the Henny started creeping back into his life, and church became a distant afterthought. No, he does not need another mother figure lecturing him. He would love to have his old one back.

His cell phone vibrates as he approaches a red light.

He knows exactly who it is, but he reads the name on the screen, anyway.

His fiancée, Lovelle…just as he thought.

The light turns green, he lifts his foot from the brake and allows the voicemail to receive the message. At the next light, he decides to listen:

*"Hey, baby, it's me. Hope you're having a beautiful morning. Give me a call when you have a moment, I want to go over with you the guestlist for our wedding and I also want to-"*

He erases the voicemail and places the phone back on his hip.

He parks the truck on the corner of East Seventeenth Street and hops out to empty the final collection box. The ice-cold January temperature does not hamper his responsibility as he opens the blue box with his arrow key and rakes the overflowing mail into his large mailbag.

A gloved finger taps him on his shoulder.

He spins around defensively, causing the startled woman to take a cautious step back.

"I'm sorry, I didn't mean to appear aggressive," he says.

"Nooo, that's quite alright," smiles the briefcase-toting lady. "I'm the one who should be apologizing for sneaking up on you the way I did."

"Oh, no apology necessary."

He awkwardly gawks over the attractive sista, stylishly dressed in winter corporate wear. He softens his stance.

Corporate Lady sticks out her gloved hand, which holds a couple of letters. "Could you make sure my bills make it to their destination on time? I wouldn't want to hunt you down because they charged me a late fee."

Her smiling eyes are as direct as her come on.

He fights hard not to give in.

"Can't have that, right?" he replies. "But you have yourself a beautiful day, Mrs.—" He quickly reads the letters. "Thompson."

"That's *Miss* Thompson," she states while holding onto his hand. "And you do the same."

Corporate Lady winks, turns around, and then struts her assets around the corner.

He shakes off the vibe and regains his composure.

*Hell, I'ma put my bid in for this truck assignment anyway—later for them.*

He nods in response to his thoughts, slams the mailbox shut, leaps inside his truck, dumps the mail inside the tub with all the other mail, and motors back to Midway Station.

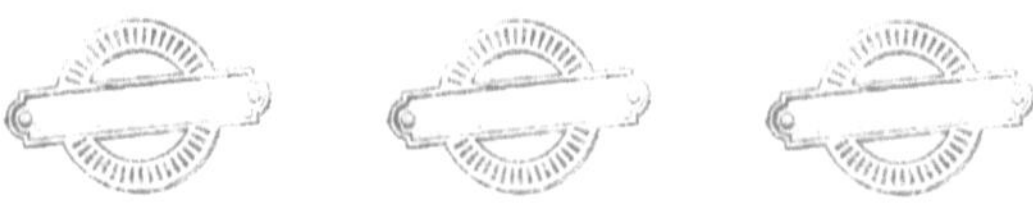

FREEMAN BACKS THE TRUCK UP AGAINST THE LOADING DOCK AND unloads two rolling tubs of collection mail onto the platform. One of the mail-handlers greets Freeman, takes the tubs, and pushes them right up against the other tubs of mail near the brick wall. He grabs a small brown bag, locks the truck, and walks inside the station.

Entering Sterling's office, he hands over his collection box scanner to the truck supervisor/computer specialist who quickly snatches it and returns to punching away at his computer keyboard. The white-frazzle-haired supervisor appears bothered by something.

"Everything alright?"

Sterling downloads Freeman's scanner information into the computer. "You would think after sixteen years, I wouldn't still be correcting others' mistakes."

Freeman cops a squat in a nearby folding chair. "Uh-oh. Who let you down this time?"

"Our boss caused quite a stir with the senior carriers' vacation bids. Now, I have the displeasure of going back into the system to undo what he's done. Word of warning, Freeman; you can forget about the Fourth of July week."

"I'm not worried about that. I'll take whatever I can get."

Sterling stops typing. He raises his droopy eyes to look at him. "That's a first. When a sub turns to regular status, they usually start demanding the most sought-after vacation slots. Should I be concerned about your mental health?"

Freeman smiles. He then peeks at the computer screen. "How do I look?"

Sterling reads the data from Freeman's scanner and points to the screen. "You forgot to scan this box, see, right here…"

Frowning, Freeman moves in closer to the computer. "Where?"

"Your last box, East Seventeenth Street. Are you sure your mind wasn't pre-occupied?"

"I don't think so," Freeman lies, thinking about the sexy corporate lady. "Damn, I hate going back out there during rush hour."

Sterling chuckles. "Don't worry about it now. You have an emergency meeting to attend upstairs.

Freeman reaches for his scanner. "I bet I know what it's pertaining to."

Sterling leans over his stack of manuals to grab the Daily Newspaper. The front-page headline reads: MAILMAN DUMPING MAIL!

"It's starting to be a trend all over the country," Sterling says, flipping through the paper to find the article.

"I bet. Later." Freeman rises from the chair and leaves the office.

"Don't forget to scan the box after the meeting!" is all he hears from the truck supervisor.

"I WON'T!"

Freeman races up the staircase, taking two steps at a time. He arrives on the "carrier work floor" and glances around at the scene in front of him. Carriers returning to their workstations, mail-handlers dispersing mail, and managers talking to supervisors.

*Damn. Missed another meeting.*

Freeman sighs while peeling out of his postal jacket. He makes his way toward Section C when he sees Velour, who is bending down in front of her workstation. His mood brightens immediately.

When she stands, she glances his way.

Their eyes intertwine.

He feels as though he is walking in slow motion. This drop-dead gorgeous woman, with a blond flip hairdo and tight, mouth-watering light-skinned voluptuous figure, sticks her tongue out at him like a bratty schoolgirl. He mimics her actions.

He walks up to her and reaches the small brown bag towards her.

"You may have to heat the oatmeal up," he says. "I bought it before I started my collection run, so-"

"It's alright," she says, placing the bag to the side. "I plan on eating it on break, anyway. But thank you so much."

"I'ma holla at my sis, I'll be right back."

"Okay."

His body fails to obey his plan. Her Dentyne smile has him captivated.

"Uh, see you in a minute."

Velour laughs. "You know where I'll be."

He breaks out of his trance and walks over to Divine's workstation, tosses his jacket over a bucket of Sports Illustrated magazines, and plops down on her stool. He watches as Divine cases the letters at a steady pace and then surveys her mail for the day. Fifteen full letter trays and fifteen buckets of oversized envelopes, magazines, and third-class bulk mail combined. He remembers a year ago when he was stuck on this dreadfully long route. *Hated it!* He does not miss it for the world. But now, his little sister suffers the same agony, day in and day out. She is in for an exceptionally long day.

Divine side-eyes him as she sorts the mail. "And yet, he somehow manages to miss another mandatory meeting."

"I got tied up in traffic during my collection run, what you want me to do-"

"Same excuse, all the time."

"What did I miss?"

She reaches to the side to snatch the Daily Newspaper. She points to the headline, MAILMAN DUMPING MAIL!

"Yeah, I read about that earlier."

"This makes us look more like fools by the day." She resumes casing the mail. "I don't understand why it's so difficult to just bring the mail back to the station and quit if you can't handle the job. That's all they gotta do! Makes no sense at all."

Even though she can be a pain in the ass, Freeman has always admired his little sister. A lot of their mother's values are instilled in her, which makes her a wise old owl at the tender age of twenty-five. She also has their mother's mouth, which, at times, is a force to be reckoned with. But other than that, he applauds her rock-hard fortitude, especially when it comes to her dedication to church. Although this job may require her to work ten to twelve-hour days, six days a week, she still manages to make it to Wednesday night bible study and Saturday night choir rehearsal. On Sunday, her only day off during her probation period, she spends the entire day with her church family in the Lord's house. That is dedication to a fault. She's stuck on a dismal route that nobody in their right mind would bid on, yet she makes the necessary adjustments to do it all.

"I see you settling into your regular status rather well," Divine says. "What's it been, three weeks already?"

"Something like that. And I'm an *unassigned* regular. So, I still can't get too comfortable around here."

"Seems like you're already cozy in your position if you ask me." Her words take on a more scornful tone now. "You come and go as you please. I don't get to talk to you like I want to, especially since you don't come to church anymore–"

"Is there a point to be made out of all of this?"

She pauses sorting and glares at him. "Yes, it is. I want to know why you stopped coming out to check on me during my heavy delivery days?"

"Huh?"

"You heard me…you know this route requires auxiliary assistance almost every single day, and today will be no different–"

"What are you talking about? Chapman sends people out left and right to make sure you're not out there all night-"

"But that wouldn't have stopped you before." Divine resumes sorting the mail. "You're so worried about Miss Thang over there that you forgot all about your sister."

Finally, it is out in the open.

He cannot deny the fact that Miss Thang, a.k.a. Velour Patterns, has taken precedence over Divine in the past couple of months. A once reserved carrier who didn't have two words to say to him when he first arrived at the station, all of a sudden, has opened up and become quite attentive to him, especially after his mother's passing. The relationship has matured to the point where the entire station is declaring the two an item. Freeman does not mind the gossip. He welcomes a refreshing presence in his turbulent life.

And justifying his every move with his kid sister is becoming a rather dull task.

"Oh, now I see where this is leading."

"That is a two-man route over there, Freeman. She and Dante are supposed to help each other, but they choose not to. And just because she says "hi" to you and wiggle her big behind all in your face, you're supposed to feel obligated to race over and help her? She doesn't even need it!"

"Here we go…"

"Well, it's true."

"What is it you got against Velour, anyway?"

She rolls her eyes but says nothing as she stuffs letters into the route-case.

"Oh, cat got your tongue now, huh? Has it ever occurred to you that maybe Velour is cool people? And you'd know that if you ever decide to get off your high horse and have a conversation with her."

"Oh, okay. But keep in mind you're engaged to one of my closest friends, alright? And why are you always up in Velour's face, anyway? What's that all about?"

"Mind your business, alright?"

"Yeah, whatever."

"FREEMAN!" Davenport yells from the supervisor's podium. "A MOMENT OF YOUR TIME, PLEASE."

"See!" Divine quips. "You should've made it to the meeting this morning-"

"Shut up."

Freeman leaves his sister's workstation but then stops short.

He discreetly turns around and cups his mouth to check his breath.

Good to go.

He walks over to the podium where Davenport is waiting.

The tall manager smiles and shakes Freeman's hand. "My *main* man…"

"Sorry I couldn't make it back to the meeting. Traffic was a beast out there."

Davenport waves him off. "Don't worry about that, son. I need a favor from you."

"Sure. What's up?"

"We're getting a new employee tomorrow and I want you to train her on the truck assignment. She needs to learn everything; collections, early drop-offs, relays–and fast. Can I count on you?"

"I gotcha covered."

Davenport beams with pride. "My man. Now, what's this I hear about you becoming a supervisor?"

Confusion drapes Freeman's expression. "And who told you that?"

"I did."

Freeman turns around and frowns at Letter Carrier Lexington VanGuard. The dark-skinned, bald head, ass-kissing protégé of Davenport struts right up to their conversation, decked out in a dark blue pinstripe suit, mimicking the station manager's appearance to the tee.

Lexington grins at Freeman. "I told Mr. Davenport you were thinking about applying for the next supervisor exam. Need I say it brought a smile to his face."

"Sure did," Davenport adds.

"The thought did cross my mind, but that was the extent of it," Freeman explains to Davenport while keeping his eyes on Lexington. "I have no intentions of becoming a supervisor. I'm good where I'm at."

Lexington's eyes darken for a split second before he re-establishes his shit-eating grin. "Well, I guess I misunderstood you, Freeman."

"It wouldn't be the first time."

"That's too bad," Davenport says, in good spirits. "But if you ever reconsider, my door is always open for mentorship. Lexington can attest to that, right, son?"

"Don't overlook this opportunity, Freeman."

Freeman's glare is his only response to the bald nitwit.

Davenport checks his watch. "And on that note, I have a meeting to attend uptown. Freeman, thanks again for your commitment for tomorrow."

Davenport slips on his gray wool coat, dons his black Indiana Jones Stetson hat, grabs his briefcase, and commandingly marches down the work floor.

Lexington beams with pride as he stares at the manager disappearing through the stairwell. That beam-with-pride smile evaporates when he faces Freeman. "Do you even have a clue on what you're passing up, bruh?"

Freeman often wonders if giving Lexington a supervisor title would prove to be a good thing in the long run. Sure, he might pass the exam easily and he could impress the board members, but it disturbs him that a person like Lex would receive that kind of authority when he is already cursed with raw arrogance which flows through his veins like dope. He has a nasty tendency of cutting people off mid-sentence; and when he speaks to someone, it is always with an annoying, superior attitude. He tries to give Lexington the benefit of the doubt, but it is difficult to reach deep inside of a person's soul, like Lexington, and bring out the good because he, in essence, doesn't really have anything positive to say about anybody, other than himself–and Davenport, of course. And Freeman knows better than to think that Lexington sincerely appreciates their friendship, but the Lord does say to "Love Thy Neighbor."

The Lord is asking for a lot.

Freeman keeps an even tone. "I want to know when I appointed you to become my spokesperson, Lex-?"

"Never mind that," Lexington snaps, cutting Freeman off. "We're talking straight leveling up, dude–fuck this letter carrier shit, ain't nothing prestigious about that position! Unless you're afraid of what people may think of you crossing over to management…is that the case?"

"That's none of your concern."

Lexington shakes his head. "Here I am thinking we're on the same trajectory with our careers because we started out together, but now I see you're no different than the rest of these cats around here–"

"And *maybe* we're not cut from the same cloth, Lex. You're already power-tripping and you're not even a supervisor yet!"

He could tell that struck a chord with Lexington. The idiot's jaws clenched.

"In three months, they're having another supervisor's exam." He leans in closer to Freeman's face. "Do yourself a favor and get with the program because this is not you…*capisce*? Now, if you'll excuse me, I have to change."

A displeased Lexington turns around and heads toward the stairwell.

Hurrying past Lexington and speed-walking straight to Freeman is Velour's route partner, Dante Maxwell, carrying a bucket of mail. He's not displaying a positive disposition at all.

"You need to talk to your girl, Free," Dante seethes, passing Freeman without breaking a stride.

*Here we go.*

Freeman follows the disgruntled coworker to his workstation.

Dante also passes by Velour without saying a word. He drops the bucket of mail to the ground and then grabs a bundle of Time magazines to sort. While angrily flinging each magazine into its designated slot, Dante turns to Freeman. "She's gonna need your assistance, you already know this. *Look* at all this shit. I'm not lifting one finger to help her out-"

"We can handle it, Freeman." She shoots Dante a dirty look. "I don't know why he's tripping; he knew I was under the weather yesterday-"

"Because we should've dealt with all of this bulk mail yesterday instead of leaving it for today, that's why!" Dante snatches up another bundle of magazines to sort. "Now Daphne is gonna wind up taking our boys to football practice *again* because I'll be two hours late getting home. This is bullshit and you know it!"

"Well, that sounds like a personal problem to me."

Dante whips his head around to face Freeman. He motions with his hands as if to say, *you see the shit I have to put up with, right?*

The intercom blares out Freeman's name. "FREEMAN SOULS, IF YOU'RE STILL IN THE BUILDING, REPORT TO MY OFFICE WITH YOUR SCANNER. THANK YOU."

Freeman says, "Well, that's my cue."

"Thanks for my oatmeal."

"No problem. Call me if you need anything while I'm out."

"I will-"

"I wanna holla at you after work, Playboy, so don't leave," Dante blatantly interrupts.

"Gotcha."

Velour rolls her eyes at Dante before turning back to Freeman.

She displays a sweet-tasting smile that sends his hormones straight to orbit.

"Catch you later."

"Okay."

Again, Freeman pries himself from her bedroom eyes to double-time it toward the stairwell.

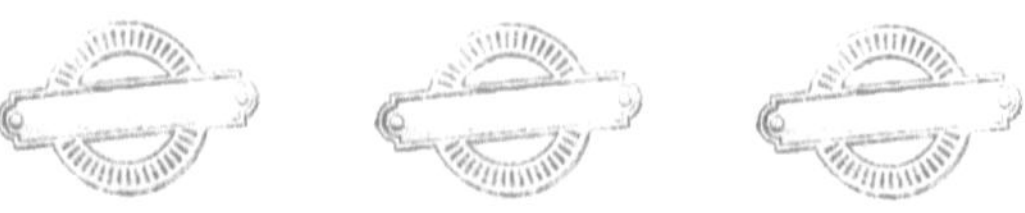

FREEMAN MUST HAVE CHECKED HIS SEATBELT A DOZEN TIMES TO MAKE sure it was secure because the way Dante is barreling down First Avenue, one would think he was competing in a NASCAR event. But you cannot steal a man's joy when his every wish has finally been granted. Still, he would love nothing more than to read his friend's approved bid notification without being jolted uncontrollably on the ride.

"See, this is the reason why my mother's gone; because of this shit right here," Freeman blares out. "Slow it down a little–"

"My bad, dawg." Dante slows his Nissan Armada down to eighty. "What's it been, three months? I can't imagine what you and Dee's been going through, but y'all seem to be holding up pretty well-"

"We're managing, alright? Don't get it twisted." Freeman finally focuses on the form. "So next Saturday is it, huh?"

"Yes! And I'll be officially out of that god-damn station!" Dante shouts in glee while beating on the steering wheel. "I swear, Free, this couldn't have come at a better time—trust me when I say that!"

Freeman glances over at his overjoyed coworker who is bobbing his head to Johnny Gill's *Rub You The Right Way*. Never can he recall in his two-year tenure seeing this low-fade haircut wearing, Bronx native this animated nor this loud. The proud father of two boys and a committed husband of eleven years to his sweetheart, Daphne, tends to successfully keep his private life away from everybody at the station. Even when he occasionally hangs out with the crew, except for laughing at each passing joke that would fly by, Dante never has too much to say about anything.

Lately, the only time anyone would know that he even has a pulse is when he and Velour get into their epic battles, and aside from those, at times, getting really ugly, he would make some of the funniest remarks anyone has ever heard. It is a shame nobody from Midway will ever catch a glimpse of his true personality. Freeman, on the other hand, gets a front-row seat to Dante's hidden dramatic side, as they converse about his sudden departure.

Freeman hands him back the form. "But you never mentioned parcel post before."

Dante mashes his horn at a slow-walking teenager giving him the finger.

"THE FUCK OUT THE WAY THEN, STUPID!" Dante calms back down. "I put in for it like a year ago, but I didn't want to make a big deal about it, you know what I mean? Folks always wanna stay in your business. *Uh, why you wanna go over there?* Cuz I want to, that's why! Nosy bastards!"

Freeman silently gasps at every turn Dante barely makes. "Got tired of the letter carrier role, huh?"

"Man, you just don't know. I'ma tell ya…it had gotten to the point where I was really thinking about quitting the whole system. Just up and leave and never look back!"

Freeman wonders if the whole Velour ordeal influenced his friend to consider that option. "For real?"

"For real, yo. But now since I have THIS!" Dante holds up his notification form like the Statue of Liberty holds her torch. "I know I'll be alright from here on out. I love driving trucks, man. You're basically your own boss. You don't have anyone all up in your grill every minute of the day, asking you stupid shit. You don't have to depend on anybody but you. You feel me?"

*It's Velour.*

"I understand that, trust me. I feel that most of us, well the guys anyway, would take a truck position over pushing that cart any day."

"True dat." A sly grin appears on Dante's face. "But now that I have THIS!" He shows Freeman the form again. "My departure will allow a certain someone to take my spot on the route, making that girl the happiest person in Midway."

Freeman chuckles. "So, we got jokes now…"

"What she be saying about me, bruh? Y'all be having them long-ass lunch dates not for her to mention about the goings-on of our route. What's up?"

"C'mon man, you know how you two are."

"I know, but I want to hear her version of it."

Knowing that Dante is going to keep pressing the issue, Freeman says, "A'ight, let me put it to you like this; she knows y'all weren't meant to be paired up. Aside from that, she did say you're a hard-working individual and a cool guy deep down." Freeman pauses for a moment. "…but you're also pigheaded."

Dante almost sideswiped a parked bus from laughing so hard.

Freeman grips the seat's armrest in fright.

"*Pigheaded*?" Dante shrieks. "Aww, man…that's okay, though. All I know is when they post that position up for bid next week, you will be the perfect partner for Velour."

"Well, actually, I was thinking about putting in for the truck assignment I'm on now—"

"Shiiiiiiit." Dante cracks up. "My man; you are not getting that truck assignment, you can forget that! Ain't it up for bid right now?"

"Yeah, and I put my name down, Jordan signed up and if I'm not mistaken, Jose must've put his name on the list today—"

"And Jose is going to get it because he has more seniority than you and Jordan put together, you know that."

"Yeah, I guess," Freeman mumbles, in partial defeat. "But I was kind of hoping-"

"You better *hope* your ass is on my route before they ship you to another station! And I know you don't want to go anywhere else, especially since ole girl would be missing the hell out of your ass! She digs you, bruh, I mean *really* digs you! That's all I hear her talk about when she's on her phone yapping to her cousin. *Freeman this, Freeman that.* And don't get me wrong, she's the bomb-diggy, but I don't need to tell you that, right? You better put in for my route, Playa."

Freeman vaguely hears the last part. He is still replaying, "*…she really digs you…*" inside his head.

"I'll give it some thought."

"What is there to think about? You've been on my route, you know how sweet it is—nice, clean buildings with doormen who take all the parcels and sign for all the valuable mail…big-ass mailboxes in ninety-five percent of my buildings. I've updated the names in all the mailboxes. My route book is up to date–what more do you want?"

"I know I don't want to be transferred, that's for sure." Freeman adjusts himself in the seat. "I kind of like the atmosphere at Midway."

"Well, then you know what you have to do." Dante merges onto the free-flowing FDR Drive Highway. "And you know homegirl is going to do her best to recruit you, so that's icing on the cake."

Freeman blushes while gazing out the window.

"Did you hit it yet?"

Freeman snaps his head back around. "What?"

"You heard me!" Dante smirks. "I SAID, DID YOU HIT THAT YET?"

"What is up with everybody?" Freeman tries to conceal his smile. "Velour and I are just cool peeps! What, I can't be friends with a fellow coworker?"

"First of all, she's not a fellow, let's be clear on that! Like you haven't noticed all that meat she's packing in her uniform pants?"

"Now, I didn't say I was blind, either…"

"You better act like you know! Shoot, you could hook a train up to her caboose and be like, ALL ABOARD! CHOO-CHOOOOO! YOU KNOW WHAT I'M SAYING? She got a big ole badunk-a-dunk!"

Freeman laughs. "You stupid, man…"

"You know I speaks the truth! And she's waiting for you, my brother…what you gonna do? CHOO-CHOOOOO! RIDE THAT PONY! THAT'S WHAT YOU'RE GONNA DO!"

They laugh hysterically while cruising down the frigid FDR Drive, en route to the boogie-down Bronx.

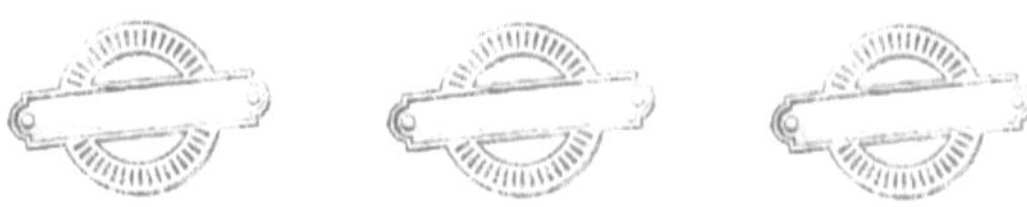

FREEMAN STEPS INSIDE OF HIS CO-OP APARTMENT AND HEADS STRAIGHT to the kitchen to place his groceries on the counter. He kicks off his work boots to avoid tracking any dirty ice into his carpeted living room area. After peeling off the rest of his uniform, leaving only his tank top and boxers on, he closes his eyes and then cocks his head back. He stands idle for a moment to allow his six-foot-one, semi-muscular, dark-complexioned frame to soak in all the welcoming heat that is simmering inside his domain; a meditating ritual he does every day, regardless of the season.

He then slides on his flip-flops and returns to the kitchen to retrieve the smaller brown bag he brought in along with the groceries. From the bag, he pulls out a pint of E&J (the liquor store did not have his Hennessy for some reason) and twists off the cap to take a quick swig.

*Ahhhhh.*

Lastly, he grabs another small greasy bag with the shrimp rolls and drags his tired body into his living room.

Before collapsing on his sofa, he presses the button on his answering machine to hear two messages he received. The first message brings a smile to his face.

It's from his pops.

*"Hey, Freeman. It's me. Just calling to see how you're making out. I'd kind of made a big dinner by accident; some baked chicken, with cabbage and rice, smothered in gravy—your favorite. You can stop by and help me and your sister woof it down if you haven't eaten yet. Give me a call back."*

Freeman stops smiling when the second message plays.

*"Hey baby it's me, um, I guess you're not at home, gimme a call as soon as you get home. I called you earlier this morning and left a message on your voice—"*

Freeman erases the message before he can hear the end of it.

Stretched on his couch, he takes bites of his dinner and heavy gulps of his liquid comforter. He fondly remembers how Lovelle would come in and decorate his apartment to her liking, adding a different, yet unique signature of her in each room. That was four months ago when feminine aromas such as perfume, hairspray, and potpourri reigned dominant. After she packed up and left, the manly and undesirable odors of feet, Lysol, Chinese food, and liquor mixtures quickly returned and settled in. He often wonders what he could have done differently to have avoided such a nasty falling out with the woman that he's been involved with for a little over ten years. And this shift in the relationship occurred a week after his mom's sudden death.

When it rains, it definitely pours.

The first thing he must do at this point is to stop being evasive with Lovelle because she is now obsessed with planning a wedding within the year—something which he feels is not going to happen. The "let's-work-it-out" plan is not working out at all; at least not on his end, and the relationship is feeling like more of a chore at this rate. He had better clear things up real soon because it won't be long before he invites Velour over to his place for some *milk-n-cookies,* and that would not be fair to either one of them. Then, as far as the job, there is the possibility of getting shipped to another station if he does not put his bid in for something permanent at Midway.

*Just too many decisions at one time.*

He takes a long swig of his drink, then another, and another, allowing the creamy contents to calmly guide him to a deep state of abyss until morning.

Lorraine rushes inside the house and quickly shuts the door to block the evening's treacherous winds which are forcibly trying to follow her inside. Dropping her bags on a nearby bench, she examines her frigid face in the bronze sunflower adorned mirror as she pulls off her full-length chocolate mink coat. After fluffing out the curly ends of her long mane, she snatches off her brown high heels, wearily advances into her living room area, and plonks down onto her plush leather couch to let out a long sigh of relief. She immediately grabs her foot to massage.

*I'm getting too old for this vain crap.*

But when the mother of two beautiful young women is constantly mistaken for their older sister, vanity gets engrained in her, after a while. If anything, she wishes she still had their stamina, as this January will mark fourteen years for her as a real estate broker, and physically it is beginning to take its toll. Her feet have taken such a beating in the heels that she chooses to wear when she is showcasing properties to her clients. At this point, however, she needs to invest in a pair of comfortable walking shoes—*fashionable* walking shoes, of course.

The delightful aroma of a home-cooked meal invades her nostrils. Now she no longer needs to order out like she initially planned because, as usual, Cadina has saved the day.

"YOU GOT THE HOUSE SMELLING GOOD, CADDY!" she yells toward the kitchen.

"HEY, MA!" a tired voice responds.

Lorraine forces herself up from the couch, returns to the foyer, grabs one of the bags, and sashays into the kitchen where her youngest daughter is holding a skillet of cornbread with an oven mitt. "What do I smell up in here, girl?"

Cadina places the pan on the stovetop. "I made barbeque turkey wings with honey garlic ginger, collard greens, yams, and of course, the cornbread. Something quick…gotta big day ahead of me tomorrow."

That statement echoes through Lorraine's head like church bells. She pours herself some apple juice and then leans against the island to watch her daughter as she fixes her plate.

Sipping on her juice, Lorraine recalls the earlier period of her life when she began prepping her, then teenage girls, to be able to know their way around the kitchen. While her oldest daughter, Camille, stuck to the very basics and became a highly regarded hair salon owner, (*My man loves my hair, not my meatloaf!* she would laugh.), Cadina grew quite fond of 'banging the pots and pans'. Over the course of time, she raised her newfound skills to newer, exciting heights by enrolling in the world-renowned Institute of Culinary Education and receiving her associate degree in Culinary Arts. To this day, she still cuts out recipes from the back of Ebony and Essence magazines to add to her culinary repertoire. Whoever spoke about food had Cadina's attention, hands down.

But unfortunately, her attention span fell short in other areas, such as holding down steady employment. Over the span of six years, she has had a total of nine jobs that she just couldn't hold onto. Three of those jobs did lay her off, but five of them she left because of lack of interest. The last one she had, did not even last a month because they fired her. That shocked everybody because not only did her father's friend hook her up with the position; it was in a popular soul food restaurant located in Harlem which provided her the opportunity to utilize her skills as a cook. Cadina never told anybody why they let her go. However, the head chef/owner told Lorraine that he had an argument with Cadina over food preparation.

She wanted to do things *her* way.

Several warnings later, the owner released her. That dismissal did not sit well with Lorraine nor her husband–at all. Now she has been given, what her father calls, one last chance. Maybe things will turn out better this time. Who knows? Then again, maybe Cadina will find a way to toss this job to the curb like all the others. Lorraine hopes not because her husband had to pull some major strings to get her a position at the post office. *Major* strings. And if Cadina ever finds it in her mind to deliberately insult her daddy again by following her free-spirited mindset, she may as well leave town.

Cadina hands her the steaming plate of piping-hot edibles.

"Thanks."

"You're quite welcome." Cadina grabs herself a seat at the dinner table. "How was work?"

Lorraine sits down and quickly blesses her food before replying, "Child, just long. Had this one couple who had the nerve to catch an attitude with one of my agents, simply because she refused to show them a two-bedroom apartment…but they have *nine* kids and another on the way."

Cadina chuckles. "You're lying…"

"I tried telling her that these landlords are not going for that. So, she got offended and they stormed out of my office. Like I said—long day."

"Shoot, the struggle is definitely real," Cadina says, letting out a yawn. "The way rent is skyrocketing in this city, it's literally impossible to live comfortably unless you *and* your other half both have two good jobs-"

"*Ohhh.*" Lorraine injects. "So, this means you're going to act like you *need* this job your father went out of his way to secure for you, right?"

Cadina darts her half-sleepy eyes at her mother. "Noooo, I'm not planning on botching up this gig, Ma. I know this is a career opportunity and I've thanked him numerous times, so I don't see why you feel the need to go there-"

"Because I *can*, that's why. Don't act like we don't know how you operate." Lorraine takes another sip before positioning her body to face her daughter. "First, you quit the banking position last year. *I* hired you, but you weren't feeling the real estate industry, so you left that, but then you get released from a place we thought for sure was right up your alley-"

"Look, I know I messed up big time at the restaurant; Dad grills me every chance he gets, so the last thing I need is for you to co-sign his guilt trip, please? Not tonight?"

Lorraine reads the pleading in her daughter's eyes and decides to let it rest for the time being. She then reaches alongside her seat for the bag that she brought into the kitchen and hands it to her daughter.

Cadina gives her mother a suspicious smile as she pulls the shoebox from the bag and opens the box top. She pulls out a pair of black Reebok Cross-Trainers and then tries to conceal her obvious appreciation.

"Maaa, now you know you didn't have to," she squeals, with one foot already in a boot.

"And that was the last pair they had." Lorraine chuckles at the fact that she's the reason her daughters are spoiled to the core. "Consider it a token of my love."

The phone rings.

With both boots on, Cadina jumps up, gives her mother a fat "thank you" kiss on her forehead, and then reads the caller ID before pressing the talk button on the handset. "Hey, Daddy...Nothing much, just admiring my first-day-on-the-job gift mommy bought for me…Some boots." Looking at her mother, Cadina asks, "He wants to know if they're postal-regulated?"

"Yes, they are," she replies between munches. "Where's he?"

"She said, *yes*. Where are you now? Okay, I'll tell her. Love you more, bye." She hangs up. "He's on his way home."

"Are you going to crash here tonight?"

"Yes, I bought my things. Wish me luck tomorrow."

Lorraine cocks her eye at her slim, yet curvaceous, brown-skinned daughter with the long, jet-black ponytail. With a straight face, she says, "Honey, I usually do a lot more than just wish."

Cadina grants her mother a fake smile before walking out of the kitchen.

Lorraine returns to her meal, all the while saying a prayer to herself on Cadina's behalf.

And for her and her husband's sanity.

# FOUR

## CADINA WILSON

After a soothing shower, Cadina tiptoes into her bedroom to finish drying off her damp body. She then sits at the bottom of the bed, and as she lotions her legs, she glances around her room which is filled with timeless memoirs of a well-rounded, if not privileged past–Portraits of her from different periods of her life hug the walls with quiet reflection, right along with posters of her favorite musical artists: the Force MD's, Stephanie Mills, Earth, Wind & Fire, and LL Cool J. Collectible items from various New York exhibitions are neatly displayed on each dresser and nightstand, highlighted by her favorite piece, the steel metal replica of the Empire State Building, which reaches a good two feet in height. Autographed photos of BellBivDevoe and other Summer Jam headliners are either framed or tucked firmly in each corner of her vanity mirror, reminding her of the days when she and Camille used to run rampant to every concert that came within the tri-state area. There wasn't a wasted opportunity in a household where parents provided infinite possibilities of enjoyment and fulfillment. Each day was an event, the next day was greater than the last and the summers were adventures all by themselves. As long as she and her sister kept grades of A's and B's, their childhood expeditions would never be shortchanged.

But just like Miss Jackson would sing:

*Funny…How… Time…. Flies…….*

The more she drifts down memory lane, the angrier she becomes at herself. Placing the cap on the lotion, she pauses in frustration. While her big sister continues to make a name for herself in the salon industry, Cadina still has the nerve to be running around like an irresponsible groupie. Living in a self-absorbed bubble for so long, she has unintentionally managed to make a mockery of the very people that she loves and respects the most. That whole restaurant disaster was the straw that damn near broke her daddy's back. Never in her entire life had she seen him so angry. And with good reason. He felt it was a slap in the face for all that he tries to do for her.

Still, he somehow managed to find her employment within the postal system. Now, that's either unconditional love from her father, or he is on a hell-bent mission to turn her into an independent woman.

Her phone rings.

It is Camille.

Cadina answers the phone and places it on speaker while slipping into her pajamas. "Whazzuuup…"

"Whazzuuup!" her sister greets. "Just calling to check up on ya."

"I'm good. Still at your shop?"

"Girl, yeah. Trying to finish up on my last customer so I can close up, but she ain't trying to go home!" Camille lets out a hearty laugh through the phone. "Ready for your big day tomorrow?"

Cadina lay across her bed on her stomach. "I guess. Nervous, though."

"You'll be fine."

"Daddy threatened to disown me if I screwed this one up."

"After what you did at that restaurant, I don't blame him one bit."

"*What?*"

"Look, we understand that you graduated with a culinary degree, okay? But who on God's green earth told you it was a good idea to create your own appetizers behind the owner's back? It was not your place to make those decisions."

"Wow. And all this time, I thought you were my ride-or-die sis-"

"I am, but sometimes you have to swallow your pride and own up to your mistakes, Boo."

Cadina rolls her eyes, but then a thought crosses her mind. "You think I'm cut out for this postal gig?"

"As long as you deliver mail to the right address…I mean, besides that, how hard can the job be?"

Cadina ponders. "I know, right? Thanks, Cam."

"Get some rest and call me tomorrow. Love you."

"Love you more."

Cadina turns off her phone and plugs it into the wall charger. She walks over to her vanity mirror and pulls out a picture–a photo of her with her daddy, taken by her mother at graduation. She is proudly displaying her culinary degree. The smile that her father displays is filled with pride. As she studies her father's face, with its hints of Cherokee blending in with strong African American features, it's as if she can hear him lecturing her through the six-year-old pic:

*Playtime is over, baby girl—time to grow the hell up!*

Another yawn escapes her as she returns the picture and climbs into bed.

Determined not to disappoint her parents again, she says her prayers and makes the promise to the Almighty Himself, as the soft seduction of the Sandman's whisper lure her closer to a world better known as a brand-new day.

# FIVE

## THE CREW

"Ahhhh, yeah. That's that Rick James shit right there..."

Cycle Floater Letter Carrier Louis Rodriguez nods his head as the classic *Cold-Blooded* instrumental beat from his boom-box slices through the quiet morning that blankets Midway Postal Station's loading dock area. With eyes closed behind his black-rimmed glasses, one can sense that the cocky Puerto Rican from Bedford-Stuyvesant, Brooklyn is about to go into full concert mode.

Forced to witness this b-boy routine are drivers and crewmembers Roy, Neville, and Shabbazz, whose purpose at this very moment is to constructively critique Lou's untested rhyming skills before he shares them with the entire hip hop world. A dream he has been longing to do for many years but has now decided to put into action.

The Latino lyricist opens his eyes wide and begins his performance...

*"Lou is what? Sexy, Sexy, Sexy Sexy...*
*But he's known to be, COLD—BLOOOOOOODED!*

*The industry is over-flooded,*
*Infatuated with cats with mumble raps,*
*The Psycho Floata, Party Promota coulda told ya,*
*I didn't come to throw bricks, son, I rip boulders,*
*I can't help but to spit fire that reaches full throttle,*
*Ricocheting through your heart from shots that's primed hollow,*
*Never lacking in confidence, I cherish my own bravado,*
*Trust me when I say I'ma hard act to follow,"*

"—Excuse me—"

*"Cuz Lou is what? Sexy sexy sexy.... Baby girl come test me,*
*Fulfilled her kinky needs with this potent Latin breed,*
*Papi Chullo has juice flowing from his floppy seed,*
*I'ma thief in the night, you might consider it a felony,*
*A midnight marauder while your broad is taking care of me,"*

"—Uh, excuse me?—"

*"Bitch keeps telling me, I pack more than Ron Jeremy,*
*She brought her flock over and we created group therapy,*
*But the stimulation factor doesn't happen in my chapter,*
*I want them hoes that can freak it just by hanging from the rafters—"*

"EXCUSE MEEEEEE!"

"WHAT THE FUCK, MAN!"

A ticked-off Lou turns around to see who has the audacity to cut his cipher short. The lanky Latino turns off his radio and joins the rest of the crew as they silently gawk over the person who has just walked up the loading dock's ramp.

Standing in front of them holding a folder and wearing a black leather jacket over a red hoodie, black jeans, a pair of Reebok Cross-Trainers, black earmuffs, and a nervous smile is a beautiful sista who stops waving at them now that she has caught their attention.

"Oh, sorry to bother y'all," she says. "...but is there another way inside your building? The front entrance is locked."

"We don't open 'til eight, Ma," quips Lou. "Come back in a half-hour."

"No, see, um, I'm supposed to meet up with Mrs. Tucker, I think she's the assistant manager. I'm Cadina Wilson."

Roy, the muscular Albino, bumps past Lou to speak to the new arrival. "You're the new sub, right? Forgive us, we didn't know. Welcome aboard. My name is Roy. This is Big Country right here…"

"A.K.A. Neville, at your service," The squatty driver greets, shaking her hand.

"My man, Shabbazz…"

The dreadlocked driver shakes Cadina's hand. "Pleasure meeting you."

Lou greets Cadina with a straight face. "They call me Lou, Da Psycho Floata, Rip-A-Party Promota—holla at your boy."

"Oh, uh, okay." Cadina politely grins at Lou.

"Don't pay him no mind." Roy points through the glass door. "Look, you go through this door, then the other door and walk all the way down towards the back and the manager's office will be on the right, she should be in there."

Cadina repeats the directions to herself. "Okay, thanks a lot. Nice to meet y'all."

"Likewise," they chant in unison.

The crew watches her walk through the main employee entrance before running over to the door to catch another glimpse of the new ponytailed employee as she makes her way down the corridor. When she enters the manager's office, they turn to each other with delighted approval.

"Now *that's* whuzzup!" Neville confirms, smelling the perfume Cadina left on his hand.

"Oh, no doubt," Roy agrees. "*And* she has a mean bow-legged walk, too? *Whew…*"

Shabbazz grabs his hand truck and states, "Fifty bucks says she won't make it past probation."

"Damn, son, she just got here!" Roy twists his face at the dreadlocked driver. "How you gonna say some evil shit like that?"

"You saw the way she was holding her folder…like she was cuddling a teddy bear. I just don't see it in her-"

"Hell, *your* ass almost didn't pass probation, you forgot about that?"

"Yeah, because they put me on that bullshit route that Dee is on right now," countered Shabbazz, locking his hand truck inside the cargo area of his postal truck and closing the door. "I was coming back to the station damn near every night-"

"Yo, fuck all that! I wasn't finished spittin'!" Lou stares at his comrades like they lost their minds. "So, what's up? Y'all feeling my joint or what?"

Neville and Shabbazz zip up their parkas and board their trucks, leaving Roy to become the unlikely spokesman. "Yo, we'll talk later, a'ight?"

Roy turns around, jumps off the dock's ledge, and then hops in his truck.

Still standing in the same spot, Lou shouts at his boys through revved-up truck engines and exhaustion. "A'IGHT! THAT'S HOW Y'ALL GONNA BE? COOL! IT'S ALL GOOD, BABY! WE'RE GONNA BE DOING A WHOLE LOTTA TALKING—"

But his tantrum goes unheard as, one by one, the three trucks roar out of the loading dock area and down the street in clouds of smoke to start the morning collections.

Alone in his funk, the aspiring rapper gathers himself, grabs his boom-box, yells out to no one in particular, "NEVER LACKING IN CONFIDENCE, BABY! Damn, it's colder than a mufu out here…", and runs into the station to start casing his route for the day's delivery.

# SIX

## CADINA

Cadina makes a right as told by one of the drivers. She sees an office with the door ajar and light conversation spilling out.

*Must be this one…*

Entering the office, she spots a lady behind a desk talking on the phone. Judging by the lady's tone, it sounds more like a personal call.

Cadina pulls off her ear-muffs and quietly takes in the award-heavy room, where achievements the station has garnered over the years hang honorably on the four walls that surround her. Her eyes land upon an oil-painted portrait of the manager-in-charge. A bald, dark-skinned man in a dark-blue suit sitting proudly behind his desk with his hands clasped together and the American flag flanked behind him. What captures her attention is the man's eyes; so self-assured, so confident, so commanding—

*So intimidating.*

The lady holds up a finger to motion that she is about to wrap up her conversation. "No? Well, look behind the microwave...See, now the next time you won't fling your keys on the counter with so much force as you did last night…Another long day, probably…

Alright, talk to you later, love you, bye." The lady hangs up the phone and then shakes her head with a smile. "Why my perfectionist of a husband struggles to find his keys every morning is beyond me."

Cadina flashes a new-to-the-job smile.

The assistant manager rises, showing her 'WNBA-type' height while her autumn-colored, cable-sized dreads rest against her long, lean back. She extends her hand to Cadina.

"I'm Mrs. Denise Tucker, the assistant manager of Midway station. You must be Cadina Wilson, right?"

Cadina winces at the unexpected strength the skinny lady possesses. "Yes, I am."

"Welcome aboard—now follow me, please."

Before Cadina can say anything, the tall manager grabs a couple of manila envelopes that were on the desk and power-walks out of the office. Cadina plays catch-up along the way.

"The first thing we must do is get you squared away on the truck."

Cadina suddenly stops. "Y-You putting me behind the wheel already?"

Tucker spins around, causing her beige buttoned-down jacket and matching skirt to flow like a matador's cape. "Well, not exactly. One of my drivers is going to train you on various assignments. It's vital you learn the truck position as soon as possible because that will be one of your duties for a while, in addition to actually delivering the mail, okay?"

Cadina deadpans, "I guess."

Tucker laughs. "Child, you'll be fine. And you'll be in good hands with Freeman Souls. He'll be your trainer for the entire week."

Cadina follows Tucker up the stairs and onto the second floor where Tucker is immediately motioned over by an impatient supervisor.

Tucker sighs, "As soon as I step foot on this floor, people claw for my assistance. Miss Wilson, do me a favor and go see the man at that podium. His name is Mr. Chapman. He'll be your immediate supervisor in Section C. And tell him I'll be right over for further briefing."

"Mr. Chapman, right?"

Too late…Tucker is already en route to her supervisor.

Taking a deep breath, Cadina begins making tracks down the work floor to her newly assigned section. As she unzips her jacket, she feels the eyes of employees all over her. She smiles nervously at some of the younger male carriers who huddle up quickly to evaluate 'the new kid on the block', while the older carriers take a brief look at the new face and return to their breakfast or their phone.

The closer she gets to the section, the more her eyes soak in; like the convoy of blue mailcarts lined up along the many route-cases that zigzag throughout certain sections. And everywhere she looks, there is mail–on the floor, on huge skids, in steel-caged post cons, leaning next to route-cases, magazine bundles on top of magazine bundles colliding with oversized priority packages, and letters overstuffed in long plastic trays.

This is her new home.

Cadina feels tired already.

She makes her way to the podium where Supervisor David Chapman is bending down over a stack of mail and scribbling on his clipboard.

The sandy-hair Irish supervisor in a brown tweed coat and brown loafers straightens up to greet her. "Cadina Wilson, right? I'm David Chapman, Section C Supervisor. Welcome aboard."

"Nice to meet you and thanks."

Mrs. Tucker arrives, glancing at her watch. "Have you heard from Freeman, David?"

Chapman smiles at Cadina. "Will you excuse us, Miss Wilson?"

Cadina nods as Chapman and Tucker veer off to the side to talk privately. But she still manages to eavesdrop on their conversation. She keeps her eyes on them.

Chapman drops the smile. "Freeman called in sick…again. Saw his name on the call-in sheet."

Tucker frowns with her arms crossed. "This is getting old, David."

"This marks, what, the third time he's called out in the past two weeks?"

"Ever since his mother's passing, he's been more off than on around here," mutters Tucker. "A line needs to be drawn because I'm not tolerating any more absences from him."

"Well, now I'll have to pull somebody off their route to get his truck from the garage and start his run which will be two hours behind schedule-"

"No. Have someone go and bring his truck back to the station and that's it," Tucker orders. "I'll get another carrier from the other section to do his relays but in the meantime, have Roy, Neville, or Shabbazz split up Freeman's collection-run and morning-drops. That should minimize the damage."

"And I can put the new kid with Lexington to get her familiar with his route before he leaves the station, altogether."

Tucker nods in approval. "When Freeman shows up tomorrow, tell him I want to see him in my office first thing."

"Will do."

They break up their meeting.

Cadina pretends she was not eavesdropping on their conversation as they approach her.

Tucker says, "Change of plans, Miss Wilson. Mr. Chapman will get you situated from this point on, okay? Best of luck to you and again, welcome aboard."

"Thank you," Cadina responds as the assistant manager marches down the work floor.

Chapman turns to Cadina. "Come with me, Miss Wilson."

While following the supervisor, Cadina glances at her new coworkers. She walks by a petite dark-skinned carrier sporting a Halle Berry hairstyle, who seems aggravated as she sorts the mail. She stifles a chuckle as she, once again, sees the Puerto Rican carrier named Lou, who is bobbing his head to some music playing in his headphones as he cases the mail. And then her eyes land upon an attractive light-skinned carrier with blond hair and a high-powered physique, who apparently has been watching her the entire time. The attractive sista smiles and waves at her. Cadina waves back.

They reach their destination and Chapman gains the attention of a male carrier who is writing something down in a ledger. The carrier peeks up at Chapman, but immediately his eyes divert to Cadina. The carrier straightens up and turns his body towards them, never letting his eyes off her.

Then the carrier smiles.

It was the creepiest smile Cadina's ever seen in her life.

"Lexington, I would like for you to meet Cadina Wilson," Chapman states before turning his attention to her. "Lexington will be leaving soon for the Supervisor's Academy, so this will become your temporary assignment, in addition to training on the truck during your probation period."

Cadina extends her hand. "Nice meeting you."

Lexington reaches for her hand. "The pleasure is *all* mine."

The moment their hands touch, Cadina absorbs all the wrong vibes from this guy who continues to blatantly probe her body with his beady eyes while bits of saliva pack the corners of his mouth.

Plus, he is getting a little too comfortable with holding her hand.

She politely snatches her hand from his slimy grip.

"I trust you will train her properly?" Chapman asked Lexington.

"I'll teach her everything she needs to know," Lexington assures, before turning his perverted eyes towards Cadina. "You can count on it."

She feels violated.

"Great!" Chapman shakes Lexington's hand and turns back to Cadina. "We'll postpone the truck assignment til tomorrow morning. Any questions, don't hesitate to ask, okay?"

"Yes, Sir."

"I'll check on you later."

Chapman pats Cadina on the back and returns to the podium.

Lexington rolls up his uniform sleeves, claps his hands together, and rubs them vigorously. "Ready to get this party started?"

She gazes at all the mail in his workstation. "I guess so."

"Have you ever worked in this type of environment before?"

"No, I haven't."

"It can be very fast-paced." He picks up a tray of letters and plops it on the route-case ledge. "The goal is to case the mail, then break it all down so you can go out and deliver to businesses and residential buildings and return back in a timely manner. And that's it. Nothing complicated at all. And I'm going to break down everything you need to know about this route."

"Gotcha." She hangs her jacket on a coat rack and then rolls up her sweater sleeves. "What do you need me to do?"

That repulsive grin returns to Lexington's face. "I like that."

She cautiously asks, "You like what?"

He folds his arms like an emperor. "The fact that you're ready to get down to business. And that's what this station needs; more hard workers like you. We have enough slackers around here who act like they can't grasp that concept. They feel as if cutting corners is the way to go and that's why the post office's name is continuously dragged in the mud. But hey, no need to dwell on any negativity, right?" Lexington sneers.

She raises her eyebrows. "Okay…"

He grabs a handful of letters. "Now, I'm going to be throwing around a lot of postal jargon so bear with me, I'll break them down as we move along." He takes a deep breath and grins proudly. "This is what we call casing or sorting the mail, which basically means placing the mail in the slots with the matching address and apartment number, okay? Now, we start with the first-class letters, then the large envelopes and magazines which we call flats and end with the bulk mail." He then says to himself, "*Yeah, I'ma get you good and ready for my route…*"

Cadina patiently listens, all the while wishing she had a piece of mint to offer him.

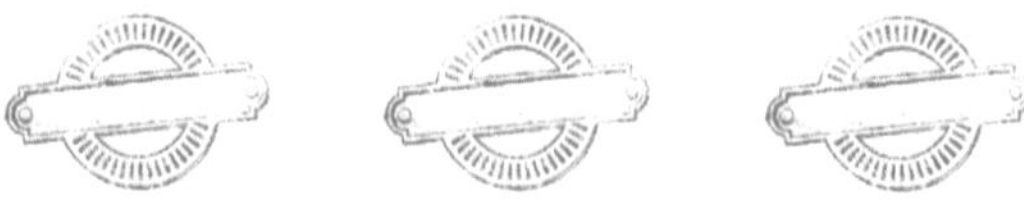

THREE HOURS HAVE PASSED, AND HER GUT INSTINCTS WERE RIGHT.

She is going to have problems with this dude.

Although he tries to come off friendly, she sees the nasty disposition Lexington possesses just by the little things he does early on–things like launching letter trays on the ledge which miss her arms by mere inches; trying to boss over people, such as an old mail-handler who distributes the mail to various workstations. She can tell that the old man dislikes coming over to Lexington's workstation because of how this arrogant fool snatches the mail from his hands and scolds him for stacking the mail the wrong way. Then, Lexington occasionally turns around to say something sarcastic on the sly about how she is casing the mail. However, nothing infuriates her more than how this nincompoop feels the need to get all up in her face to say something, giving her the impression that he wants to kiss her. At one point, she has no choice but to politely check his behind. This slightly offends him, but he gets the message. Now that the mail has been cased up, she wants the day to hurry so that she no longer has to be in his 'self-absorbed' presence.

"So, what do we do now?" she asks, pushing up her sweater sleeves.

"Well, we wait to see if there is more mail arriving to the station," he explains, with his chest puffed out and his arms crossed. "Normally, you would take care of your return-to-sender mail and forwardable mail like I did while you were casing up those magazines. Now, remember to always check the hot case every half hour for loose mail, even right before you leave the station, alright? And always remember to case up your first-class letters before you case up anything else, then your second-class envelopes and magazines, then your bulk mail, and please remember that you do not case up the DPS mail, which is short for delivery point sequence mail since it's already in order—"

Cadina watches Lexington do about three double-takes at Lou, whose workstation is across from his. With his headphones blasting, the Latino carrier dances and sings to himself while closing his relay bags and throwing them on the relay skid next to him.

"*Teh-leeee-foooo-noooo…suena, suena, suena, suena, suena,*
*Teh-leeee-foooo-nooooo…penas, penas, penas, penas, penas…*"

Lou does a couple of two-step moves before he loads up another bag of mail, causing Cadina to chuckle. Unfortunately, she notices Lexington, who is not finding it amusing at all.

"Excuse me for a moment," mutters Lexington.

He squirms his way between relay skids and steps over a couple of empty letter trays to tap his dancing coworker on the shoulder.

By the way Lou spins around and rips off his headphones, Cadina gets the feeling he does not appreciate Lexington killing his salsa mood.

"What?" barks Lou.

"What you mean '*what*'? You and your loud singing and dancing—that's what! Can't you see I'm training a new sub over here?"

"First of all, you're not supervising today, Papa, so don't bring that bullshit over here-"

"I don't have to be supervising to tell you that your little sideshow act is becoming a major distraction-"

"Are you *serious*? How am I disrupting you from *way* over here, huh?"

"Do I need to call Davenport up here to tell you to tone it down? Because I will if you—"

"YO, TAKE YOUR NON-SUPERVISING ASS BACK TO YOUR ROUTE AND LEAVE ME THE HELL ALONE! I DO THE SAME SHIT EVERY DAY, BUT NOW SINCE WE HAVE A CUTIE UP HERE, YOU WANNA GET ALL BOUGIE AND SHOW YOUR ASS! BUT I GOT NEWS FOR YOU—YOU COULD KISS MY GOYA ASS TWICE! YOU HAVE NO BUSINESS IN MY SPACE, PAPA!"

"OOOOOOOOOOOOOOOOOO!"

An embarrassed Lexington peeks around to see the other carriers laughing. He turns back to Lou. "You're ignorant, you know that? I can't even talk to you like a mature adult-"

"Fuck outta here, man." Lou returns to loading his relay bags while making it his business to sing even louder. "TEEH-LEEE-FOOO-NOOOOO...."

The entire section sings in unison, "SUENA, SUENA, SUENA, SUENA, SUENA, SUENA-"

"ALRIGHT, SECTION C, KNOCK IT OFF!" yells Chapman, returning to the section. "THAT'S IT FOR THE MAIL! LET'S TIE DOWN AND HIT THE STREETS!"

Cadina watches Lexington retrace his steps back to his workstation.

"We're going to start tying down the route now," he says in a low, aggravated tone. He points to the panel on the top. "Start from up here."

"Okay." Cadina begins to place rubber bands around the mail bundles.

"And after we finish tying down, we'll go downstairs to get our arrow keys, scanners, and our valuable mail, which consists of certified mail, registered mail, and Express Mail." Lexington then grumbles under his breath, *"I'll be glad when I get the hell outta this station."*

Cadina tries hard not to laugh as she prepares her bags for her very first mail delivery.

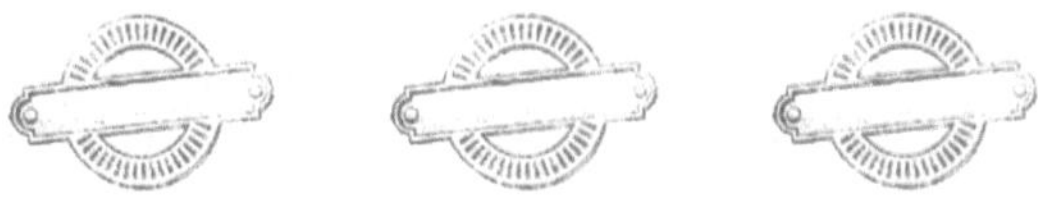

PUSHING THEIR MAILCARTS THROUGH THE SIDE ENTRANCE OF THE FIRST stop of their day, a mid-century architectural-styled Co-op on the corner of Eighth Street and Fifth Avenue located in the Greenwich Village area, Cadina follows her trainer into the well-maintained lobby area. Her eyeballs bounce from one wealthy tenant to another, who is either leaving through the revolving doors or rushing in from the cold and waiting on the elevators.

Lexington shouts, *"VINNY, WHAZZUP?"*, to the young Italian doorman wearing a red jacket and sitting behind the front desk, who in return, peeks up at Lexington, and gives him the finger before returning to his phone.

"He always plays around like that," Lexington says.

Cadina rolls her eyes.

They swerve around a circled desk with their carts into a spacious, well-lit room where fourteen silver mailbox panels stretch across three walls, and a large oakwood island nestled in the center. They peel off their jackets and begin grabbing numbered mail bundles from their carts to place in front of its designated panel.

"You start over on that end, and I'll start over here and we'll work our way towards the middle," Lexington orders.

Cadina, promising herself to say as little to this guy as possible, does as told.

An hour passes and she struggles with finding names inside the mailboxes while Lexington, on the other hand, zips through each panel on the opposite end and slams the panel doors to emphasize a point he made earlier en route to the building:

*I'm the fastest carrier at Midway!*

What a way to start off her first day, with this type of nonsense. Even when she asks him about letters that do not have an apartment number, he brushes her off by commanding her to *just put them off to the side and I'll get to them after I finish;* like she's bothering him, while he makes it his business to kiss every tenant's ass that walks into the mailroom.

A distinguished-looking gentleman wearing a puffy ski jacket strolls in and opens his mailbox which is next to Lexington.

"PAUL! HOW'RE YOU DOING, MAN?"

Lexington shouts so loudly that Cadina could have sworn the poor man jumped an inch off the tile floor.

"Oh, uh, I'm doing just fine," Paul politely replies, while retrieving his mail from the box. He strains his eyes as he points at Lexington. "It's Lenny, isn't it?"

"C'mon, you know my name…*Lexington,*" he says with a stupid grin. "You're funny, Paul!"

"Oh, I see you're training a new person…"

"Yeah, she's a cutie, isn't she?"

Cadina stops immediately and faces the smiling fool.

Flipping through his letters, Paul pulls one out and hands it to Lexington. "This one's not mine, I think it belongs to the other Williams guy in 4-B."

He takes the letter, examines it, and then reaches it out to her. "Here, it goes in 4-B."

*You put it where it belongs, Mister Flash—you're the one who did it!*

She ignores him while working her panel.

"Never mind, I'll handle it." Lexington tosses it onto the island and turns back to Paul, who is now leaving the mailroom. "Hey, Paul! I didn't see you this past Christmas. Did you have a nice holiday?"

Turning around, Paul displays a huge phony grin. "It was wonderful, Lenny-"

"It's Lexington-"

"I'm sorry…*Lexington.* I took the family to Aspen!"

"Really? How was it?"

"Beautiful! It was my daughter's first time. Now she thinks I'm the coolest person, next to Chris Brown, of course-"

"That's nice, that's really nice." Lexington nods while rubbing his sweaty palms together. "Because I didn't get a chance to *see* you before the holidays, you know…"

"Ohhh, right, I totally forgot about you, didn't I?"

From the corner of her eye, Cadina watches Paul dig deep into one of his corduroy pants pockets and pull out a thick wad of cash. He flips a crisp hundred-dollar bill over, then another hundred over, then a fifty.

She peeks at Lexington, who waits patiently.

Damn near salivating.

Paul finally flips over to a wrinkled five-dollar bill. He pulls it out and hands it to Lexington, who accepts the shabby-looking bill with a stupid look on his face.

She fights hard to conceal her laughter.

"I'll remember to stick it in a Christmas card the next time, Lenny," Paul says, patting Lexington on the shoulder. "Keep up the good work…and train your new coworker well!"

"It's *Lexington,*" he mumbles, but, by now, Paul has already left the mailroom.

Fighting hard to keep a straight face, Cadina grabs a batch of the letters without apartment numbers and walks over to Lexington. "These are the ones whose names I couldn't find inside any of the boxes—"

He snatches the letters from her hand and storms over to the panels where she had been working.

*Oh, no he did not snatch those letters outta my hands-*

That was it.

She's had about enough of this guy's rude behavior and decides to confront him.

"Lexington, I need to have a word with you" …but, she cuts herself off in mid-sentence.

Cadina stands motionless as she listens to Lexington grumble to himself while shoving the letters inside the correct boxes.

*"'Keep up the good work,' he says. Yeah, I go above and beyond the call of duty every day, ALL DAY, but you can't break a brutha off better than a five-spot? What am I supposed to do with that? Buy bubblegum? You could've kept that raggedy bill…stingy bastard!"*

He slams the panel door so hard that she feels the rattling sensation vibrating through her bones. He turns around to face her and in a surprisingly calm manner says, "Were you about to ask me something? I didn't mean to cut you off-"

"Uh, nooo, you're good." She decides it is best not to say anything to this crazy-ass coworker of hers until he is in a better place emotionally–and mentally.

"Okay. I believe we're done here." He grabs a mail bundle from the island. "I'll be back, I'm going to leave this with the doorman. You did good in this building, Cadina."

She acknowledges the compliment, all the while, watching him stare at her with that Grinch-like smirk she is beginning to loathe. But as he smiles, he also balls up the wrinkled five-dollar bill and flings it into a wastebasket that's underneath the island before he heads to the front desk.

She begins to collect the rubber bands and the return-to-sender mail from the island to place them back into her pushcart. Then she bends down to retrieve the five-dollar bill from the waste bucket, stuffs it in her pocket, and waits patiently for her looney trainer to return.

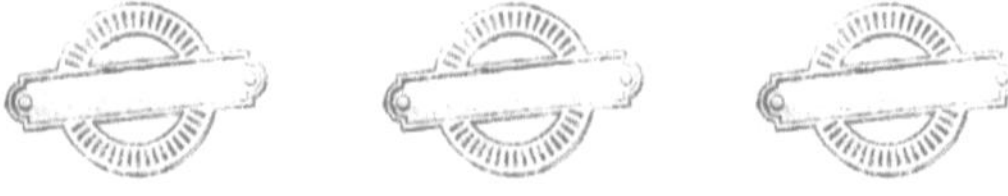

THREE O'CLOCK ROLLS AROUND WITH CADINA AND LEXINGTON returning to the station. She pushes her mailcart at the speed of light down the slick sidewalk, trying her best to distance herself from her yapping trainer. But he matches her speed, stride for stride. On and on, he babbles about himself, dulling her senses. And now he is asking questions pertaining to her personal life.

*God, why'd you do this to me?*

"What did you say you used to do before coming to the p.o.?" he asks.

She cuts her eyes at him. "I said I worked at a restaurant for a while and decided to leave."

"What made you leave?"

"I dunno. Just left."

He grins. "I see you're not really big on conversation."

"It's not that, but could you do me a favor?" She stops walking and faces Lexington, who stops pushing his cart, as well. "Ease up on the flattery when we're amongst people? It's kind of embarrassing and I didn't appreciate that remark you made to that tenant earlier-"

"My bad, Cadina," he apologizes. "I saw it on your face and definitely didn't mean any harm by it."

"Thank you."

They resume pushing their carts down the sidewalk.

"But don't act like you don't warrant that kind of attention," he adds. "I was merely stating the obvious-"

"Lexington, just behave. Alright?"

His pompous smile shines on his face. "Lexington is now behaving himself."

Cadina shakes her head.

As trainer and pupil turn the corner en route to the station's loading dock, they bump into Mrs. Tucker. Right behind her is the person Cadina saw earlier in the oil painting—Mr. Davenport. Even buried underneath his wool coat and Baldwin hat, she can feel his commanding presence. When she shakes his hand, she feels herself becoming paralyzed by his dark, glowing eyes, and his outrageous smile.

"Did I just talk her up or what?" Davenport gleefully says to a smiling Tucker. "I was just telling Denise that my day was about to close, and I didn't get a chance to meet our new employee! Cadina Wilson, I'm Michael Davenport, the manager-in-charge; welcome to Midway, and how was your first day of delivery?"

"I-It was good," Cadina stutters.

Davenport's eyes intensify. "He talked you to death, didn't he?"

Cadina's hesitancy causes everyone to laugh.

"Now I wasn't that bad, was I?" Lexington asks.

"Oh, you *are* a talker," Cadina confirms. "Don't act like you're not."

"Well, I'm glad your first day here was a positive one." Davenport pats Lexington's shoulder. "You mind if we have a moment with the future supervisor?"

"No, go right ahead."

The managers huddle up with Lexington on the corner.

Cadina pushes her cart toward the loading dock ramp and waits until they are done with their prized pupil.

"Hey, newbie! Welcome home!" greets a couple of senior letter carriers, leaving the station for the day.

Cadina smiles while waving at them.

Her eyes just happen to gaze across the street.

And the sight she sees causes her to scoff under her breath.

*No, he did not show up at my job…*

Leaning on his black 2013 Cadillac CTS Coupe with his arms folded is a tall suave-looking man wearing a black wool trench over a black suit. With black shades covering his strong African American and Cherokee features, the gentleman with the cool Malcolm-X fade smiles at her. She simply shakes her head. The man glides across the street with his trench coat flapping in the cold wind and gives her a warm embrace. He is known to the world as Vernon, but she simply calls him daddy.

Cadina takes off her father's shades and hands them to him. "I see you didn't waste any time."

"Actually, I was on my way to buy a new laptop."

"But you just so happened to make a pit-stop to check up on me, right?"

Vernon's sculptured smile says it all. "Somewhat."

Lexington pushes his cart towards the ramp and then joins in on the conversation. "How're you doing, Sir."

Cadina smirks at Lexington and says, "Daddy, this is my instructor for the week, Lenny VanGuard—"

"The name is *Lexington* VanGuard, Sir." Lexington cuts his eyes at Cadina. "And I'm proud to report that your daughter is learning rather quickly for her first day on the job."

Vernon stares at Cadina. "Don't let up on her, young man."

She twists her face.

"I won't let you down, Sir." That Grinch-like grin returns to Lexington's mug as Cadina hands him the certified letter receipts. "I'll see you upstairs."

Lexington pushes his cart up the ramp and onto the elevator lift.

Cadina shudders. "Of all the people they could've paired me with, my supervisor chooses that looney-tune to train me."

Breathing on his sunglasses, and then wiping them off, Vernon asks, "Oh, really?"

"Oh really, what?"

"Well, it appears to me that no matter where you wind up, you seem to have issues with management. You tell me who's the common denominator in all of this?"

"Are you going to make this a daily routine? Swinging by the station to evaluate my every move?" She pauses and peers down the street to maintain her composure. "I think I've learned my lesson from that whole restaurant disaster, so there's no need to babysit me, okay, Daddy? I can handle this job."

Vernon slides his shades back on, turns around, and without looking back at his daughter, says, "Finish up so we can go get my laptop."

Cadina watches her father return to his vehicle. She mutters to herself and then rushes her mailcart up the ramp to enter the open elevator lift. As she waits for the gate to close, she pulls off her earmuffs and makes a mental note to bring her earbuds tomorrow–just in case she is paired up with Lexington again. She hopes this is not the case, for this will be the ultimate test of her patience. Worse, it could also determine her fate in keeping her promise to her parents.

The gate finally closes, just like her unappealing first day at her brand-new job.

# SEVEN

## FREEMAN

Freeman stumbles through his apartment door with the force of a clumsy bull and throws his groceries onto a kitchen chair. Pulling off his snorkel jacket, his eyes dart around the kitchen area and the realization hits him—it has been cleaned up. All the dishes have been washed and put away. The counter is clear from opened cans and cereal boxes.

He slowly enters the living room and continues to scan his surroundings. Chinese food containers are gone, rug vacuumed, pillows fluffed, and properly placed back on the sofa and recliner. He takes a couple of whiffs in the air.

Potpourri?

*Damn.*

Freeman grumbles to himself as Lovelle Taylor steps out of the bathroom and approaches him to plant a kiss on his lips. Never breaking stride, the chocolate-skinned lady, still dressed in a beige cardigan sweater draped over a white dressy blouse and brown-pinstripe flare-legged pants covering up brown boots, walks over and sprays leather cleaner all over the couch and recliner.

"One of these days, you're going to wake up and find a roach crawling inside your mouth; this place stays a hot mess." Lovelle pushes the vacuum into the closet. "Sink full of dishes, food containers all over the place, Chinese rice in and under the sofas, and it *stinks* in here! But are you going to change your ways? Probably not."

"You paint a lovely picture, Bee-Bee."

The elementary school teacher, with the full bob hairdo that covers one of her slanted eyes, stares at him. "I haven't heard you call me that in a while."

His original pet-name for his fiancée was Bee-Bee, short for "Brown Buffy", on account of her plus-sized frame. Lovelle, on the other hand, despised her lifelong weight problem. Thanks to Shaun T's DVDs and a strict low-carb diet, she rigorously pushed herself into losing the sixty pounds she marked as her goal in less than two years and remarkably succeeded. Now "Brown Buffy" transformed into "Tootsie Roll" which became his second pet name for her. Suddenly, Lovelle, sixty-three pounds lighter and beautifully toned, began to exude the self-confidence that she never had in her younger years.

On one hand, he applauded her efforts, for he could not imagine anyone *not* putting an extra pep in their step after accomplishing such a huge personal goal. But on the other hand, it came with a heavy price.

"It has been a minute, right?" Freeman recalls while pulling off his hoodie. "Thought you were getting your workout on at the gym."

"I went this morning before work. Heading to choir practice in a few."

"So…how was school?"

Lovelle, who continues to clean, drags a heavy garbage bag next to her, and says, "Well, aside from Antonio bouncing off the walls because he forgot to take his medication again, the other kids were actually on their best behavior for a change, so I had a good day."

"That's good." He forces a smile as falls back in the recliner to untie his Timberland boots.

"I wanted to stop by and see how you were doing and if you needed anything, but it's obvious you're feeling much better."

"Why wouldn't I be?"

"Well, according to your sister, you caught a stomach virus this morning."

He peeks up at her, confusingly. Then it dawned on him about the lie he told Divine earlier that morning on why he did not make it to work today.

"Oh, yeah…*Yeah.*" Freeman sits up to embellish on the untruth. "Came outta nowhere. But I went to the bathroom a few times, flushed it right on out. Feeling much better now-"

"Really…"

She digs into the garbage bag and pulls out an empty bottle of Hennessy and holds it high for him to see.

He twists his lips and returns to unlacing his boots.

"So, I guess this cured that little virus of yours, huh?" she asks, but not waiting on a response. "Or was this the actual *virus* that made you miss another day of work?"

He pulls off one boot. "I'm not in the mood for one of your little lectures, Lovelle-"

"Freeman, either you let me schedule you an appointment with a counselor or at least talk to Pastor about your obvious drinking problem-"

"I don't want to talk to your *father* and I damn sure don't want you making any appointments for me. Why? Because I don't have a drinking problem!" He yanks the other boot off with so much force, it goes airborne. "Let this be the last conversation we have about this-"

"Well, if you don't want to hear my mouth, then I suggest you start throwing away these empty bottles I keep finding underneath your bed-"

"Maybe there's a reason why I like to have a taste every now and again. Ever took that into account?"

She fixes her lips to say something, stifles it immediately, and places the bottle back inside the bag.

He knew that would shut her up.

She then walks over to retrieve her purse, which was laying on an end table. Eyeing her every move, he observes her digging into her purse for something. She returns to him with a forced smile.

He remembers when her smiles were infectious glows of light that used to make him feel like he was sitting on the moon, looking down at the world. These days, her smiles are filled with hope. Hoping to recapture that unbreakable union they once shared so deeply because everything now seems so off-kilter.

Kisses are now bitter.

Touches are cold and awkward.

Conversations strained and pointless.

He knows it has been her strength alone that has been keeping the relationship afloat this far. It is only a matter of time before he finds a way to just let it go, but for now, the charade drags on.

"I didn't come over here to argue with you." She opens his hand and places two tickets in it. "You remember that musical at the Palace Theatre, *Holler If Ya Hear Me*, you said you wouldn't mind seeing? Well, two tickets for next Saturday, front row at eight o'clock."

He studies the tickets for a moment and then tries to hand them back to her. "Nah, take one of your homegirls. Hell, take Dee, she digs stuff like this."

"Freeman…" She ignores the tickets as she stares at him, baffled. "You were very adamant about going to see it before-"

"That was then, this is now. I don't want to go see it-"

"You know what? This is crazy. This, this whole thing is just crazy!"

She takes a deep breath to regain her composure. She then sits on the recliner's armrest, next to Freeman. "Are you sure you're ready for this?"

"Ready for what?"

"The *wedding*, *married life*, you know what I'm talking about. It's less than six months away-"

"How many times are you going to ask me the same question?"

"Until you give me an honest answer-"

"That rock on your finger ain't enough for you?"

"But that was the extent of it!" She strains to keep her voice at an even keel. "You act like you never have time to sit down with me and talk about how many people we're inviting to our wedding. We haven't even settled on a color nor a particular theme-"

"We're sitting down right now," he affirms with a blasé tone. "Cancel choir practice and let's talk-"

"No, no, see, this is what I'm talking about. You don't seem to be the least bit excited about any of this and I'm sick and tired of having to track you down just to have this conversation. The last thing I want is the both of us wasting each other's time because I'll tell you right now, I could focus my energy elsewhere-"

"Yeah, well, we all have our options now, don't we?"

She glares at him. "And what does that mean?"

"It means, I'm tired and I'm hungry. If you want to talk about the wedding, fine, let's talk. If not, don't be late for choir practice."

He reclines in the chair and grabs the remote from the end table.

Lovelle shoots him a *'I can't believe you're acting like this…"* look before grabbing her purse and heading to the closet to retrieve her coat.

"You forgot these."

He extends the tickets towards her.

She thrusts her arms through the sleeves and then buttons her coat, all in a heated fashion. "Like I said, I bought them for you. And the next time we have a conversation, Freeman, at least *act* like you care about what the hell we're talking about. Alright? Have a good night."

Lovelle storms out the front door.

Freeman sighs as he tosses the tickets on the end table. He straightens the recliner and trudges towards the kitchen. He grabs a small bag and pulls out a pint of E & J Brandy, the apple flavor. He quickly screws off the top and downs a big gulp. He wipes his mouth and then turns his attention to a photo magnetized to the refrigerator. A year-old memory of him and Lovelle hugging each other and acting goofy at a skating rink.

A happier moment in time.

Seems like centuries ago.

He takes another swig, grabs another bag, which contains Jamaican food, and trudges back to the living room to watch some television.

The phone rings.

He checks the caller I.D. to see if it is Lovelle, deciding to give him a piece of her mind after his smart remark. Instead, it is a number that brings a smile to his face. He wipes his hands before touching the handset.

"Hey Velour, I didn't expect to hear from you until tomorrow… Nothing, just sitting here, about to watch a little tele…" Freeman belts out loud laughter. "Nooooo! Not another Dante episode! What happened now?"

Rejuvenated and liquored up, Freeman's conversation with Velour, along with the E & J Apple Brandy, is finished precisely at two o'clock in the morning.

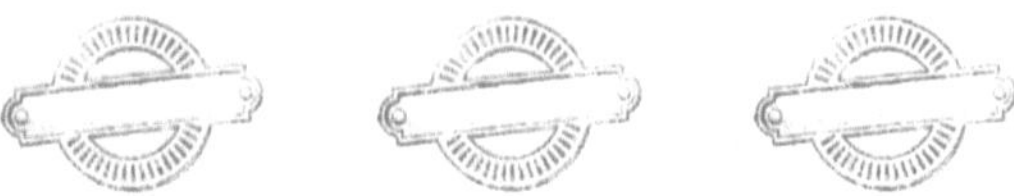

THE SCREAMING PHONE JOLTS FREEMAN OUT OF A DEEP SLEEP. HE reaches to get the handset from the floor and then presses the talk button. Grogginess takes hostage of his voice. "H-H-Hello?"

"The hell with '*Hello*'!" Roy yells on the other end. "You know what time it is?"

Freeman rubs his eyes to focus on the clock on the cable box—6:05 am. He yanks the covers from his body and springs up from the sofa. "Shit! Where you at?"

"At the garage, staring at your truck without you in it. This is getting old, Free."

"Shit! Shit!" is all he can mumble as a sharp pain detonates inside his head, causing him to double over in agony.

"Yo, I went ahead and fueled your truck and loaded the back with empty tubs and buckets, so the only thing this truck needs is *you*."

Freeman struggles to slip into the only decent uniform he can find. His head is pounding with the force of a sledgehammer. His eyes are blurred from interrupted sleep. *Lord, help me get through this day!* "Yo, I owe you big time, man-"

"Fuck all that! Just get your ass here, Tucker is pissed!"

"Wh-What she say-"

Roy hangs up on him.

After lacing up his dusty boots, he sits on the edge of the sofa waiting for the room to stop spinning. As his drunken world continues its carousel, mournful images of his mother's funeral are summoned from his subconscious.

His heavy eyes begin to close.

Other images follow suit, such as he and Lovelle racing against one another on rollerblades throughout Flushing Meadow Park in Queens.

He begins to drift away.

The final image is Mrs. Tucker on the phone leaving him a brutal message on his answering machine.

His eyes pop open like a surprised owl.

Throbbing head and all, Freeman grabs his postal parka, his hat, and staggers out of the apartment.

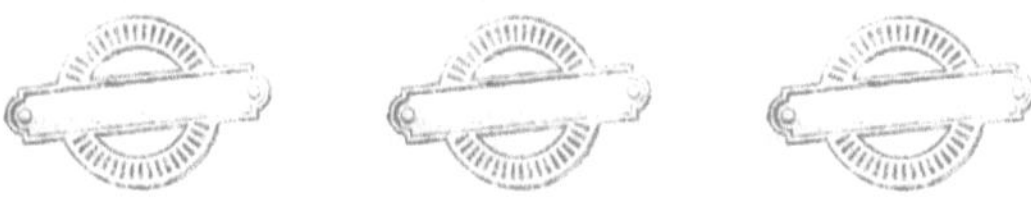

*"NIGHTS LIKE THIS, I WISH, THAT RAINDROPS WOULD FALL…"* ECHOES around Freeman's brain, along with streams of pain that blast off like roman candles. The agony causes him to swerve his truck from side to side all the way down Third Avenue.

As he makes a right on Eleventh Street, he has already accepted the fact that today is going to be one of those days. He's already had to absorb a vicious tongue-lashing from the cab driver for puking in the back seat of his car, so the last thing he needs is Tucker and her verbal heat chastising him.

He pulls up behind Roy's postal truck which is parked in front of Webster Hall. He turns off the engine and sits there for a moment to sober up.

Roy hops out of his truck and trots over to see Freeman slumped over the steering wheel. "Yo, for a minute, I didn't think you were gonna make it here on time."

"I didn't, either." Freeman pushes himself off the steering wheel, steps out of the truck, and welcomes the fresh, freezing air. "Yo, I appreciate this, man—"

"WHOA, SON!" Roy repels a few feet from him, holding his nose. "I know you're going upstairs smelling like ass! And Tucker's upstairs waiting on you, too! You better go gargle and throw on some cologne. Shoot, *gargle* some cologne, do something!"

Roy's advice falls on deaf ears as Freeman beelines it through the employee entrance, stumbles up the staircase, and then pauses for a second to allow the queasy feeling in his stomach to pass before he speed-walks the rest of the way to his section, and finds Tucker and Chapman standing at the podium.

The assistant manager and supervisor trade glances, giving Freeman the impression that they do not like what they see. Freeman checks his appearance. *Shit.* His uniform shirt buttons are not aligned with the holes, plus his shirttail is sticking out of his zipper. Tucker's eyes are about as dark as the two-piece pantsuit she is wearing.

"Walk with me over to the timeclock," Tucker orders through clenched teeth.

Feeling more agitated than embarrassed, he snatches off his beanie, rubs his hand through his afro, and glances at his nosy coworkers, who are watching the play-by-play drama unfold at the podium.

"NOW, FREEMAN!"

He drags his body over to the timeclock where Tucker stands with arms folded.

"Haven't I spoken to you about this matter before?" she asks.

He tilts his head to brave a sharp pain. "Yes, you have, Ma'am."

"But yet, you're not comprehending. Look at you! You come waltzing up in here late and looking like a hot mess–"

"What difference does it make now, Mrs. Tucker? I'm here, right? Who am I training?"

He watches Tucker swing over to an attractive lady with a long ponytail, wearing an orange hoodie, and staring at him like he has lost his mind.

"Miss Wilson, help the mail-handler give out the mail, and then report over to Lexington's route, thank you."

The new sub slips on her gloves and mumbles to herself before assisting the elderly mail-handler.

"I know what you're thinking, but I'm really okay!" Freeman states. "You see I drove the truck over here without any problems, so you don't have to make a big deal out of this—"

"Don't you dare tell me what I need to be doing, Mr. Souls, who do you think you are?"

"Look, if you don't want me to train the new sub, can I at least do my collection run without all the drama?"

Tucker turns to Chapman. "Are all of our drivers gone?"

Chapman checks his watch. "About an hour ago. And the transporter truck will be here soon to pick up the early collection mail." Chapman leans closer to Tucker and in a low voice, advises, "I know what you're thinking, Denise, and if I were you, I wouldn't have him on the road in the condition he's in-"

"But I'm telling you both I'm fine," Freeman desperately reiterates between yawns. "Just let me do my job, that's all I ask."

Tucker glares at him, pondering a critical decision. She then moves closer to his face and whispers, "When you are finished with your collection, you don't do anything else except report to my office—do I make myself clear?"

"Crystal."

Freeman spins around and marches down the work floor. He feels the weight of everybody's eyes on him, which prompts his legs to nearly trot to the stairwell. As he does, he almost collides with Velour, who stops short of him with two steaming cups in her hands.

"Hey," she says, scanning Freeman up and down. "Are you okay, Baby?"

Her voice, as soothing as aromatherapy, sobers him up just a bit.

"I'm good. Just in a rush, that's all."

"I caught you at the right time. I knew we were going to pay for all of that talking we did last night so I went ahead and bought you this. It's your favorite, French vanilla espresso."

She hands him the toasty cup. He gulps on the espresso feverishly.

"This was much needed, thanks."

"I know you gotta run, our boss is eyeballing us as we speak."

"So what else is new?"

She caresses his hand. "You need anything else from me?"

That was a loaded question, and she knows it.

"I'm good…for now."

"Call me if you do."

She gives him another long, knowing stare before letting go of his hand.

His eyes gravitate to the hypnotic sway of her hip-hugging postal pants walking away.

In his line of vision, he also captures Tucker, who is monitoring his every move. She gestures with a pointed finger, making it loud and clear-

*Why are you still here? Get To Work!*

He snaps out of Velour's bootylicious spell and spirals down the staircase.

FREEMAN BARRELS THROUGH HIS MORNING COLLECTION RUN AT A torrid pace. After every mailbox he empties, he makes sure he scans it, and then slams the door with enough force to wake up the entire village area. As his hangover fades away, frustration takes its place. Never has he disrespected anybody the way he did Tucker, who, by his own admittance, has been very patient with him and his personal drama. But that is all about to come to a crashing halt. The scales have been tipped by his smart mouth and whatever Tucker has waiting for him in that office will be justified because of his dumb actions. Freeman shakes his head in shame. His moms taught him better than that.

He parks in front of his last collection box on Cooper Union. He hops out, opens the mailbox, and shovels all the mail into his bag. From the corner of his eye, he notices a lady flagging down a taxi a few feet in front of his truck. That reminds him to bum some money from Divine until he can get to the ATM. His vomiting inside of the taxi that morning was costly, and it caused him to shell out an extra twenty, the last he had in his wallet, which went towards tipping and cleaning.

After throwing the bag into his truck, he slides behind the wheel and pulls out slowly to swing around the taxi.

In a split second, the taxi, unaware of Freeman passing by him, begins to bolt off.

"What the..."

Freeman bangs on his horn, but it was too late.

BAM!

"Oh, no…No...*NOOOOO*!"

He slaps the gear in park and flies from the truck to see the rear right side of his truck and the front left side of the taxi crushed against one another.

"*Stupid muuufucka, man*!" he screams in outrage.

Hopping out from the passenger side of the vehicle, the skinny cab driver raises his fist at Freeman with equal fury. "What the hell is wrong with you? You didn't see me pulling off? Are you blind?"

"Am *I* blind? You slammed into *me*, idiot! Jesus, I can't believe this shit!"

The driver quickly sizes up Freeman and senses victory in his favor. "You drunk! I smell it all over you! Ohhh, you in big trouble, your company is paying for this!"

*This is not happening, it can't be happening!*

Freeman stands with his hands on the top of his head in disbelief. When he sees the cab driver pull out his cell phone and storm off to the side, panic grips in, and Freeman frantically digs his phone out of his pocket to call the station. Chapman is going to have a fit. And that would be peaches and cream compared to what Tucker might have in store for him. He was right all along.

It was going to be one of those days.

# EIGHT

## DENISE TUCKER

Rocking back and forth on the podium's chair, Tucker monitors Chapman's section while he investigates Freeman's accident. As carriers approach her with loose mail they've received from the hot case, she jots down the count and smiles. But deep inside, she is a nervous wreck, blaming herself for allowing Freeman to drive a company vehicle under the condition he was in. He could have killed somebody or himself for that matter. All because she was more concerned about having the collection mail ready for the transport truck rather than her own employee's wellness. Her body shudders, causing her to spill a little coffee on her blazer.

The intercom blares out her name.

"MRS. TUCKER, YOU HAVE A CALL ON LINE TWO. MRS. TUCKER, LINE TWO, PLEASE."

She lunges for the phone, almost knocking the base to the floor. "Midway Station, Tucker speaking."

"Shouldn't that be Assistant Manager Tucker or are you still having trouble grasping that esteemed accolade?"

If there is one person other than her husband that can make her smile in a time of distress is her longtime friend, Dexter Whitehead. Both started out as letter carriers in the late nineties before becoming supervisors at the same post office in the Bronx and then branching off into different fields within the postal system. She has not heard from him in almost a year but after hearing his baritone voice, she can still visualize the portly little man with bulging eyes standing flat-footed in front of her.

"Dexter, I'm going to slap you the next time I see you! How're you doing?"

"I'm doing just grand. Now, tell me why I'm hearing about your promotion through a third party?"

"My apologies, Dexter. Been swamped with paperwork, learning my new position, you know how that goes. What about you? You still supervising at Cooper Station?"

"Well, no. Actually, I've been supervising over at VMF for the past eight months."

VMF?

*He's the Vehicle Maintenance Facility Supervisor, which means he must be at the scene where Freeman and Chapman are to investigate the accident.*

Tucker's smile drops from her face.

"Okay Dex, lay it on me; how does it look?" She asks, holding her breath.

"Well, I've seen worse. I don't know if you were aware of it, but your supervisor allowed your driver to operate a vehicle, despite his condition—"

"I allowed him to resume his duties, Dexter, it was my call."

"But, *why*? You put this man in an extremely dangerous position. This is not like you-"

"I know, I know." Tucker rubs her forehead. "If we weren't so short-staffed around here, things would've been different—" She cuts herself short to avoid making any excuses. "I take full responsibility for his actions."

"Be grateful. The accident wasn't his fault. The other driver smacked into the back of the truck, plus his license was suspended, so that clears Freeman of any violation."

"Thank God." Tucker exhales. "I promise you; this won't ever happen again."

"I know it won't. Starting tomorrow, he is prohibited from driving any company vehicle for at least a year. I don't care if he's the only employee you have left in the building. Understood?"

"Yes."

"Now, as a friend, I'm going to omit that part from my report. But I strongly suggest you send a stern message to your driver regarding his condition and the horrible repercussions it could have led to–follow me?"

"I owe you big time, Dex."

"And you can start by treating me and Pearl to a bowling match. And tell your husband to bring his A-game with him."

"Will do and thanks so much. Bye."

Tucker hangs up the phone. The trembling in her hand flares up again as her emotions try to get the best of her. She takes a couple of deep breaths.

*Relax, relate, release…*

She vows not to let Freeman and his personal baggage drive her to a sudden demotion or to an early grave, whichever would come first. She has too many personalities to deal with at this station to focus on just one. No, this time around, she is going to deliver the kind of ultimatum that is going to send an unexpected jolt into Freeman's diluted reality.

But first things first. She must figure out if she is going to tell Davenport the whole truth behind Freeman's unfortunate incident or handle it her way.

In her mind, she has no choice but to choose the latter, or she'll risk looking like what Davenport describes as an incompetent individual who is unprepared to make critical decisions, let alone run a station.

Regaining control of her bearings, Tucker takes Freeman's badge, walks over to the time clock, ends his day with a single swipe, turns around, and roars at the top of her lungs, "*BREAKTIME, EVERYBODY!*"

# NINE

## CADINA

At the sound of the assistant manager's thunderous voice, Cadina hurries to finish passing out the final letter trays located inside the caged post-con. She picks up a tray, reads the label, and approaches Velour's workstation where she finds the statuesque bombshell sitting on a stool, quietly eating a cup of oatmeal, and flipping through an Ebony magazine.

"Hey," Cadina greets. "Where do you want me to put this?"

"You can slide it right under here, that would be fine."

Velour scoots over to allow Cadina room to slide the tray underneath the letter case. When she stands back up, Cadina quickly sizes up her glamorous coworker–a flawless-complexion, light honey-skin woman, sporting a blond Farrah-flipped hairdo. She's donning a super-tight postal shirt that generates significant attention around the bosom area. No stomach to be found over her belt and hips curved to perfection. And Cadina had already taken notice of the booming derriere Velour is blessed with. By and large, the quintessential hourglass figure that every man dreams of sporting proudly by his side.

"Thanks," Velour replies, with a tropical smile.

"No problem."

Cadina begins to walk away.

"Now, if I see you pick up another tray of mail during breaktime, girl, I'm going to scream. You hear me?"

Cadina turns around. They both break into laughter.

The diva-carrier extends her hand. "Velour Patterns—welcome aboard."

"Thanks. Cadina, uh, Wilson." She shakes Velour's hand. "Excuse my nervousness—"

"Please," Velour casually dismisses. "We all get the willies on our first week at work. Shoot, I just don't want to see you pick up another tray while you're on break."

"I don't mind, really. I only have two more trays left in that cart, and then I'll chill for a minute—"

"Allow me to school you, Newbie." Velour holds up her hand to motion for silence. "First and foremost; always and I do mean *always*, take your breaks and your lunches. Trust me, when you're out on your own delivering the mail, you're going to value those breathers, okay? Now, repeat what I just said. Come on now, I don't hear you…"

Cadina laughs. "Okay, okay! I promise to take my breaks and my lunches."

"You better. I'll be watching you."

Something or *someone* catches Velour's attention, causing the diva to smile.

"I see someone's back from vacation."

Cadina turns her head to see who she is referring to.

That is when her jaw drops, and her eyes widen.

Making their way towards the section are two letter carriers: an older white gentleman and a black gentleman.

A very *handsome* black gentleman, at that.

Cadina stares at the brother with thirsty intentions.

The two men wrap up their conversation and the older gentleman veers off, heading to the supervisor's podium. The handsome brother remains on course to Velour's workstation.

She wipes the gawky expression from her face and says "Hi" to him as he approaches. He politely greets her and then continues forward to greet Velour.

"James is in the building!" Velour announces as she gives him a warm hug. "How was vacation?"

"It seems like I was never on one." He places his shoulder bag down and peels out of his postal jacket. He then motions to Cadina. "New sub?"

Velour turns to her. "Cadina Wilson, meet James Richards, one of the coolest brothers to ever deliver the mail."

James chuckles as he shakes her hand. "I don't know about all that, but welcome aboard."

As she shakes his firm grip, she can barely look at this five-foot-nine, caramel-colored, thick eye-browed, juicy lip specimen, without blushing. But her poker face remains intact. "Thank you."

"Alright, James," Velour says, with pending excitement. "You know what I'm about to ask you, so let's hear it…"

He locks his arm out and shows off a set of keys. "Me and Moms move in next week!"

"That's what's up! Congratulations, Mr. Homeowner!"

Velour slaps James a high-five and he pumps his fist in the air, further exemplifying his elation.

"Thanks. I'm so glad this week is over. Dealing with the loan officer and home inspectors, stressing my ass out! But I'm happy my moms can finally move out of her apartment, so this is a beautiful moment."

"Awwww," both ladies chime in admiration, and they began to laugh.

"That is sooo nice," she says.

"Thank you, Cadina." James stares into her eyes. "That's a unique name, I like it."

"Why, thank you. I'll tell my parents you approve of it."

"You do that."

They both smile at each other.

"I know a housewarming is in the works, right?" Velour asks.

"I'm already on it."

"Good. Cuz I need to go somewhere and look cute. You know how we do, right, girl?"

Cadina laughs. "*You* are crazy."

"BREAKTIME IS OVER LADIES AND GENTLEMEN!" Tucker blares from the podium. "LET'S GET BACK TO WORK! Miss Wilson, come to the desk, please?"

"Okay!" Cadina turns to Velour and James. "That's my cue. Talk to y'all later."

"Alright," they simultaneously respond and resume their conversation.

Cadina approaches the podium. "Yes, Ma'am?"

"This way, please."

She follows Tucker over to the older letter carrier's workstation. The tall man with the ghoulish-looking eyes behind a pair of thick bifocals does a double-take at them both.

"How're you feeling this morning?" Tucker asks.

"Fine," the carrier grimaces while organizing his area. "I placed my ninety-six form over on the desk for an hour of overtime, that's all I'm going to need to finish up today."

"I have the form right here." Tucker holds it up to show him. She then turns to Cadina and says, "Miss Wilson, this is Marc Speid, our senior carrier at Midway. Marc, this is Cadina Wilson, our new sub."

Cadina sticks out her hand. "Nice to meet you, Sir."

After running his fingers through his buzz-sawed military-style haircut, Marc straightens his pocket-pen protector, adjusts his thick glasses, stares at Cadina without shaking her hand, and finally glares at Tucker. "What's this all about, Denise?"

"I read the doctor's note you threw on my desk this morning stating that you're fit for duty and while that may be true, I'm going to have Miss Wilson assist you at the end of your route-"

"If I wanted somebody to help me, Denise, I would've requested it," the old-timer counters. "I'll be just fine-"

"Look Marc, I really don't feel like debating you on this one. Do I have to remind you about the brief encounter you experienced last week?"

"My medication had to be adjusted, Denise." A tempered expression arises on Marc's face. "That was the problem all along. Trust me, I feel a hundred percent now-"

"Miss Wilson is going to assist you and that's final-" Tucker finds herself raising her voice, so she quickly pulls back. "I want you to retire next year in one piece, okay? Please, it's been a long morning already."

Marc grumbles as he resumes his work.

Tucker turns around to depart from his workstation. Cadina follows suit.

When they return to the podium, Tucker turns to her. "Don't let the mean look fool you, he's a teddy bear, trust me. Now, Chapman has you assisting Lexington and once you're done, you'll pivot over to assist Marc on his route. Any questions?"

"So, I won't be training on the truck today?"

"In due time." Tucker smiles. "Continue handing out the mail, please, thank you."

The assistant manager grabs a manila envelope from the podium and marches down the work floor.

Cadina slips on her gloves to pick up a tray of letters. She takes a couple of steps and then stops. She does a slow three-hundred-and-sixty-degree turn to soak up the busy scene occurring at her new job. Almost all the carriers are either talking amongst each other or singing and dancing in their own private worlds, but the one thing they have in common is that they are casing their mail at phenomenal paces. And she can see why.

It seems as if the mail never stops coming.

Cadina snaps out of her trance and scurries over to a workstation to hand a carrier his letter tray. When she turns around, she catches James peeking at her, as he continues to converse with Velour.

Picking up another tray of letters, she keeps her poker face intact, but her insides tingle with glee.

 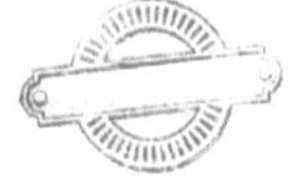 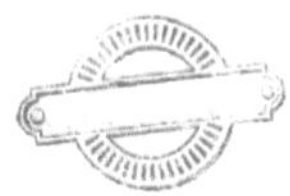

Two-thirty in the afternoon and Cadina pushes her mailcart down Sixth Street. Her face feels like a thick sheet of ice due to the frigid wind whipping around in the area. She doesn't mind one bit. She will take this over the company of Lexington any day.

She arrives at the corner of Sixth Street and Second Avenue. She pulls out her arrow key to unlock the two large green relay boxes on Marc's route. She opens the first one; nothing is in it. She opens the second one…same thing; empty.

Puzzled, she pulls out a form from her coat pocket to make sure she is at the right location. She reads the form and the street signs twice before confirming to herself that everything is correct.

A lady in a two-piece business suit rushes out of a garden apartment, waving a couple of letters in the air. "I'm so glad I caught you. Could you take these for me, please? I'm in a hurry."

A blank expression appears on Cadina's face. "Huh?"

The businesswoman quickly withdraws her mail. "You *are* the mail-lady, right?"

"Uh, yeah, I'm the mail-lady, but what do you want me to do with those?"

"*Excuse* me?"

"I'll take them off your hands, Mrs. Baker."

Cadina turns around.

Marc Spied pulls up and accepts the mail from the businesswoman.

"Thank you, Marc," the businesswoman says, while slowly backpedaling. "She must be new."

Cadina notices a stark difference in Marc's demeanor as compared to the attitude he displayed when she was introduced to him earlier.

There is actually a *twinkle* in his ghoulish-looking eyes.

"She's a motivated prospect with a bright future ahead of her," he states with a rugged smile.

"Well, she looks scared to me." The businesswoman slides into her running BMW. She shouts to Cadina, "No worries, dear, Marc will get you right! Tah-Tah!", before she pulls off down the street.

The senior letter carrier lets out a hearty laugh before speaking. "You better get used to people handing you mail and asking for directions; that's Carrier 101."

Cadina cracks a smile, welcoming his jovial spirit. "Gotcha. But wasn't I supposed to deliver your last block? I looked inside the relay boxes, but didn't see any bags in them-"

Marc shows her a couple of empty bags in his hand and then stuffs them back inside of his pushcart. "I trust you won't tell anyone." he winks.

Cadina shakes her head. "Marc…now you know I have to get familiar with my position before my training period ends. That's the only way I'm going to build my speed up."

The senior carrier snatches off his thick glasses and wipes them clean, all the while, maintaining a mischievous grin. "I totally understand."

He slides his glasses back on and then digs into his postal shoulder bag. He whips out a vintage postal winter trooper cap, still in its package.

"You need this more than me."

He rips the plastic open, walks over to take off her earmuffs, and places the furry cap on Cadina's head. "There. Now you're official, at least from the neck up."

Adjusting the hat and blushing, she says, "Thanks, but you didn't have to—"

Marc waves her off. "Ah, it's a token of my apology regarding my behavior this morning. And it's one of the original winter caps from back in *my* day. I bought it off eBay, mind you, so it wasn't cheap. Wear it in good health." He turns his mailcart around, preparing to leave.

"I will." She stuffs her earmuffs in her pocket. "Now what am I supposed to do in the meantime?"

Pushing his cart down the street, Marc yells, "Did you eat yet?"

"Well, no, I was about to—"

"Go eat!"

Marc points to a little 'hole-in-the-wall' restaurant called The Stage across the street.

*Might as well.*

As she waits for the light, she glimpses at the senior carrier slipping and sliding down the street at the speed of light, especially for a man his age.

"*I want you to retire next year in one piece!*" That is what Tucker said to the old-timer.

*But denial can be a mutha,* Cadina muses.

The light turns green.

Cadina crosses the street, heading straight to the restaurant for some welcomed heat.

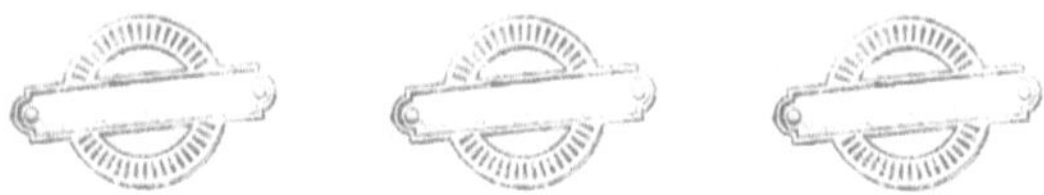

Sitting at the counter, Cadina sips on a hot chocolate with marshmallows. She evaluates her second day on the job. She was supposed to be trained on the truck, but that did not happen because her driving instructor appeared to be dealing with a massive hangover. She met a cutie by the name of James, who seems to have *his* eyes on her, as well. Later, she enjoyed delivering the mail with Lexington because she could successfully drown out the lunatic's babbling with a custom Pandora playlist on her phone. Lastly, Marc, the old-timer had finished the buildings she was scheduled to do and told her to have a nice lunch.

Like Ice Cube would say, *Today Was A Good Day!*

The homely Polish restaurant begins to pick up a little crowd as she pays the cashier for her order. She glances out of the frosted window and observes Divine parking her loaded mailcart under a tree before rushing inside of the restaurant. The petite carrier removes her postal parka and then plops in the front booth over by the window.

The chubby cook behind the counter yells out, "*...your food is ready!*" to Divine. She nods and at that moment notices Cadina. The petite carrier flashes a weary smile and motions her over. Cadina grabs her new hat and makes her way to Divine's table.

"You know, for a while, I was the lowest employee on the totem pole at Midway, so you know *I'm* glad to see you!" Divine sticks out her hand. "I'm Divine."

"Cadina." She shakes the tiny hand while taking a seat across from her.

The waiter arrives with the food.

"Appreciate you," Divine says to the waiter. She then smiles at Cadina. "Girl, all I had was a banana this morning, so I'm about to put a hurtin' on this right here, you hear me?"

"Go right ahead!"

Cadina laughs as her new coworker begins buttering her pancakes. A beautiful young lady with a stubby little nose, feline eyes, and a smile which illuminates her almond-colored complexion like a burning candle on a cozy Christmas Eve.

"So, you haven't been a carrier that long?"

Divine takes a sip of orange juice before answering. "Just a little over a year. My brother, Freeman, told me the post office was hiring, so I took the test and here I am."

"Freeman…" Cadina repeats. "Isn't he supposed to train me on the truck?"

Divine frowns. "He was, but I don't think he'll be training anybody anytime soon. He was involved in an accident this morning."

"Oh, my God…" Cadina's mouth hangs open. "Is he okay?"

"Other than his pride, he's alright. No one was hurt."

"See, that's why I'm hesitant about driving any kind of truck," Cadina confesses. "I know *I'll* be a nervous wreck…and dealing with the psychopath drivers out there, too-"

"Tell me about it. We lost our mother to a hit and run just three months ago."

"Nooo!" Cadina cups her mouth. "I'm *so* sorry-"

"Thanks. It's been rough, Lord *knows* it's been rough." Divine slows down eating while reflecting. "But I'm dealing with it the best way I can, you know? But as for Freeman? He has his own way of mourning, which is why he's in the predicament he's in now."

Cadina nods in sympathy.

"I see you're making a lot of friends already."

"Lexington is going to be a handful; I see that already," Cadina admits. "But everyone else has been really cool."

"Including Velour?"

"Especially her. She really embraced me with opened arms, schooling me on the do's and don'ts in the postal world-"

"That's cool and all but let me school *you* on a little something." Divine leans in closer to Cadina, staring dead into her eyes. "Everything that glitters, ain't gold, especially when it comes to the likes of her. Not hatin' or throwing any shade, just watch the company you keep, that's all I'm saying."

By the tone of the petite carrier's voice, Cadina has the feeling Divine is not particularly fond of the station's diva.

She decides to change subjects.

"Well, I'm done for the day, but it looks like you can use a helping hand."

Divine shakes her head. "I'm good. I only have two bags left. Enjoy the moment, it'll be over soon enough and that's when the fun really begins."

"I guess I have a lot to look forward to." Cadina rises. "I'll see you tomorrow."

"It was nice meeting you, Cadina."

"Likewise."

Cadina pulls her new cap-flaps over her ears, slips on her gloves, and heads outside to face the bone-chilling temperature. She retrieves the empty mailcart from the side of the building and then sneaks one more peek through the restaurant's window at Divine.

The petite carrier opens a small bible to read while gobbling down her pancakes.

*So, Divine despises Velour for some unknown reason.*

The stiff winds release an unwelcoming swirl around Cadina, blowing newspapers and other sidewalk debris at her boots, prompting a fast-paced journey back to the station.

# TEN

## FREEMAN

Freeman waits at the door of James' apartment for someone to answer. The door whips open and James, still dressed in his postal uniform, with the phone stuck to his ear, motions him in. Freeman pulls off his snorkel, hangs it on the opposite side of the front door, and walks past the dining room area, which is crammed with large cardboard boxes, clear plastic containers, and overly packed garment bags. He notices furniture disassembled and placed next to the wall. But they still have decades worth of items to break down before the big move date. The purchase of their new house was long overdue.

Entering the living room to join James and Freeman, wearing a blue Patrick Ewing jersey and a melancholy expression, is James' daughter, Janae. "Hey, Uncle Free."

Freeman extends his arms wide. "How's my favorite girl?"

"Meh."

"Everything alright?"

She shrugs. "I've seen better days."

Freeman hugs the skinny nine-year-old tomboy, and the stench of secondhand smoke rushes up his nostrils, catching him off-guard. She hands him a game controller, turns on the Xbox One, and challenges him in NBA Live 14. As Janae methodically dominates the match, Freeman tunes his ears to a scathing, one-sided phone conversation James is having while pacing the floor.

"No, you tell me why my daughter was in some hookah lounge when she was supposed to be with you?" James yells into the phone. "You damn right I'm making a big deal about it! My baby coming home smelling like smoke is a big deal! She was in good hands? The hell you mean she was in—? You know what? She's not going over there anymore. Because you're still not showing me you know how to handle responsibility and she's *your* child! Oh, really, word? I'd like to see that happen! You know what? I can't even talk to you anymore. That's right, I have better conversations with a freaking cat!"

James flings the phone on the sofa and tosses himself right next to it.

Freeman had the unfortunate role of sitting courtside to watch the relationship between James and Janae's mother, LaToya Feldman, deteriorate to the point of no return. Since the day Janae was born, LaToya has proven to be anything but a good parent. Focusing initially on jumpstarting a floundering model/actress/singing career, she eventually decided to pursue the sought-after role of 'video girl'. Landing an appearance in only three videos was enough for LaToya to totally neglect her motherly responsibilities and chase every casting call available with hopes of becoming the next Melyssa Ford or La-La Anthony. The chance of that happening being slim to none, due in part to LaToya's conceited attitude, those embarrassing "casting-couch" rumors, and from what James has confided to Freeman in secrecy, her experimenting with drugs. James has given LaToya enough chances with their daughter, and Freeman feels his homeboy is about to drop the sole-custody bomb on her any day now.

"Yessss!" shouts Janae, with her arms raised in the air. "Victory is mine!"

Walking into the living room wearing blue nursing scrubs and a worn expression on her chubby face is James' mother, Grace. With her stubby hands on her thick hips, the short, brown-skinned woman turns to her grandchild. "Okay, young lady, get out of them stinking clothes and hop in that shower."

"Can I play one more game with Uncle Free, pleeeeze?"

"That will have to wait; you got school tomorrow. Let's go."

"I won't hold back next time," Freeman warns.

"We'll see." Janae hugs Freeman. "Love you."

Grace watches her granddaughter pout her way to the bathroom before turning to James. "What was LaToya's excuse this time?"

"She had the nerve to tell me she had a five o'clock hair appointment for an upcoming video shoot, and she didn't want to bring Nae with her because she would get bored, so she left our daughter with one of the bottom-feeding lowlifes she hangs out with at some hookah lounge. Then she tells *me* that I'm being too overprotective, and I need to stop acting like somebody's grandpa! I tell you this; the next time LaToya sees her daughter; it will be in court. I'm sick of her mess…"

James pushes himself from the couch and storms into the kitchen.

Grace shakes her head as she looks at Freeman. "If it's not one thing, it's another with that child's mother." She then heads to the bathroom to check on her grandchild.

In the late eighties, Brooklyn's Raphael Cordero Junior High School I.S. 302 had been the launching pad for James and Freeman's solid relationship. Even in those scholastic years, Freeman saw in James, the same old-school values that he possesses. Freeman also saw his homey follow his father's footsteps and join the Army, even though the Vietnam vet's life was cut short when James was only one. This left Grace to raise him by herself. After three years in the military, James confessed to Freeman that he was not as gung-ho about the service as he thought he would be. Years later, after working a range of jobs, James accepted a position as a temporary postal clerk. During that period, he had a brief fling with a once shy, but incredibly pretty, LaToya. Soon after their love affair dwindled, LaToya announced she was pregnant with Janae. Now nine years later, James realizes that his baby girl is the only blessing that came out of their acrimonious relationship.

James returns to the room with two long-neck Coronas and hands one to Freeman.

"She left my baby in a damn *hookah lounge*," James repeats to Freeman in disgust. "For a video shoot? Just last month, she left Nae with her cousin and told her that she was going to get a pedicure that wouldn't take long. Six hours later, her cousin found out that she had gone to the club! What the hell is wrong with her, Free? She hollers that she doesn't spend enough time with her own daughter, but then she pulls stupid shit like this."

Popping the top off the beer, Freeman asks, "Are you sure taking it to court is the best thing to do? Mess around, LaToya might throw a brick and shatter your whole game plan, and you wind up losing the joint custody you share now-"

"Nah, bruh. Me and Moms have been documenting her negligence for the past two years. And what the hell am I doing—"

James snatches the Corona from Freeman's hand before he can take his first sip.

"What's up with you?" Freeman shrieks, grabbing for the beer.

"You're on punishment—that's what's up. You forgot about what happened this morning?"

Freeman leans back in his chair. "How many times do I have to tell you the man drove his car into *my* truck—"

"It's not just about that, Free. I really hate to pull your coattail, but you've been trippin' ever since your mom's passing. Supervisors questioning me about your behavior, what am I supposed to say to them?"

"You don't say anything; simple as that. Now, can a brother get some water? Or do I need permission for that, too?"

James side-eyes Freeman before heading back to the kitchen. When he returns, he throws an icy bottle of Aquafina on Freeman's lap. "Tucker wants to see you first thing in the morning. Now, I don't know what that sounds like to you, but it definitely sounds like you need to get your shit together and fast."

"I know." Freeman cracks open the water. "And that's why you're going to give me the best shape up you ever cut in your life."

Grace returns to the living room and sits next to James. "And when he's finished with your hair, Freeman, can you drop me off at work, if you have time?"

"I don't know, Ma," James quips. "Another taxi might hit him."

"What's he talking about, Freeman?"

"Oh, nothing. I'll drop you off."

"Thanks. Now, James, last year we had this same conversation about custody, but you reneged, giving LaToya the benefit of the doubt. You sure you want to go through with it this time because once the process begins, there's no turning back."

"I don't know what else to do, Ma. I tried working with LaToya, but she's proven over and over that she's just an unfit parent." James shakes his head. "I have to focus on Janae's well-being from here on out."

"Okay, well, my coworker has a brother who's a family lawyer. I will get his number and we'll start from there."

"Cool."

Grace pushes herself to her feet. "I have to leave in an hour, so get to cuttin'. I'ma check on Nae."

As she leaves, James shuffles to the closet and returns with his barber kit.

"Grab one of those chairs over there," James orders while flapping open his barber cape.

Freeman pulls up a dinette chair and takes a seat. James wraps the cape around Freeman's neck and fastens it.

James grabs a hair pick and goes to work on Freeman's afro. "You know, Tucker sees potential in you, possibly as a future supervisor."

"How do you know that?"

"She told me this, like six months ago."

"What'd she say?"

James brushes his clippers. "Well, she said, '*your friend has leadership qualities.*' And I said, '*yeah, he's always telling people where they can go…*'"

Freeman laughs. "I guess they all want me to follow in Lexington's footsteps, but they can have that. I'm not letting nobody stress me out."

"Like the way you're stressing out Tucker and Chapman?"

Freeman peeks up at James. "Just cut my hair, alright? Your Moms is waiting on me."

"Look, all I'm saying is Tucker is an assistant manager now; meaning she's going to have less tolerance for people's bullshit with this new position. So, you better start thinking about something else to win her over with besides a simple haircut…you feel me?"

James powers the clippers.

Leaning his head to the side for James, Freeman stares into space, with his mind formulating a game plan to get back on his assistant manager's good side.

"I'll think of something."

FREEMAN CLIMBS OUT OF THE FOURTEENTH STREET/UNION SQUARE subway station and dips into the first deli shop he sees. He tells the cashier he wants a toasted sesame seed bagel with cream cheese. He grabs a pint of Tropicana orange juice from the cooler and places it on the counter. While waiting for his order, he grabs a batch of red roses from the front of the store window.

Near the magazine rack is a full-length mirror.

He quickly checks his appearance.

Crisp, dry-cleaned uniform underneath his postal bomber. Boots polished to a mirror shine. He turns his head from side to side, admiring the professional tapered job James did to his hair and goatee. Pleased with the overall results, he pays for his items and exits the store.

Feeling about as fresh as the cold morning air, Freeman diddy-bops down Fourth Avenue, full of purpose and vitality. When he turns down Eleventh Street, he spots Shabbazz, who is showing Cadina the morning collection board in front of the station's bay area.

Freeman sizes up the physical beauty of the ponytailed sub in her bright yellow hoodie, blue jeans, black leather coat, and matching black boots.

*Man, she fine...*

Shabbazz mocks a surprised look and gives Freeman a hearty, half-hug pound. "Please tell me the old Freeman is back and not the one that is causing accidents!"

"Be nice," Freeman smiles. "I'm back and in a better place."

"I heard that. Have you two met?"

"Not properly, no." Freeman sticks his hand out towards Cadina. "I'm Freeman, the one who was *supposed* to train you on the truck yesterday. And you are?"

She shakes his hand. "Cadina Wilson. Nice to meet you—finally, I guess."

They all laugh.

"I know," Freeman says. "And I want to apologize for my actions and my appearance yesterday, that's not how I roll at all."

Cadina reaches for the flowers in his hand. "Awww...now, you didn't have to buy me flowers! I mean, I totally understand—"

"Oh, these aren't for you." Freeman jerks his arm back.

"Oh." Cadina turns beet-red.

"AH-HAAA, HAAAAAA!" Shabbazz doubles over in laughter, with dreads flying everywhere. "Yo, that was cold, Free."

Freeman pulls out a single rose and hands it to Cadina.

"Awww, thank you." Cadina blushes, smelling the rose. She turns to Shabbazz and mocks him. "A-HAAA, HAAA!"

"I see she's fitting in already," Freeman says to Shabbazz.

"Without a doubt." Shabbazz hands Cadina the truck keys. "She'd better not hit anybody out on the street, that's all I'm saying. We'll see you at Wang's for lunch."

"Cool."

"Ready, Cadina?"

"Ready as I'll ever be."

She hands Shabbazz the rose and then pulls herself up behind the steering wheel. She cranks the engine, shifts the gear into drive, and jerks the heavy vehicle out of the bay. "*WHOA!*" is all Freeman hears from Shabbazz, who holds onto dear life as Cadina stutter-drives the truck down the street.

Freeman heads into the station and makes his way toward the manager's office. Suddenly, all the fears he had been subconsciously avoiding, come rushing up to him like an angry linebacker. He calms himself down before knocking on the door.

"*COME IN!*"

He opens the door and steps inside the office, where the humming of the computer keeps the room from appearing mortuary quiet.

Tucker sits behind the desk with her dark brown eyes fixated on him.

He tries to trade smiles with her but fails miserably as the assistant manager remains stoic, with her fingers planted firmly on the desk.

Clearing his throat, he says, "Good morning, Mrs. Tucker."

"Good morning, Mr. Souls."

He swore he did not see her lips move.

She sits behind the desk with about as much life as a puppet.

*Just get it over with, Free.*

"I'ma just come on out and say I am truly sorry for the way I spoke to you yesterday and the way I've been acting around here as of late. You know that's not how I operate, and I hope you find it in your heart to forgive me." He hands her the roses and the breakfast bag. "I, uh, took the liberty of buying you breakfast, a toasted bagel with cream cheese and orange juice. And these roses. Tokens of my sincere apology."

She examines the roses. "Thank you, Mr. Souls."

"Hey, no problem at all."

He grabs a seat, feeling relieved.

She places the roses in a nearby empty vase. She then digs into her purse to pull out an envelope and hands it to him.

Flipping the envelope over a couple of times, he peeks at the tight-lipped manager. "What's this, a check or some sort?" he jokes.

She says nothing. Her eyes remain glued on his every move.

He opens the envelope and pulls out the form to read. He then jumps out of his seat as if his pants had caught on fire.

"You can't be serious, Mrs. Tucker! A two-week suspension?"

She rockets out of her chair, displaying every aspect of her authoritative position.

"The suspension is effective today, Mr. Souls, and you will report back to duty the following Monday and not a minute later or you'll be suspended indefinitely."

"This is a joke, right?"

"You see me laughing?"

He plops back in his chair. He cups his mouth to avoid arguing further, as he knows she is just doing her job. He made the bed that he must lie in, so he has no choice but to accept the strict penalty which could have been a whole lot worse.

Still, his stubbornness overrides his common sense.

"Don't you think that's being a little too severe? It's not like the accident was my fault-"

"You're right! It wasn't your fault, Freeman—it was *mine*!" She points down on the desk. "I should've never put you in a situation where you could have harmed someone, including yourself. That was my crucial error. But what I will not tolerate is you challenging my authority like I'm one of your peers, you understand me?"

An uncomfortable silence mounts.

He stares at the wall.

Ashamed.

Tucker returns to her seat. In a calmer tone, she resumes, "Look, we know you and Divine have been going through a rough period with your mother's passing. I've been down that road in my own life, with the passing of my father, so I know the pain. But you're using that pain as a crutch, and it's affecting your job security. You're *way* stronger than that, Freeman. Due to the fact you were raised by a strong, beautiful woman. But is this how you want to represent her legacy?"

He avoids eye contact as tears stream down his cheek.

"I asked you a question, Freeman."

"No, Ma'am."

She hands him a tissue box.

Freeman snatches a couple of tissues and then asks, "So, I start this suspension now or what?"

"Hand me that form."

"Excuse me?"

Tucker hastily motions for the suspension paper. "The form. Hand it to me."

Freeman hands it to her.

Tucker stands to her feet.

"Promise me, Freeman, from this day forward, you're going to revert back to the carrier we hired two years ago; the one that comes to work on time and comes to work *correct,* like you are now." Tucker points the paper at him. "Because I don't like giving these things out. Promise me that."

"You have my word."

She rips the form in half and throws it into the wastebasket. "If that other Freeman ever decides to show his face around here again, the next form will automatically be faxed uptown and that one will be for a month…do I make myself clear?"

"Yes, Ma'am—and thanks."

"One more thing…"

Tucker goes inside the desk and pulls out a business card. She reaches it to him.

"I have a friend who counsels individuals with alcohol use disorders. I encourage you to give him a call."

Freeman shakes his head. "I appreciate your concern, Mrs. Tucker, but I'm not suffering from any kind of disorder-"

"Freeman, from my twenties, well into my thirties, I was in denial about a serious nicotine addiction. I overcame it, thank God, but not without help. There's no shame in being transparent."

Tucker insists on the card.

He reluctantly takes it.

She quickly opens the small bag, pulls out the bagel, spreads the aluminum foil, and then takes a hefty bite. "Thank you for the food, I was *starving.*" She takes a huge gulp of her orange juice before returning to her seat behind the computer.

"Should I clock in today?"

"Yes. And I believe Chapman has you assigned to Velour's route. Dante took the rest of the week off to prepare for the parcel post position. Oh, and Freeman..."

"Yes?"

"This conversation stays between you and me. Davenport doesn't know about your condition yesterday and I prefer it stays that way, understood?"

"Uh, yeah."

"Good. Now close the door behind you when you leave."

She explains all of this while focusing on the computer.

Freeman throws his backpack over his shoulder and walks out of the office. As he closes the door behind him, he pauses for a moment and stares at the business card she gave him. He crumbles the card in his hand and tosses it into a nearby trash can.

Exhaling relief, he begins his stroll upstairs to start his new day off on the right foot.

# ELEVEN

## CADINA

From Cadina's perspective, time plays a major factor with Shabbazz. The moment they left the station, the dreadlocked instructor turned his radio to Power 98, slapped his game-face on, and proceeded to train her on all the various driver's assignments without compromising the dizzying pace he had set up for himself for the day.

The morning was somewhat of a blur to her as Shabbazz taught her how to do a mailbox collection run. Shabbazz opted to do the first half of the run so they would not fall too far behind, and that allowed her to get a comfortable feel of the truck while the traffic was still light.

At each mailbox she screeched up to, Cadina watched her instructor dash out of the truck, open and empty out the box, scan it, and close it back up. He would then zoom back into the truck and with wild eyes behind his glasses, point to the next mailbox down the street.

When it was her turn, she felt as if she was on a timer. Every mailbox she opened had an avalanche of mail pouring out of its door. As Cadina bent down to rake the letters inside of the bag, she would cut her eyes at her instructor and muse: *He's got another thing comin' if he thinks I'm gonna rush through this.* When she would fill the bag and drag it back to the truck, Shabbazz would ask, "Did you scan the box?" Rolling her eyes, she would find herself racing back to scan the inside of the mailbox. That question was asked two more times before she finally caught on.

After that assignment was complete, they raced back to the station, handed the collection mail to the mail-handlers, and prepared the truck for the next assignment, which Shabbazz called the early mail-drops. They both loaded buckets of mail into the back of his truck, as well as two hand trucks, before heading down the road for the second time that morning.

If the collection run had not awakened Cadina's dormant muscles earlier, the early-drop assignment all but popped whatever biceps she had in her shocked body. With mail stacked six-buckets high on each of the hand trucks, Shabbazz would lead the way as he swiftly moved his load into numerous buildings on Fifth Avenue and into their huge mailrooms. Cadina, however, struggled to prevent her loaded hand truck from rolling away from her each time.

After that two-hour workout, an exhausted Cadina drives back to the station with Shabbazz, who looks almost as refreshed and relaxed as he did when he clocked in. He cocks his feet up in the passenger seat and scrolls through Facebook along the way.

When they arrive, bundled-up carriers from their section push their carts out onto the sidewalk and stop to yell at Shabbazz, "... *Don't be late with my relays, 'Bazz!*" He smiles and gives them the finger, as he and Cadina rush up the steps to the work floor.

They push skids of heavy relay bags to the elevator lift and down to the loading dock area where they see Roy and Neville, who wave and laugh at them. "*Yo, Cadina, don't let him overwork ya!*" Shabbazz flips them the bird, as well.

After a few back-and-forth trips from the work floor, they finally load the truck to the maximum. This time, Shabbazz sits behind the wheel and pulls off as Cadina peels out of her leather jacket to enjoy a relaxing moment of not doing anything. That moment becomes short-lived as Shabbazz whips around Second Avenue and parks in front of their first relay box. They hop out and open the back of the truck. Shabbazz jumps in the back and hands her about six heavy relay bags to toss into the green box. Trying hard to show her instructor that she is unfazed by the strenuous work, she drags the heavy bags to the relay box and throws them in, one by one. After bouncing from relay box to relay box, stretching from Fourteenth Street to First Street, and then those same streets on First Ave, Cadina is virtually whipped.

She places the last group of bags inside the final relay box, climbs back in the passenger seat, and lets out a deep sigh while wiping the cold sweat from her brow with her forearm. She glances over at Shabbazz, who is trying to conceal his amusement.

"Please tell me you're not laughing at me over there," she says in a tired drawl.

"I'm sorry, Cadina, but the look on your face suggests that you might wanna apply for another less physical job."

*And disappoint my father again? Not in your life!*

"I'm alright. But please tell me we're through for the day."

"Yeah, that's basically it. We've got the brunt of the work out of the way so now what me and the crew would usually do is either return to the station and wait around for them to hand us more work or go grab something to eat."

She squeezes hand sanitizer in her palm and begins rubbing vigorously. "I have a confession to make."

"What's that?"

"Well, ever since we started this morning, I thought you were rushing because you didn't want to train me, but now I see you don't have time to play around. This ain't no joke!"

"I'm trying to tell ya. It's all about getting off to an early start because, at the end of the day, you wanna get those relays out to the carriers, or they gonna pitch a bitch, trust me. But you did alright for your first day on the truck. I'ma brag about 'cha."

"You think I'll be driving by myself anytime soon?"

Shabbazz nods. "And when you do, just pace yourself. Don't rush for nobody, because you don't wanna have to double back to the station for a missing relay bag or you delivered early drops to the wrong building, especially when the traffic gets crazy."

Cadina leans her head back and sighs. "This is going to be fun."

Shabbazz laughs. "Welcome to the post office! Now let's join the crew for some lunch."

He floors the truck and they roar down First Avenue.

She closes her eyes and enjoys the peaceful ride.

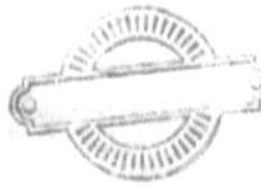 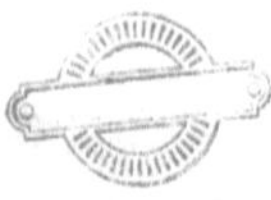 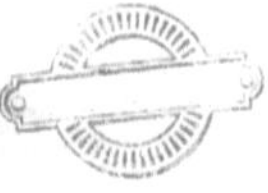

*I'VE SEEN HIS FACE SOMEWHERE BEFORE.*

Sitting inside Wang's Chinese Restaurant, Cadina quietly sips on her wonton soup as the crew—James, Lou, Roy, Neville, Shabbazz, and Divine—partake in noisy conversations over their steaming entrées. She tries not to overtly stare at the wannabe rapper, but he reminds her of somebody from the past. She can't quite put a finger on what period of her life, though. But she won't be asking him anything any time soon as the Latino letter carrier is in a heated exchange with James over his lyrical content.

"But why you gonna call my rhymes garbage?" Lou contests, woofing down his fried rice. "I don't understand that-"

"You *never* understand; that's the problem!" counters James. He turns to Roy. "Why do I keep putting up with him?"

Roy licks his fingers from the ribs' sauce. "I ask myself the same question."

"Because you try to clown me, Roy, that's why I don't ask you anything," Lou retorts. He turns to James. "But I do value *your* opinion-"

"No, you don't," James snaps. "Because if you did, you would've heeded my advice the last two times we spoke, but did you? Nope. If anything, your lyrics got way worse."

"How?"

"*How*? News flash, Lou, we don't call our women, *bitches* like that, we've evolved from that era."

"Man, you know damn well there're bitches all over the world scheming on niggas, and that's a fact, so don't come over here with that, *all women are queens,* shit!"

"He has a point," Neville adds, sipping on sweet tea. "I have a few in my family…just ruthless."

"First of all, Lou, your argument is weak." James drizzles duck sauce over his rice. "All you're doing is falling in line with the rest of the cats who just want to cash in on our culture while compromising our cultural integrity."

"Oh, so now you're calling me a *follower*?"

James turns to Roy. "Yo, what was one of his verses?"

Roy wipes his mouth and comically imitates Lou's rapping style. "*'I'm packin' more meat than Ron Jeremy'.*"

Everyone laughs.

Except for Lou.

"And what about, '*I want those hoes hanging in the rafters.*'? You're married, Lou. You're not embarrassed by any of that?"

Lou shrugs. "Why would I be?"

"Damn!" laughs Neville.

James shakes his head. "Man, if it's like that, you should stick to the party joints you used to write. They're way better than that crap you've been writing lately."

"What y'all fail to realize is, I'm trying to get myself in the industry, by any means necessary." Lou glares at all of them. "Once I'm in, *then* I can flip it to the party joints you like. I'm playing chess, son, not checkers."

"Like I said; you're selling out."

Divine turns to Cadina. "What's your take on it, girl?"

Catching her off-guard, Cadina glances around the table.

All eyes are now on her.

Cadina cuts her eyes at Divine.

*Alright, Sister Souljah, don't get stupid now.*

Cadina wipes her mouth and says, "The way I see it, Lou, is to stay true to yourself and trust the process because the right audience will eventually find you if you're authentic and you'll wind up enjoying a glorious career. That's my take on it."

"And there you have it," James affirms.

*Damn, he's fine!* Cadina muses about James while returning to her tea.

Lou eyeballs everyone at the table and waves them off. "Whatever, man. All I know is I'm not trying to solve the world's problems. You think I wanna be a mailman for the rest of my life? I got dreams that are way bigger than this uniform and if that means blending in with the new millennials, so be it. I'ma do *me,* regardless."

"Nobody's shooting down your dreams, Lou—"

"Nah, you said your piece, now let me eat in peace, a'ight?" Lou holds up his hand to silence James and then returns to his food.

"You know he won't talk to us for the next two days," Roy says.

Neville snickers, "Hey, that might be a good thing."

"Here comes your brother, Dee." Shabbazz points toward the front window. "Yo, Free came to work with a pity package for Tucker. Roses, food, looking all sharp; he wasn't playing."

"That's because he knew he'd crossed the line," Divine says.

The entire table turns around to greet Freeman and Velour as they enter the restaurant. They take off their coats and join the packed table.

Roy asks Freeman, "So, how'd it go with Mrs. Tucker?"

"Well, it wasn't pretty, I'll tell you that much." Freeman places his order with the waiter and then directs his eyes around the table. "I was facing a two-week suspension."

"Word?"

"Yep. She let me read the letter first, then she read *me* for about a minute, and finally she tore the letter in half and gave me my last verbal warning. And that was about the gist of it."

"Damn, you are lucky. Had it been Davenport—well, who knows. He likes you, too, Free. You one of them likable muthafuckas, you know that? That's why the crew is always doing shit for your dumb ass."

They all laugh and agree wholeheartedly.

Cadina glances around the table. She can tell these guys have genuine love and respect for one another.

"Yeah, well, it was a humbling experience that I don't ever want to encounter again," Freeman says. "I have to stay focused from here on out and for starters, lunch is on me today for all the times y'all covered for me."

"What about tomorrow's lunch?" Shabbazz asks.

"You better make it a whole week," Neville laughs. "You owe a lot, son!"

Freeman smiles. "Whatever. I got y'all."

"Personally…" Velour injects. "I think the only reason Tucker let you off the hook is that she knew she was in the wrong herself."

Cadina glances at her male coworkers.

They all stopped laughing.

And their eyes are planted on Freeman's little sister.

"Really?" Divine wipes her mouth. "Why would you think that Velour?"

"Well, because she knew about Freeman's supposed condition before he left the building, and her job would have easily been in jeopardy had the wrong people found out about it, so instead of just sweeping the whole incident under the rug, she wants to threaten him with a suspension? I just think it was totally unnecessary."

"Well, I think it was *very* necessary if you ask me," disputes Divine.

"But why? The accident—"

"—*My* brother needed—"

"—Wasn't his fault to begin with—"

"—Some discipline thrown his way—"

"So, she just wanted to cover up her own misdoing. That's all, Dee—"

"I'm not talking about the accident, Velour!" Divine barks. "I'm referring to everything else prior to that. The excessive drinking, tardiness, or not showing up for work at all. If she had given him that suspension, it would've been justifiable, trust me."

Cadina watches the intense conversation the way she would watch Serena and Venus vie against each other in a title match. But unlike the Williams Sisters, there is no love between these two coworkers, especially on Divine's side of the court.

"But you gotta admit, she's treating your brother like he's never done her any favors in the past."

"*Favors*? What are you talking about?"

"Going to the store to get your boss breakfast or getting her clothes out of the nearby cleaners; these are not listed in the carrier's manual. I'm sorry."

"If that ain't the pot calling the kettle—!" Divine shifts her chair and her whole attitude directly at Velour. "And what about *you*? Every time you see my brother, you ring your little bell, shake your big ass and he goes galloping over to you like a dog in heat! Is *that* in the carrier's manual, Velour?"

Cadina's eyes widen in shock.

The rest of the crew try to conceal their snickers.

Freeman immediately jumps in. "Dee, I think you've said enough, okay?"

Divine turns to her brother. "No! This is between me and your little side-piece, so stay outta this-"

"Look, Dee…" Velour resumes. "I'm not trying to be your enemy here. I'm just as concerned about your brother as everyone else is at this table—"

"Please, he already has a fiancée for that role. He doesn't *need* you-"

"I think you need to shut the hell up before I do it for you," Freeman warns.

Divine eyeballs her brother. "So, you're gonna side with this chick over your own sister? Really?"

"Yes, *really*! Because she's just voicing her opinion like everyone else around this table, but when it comes to *her*, you seem to always have a problem! And who are you to be putting my business out in the open like that?"

"As if that was top secret! *Everybody* knows about your-"

"Everybody knows what, Dee? Huh? And that's another thing with you; you flap your gums a little too much about stuff you don't know and I'm getting sick and tired of that shit! You're not my mother, okay, so stay in your damn place!"

The snickering from around the table ends.

Divine embarrassingly peeks around the table before standing up to grab her coat from the back of her chair.

"Nah, Dee. Sit back down and finish your food," James pleads.

"You heard your friend; I need to stay in my place." Divine digs into her pocket to pull out a ten-dollar bill. She slaps it in the middle of the table. "I have a hair appointment to make, anyway."

Freeman picks up the money and tries to hand it back to her. "I told you, I got the bill—"

"Please…your pockets stay on broke." Divine pushes Freeman's hand aside. "And since I'm getting on your nerves so bad, you can start coming up with your own lies when Lovelle, your *fiancée,* wants to see or hear from you, okay? I'm quite sure you can squeeze her in between some of y'all's conversations."

Divine shoots a dirty look toward Velour before stuffing on her furry postal hat and storming out the front door.

A hush is cast over the lunch table.

"I am so sorry if I said anything out of context," Velour whispers to Freeman. "I mean, I wasn't trying to argue with her or anything."

"You don't have anything to apologize for…that's just Dee."

"I can tell you what's the real problem here," Neville says.

"And what's that?" Shabbazz asks.

Neville points at Lou, who is eating. "If he didn't have them hoes hanging in the rafters, we wouldn't be going through this mess!"

The table erupts in laughter.

"Yo, keep my name out your mouth, a'ight?' Lou cautions.

"Y'all are too crazy around here." Cadina wipes the tears from her eyes.

"You're just now figuring that out?" snickers Neville.

James holds up his glass. "Alright, y'all. Let's switch up the mood with a quick toast."

Drinks are raised, except for Velour's, who stirs a straw around and is still in a funk.

"Let it go." Freeman turns to her. "Dee's skin is thicker than most, trust me, she'll be okay."

Cadina watches Freeman as he caresses Velour's hand.

*Okay, Mr. Fiancé.*

Velour cracks a smile as she holds up her glass.

James begins his toast. "To our boy, Freeman, for returning back to his former self before he got that ass terminated."

"HERE, HERE!"

"To our new coworker, Cadina, who, on her third day of employment, hasn't thought about quitting just yet."

"HERE, HERE!"

Cadina laughs.

"I got this last part, Jay!" Neville begs.

"Go 'head."

Neville smirks at Lou.

"Say something stupid, Papa-"

Neville stands up. "This is a toast to you, Lou! For showing us that you, too, can have hoes hanging from the rafters and be proud about it!"

"When we get outside, it's gonna be me and you, bitch!"

Instead of getting full from the wonton soup, Cadina was unintentionally fed an abundance of newfound information regarding her coworkers during their round table session–from the questionable lyrical content of the wannabe rapper to the beefy catfight between Divine and Velour, and the obvious "courting" between Velour and Freeman.

As for Cadina, her bright spot was James, who she finds at this very moment, staring into her eyes with about the same amount of passion as she is giving him in return.

And that is a good thing all by itself.

James announces, "If all is said and done, cheers!"

"CHEERS!"

*Clink!*

Freeman waits in front of the post office building for James to clock out for the day. As he checks his watch, the employee entrance door swings open. Velour steps out wearing an all-white booty-hugging denim outfit with a white goose jacket draped over it. With a white skullcap pulled over her hairdo and white knee-length Ugg boots completing the wintry look, she resembles a sexy poster-girl advertising for a ski resort.

She saunters right up to his face. "Waiting on James?"

Her words fall on deaf ears.

All he wants to do is throw his tongue down her throat.

"Freeman?"

"Oh, uh, yeah, we're about to secure a U-Haul truck for next weekend."

"I am so happy for him. He deserves it."

"I know. Heading home?"

She glances at her watch. "Yeah, my brother is picking me up. I thought he would've been here by now."

He rubs his chin. "Listen, about my sister's verbal assault on you earlier, she's just-"

"That's water under the bridge," she chuckles. "I, too, have thick skin, so we're good."

"Good, because Dee and Lovelle are extremely close, and…you know how that goes."

"Well, can you blame her for having your best interest at heart?" She grabs his hand. "I mean, c'mon, if I had the privilege of being your woman, I'd love the fact that she would go out her way to defend our relationship. So, I'm okay."

Her underlying message sinks in as they swing their arms in sweet silence. Still, he visions his tongue caressing her caramel-colored lips and struggles mightily to fight back those strong urges.

Out of nowhere, a candy apple-colored Bentley Coupe roars down Fourth Avenue and pulls up in front of them. As the limousine-tinted passenger window rolls down, Raekwon the Chef's classic gem, *Incarcerated Scarfaces,* escapes from the pulsating speakers causing pedestrians to peek in to see if the car belongs to someone famous.

Velour rolls her eyes in obvious admiration. "He just *loves* to make an entrance. Come, let me introduce you to my brother."

He follows her to the luxurious vehicle. She circles around to the driver's side as Freeman bends down to peer through the opened passenger window.

"Give me a minute," she says to her brother. "I need to get a money order."

"You should've done that before I even arrived," he quips.

"I'll make it quick, geez."

"Well, get a move on! Time is money!"

"Freeman, this is my brother, Vincent. Vincent, this is my new route partner, Freeman. You two get acquainted while I run back inside." Velour hustles into the post office's lobby.

"Nice to meet you." Freeman reaches his hand through the window.

Judging by Vincent's iron-clad grip, Freeman assumes he works out a lot. And by the rest of his flossy appearance—a dark-grey wool Kangol cap turned backward, a thick red turtleneck sweater underneath an even thicker butter-soft grey leather jacket, plus a red toothpick roaming in and out of his mouth—Vincent appears to be financially sound.

"Heard a lot about you, Playboy—so what's popping?" Vincent inquires.

"Nothing much. Just trying to keep my head above water."

"Aren't we all."

"I see you're doing quite well for yourself." Freeman's eyes take in the white leather seats with red piping and wood grain interior. "This is sweet."

"Appreciate it. I don't get to play with my toys often, due to my hectic work schedule. So today, I felt like taking this one out and letting it breathe, you know what I'm saying?"

"I can dig it."

"Velour is really excited about you replacing Dante on her route."

"Yeah, I guess she is. But if I had my way, I'd prefer driving over delivering any day-"

"By the way, Playboy; have you seen or heard from that water head fuck lately?"

The question stuns the hell out of Freeman.

He takes a second to size up Vincent's overall demeanor.

Cold, unwelcoming eyes combined with a toothy grin that seems to sneer at him as he waits for a response.

"Excuse me, but who are you referring to?"

"*Dante*," Vincent stresses as if he is offended by having to repeat himself. "Velour told me he'd transferred to another station, but I want to know if his bitch-ass still swings by here from time to time?"

Freeman quickly confirms to himself that he has zero tolerance for this dude's vibe or his line of questioning.

"Is there a particular reason you're asking?"

Vincent belts out a condescending laugh directly at him.

*Is this dude mocking me?*

The car phone rings.

Vincent stops laughing, pulls the toothpick from his mouth, and points it at him. "Don't worry yourself about it, alright? Just be a better route partner than Dante was. I have to take this call, peace out."

Vincent answers the phone while rolling the passenger window up in Freeman's face.

Velour returns and pauses for a moment to admire her brother's vehicle. "Is this Bentley nice or what?"

Freeman heard her but was still trying to wrap his mind around the Vincent interrogation concerning Dante. "Yeah, uh, real nice."

"Just wait until you see what *I* pull up in at James' housewarming!"

Freeman cocks an eyebrow. "Oh, so now *you're* balling on this level…on a postal check?"

"Hey, I have no kids, I live with my brother practically scot-free, and with all that overtime we're accumulating…the sky has been the limit, you hear me?"

"In other words, you got it like that."

"I believe I do."

Freeman dwells on a certain proposal before mustering up the courage to speak on it. "Check this out; I have a couple of tickets to this play called, *Holler If Ya Hear Me,* that's playing off-Broadway. Are you into plays?"

"What?!?" Her eyes light up. "I've been dying to go, but I could never get my hands on any tickets!"

"Well, would you mind accompanying me to the show?"

Velour blushes. "Wow. I'm flattered, Freeman, but I feel like this is something you should take your fiancée to-"

"Something came up and she won't be able to attend," he lies. "So, I'm just asking a *friend* out for a night on the town–no strings attached."

She grins down Fourth Avenue before turning back to him. "You have yourself a date."

He nods and smiles. "Cool."

"Let's go!" Vincent barks through the window.

She rolls her eyes. "Let me go before I have to hurt somebody."

"I'll call you later."

"I expect you to." She slips into the car and rolls down the window. "And thanks for thinking about me."

"I always do."

She beams.

Taking a deep breath, Freeman searches for enough strength in his heart to at least say goodbye to her brother. "It was a pleasure meeting you, Vin—"

*VRRRROOOOMMMMM!!!!!!*

The gleaming red Bentley leaves a blood-streaked path down Fourth Avenue, just beating the light.

"I see you met Mr. Personality."

Freeman turns around to James, who is standing a few feet behind him, observing the entire scene. They begin their trek down the block.

Freeman shakes his head. "Dude is a character."

"He's something alright," James shrugs. "He used to drop Velour off and pick her up almost every day, right before you started working here, but then it slowed down to only once in a blue moon."

"It's crazy," Freeman ponders. "She always seems to be curious about my family background, but not once has she talked about hers."

"As if you really care about her upbringing. You ain't slick!"

"Don't start that mess. I hear enough from Dee to last a lifetime."

"Yeah, but you can't deny the fact that she was hitting on the truth a little at the restaurant."

Freeman side-eyes James but says nothing.

"Yo, I don't want to be all up in your business because what you do *is* your business, but are you and Velour—?"

"We haven't done anything, okay?" Freeman bluntly states. "But keep that to yourself; let them other cats keep guessing."

"Gotcha. I mean, because if you two are, then that's your—"

"Damn, Jay!" Freeman stops in his tracks. "If I said we didn't do anything, we didn't do anything-"

"A'ight, chill," laughs James. "Getting all defensive and shit."

"But she keeps knocking on my door, yo."

"Yeah, we can see that."

"And I'ma keep it real with you; sooner or later I'm going to invite her in."

"So, what about Lovelle?"

"What about her?"

"Whoa, it's like that now? I thought y'all were trying to make it work this time."

"Let's not go there, if you don't mind."

"Alright, I'll drop it."

They turn the corner on Twelfth Street and walk across the street.

"Yo, what do you think about our new coworker, Cadina?" Freeman says. "Yo, she is mad *fly*. I had a chance to talk to her this morning and she seems really cool, too…Jay?"

Freeman glances to his side and finds himself walking alone.

He turns around.

James is a few feet behind him halted in one spot, with the goofiest grin Freeman has ever seen in his life.

"The hell is wrong with you?"

"Yo, Free, promise me you won't think I'm talking out my ass, please, hear me out."

"What the—what's up?"

"I think she likes me!"

Freeman bursts out laughing.

"I'm serious, Free…you can stop laughing any time now."

Freeman holds his chest and calms down. "And how do you know this?"

"Yo, ever since we met, she's been staring at a brutha! *Hard!* Even at Wang's when everyone was talking, she kept giving me that look the entire time, I kid you not!"

Freeman waits as James unlocks his doors and they both throw their bags onto the backseat. "Okay, if she's throwing all of this unspoken rhythm at you, then maybe you should step to her."

"I don't know, man. I'm not the smoothest brother in the world. I'll probably get all tongue-tied and say some stupid shit trying to be funny."

"Well, that's on you, Playboy," Freeman jumps into the passenger seat. "She's doing her part by giving you an open invite, now it's up to you to do *your* part. And really, just be yourself, that's half the battle right there."

"I know, I know." James slides in, cranks the engine, and then sits back in his seat, staring out the front windshield. "But she's got those soft, bubblegum lips that always seem to stay wet for no reason…it just makes me wanna grab her by her ears, pull her head towards mine and suck on them bad boys! And she got those curvy hips on that slim frame of hers. Yo, did you peep out her walk? She got that walk—that *strut*, mind you—like she just hopped off a thoroughbred with her bow-legged self…DAMN SHE FINE!"

Freeman chuckles. "If she has you sprung like that, then you need to start making moves, dawg."

"C'mon, man. You know I'm shy."

"Shy my ass! That didn't sound like you were shy a second ago when you wanted to grab her by her ears!"

"Hey, at least I don't have hoes hanging in the rafters like somebody we know."

"And packing more than Ron Jeremy!"

"Hey, that's *way* too much information to be sharing with the bruthas."

"Especially when we know his ass is lying!"

The two childhood friends double over in laughter as James peels off down the street.

# THIRTEEN

## CADINA

Balsamic glazed steak tips with mushrooms, garlic sauteed spinach, loaded baked potatoes and a fresh tossed salad with walnut dressing is the cuisine for the evening at Cadina's parents' home. She woofs down her plate and guzzles a glass of Ocean Spray cranberry juice in one shot, all the while sharing her journey as a postal employee to her sister, Camille.

"I swear, Cam, I even had help today from my instructor and my back still wanted to lock up on me. I can't imagine me doing that truck run by myself."

So, let me get this straight…" Camille, five years older than Cadina, and beautifully full-figured, sporting a braided swirl hairdo, and a Spelman College sweatshirt, pours herself some juice. "You drive a big postal truck around town and drop off heavy sacks of mail to your coworkers?"

"Yep." Cadina leans back in her chair. "*And* empty out those mailboxes you see on every other corner. That's the first thing on my long list of to-dos every morning."

"You sure you don't want your old job back at the restaurant?"

"Not in this lifetime."

"Well, maybe at another restaurant where you can maximize your culinary skills. What I can't understand is how someone as passionate about cooking as you are, opts to work at a place where you have no desire to be-"

"I never said I had no desire to work at the post office, that's coming out of *your* mouth-"

"You know what I mean. That's why Pops stay on your case so much. You have no sense of purpose, what-so-ever."

"Well, he doesn't have to stay on my case anymore because I have a job to do and I'm going to see it through to the end. Next topic, please."

"Well, at least tell me you have some eye candy to look forward to when you're moving all this mail around."

"There's a few," Cadina's eyes gleam. "They are crazy as hell, though."

Camille jumps to her feet in a dramatic fashion. "See! You said it yourself! The people at the post office are deranged and they're going to drag you all the way *down* to the sunken place! GET OUT! WHILE YOU STILL CAN, GIRL!"

Cadina hollers. "You stupid, you know that?"

"Just looking out for my little sis." Camille throws her coat on and grabs a plastic bag from the counter. "Thanks for dinner!"

"I'll call you later."

Camille leaves out the back door.

Cadina pushes herself out of the seat to take care of the kitchen. As she washes a few dishes, the house phone rings.

She wipes her hands before picking up the handset. "Hello?"

"Hey, Cadina! this is Bianca."

"Heeeeey, Bianca!" Cadina cheerfully greets a childhood friend. "Haven't heard from you in a minute! How's NYU treating you?"

"Girl, I finally completed my master's program in business management, so I'm officially done with school, thank you, Jesus."

"Oh, my God. I didn't know this was your last year?"

"Yep. And I'm so glad it flew by."

"Well, congratulations to you!"

"Thank you! And let me congratulate you on your new job, Miss Mail-Lady! How do you like it?"

"So far, so good." Cadina rubs the lower part of her aching back. "I'm really blessed to have it."

"I know that's right. Listen, the reason I called is that I was kind of hoping you would be interested in catering for my mother's sixtieth birthday which is coming up soon."

Cadina pauses briefly. "You want *me* to cater this event?"

"Girl, yes! I had you in my mind ever since I attended your family reunion last year and was told you were responsible for all the amazing food! I didn't know you could throw down like that! I mean, everything was so delicious and the potato salad? Oh, my God! You just can't eat everybody's potato salad, I'm sorry."

Cadina beams with pride while resuming with the dishes. "Why, thank you!"

"Now, I'd understand if you can't do it, being that you've just started your new job-"

"I would be honored to cater this event for your mother. Just give me the menu, headcount, the date, and I'll fit it in."

"Excellent! Now, let's talk about your fee. We're prepared to offer four thousand for your services. And we'll take care of the food expenses and servers."

Cadina almost drops a plate. "Excuse me, but did you say *four* thousand dollars?"

"The family is willing to negotiate if you decide to counter, but it wouldn't be an issue because I personally want your services-"

"Nooooo, noooo, I'm cool with that, thank you! And I promise I won't let you down, either."

"Girl, you couldn't let us down even if you tried. I'll have the itinerary ready for you by tomorrow. Be blessed and have a good night!"

"You as well!"

Cadina hangs up.

*"WOOOOO-HOOOOOOO!"*

She does the cabbage patch dance right where she stands.

The momentum of her mood shifts from feeling drained to that of elation as wipes down the kitchen counter. Four thousand dollars, for a day of doing something she absolutely loves. Her heart beats like that of a funky drummer but settles down quickly with fear of what-ifs:

*What if I undercook or overcook something? Worse, what if I make something and they think that it's just alright and not worth the money?*

But she trashes the negative bashing.

Especially when it comes to her forte.

Not only is she going to wear Bianca's praise as a badge of honor, but she's also going to make damn sure her name is on everybody's tongue before, during, and after that event—

*Ohhh, but James' big juicy lips, though...*

Cadina struts up the stairs with thoughts of new acquaintances and lucrative beginnings.

# FOURTEEN

## JAMES RICHARDS

"No, I said *this* Saturday, not next Saturday…Skillet, listen to me…I know what day I said because *I'm* the one who's moving…so what time are you gonna get to the Bronx? YES, I STILL NEED YOU!...I'm not yelling at you…just be on your way and bring Curtis and Simon with you…yes, I'll pay you when we're done, but meet us in the Bronx, not over here…bye."

*Fuck*!

James pockets his phone as he trudges out of the tenement building and into the cold Saturday afternoon. He blocks the sun from his eyes while glancing up and down Atlantic Avenue, knowing this will be the last weekend the Richards family will spend in Brooklyn before settling into their new home in the Bronx.

He then stares straight ahead at the U-Haul truck parked in front of the building's entrance. His crew, dressed in either worn sweatsuits or army fatigues, congregate at the rear of the truck.

Tired.

Hungry.

And when he shares his recent news, they are going to be pissed.

*Oh, well.*

James slaps on a positive smile and joins his cohorts behind the truck. He peeks inside the packed cargo area if only to properly gather his next words. He then turns around and faces his friends.

All eyes are on him.

Impatient eyes.

He clears his throat while maintaining happy eye contact with the crew. "Well, judging by our current situation, we probably need to make two more trips and we'll be done-"

"BULLSHIT!"

Roy, wiping his steaming forehead, fires off first. "Dude! I told you four hours ago; we're not going to be able to finish moving all of your furniture today!"

"Word. And we started late, too?" Shabbazz adds, kicking a rock down the street. "Yo, why did you pick this size truck, to begin with?"

"I was about to ask the same thing!" echoes Neville, sitting on the truck bumper. "You should've rented a moving company for all the shit you got upstairs."

"Yo, all I know is come eight o'clock, I'm ghost." Lou blows out a cloud of frustration into the frigid air. "You said your uncles and cousins were coming; where your peoples?"

James checks his watch. 5:10 pm. "They're on their way, relax."

"They've been on their way since noon, Jay. Where they coming from, Alaska?"'

Grace arrives from the building with a blissful smile.

"Alright, men," she begins, bubbling with misty-eyed pride. "I just want to say that I really, *really* appreciate you all taking time out of your busy schedules to come help us out. It, it really means so much to us—*oooh*!" She sheds happy tears and then wipes them away. "I'm sorry, it's just that this is the biggest day of our lives and because of friends like YOU!" She points to each crew member. "You all are making our dreams come true by being true servants of the Lord! So, when we get to our new home, I will have the best cheeseburgers and crinkle-cut fries ready for everyone, and for an added treat, Neapolitan ice cream for dessert! You know, the kind with the three flavors; chocolate, vanilla, and strawberry—how does that sound?"

The crew glares at James.

"Sounds good, Ma," he responds, looking the other way.

"Great! Again, thank you. And may God bless each and every one of you." Grace wipes her eyes again before skipping back into the building.

Freeman joins the group with a garment bag over his arm and casually dressed for an evening out on the town.

He turns to James. "Thanks for letting me use the bathroom to freshen up before I leave."

"No problem."

"And where the hell do you think you're going?" Lou asks.

Freeman smiles. "I had a prior engagement that unfortunately fell on today."

Lou turns to James. "Yo, Jay, this ain't right-"

"The man has tickets, Lou. What do you want me to do?"

Lou throws his hands in the air. "This is straight cah-cah, Bro. Eight o'clock, I'm out!"

"You ain't the only one," Roy moans.

Lou, Roy, Neville, and Shabbazz grumble their way towards the front of the truck.

Freeman turns to James. "Hey, if you want me to stay until your cousins arrive, I will-"

"Nah." James sits on the bumper. "This will be the last trip for the day. As you can see, the natives are getting restless."

"Put some food in their bellies, they'd calm down."

"I know, right?" James wipes his brow. "But I am surprised you bought tickets on the same day you knew I was moving."

"I didn't. Lovelle ordered them a while back, but it never occurred to me that it was on the same day-"

"Hold up." James stares confusingly at him. "You said Velour is coming to pick you up, right?"

"Yep."

"So, she's gonna drop you off somewhere to meet up with Lovelle?"

"Actually, I'm taking Velour to the show."

"With the tickets Lovelle bought?"

"With the tickets Lovelle bought for me to use at my discretion."

James shakes his head in amazement. "Wow. Does Lovelle know you're taking someone else?"

"At this point, it doesn't matter."

"But does she *know*–"

"Nope. And I'ma tell you why, since you're so determined to know."

"I'm not picking sides, Free, I just asked a simple question."

"Look, people may have their opinions about Velour and it's cool…that's their right. But for me, she's been a breath of fresh air ever since my mom passed and she's been sincere. Unfortunately, I can't say the same for the person that I'm *supposed* to be engaged to. Hopefully, that answered your question."

James studies Freeman for a moment and decides to let it go.

For now.

A taxi rolls up and double-parked behind the truck.

Velour sticks her head out from the backseat window.

"Hey, James! How's the moving coming along?"

"It *was* going good, but you're taking one of my helpers."

"Hey, it was all Freeman's idea. I'm just going along for the ride."

James faces Freeman. "So, I was told."

Freeman hugs James, all the while whispering in his ear. "I can handle my affairs, Jay. Concentrate on moving into your beautiful home."

He winks at James before climbing in the backseat of the taxi.

"I know the housewarming is going to be lit," she says in excitement. "I can't wait!"

"You know how I do. Y'all enjoy."

"We will!"

The taxi pulls off.

Skepticism creeps into James' memory bank.

He recalls not too long ago when Velour barely had two words to say to any of the crewmembers, including Freeman. Basically, she was on some prima donna shit. But no sooner than the passing of Freeman's mother, she made it her business to be his comforter, knowing full well he was spoken for. Freeman may say Velour's actions are sincere, but he's in a state of denial...because no one else is buying it.

And if Velour's actions are motive-driven...*why*?

*They are grown-ass people. No need for me to worry myself about it.*

James reaches up and closes the cargo door, locking it shut.

A group of teenage boys burst from the building, tossing a football to one another. One of the boys throws a bullet to James, who catches it and immediately launches a Hail Mary toward another boy who is sprinting down the street. The rest of them follow suit.

Jubilation sweeps over him as he now experiences a severe case of the *no mores*. No more listening to those same teenagers running up and down the hallway like a wild stampede late at night. No more bumping into drug transactions inside the building's stairwell. No more street news of so-and-so got shot by whomever on what floor. No more broken, urine-infested elevators to deal with.

And the list goes on.

*We are finally out of this friggin place.*

"IT'S GETTING LATE, PAPA!" Lou shouts from inside the truck. "LET'S ROLL!"

James snaps back into the present, circles around the truck, jumps behind the wheel, and pulls off, with Roy trailing them in his SUV.

# FIFTEEN

## FREEMAN

"Stop playing…" Freeman says, in awe.

Velour giggles. "I told you."

"You live right *here*?"

"This is where I lay my head every night." She grabs her purse and slides out of the backseat. She turns back to him. "Are you going to walk me to the door?"

Freeman grabs the uber driver's attention. "I'll be back."

Deep in the heart of New Rochelle, New York, he just assumed the uber driver was being a slickster by taking the scenic route to Velour's home as he drove through the ritzy neighborhood known as Bonnie Crest. Somehow, he never envisioned her living in *this* area which is famous for its luxurious English Tudor-style homes.

Sliding out of the vehicle, he never takes his eyes off the two-tone brick, three-storied, castle-like mansion, complete with a three-car garage nestled in the rear.

Velour leads the way through the colossal Victorian iron scroll gate and along the cobblestone walkway to the front entrance. He notices her brother's Bentley parked in front of the garages, along with a Ferrari, A Rolls Royce Phantom, and other luxurious vehicles.

"What did you say your brother does for a living?" he asks.

"He owns a chain of custom car shops."

"Oh, word?"

"Yep, from rims to detailing, to accessorizing rides for several recording artists and actors as well; trust me, he does it all. Been doing it since the late nineties, and as you can see, it's been paying off quite lovely."

"You got that right."

Before she can stick her key into the lock, the door swings open. A tall, dark-skinned brother, wearing a black mock-neck shirt over his rock-solid frame and matching doo-rag, greets Freeman with a tight-lipped thuggish glare.

"Hey, Stanley." Velour pockets her keys. "Freeman, this is Stanley, better known as Strong. Strong, this is my coworker, Freeman—"

Stanley quickly slams the door before giving her the chance to even finish her sentence.

Freeman gives her a puzzled look.

"A close friend of the family," she explains while shaking her head. "Don't mind him. He just wants to show his ass, that's all."

"Well, the way he was grilling me a second ago, it looked like he could be more than just a close friend."

"*Please.*" She inches closer to his lips. "He's like another overbearing brother I don't need in my life right now."

Freeman momentarily stares at the door before meeting her halfway towards her lips. "Well, what *do* you need in your life right now?"

She grips his face and thrusts her tongue inside his mouth, and they taste each other for the very first time. He matches her intensity to such a degree, they begin play-fighting for tongue domination. They wrap up the passionate moment with laughter and a long, comforting hug.

"You had a good time tonight?" he whispers in her ear.

"The best night I've had in a while."

Between her nibbling his ear and inhaling her enticing perfume, he manages to say, "I'm glad."

She pulls away while still holding onto his hands. "But now I have to get ready for tomorrow. We had a shipment arrive today and we must put the new rims and accessories on display, sooo, that means-"

"Long day tomorrow."

"But don't let it stop you from calling me tomorrow evening."

"And what if I decide not to?"

She purses her lips. "Then, I will pout and call you all kinds of names."

"Oh, really…"

"Yes, really."

They share another long, sensual kiss.

He peeks down at his crotch area. "Okay. Something's popped up. I'll see you Monday."

"Bye, Silly."

After a quick kiss, Freeman double-times it to the waiting uber. "To the Bronx, please. Co-op City."

Freeman turns on his phone.

Thirteen messages.

Eleven from Lovelle. Two from Divine.

Out of nowhere, he hears a loud disturbance.

He turns his head and witnesses Velour having a heated discussion with Vincent that apparently gets out of hand when the muscle-bound sibling repeatedly points his index finger in Velour's face. She, in turn, slaps his hand away from her and stomps her way inside of the mansion. Vincent then turns his attention towards the uber and locks his eyes on Freeman.

*What the hell…*

After a long and unsettling stare down, Vincent rolls down the sleeves of his black shirt and storms back inside, slamming the door behind him.

"Ooooh, he looked like he wanted to kick your ass, my friend!" the nosy uber driver states. "I hope you have good health insurance—"

"Co-op City, the Bronx, please—thank you."

The uber driver rolls his bloodshot eyes and drives off.

His phone vibrates in his hand.

It's another text from Lovelle.

Instead of responding back to his fiancée, he texts Velour to see if she's alright.

She immediately responds by saying she's good, along with a winky-kiss emoticon.

Lovelle now calls him and he immediately turns the phone off. He does not want to hear her mouth about anything, especially if it pertains to those tickets. If anything, he would love to thank her for purchasing them. But that would be tacky.

Right now, he could care less about his fiancée or Vincent, for that matter. He and Velour had too much of a blast for him to let anything or anyone spoil his erotic high.

Freeman gazes out the window and smiles at the clear blue night.

# SIXTEEN

## MICHAEL DAVENPORT

Monday morning at Midway Station and Davenport strolls down the work floor toward Chapman's section. With his obligatory 'good mornings' and a politician's 'wave-and-smile', the station manager's professional charade is in full effect.

Behind his pasted grin, however, lies displeasure.

As soon as he gets his station operating at full potential, the powers-to-be from midtown shatter Davenport's stability. This time it happens to be a valuable component of his operation. Supervisor Sterling, his truck/computer specialist, who also possesses the experience needed to manage another station, will be used in that capacity for a three-month period until the folks from midtown can permanently assign someone else.

The aggravated manager takes off his coat and shakes Chapman's hand. "How's it going?"

"It's going. Denise told me the jolly news about Sterl."

"They just can't keep their hands out of my cookie jar," Davenport gripes. "I must be doing something right if they're always willing to pull people from *this* station instead of the other stations in this city."

"I agree with you on that. When's he leaving?"

"In another month. And you'll be taking Sterling's spot downstairs for the duration of his absence."

"Who's going to take my spot up here?"

Davenport crosses his arms. "Take one guess."

"Someone straight from the Supervisor Academy. Can you say *sacrificial lamb*? I feel sorry for the person already."

"I know. How're we looking around here?"

"Marc called earlier this morning, saying he couldn't make it in today."

Davenport lowers his brow. "What's wrong *this* time?"

"He said he has to change medications because the ones he's currently taking are making him sick."

The manager grimaces.

"I specifically asked him to consider either staying home until he was one hundred percent healthy or taking a light-duty position, to avoid putting too much strain on his body, but he wants to play this on and off crap and I'm getting a little tired of it. Who is on his route today?"

"Miss Wilson."

Davenport nods. He makes his way over to the workstation where an overwhelmed Cadina is standing in one spot watching the mail handlers stack up two columns of overly packed letter trays that measure up to her waist.

"Miss Wilson!" he greets in a jolly tone. "How're we making out over here?"

"Okay, I guess."

"From what I'm hearing, you're doing a magnificent job. Keep up the good work, okay?"

"Thank you."

Davenport returns to the podium where Chapman prepares to brief him.

"I spoke to Freeman and Lou about pivoting over to help Cadina when they're done. James is going to swing by Divine's route after she's finished, so everyone's covered."

Davenport nods. "Good. We need to bring everyone back early to the station as soon as possible. The folks at midtown are hounding me about the excessive overtime we accumulated after the holidays and they want things to start smoothing out now. What they need to do is to stop taking my staff away from me so that I can successfully follow through with what they want."

"I'll make a note of it." Chapman scribbles on his clipboard. "I'll keep you posted with everyone's whereabouts."

"Thanks, David. I'll be in my office if you need me."

Davenport makes his way down the work floor, shaking hands, smiling, and waving. Yet, as he hits the stairwell, he thinks about how nice it would be if he could persuade the folks at midtown to leave his staff alone.

# SEVENTEEN

## CADINA/LEXINGTON

Aches and pains travel throughout Cadina's body as she labors up the loading dock ramp and onto the elevator lift. When the doors close, so do her eyelids. She summons enough nerve to pose a daring question to Chapman pertaining to the party she is supposed to cater for the upcoming Saturday. The thought of calling in sick did cross her mind, but she quickly dismisses the notion. After that whole restaurant debacle with her father, she is sticking to the promise of cleaning up her act, which means no more doing what she wants to do when she wants to do it.

*But we're talking four grand, Boo.*

Her heart flutters with the possibilities.

She quietly recites to herself; "*I would like to have this Saturday*... nah, that's too direct... *Would it be possible to have this Saturday off for an event I was asked to cater?*"

The elevator reaches the second floor.

The doors open and there stands Lexington, dressed in a two-piece gray wool suit, a greased-down baldie, and an even greasier-looking smirk on his face.

He swaggers onto the elevator with one hand in his pocket and the other holding a cellphone. "Good morning, Cadina. Today's the big day!"

She stares right through him. "Excuse me?"

"The supervisor exam; I mentioned this to you on several occasions. Don't tell me you forgot?"

"I didn't know I was supposed to remember. But good luck, anyway."

She walks off the elevator lift.

"Chapman told me you're going to be on my route today." Lexington presses the button. "Don't make me look bad."

Cadina spins around to the shiny-face rascal. "That was really encouraging, Lex."

"Just messing with you. I'm sure you're going to do what you can."

Lexington smiles down at his phone as the doors close.

*Asshole.*

She gets her mind right before walking down the work floor, en route to the podium where Chapman is hanging up the phone.

"Good morning, Mr. Chapman," she greets, while also measuring the supervisor's mood. "I was told I will be covering Lexington's route today?"

"Shabbazz won't be coming in, his car broke down on the highway this morning." He explains this while erasing something from his clipboard. "Which means you'll be covering his truck assignment."

Her heart sinks completely through the floor.

"B-But I only trained a few days with him on the truck–"

"We know. This is his collection board." He hands her the folder. "You're only doing that and his relay runs today. Roy is going to drive you to the garage to pick up the truck, so meet him downstairs, he's waiting on you."

This was not the type of morning she was anticipating.

"Wow, okay. Um, but I have a favor to ask from you."

Chapman continues jotting on his clipboard. "What is it?"

"I was wondering if it would be possible to have this Saturday off?"

His eyes pop up at her.

You would have thought she cursed at him.

He shakes his head. "I'm sorry, Miss Wilson, but being that this is your probationary period, I have you locked in on every Saturday for the next three months due to filling in vacation spots, carriers' three-day weekends, plus the fact that we're still undermanned in this station. I'm afraid I can't give you this Saturday off."

Her mind goes to work.

"I understand, Mr. Chapman, I really do, but I'm supposed to cater my aunt's birthday this Saturday and my family is counting on me to do this. I promise I won't bother you about any more days off, I swear."

She hits him with her best puppy dog expression.

At that crucial moment, Tucker joins them at the podium.

"Did you hear from Shabbazz?" the assistant manager asks Chapman.

"Just got off the phone with him. Cadina is going to cover his truck assignment today, but only the collections and relays. Roy and Neville are going to split up the early drops. And I know you heard the news about Marc…"

"Yeah, the doctor prescribed him the wrong medication. I tell ya, if it's not one thing, it's another." Tucker gives Cadina a once-over look. "Good morning, Miss Wilson. Are you ready to go?"

"Yes, Ma'am."

For some reason, Cadina is not feeling any positive vibes from Tucker at all.

But then, the unthinkable is about to happen.

*Don't you dare ask her, Chaps, please don't ask her—*

"Not to jump subjects, Denise," Chapman says. "…but Miss Wilson wants to know if she can have this Saturday off to cater a family event."

Tucker furiously shakes her head. "Your Saturdays are booked for the next couple of months, my dear. Didn't you see the schedule before you made plans for this event?"

Cadina starts fast-talking.

"I know this is short notice, Mrs. Tucker, but I wouldn't be asking if it wasn't important."

"Well, I'm sorry, Miss. Wilson, but they're going to have to find another caterer for this affair. It's only Tuesday, they'll have enough time."

"But they don't want anybody else, they want *me.*"

"They do know you just started a job that requires you to work on the weekends, right?"

"They know this already, Mrs. Tucker, but I—"

"But you went ahead and made a commitment, knowing you were scheduled to work this Saturday?"

Cadina pauses for a second to get her answer straight. "Well, yes, but only because I didn't think it would be too big of a deal to have that day off—"

"Let me explain something to you, Miss Wilson," Tucker tightens her lips. "When we hired you as a part-time flexible substitute, it meant just that. You must be flexible with *our* schedule, not the other way around. You see what's happening around here. Lexington is about to leave soon for the academy. Marc is dealing with health issues and then you run into situations like Shabbazz's. So, if I were you, I would call your people and tell them you can't fulfill that obligation, okay? I'm sorry. I'm so sorry."

The expression on Tucker's face suggests that she is not really sorry at all.

"Now, if you run into any problems during your collection run, don't hesitate to call us or one of the drivers, they would be happy to assist you. And please be safe out there."

Tucker turns around to continue chatting with Chapman.

"AYE, CADINA! LET'S GO!" Roy yells from the elevator lift.

Cadina turns around and marches down the work floor.

Each stride is fueled with anger and resentment.

*She could've given me the damn day off. It's not like the whole station is going to suffer because of my absence.*

Despite it all, she must push those bitter emotions aside to concentrate on a truck assignment she has no desire of doing.

She quickens her pace to the elevator.

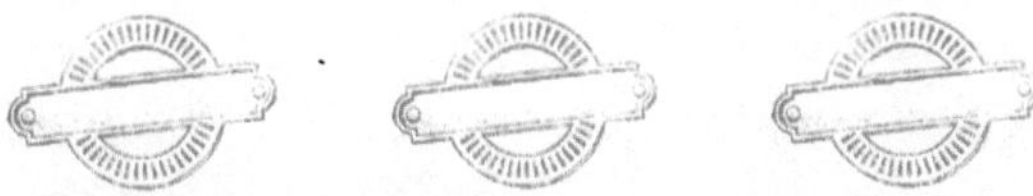

INSIDE MIDTOWN MANHATTAN'S GENERAL POST OFFICE ON 33RD AND 8th Avenue, the examination room is crowded with jittery supervisor-hopefuls, who quietly wait for the test administrator to signal the start of the first part of the exam.

An attractive Dominican woman becomes so annoyed with Lexington trying to gain her attention, that she boldly displays her wedding ring. He turns around in his seat and stubbornly adjusts his bowtie.

"Okay, everyone!" the tester says, motioning for the classroom's attention. "You will have thirty minutes to complete the first part of this exam. When I say time's up, you put your pencils down immediately and close your booklets. Any questions?"

Adrenaline rushes through Lexington's body every time he thinks about his future transition from a person delivering mail to a person who *oversees* the people who deliver the mail. His mind travels four to five years down the road where he sees himself navigating in the supervisory field until he has gained the time and knowledge needed to achieve his ultimate goal –becoming a station manager. The endless opportunities cause him to tremble in sensation.

"You may open your booklets and begin."

The flapping sounds of pages turning echo throughout the large room.

Lexington grabs his pencil and focuses on the task at hand.

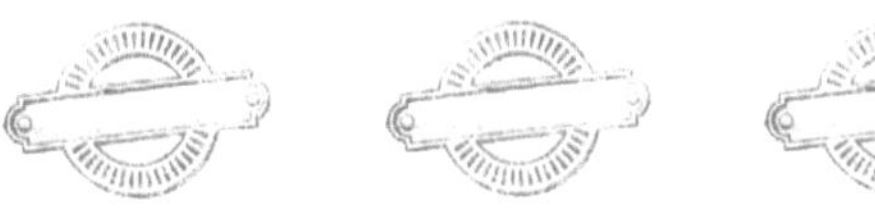

HOOONNKKK!!!!!

Cadina snaps out of her trance and realizes the light has turned green. Before she can release the brake, the truck behind her blows its horn again.

"OKAY, ASSHOLE!" she screams from inside the truck as she drives down Second Avenue on her way to drop off the last of the relays.

*What a day.*

Everything that could've gone wrong, did. Not only did the early collection go haywire (letters flying into the streets because of rapid winds, a couple of mailboxes she couldn't locate on the streets only to find out they were inside buildings, and she had to turn right back around to scan a couple of boxes she missed), but with the few early mail drop-offs she had to deliver, she took them to the wrong buildings-

*This address is 30 East 9th, my dear, not 30 East 10th.*

And that string of unfortunate events made her late getting the relays out to her coworkers. Each carrier she met up with either gave her a compassionate look or was obviously ticked off by receiving their relay bags an hour late. A few carriers were happy with the slow relay delivery, only for the sake of overtime. But she wasn't happy at all. Only tired.

Pulling up to the final relay stop for the day, Cadina watches an older female carrier near the relay box swing her arm impatiently as she talks on her cell phone.

Cadina can only assume that the conversation is about her.

She parks the truck, stumbles out of the passenger's side to open the back door. The woman carrier hastily motions for Cadina to bring the bags over to her opened mailcart.

The woman carrier snaps in the phone, "Noooo, she's here now, so what do you want me to do? An hour is definitely not cutting it." She swings around to Cadina. "Are these your last relays?"

Exhausted, Cadina nods yes.

"Yeah, I'm her last stop…Yeah, I'll tell her, bye."

The woman carrier pockets her phone and releases a disappointed sigh while shaking her head at Cadina. "Chapman wants you to help me finish up my route so I can get back within the hour, as if that's going to happen. Did you eat yet?"

"I'm alright."

"What does that mean?" the woman carrier huffs. "Yes or no? You're entitled to your lunch, you know?"

"I said I'm alright."

"Okay."

The two ladies load up the cart with four relay bags.

"Your name is Cadina, right?" the woman carrier asks, pushing up her glasses on her nose and sticking out her hand. "My name is Gladys. I just don't want you dying out here on me, alright?"

"I understand."

"Well, you ready?"

"Let me lock the truck."

Cadina just lied to the lady. Her stomach is grumbling up a storm.

But she prefers to wait until she's at home to eat. That way, she can soak in a hot bubble bath afterward and then jump into her cozy bed which is calling her with each passing minute.

Cadina wipes her face with a small towel, grabs her jacket, and then locks the truck. She turns around and watches Gretel push her cart down the sidewalk, which is fine by her. At this very moment, she is not in the right frame of mind to get acquainted with another one of the elder carriers.

Tucker killed that mood earlier that morning.

She purposely trails behind Gretel with hopes of a better tomorrow.

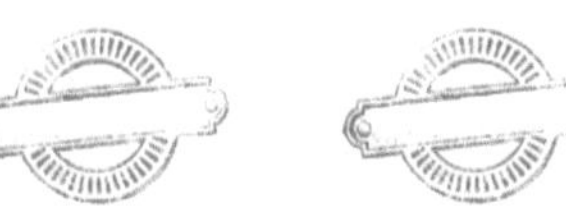

The next day does not do Cadina any justice at all.

In fact, it starts off on the wrong foot in a hurry, as the relaxing bath she took the night before evidently overdid its job. She wakes up late, hurries a shower, throws on some clean work clothes, and bolts out the door without even applying make-up.

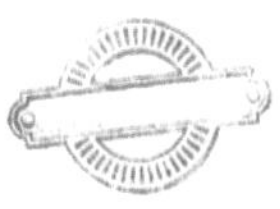
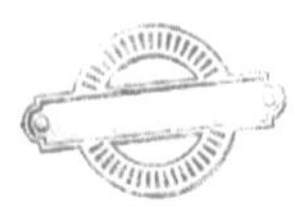
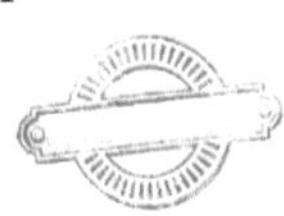

As Lexington sits on his bed to tie his shoes, the radiance of the sun blasting its way into his bedroom, causes him to chuckle with delight. His future appears just as bright.

He knows he aced that test.

He can just *feel* it.

Now, all he has left to do is to impress the members of the board, which to him, is merely a welcome wagon for the future elite, and his mission will be completed. He laughs as he checks his neat appearance, grabs his leather trench, and struts out the door.

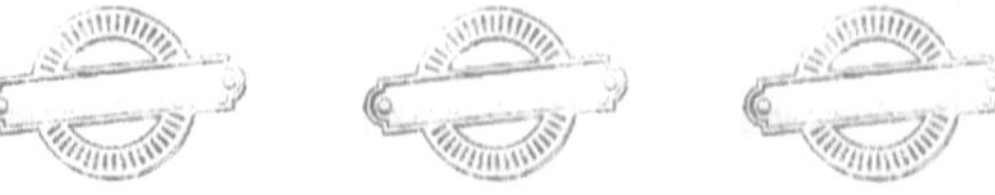

"*DUMB-ASSES...*" MUTTERS CADINA AS SHE WASHES HER HANDS AND ARMS.

Another day. Another truck assignment. Another dramatic episode. It was bad enough that every collection box on Neville's run was stuffed with oversized mail, but she failed to see the humor in finding a mushy Big Mac sandwich inside the last box. This caused her to squeeze secret sauce over some of the mail and her arm. After cleaning herself off, she hurries downstairs to load up the truck with the early drops. Repeating to herself simply to take it easy, she does exactly the opposite. She rushes through her early stops only to find out that some of the mail was delivered to the wrong buildings—again.

*These people are going to think I'm stupid.*

More time wasted. Extra energy spent. After correcting those errors, she high tails it back to an empty station. Panic overtakes her body as she pushes heavy relay skids to the elevator. She does not want a repeat performance of yesterday's disaster. When she arrives at the loading dock, she launches the heavy bags into the truck, slides behind the wheel, and takes off down the street.

Just like the previous day, carriers wait by their relay boxes for her arrival. She apologizes to each carrier for being late and again she receives mixed reactions. This time, however, it doesn't faze her as she delivers the last of her relays. She parks the truck on a side street, turns off the engine, and closes her eyes.

*Whew.*

Finally, she gets to rest.

With her heartbeat settling down to its regular pace, she cannot recall ever working this hard in her life. She never had to. Everything was inadvertently handed to her on a silver platter. Slowly those pampered walls are being broken down by the physical realization of her current job.

Cracking her eyes open slightly, her attention is drawn to her feet. She reaches for an item tucked behind her route board.

She stares at it in horror.

An Express envelope needed to have been delivered by noon.

And it's now three in the afternoon.

She cranks the truck, slaps the gear into drive, mashes the gas pedal, and roars down the street, desperately repeating, *"oh my God, oh my God!"*, to herself. As she drives the late item to its destination, she is cut short by a construction flagger, who furiously waves his stop sign as if he is about to hit the front of the truck.

She looks left.

A funeral convoy, stretching a mile long, creeps through the busy intersection.

*You're in big trouble, Caddy.*

She shifts the gear in park and slouches back in her seat to watch the limousine-led vehicles, shining their bright lights, pass by.

In Cadina's eyes, failing to deliver the Express envelope, which she now held in her trembling hand, was like watching her own funeral take place.

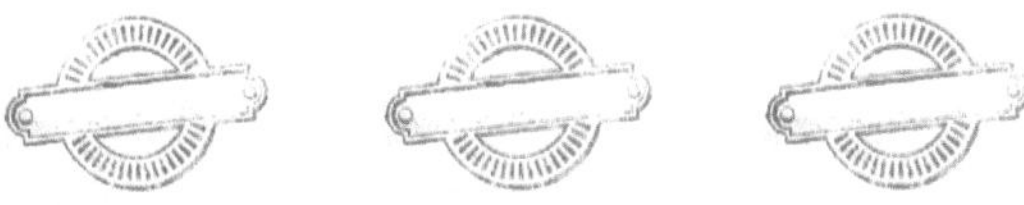

LEXINGTON IS LOVING EVERY MINUTE OF IT.

He now stands proudly before three board members.

Armed and ready to show them he possesses the proper skills needed to lead the masses.

From the first question, "*Why do you want to become a supervisor?*", to the last, "*What is the number one goal of a supervisor?*", Lexington confidently answers with integrity and professionalism. He wishes Davenport was present to witness his student emulate his style. He would be proud.

The board members rise to their feet to shake his hand and commend him on a job well done. He holds back his emotions until he leaves the room.

Mission complete.

In the hallway, he feels like he's floating in air. He tries to hold back his solo celebration but cannot contain himself.

*"YEEEEEEEEEEEEAAAAAAAHHHHHH!"*

His reaction scares a lady custodian half to death.

"Sorry!"

He laughs out loud, as he runs down the corridor, pumping his fist in the air in victory.

# EIGHTEEN

## CADINA

Cadina sanitizes her hands and digs into the corners of her eyes to make sure there is no crust buried in them. Then she applies her lipstick. Afterward, she checks her face one last time in her compact mirror and then hops out of the truck. She locks the door, and turns around to take a deep breath, for this will be the first time that she has ever worked with James alone and she plans on keeping her emotions under control.

She pushes through the revolving doors of an impressive co-op building and is quickly greeted by a pot-bellied, black uniform-wearing Spanish doorman, who is handling luggage.

"May I help you, Ma'am?" he asks, under his thick mustache.

She flashes her postal badge.

He smiles. "James is in the back." He points her in the direction of the mailroom.

"Thank you."

Cadina walks to the back room. She observes James as he places bundles of mail in their designated panels.

With his headphones on, he bobs his head to his music before doing a quick double-take at Cadina. His surprised gaze turns into a welcoming grin as he pulls off his headset.

Her heart flutters in delight.

"I thought you'd be on your way home by now," he says.

*Hmmm. He's been thinking about me.*

"I thought so, too." She leans on the ledge. "But Chapman wanted me to check on you to make sure you were alright out here."

"All I have left is this building, so if you want to give me a hand, you can start on the other end."

"Sure, no problem."

She heads to the panel but turns around immediately. "Uh, James, question; would I be in trouble because of this?" She pulls out the Express receipt from her jacket and shows it to him. "It didn't get there before twelve."

James examines the receipt. "Nah, it was attempted yesterday."

"What does that mean?"

"It means that somebody tried to deliver it yesterday, but no one was home, which means the next day you don't have to rush trying to deliver it before noon. So, you're good."

"Thank God."

"You were shook for a minute, huh?"

"Man, you don't know the half!"

Their hearty laughter slows to a light chuckle. The attraction she feels for him is too overpowering to conceal. She sees it in his eyes as well. They quickly head to opposite panels and begin working.

For the next ten minutes, the only sound in the mailroom is the opening and closing of the panel doors. They talk for a brief spell about the job, but then silence again fills the room.

She analyzes the challenge that lies ahead and takes it upon herself to jumpstart their flat-lined conversation.

She did not dig the crust out of her eyes for nothing.

She picks up a letter that does not have an apartment number on it and strolls over to him.

"Uh, 16B."

"Thanks." She returns to her panel and then turns around. "What's the name of that cologne you're wearing?"

Beaming with pride, James replies, "It's called Iceberg Twice. Why? You like it?"

"Well, you sure sprayed a lot on."

She resumes delivering the mail.

From the corner of her eye, she is pleased to see the results of her smart remark.

Laughter.

*Yes!*

He turns to her. "Now, I know you're not cracking on my cologne over there."

She turns around and smiles. "I'm saying, though. Just a little dab will do you, James, not half the bottle, c'mon."

"I see you come with jokes. Okay, you got that one."

"I'm only messing with you. It smells nice."

"I know damn well it smells nice! And for your information, I didn't spray half a bottle on me, either."

"Then how much did you put on, a quarter of a bottle?"

"Let's just say I sprayed enough to grab *your* attention."

*He's flirting...about time!*

She grins. "I'm scared of *you*."

"You don't have to be."

The tingling sensation hits the Richter scale in her body.

"Alright, now."

Earth, Wind & Fire's classic song, *Devotion*, softly harmonizes from the lobby/mailroom speakers.

"Ahhh, yeah." Cadina sways her head and snaps her fingers. "This is my jam right here!"

"What do you know about Earth, Wind, and Fire? That's *my* group–"

"Mine, too! That's all my father played growing up! Them and the Isley Brothers."

"So, you got it honestly, huh?" James croons in a high falsetto, "*Through Devotion...*"

*"Blessed are the children!"* Cadina joins in, with her arms stretched out in dramatic fashion.

They sing so hard that they catch the eye of a tenant who walks in on their serenading act. The tenant retrieves her mail from the box, smiles at both James and Cadina, and then exits the mailroom.

"You crazy, you know that, right?" he says.

"Well, you started it!"

"Can I get your opinion on something?" He digs in his hoodie pocket.

"Sure. What's up?"

She strolls over to him and for a moment, gets lost in the scent of his cologne, which she is already growing to love. He opens a flyer and points to two pictures.

"I'm having somewhat of a dilemma here. I want to surprise my daughter with a bedroom theme for the new house. Now, she loves Beyonce, but she's also a devoted Knick fan. I can't decide between the two."

She smiles half-heartedly at the flyer.

"Well, I mean, does my opinion really matter? What does her mother think?"

"Her mother isn't around anymore."

Her mouth gapes out of sheer stupidity for sounding jealous. "I'm so sorry, James. I didn't know she had passed—"

"No, no, no…" He waves off her assumption. "Let me rephrase that. When I say she's not around, I mean she's…she's just not active in her daughter's life. As crazy as it sounds, that's the reality I'm dealing with, so…" He stuffs the flyer back into his pocket and resumes to his panel.

"Oh."

Too judgmental, too soon.

*Clean it up, Cadina, switch topics.*

"So, do you have a picture of your little angel?"

James turns around. He grins like a proud father. "I sure do."

He pulls out his wallet, fingers through his credit cards, and business cards, to no avail. He gives her a sheepish look and flips through his wallet again. "It's in here somewhere."

She folds her arms. "Now that's a shame."

"I just bought this wallet two days ago and I thought I transferred everything from my old one—"

"You know, there should be a *law* against this type of foolishness."

"You know what?" James pockets his wallet. "Just for that remark, you're coming to my housewarming party this Saturday so you can meet her yourself, and I'm not taking no for an answer, either."

She laughs but then studies his face. "You sure it's cool?"

"What did I just say?"

His sense of humor matches hers to the tee. Even though she knows to take this one day at a time, she has a good feeling she is going to enjoy the beginnings of this newfound friendship, and whatever else it may lead to. She just hopes he is on the up and up about this "supposed" baby-momma drama. Nothing in life is what it seems these days. She knows this for a fact. But her inner voice has already confided in her.

He is the chosen one.

"Okay, but I'm not coming over empty-handed, so can I bring over a dish?"

"You cook?"

"I dabble a little."

"A little…"

"Well, a lot. I enjoy cooking."

"Well, surprise me with your culinary skills."

"I will do that."

"Cool."

All the qualities of what a man should be are being portrayed right in front of her eyes. Confident, but low-key. Gentle when he needs to be. Strong when he has to be. And the ability to laugh at himself and not take life so seriously. She is digging him more and more with every passing second.

"James..."

He stops working and turns her way.

"Go with the Beyonce theme. She's doing a lot better than the Knicks these days."

James' face lights up from laughter.

They continue to work and converse in pure harmony.

Like life-long companions.

# NINETEEN

## LEXINGTON

Outside of Midway Station, Lexington leans on the building as he impatiently waits for Tucker to stop chatting with James' mother, Grace, and daughter, Janae. He checks his watch. She said to give her five minutes. Yet, fifteen minutes have blown by, and the two ladies haven't stopped to catch their breaths.

The rumbling sounds of a truck bend Lexington's ear.

He turns around and watches Cadina park the postal truck on the curb and hop out on the driver's side. He smiles but then frowns once he sees James jump out of the passenger's side. The two carriers walk in his direction, laughing and smiling at one another.

He immediately waves at her. "Hey! How was your day-?"

They stroll past Lexington and join the gathering on the corner.

Lexington grimaces as he checks his watch again and stubbornly listens in on their extended conversation.

James embraces both his mother and daughter. "Cadina, these are my two sweethearts. My queen, Grace, and our future WNBA first-round draft pick, Janae."

"Nice to meet you," Grace said, vigorously shaking Cadina's hand.

"Nice to meet you, too, Ma'am." Cadina turns to Janae. "Hey, Pretty."

"Hey."

The pigtailed young lady, in her pink goose jacket and matching Nikes, slowly encircles Cadina, inspecting her body.

Confused, Cadina looks over her shoulder. "Is something on my back, Sweetie?"

Janae turns to her father. "Daddy, why did you tell Uncle Freeman she has an onion booty? Clearly, her booty doesn't look like no onion."

James turns red from embarrassment.

Cadina blushes.

Lexington fumes by the wall.

*Cock-blockin' bastard!*

"I don't know what she's talking about," James responds, chuckling. "But I, uh, invited Cadina to our housewarming Saturday, Ma."

"Oh, she's already welcomed." Grace smiles at Cadina. "And I'm happy Denise is coming, as well!"

"Wouldn't miss it for the world." Tucker hugs both Grace and Janae. "Now, if you'll excuse me, I have to finish up for the day. It's always good seeing you, Grace."

"Likewise."

*About time.*

Tucker walks over to him with a grand smile. "Sooo, Mr. VanGuard, are you ready to spring the good news on Davenport?"

Despite being annoyed by James and his family's presence, Lexington cannot stifle his giddiness any longer. "Let's do this."

They make their way inside the station.

Lexington overhears Cadina relieving herself from James and his family.

He approves of a thought that enters his mind.

"On second thought, why don't you go and break the news for me while I use the bathroom."

Tucker gives him a curious look. "I can wait. I'm quite sure he'd want to hear the big announcement from you."

He hears Cadina walking up the ramp. "I'm cool with you doing it. It's no big deal, either way."

"Well, if you insist. Shoot, I think I'm more excited than you are at this point! Meet me in the office." Tucker winks at him and then double-times down the first floor.

With his heart racing, Lexington waits to hear the door behind him open so it won't appear as if he was waiting for her. The next five seconds seem like an eternity to him. Finally, the door swings open and Cadina enters the building's stairwell.

He turns around and mocks a surprised expression. "Oh, hey Cadina!"

"Hey."

She passes by him and approaches the area called the valuable's cage to return her arrow key and registered mail receipts to the clerk.

Lexington obsessively appraises Cadina's toned profile.

Her long, black ponytail that rests on the back of a track athlete's frame.

Her cute bow-legged stance.

Her firm onion booty.

He has been craving her body from the moment he first laid eyes on her. But due to his tight schedule and her training sessions on various truck assignments, he has never had the chance to establish any kind of connection with her. Therefore, he must act now.

She tells the lady clerk *thank you* and heads back to the stairwell. And just when she's about to take the staircase, he cuts her off.

"Guess what?"

Annoyed, she asks, "What?"

"I got a ninety-eight on the exam!"

"You got a ninety-eight on what ex…ohhh! The supervisor's exam! Congratulations! That *is* good news! I'm so happy for you!"

"Really?" The excitement in her voice makes his private jump. "Thanks! That test would've been a beast had I not prepared for it with Davenport's help."

"Good for you, Lex. That is really major! Congratulations again."

She tries to go around him, but again, he blocks her path.

"Lexington, what do you want from me?"

"Well, I was wondering if you wouldn't mind accompanying me to a celebration dinner later this evening—"

His proposal is met with a declining headshake.

"I'm sorry, Lex, but I have a ton of stuff to do when I get home, so–"

"I know this was short notice, but what about tomorrow? I'm free as a bird!"

"Lexington…can I be honest with you?"

"Noooo, I'd rather you take me up on my offer."

"But I'm not interested in you in that way."

"Oh, really?" His tone stiffens. "You haven't been around me long enough to form a true opinion about me."

"Hold up, Lex. How are you going to tell me about my own feelings towards you?"

"Because you don't know any better, that's why."

"Excuse you?"

The intense exchange is cut short when James enters the stairwell.

"Hey," James says to Cadina while squeezing in between the two of them. "I told my moms you're bringing a dish to the party and she wants to know what it is."

Cadina rubs her chin. "I was thinking about making oxtails–"

"*STOPPP!*" James takes a step back, almost scuffing Lexington's shoes. "Now, you know that's my favorite, right? Don't disappoint me."

"I think you will enjoy them."

"Then, I will see you tomorrow." James turns around to a seething Lexington. "What's up, Lex? Nice suit."

James walks back outside.

"Clearly, he wasn't raised with any manners," Lexington huffs while adjusting his cuffs. "Anyway, back to our conversation–"

"Listen, Lex, I don't want this conversation going any further than it needs to." She places her hand on his shoulder. "I'm happy for you with your test results, okay? So, let's leave it at that and you have yourself a good afternoon."

Cadina pats his shoulder like an old chum and trots up the staircase.

Watching the way her ponytail bounces off her back, he suppresses the thought of yanking her ass back down those stairs.

*Bitch, you ain't the only fish in the sea.*

# TWENTY

## DAVENPORT

*Tap…Tap…Tap…Tap…Tap…*

Lounging behind his desk, Davenport subconsciously beats his pen to the cadence of the clock that ticks the afternoon seconds away. He is a bit ticked off himself. Rising from his desk, the manager rubs his head as he stands in front of the big calendar on the wall. Earlier, he received a call from midtown informing him that Sterling's status has been upgraded to managing another station for an indefinite amount of time.

He knew this was going to happen.

Still, he does not find it too pleasing that the powers-to-be would disrupt the mechanical rhythms of his reputable station without sending a competent supervisor who would possess half of Sterling's caliber to replace him. Somebody who could monitor all the truck routes without the chaos, run the computer operation, and relate to the carriers while simultaneously earning their respect. That's the person they're taking away from Davenport. The sheer thought of a 'wet-behind-the-ears' supervisor coming straight from the academy and into his station provokes him to rub his head even more.

Tucker breezes into the office with a song and two-step dance shuffle.

"*We're gonna have a gooood time tonight! Let's celebrate...it's alright!* Be the background vocals for me, Michael..."

He manages a weary grin at Tucker who, with her dreadlocks twirling around in the air, has every reason to be jovial.

Tucker stops dancing. She leans on the desk and then clasps her hands. "Come on, Michael. It was bound to happen sooner or later. Sterling has been in this profession almost as long as you have, and I wouldn't be too surprised if he accepts the job permanently."

"I know." Davenport circles around his desk and plops back in his seat. "But can I be selfish for once? Shoot, I mean, I had the perfect staff in place. The better the staff, the better the numbers look in the long run. I live and die by that mantra."

"Will you put your numbers to the side and focus on Lexington?"

He finally cracks a smile. "He damn near aced that test. A *ninety-eight* percent?!?"

"So you *have* heard about it!"

"I got the call about an hour ago."

"Our boy topped them all!" Tucker rejoices by pumping a fist in the air. "Oh, and he also did a good job today in front of the panel, as well."

Davenport raises an eyebrow. "You heard about that already?"

"I sure have. They confided in me that he was a little green in certain areas of the interview, but overall, they said he did an exceptional job and carried himself like a true professional."

"That is good news."

"Now, where are we treating him because I'm ready to eat!"

"Let's go to the Sugar Bar uptown. They have live music, plus the food is incredible."

"Sounds good to me. I'll tell the future supervisor." Tucker retrieves her coat and briefcase. "Oh yeah, one more thing..."

"What's that?"

"*We're gonna have a gooood time tonight! Let's celebrate! It's alright!* That's okay. I'll be my own background chorus. *Ceeeeeeelebraaation time, come on!*"

She dances her way out of the office.

The room is quiet again.

Davenport's brooding picks up where it left off.

Then out of nowhere, an idea overwhelms him, causing him to quickly grab the phone and dial a number.

He waits.

The receptionist answers.

"Yes, is Elgin in?" he asks. "Tell him it's Michael…yes, I'll hold… Elgin? Hey…man, I can't call it…oh, yes, I'll be at the Knicks game tomorrow…listen, I'm in a bit of a bind and hopefully you can help me out…his name is Lexington VanGuard…" Davenport grins. "My man…"

Failing to understand why he didn't think of it sooner, Davenport starts to tap his pen even faster.

*Tap, tap, tap, tap, tap, tap, tap, tap….*

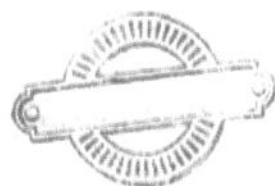 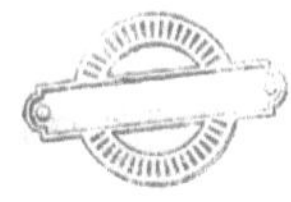 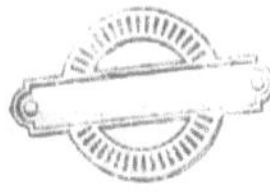

"AND WHAT CAN I GET FOR YOU, SIR?"

Davenport slides his glasses on before reading the menu. "I'll have the grilled jerk pork chops with ahhh, let's see here, oh, collard greens and mac and cheese, thank you."

"You're welcome. Will there be anything else?"

"Some more yeast rolls, please, thank you," Lexington says, eyeing the cute waitress.

"You're quite welcome."

She cheerfully takes the menus and returns Lexington's stare before leaving.

The men stretch their necks to watch the sonic movement of her bubble butt bounce all the way back to the restaurant's kitchen.

"When she comes back out, try closing your mouths, please, it's just way too obvious," jibes Tucker.

They all laugh.

Lexington continues. "...like I was saying, when the third panelist asked me what the number one goal of a supervisor was, and I said, *'keeping the carriers' overtime hours to a minimum,'* you should have seen the look on their faces!"

Davenport smiles and then says, "They were impressed, huh?"

"That or they knew I was coached well by you. Either way, I got the job done."

"I heard that."

The waitress returns with a platter full of drinks and yeast rolls. "Be careful with the rolls, they're pretty warm."

"They're not the only thing that's pretty around here." Lexington coyly smiles at her.

"You must be having a wonderful day today."

"Actually, I am. You're just adding to it."

The waitress blushes. "Your food will be out shortly. Can I get y'all anything else?"

Davenport and Tucker say no.

"What about you, Mr. Happy?"

"I'm good, thanks."

"Okay. I'll go check on your food."

She gives Lexington a lingering gaze before returning to the kitchen.

"My man is batting a thousand today!" Davenport nudges his shoulder.

Lexington leans back in his chair. "Whoo, she is *fine*."

"Both of y'all hush while I make a toast," Tucker says.

The trio raises their drinks.

"To Lexington, as he sets forth to excel in management. Allow the advanced knowledge you're about to acquire from the Academy to become the beacon of light that will enable you to help others succeed in their journeys, as well. Cheers…"

"Cheers!"

*Ting!*

Davenport takes a sip of his whiskey ginger and then clears his throat. "My sources told me an unusual amount of people took that exam yesterday."

"Man, there were so many people." Lexington butters one of the rolls. "I even heard one of the examiners say they may hold two separate classes if the majority of the people that took the test passed."

"That person was correct. The first class will be given in a couple of weeks while the second class will take place during the summer."

"Hey, as long as I'm in the first class, I'm good. I'm ready to leave Midway, like right now."

"I'm afraid you're in that second class, Lex."

Tucker and Lexington stop drinking.

Tucker turns to Davenport, confused. "Did I hear you clearly, Michael?"

"Yes, you did."

"Hold on now. I didn't make the first class?" Lexington asks, with equal perplexity. "How can that be?"

"When did you hear about this, Michael?" Tucker quizzed.

Davenport wipes his mouth with a napkin. "Right before you came in the office announcing his test score."

"But why didn't you mention this to me then?"

Davenport laughs. "You never gave me the chance! You danced into my office, we spoke briefly about his test results, and then you danced right back out! It probably slipped my mind, I'm sorry."

"But I got a *ninety-eight*." Lexington places his drink on the table. "I thought I'd be the *first* one to be slotted in the first class since I scored so high."

"The one area the program is focusing on right now is effective leadership skills. The people chosen for the first class have prior knowledge in the managerial and supervisory fields. You said it yourself, Denise, the board felt he was a little green in certain areas of their questioning."

"*Green*?" Lexington repeats. "What did they mean by that?"

"It means that by the way you answered your questions, the panel knew you weren't seasoned enough in supervision," Tucker explains before turning back to Davenport. "But I also said he did an exceptional job overall before the panel."

"You're making it seem like it was my doing, Denise." Davenport stirs his drink with a straw. "This is something they implemented as a priority because of the enormous amount of people that passed. I can't change that."

"I see you're taking this bit of news rather comfortably. *Too* comfortable for my taste."

"*Denise*, what do you want me to do?" Davenport sips his whiskey. "Rules are rules."

"Correct me if I'm wrong, Michael, but if they claimed he was exceptional and scored damn near a hundred on the exam...I don't know, I just see things a lot differently than you."

"Damn." Lexington now sulks in his seat. "And I was so ready to go *now*."

Davenport breaks into a gut-busting howl. "You two act like I just announced a death sentence. Did y'all forget why we're here in the first place? You made it, son!"

"Well, I just didn't think my departure would be prolonged."

"Well, since it has, I'm not going to waste any time promoting you to permanent 204B Acting Supervisor." Davenport inches closer to Lexington. "And with the proper guidance from our staff, you will be able to leave Midway altogether with supreme confidence in your advanced abilities. Now, how does that sound to you?"

Lexington sighs. "Well, if that's the road I have to take, I have no other choice, right?"

"Good, then it's settled."

The waitress arrives with their entrées.

As she places a sizzling plate in front of each person, she smiles and asks, "Do y'all want me to bring out more rolls?"

"Yes indeed, young lady!" Davenport claps. "They are definitely scrumptious!"

"Aren't they?" The waitress turns to Lexington. "What about you, Mr. Happy? You need me to bring you anything else?"

"Uh, no, I'm good, thanks."

"Are you *sure*?"

"I *said* I'm good, alright?" he snaps. "Thank you."

The waitress stops smiling.

Embarrassed, she manages to maintain her professional manner. "Okay, um, I'll be back with more rolls." She half-smiles at the managers and then shoots Lexington a confused look before walking off towards the back.

Tucker slowly picks at her grilled salmon.

Lexington doesn't touch his catfish plate.

Davenport leans in closer to his prized pupil. "If I were you, I wouldn't leave here without her phone number."

Davenport roars into laughter as he tears into his piping hot pork chop.

# TWENTY-ONE

## LEXINGTON

Lexington stands in front of his letter case, still processing the unexpected news he received the previous evening. The ball of confusion nestled inside his throat stands out like a swollen Adam's apple. He just knew he was about to kiss this station goodbye. Now he must suck it up for another five months. Five *long* months. He snaps out of his funk when Chapman walks over to him with his hand extended.

"I believe a congratulation is in order."

Lexington shakes his hand. "Thanks. I guess I won't be cleaning out my locker any time soon."

"Awww, you'll be fine. The second class will be here before you know it and you'll be well on your way."

"That day can't come quick enough if you ask me." He ponders for a moment. "You know, I only did the acting supervisor role twice here, but both times these people wanted to jump down my throat every time I gave them instructions. How do you maintain your composure when they come at you like that?"

"Good question." Chapman mulls for a moment. "Three things; one, everybody is not going to always agree with you, so stand firm with your decisions. Two, don't take any work-related stress home with you. And lastly, have integrity, especially when you make a mistake, and you will make some…we all do, but own up to them and move on. I was a carrier many moons ago before making the transition, so they're going to test you, there's no denying that. But if you stay consistent with those three things, you should fare well."

Lexington nods. "Appreciate it."

"And since this is your last day in a carrier uniform, how about doing me one last favor?"

"Who do you want me to bail out now?"

"Cadina. She's on Marc's route again and she will need all the help she can get."

The mere mention of her name sends angry ripples throughout his being. At this point, he does not care to do *anything* for that stuck-up broad, but he keeps that to himself.

He fakes a smile. "Yeah, I'll help her out."

"Thanks. Lunch is on me today."

Chapman pats him on the back before returning to the podium.

Lexington leans back on the ledge for a moment. As much as he hates to admit it, Davenport was right. These next few months are going to be very crucial for him to get his leadership skills up to par.

He finally mans up.

*If Chapman can deal with these people, so can I. I'll show them. I'll show them ALL what I'm really made of. Yeah, the next five months are mine to conquer!*

Cadina catches his eye.

He watches as she helps the mail-handler give out the mail.

Out of nowhere, James enters the scene. He pulls out his wallet and shows Cadina what seems to be a photo. They both laugh. James slides the photo back into his wallet and walks to his workstation. Cadina continues to smile as she resumes handing out the mail.

Jealousy grabs him by the jugular.

*Yeah, I'll help her out. But I got a trick for that ass, though.*

He swings back around to case the letters, with resentment flooding his eyes.

Cadina slams the mailbox panel shut and locks it. She gathers all the returned letters from the brownstone's hallway table and walks outside to release a sigh of relief.

She is finished for the day.

Observing the sun beating down on the pavement produces a smile across her face. The last time she finished this early was when she first started. Some of her coworkers have amusingly labeled her as the station's current nocturnal carrier, which doesn't really bother her. However, feeling the afternoon sun rays upon her wintered face is a welcomed change from her normal routine.

Pushing her mailcart down the sidewalk, she reflects on her catering dilemma. Somehow, she has convinced herself that taking tomorrow off will not hurt anybody and that she'd never do it again.

Old habits die hard.

She pulls out her phone to call her mother. It rings four times before she answers.

"Hey, girl, what's up?"

"Nothing much. How long have you been home?"

"I just walked in the door. Why?"

"I'm about to clock out in a half-hour and when I get home, I want us to go grocery shopping."

"I see you're having an early day today, that's good."

"It's about time. And it couldn't have fallen on a better day."

"You mean with Bianca's surprise party tomorrow and all…"

"Exactly."

"I know you're glad they gave you the day off, right?"

"Uh, yeah, right."

Guilt does not begin to describe how she feels lying to her mother about having permission to take this Saturday off. But she could live with that for right now. "Did you see the list I left on the fridge?"

"Didn't I tell you I just walked in the house?"

"My bad, jeez."

Cadina stops at the corner on Seventh Street.

She happens to glance at the relay box and notices long relay bag strings hanging from outside its door. Curious, she opens the relay box door and sees four stuffed relay bags she had left for Lexington to deliver.

"Bianca *did* give you the money to buy all of this food, right?" Lorraine asks. "My Lord, she has you cooking for an army!"

"That's what I'm known for, remember? Let me call you back, okay?"

"Call me when you're on your way home, bye."

Cadina ends the call and then speed-dials her station.

Chapman answers the phone.

"Midway Station, Mr. Chapman speaking, may I help you?"

"Hey, It's Cadina. Look, I don't know if you need to be concerned with this, but Lex—"

"Cadina! I'm so glad you called. Listen, Lex came back to the station feeling a bit under the weather, so he went home. I need you to get started on those bags right away and I'll try to send the next available body out there to give you a hand, okay?"

A ton of bricks just rained on her parade.

"Are you *serious*?"

"I wish I wasn't, but I can't have those bags just sitting out there without getting delivered."

"Well, how long will it take for someone else to arrive?" She hastily checks her watch.

"I can't tell you off-hand, but someone will be sent out there to assist you, okay? I have another call to take, call me if you run into any problems, okay? Thanks."

"But, Mr. Chapman-"

*Click!*

"Shit!"

Cadina stands in front of the relay box, stunned. Those four relay bags equal out to two more hours at the very least! She did not expect karma to catch up to her this quickly. Chewing on her bottom lip, she contemplates her next move when a wrinkled hand taps her on the shoulder.

"Excuse me, young lady..."

She turns around to a troll-sized elderly woman wearing a multi-colored headscarf and a smelly brown wool coat. Her rubbery, squinted face resembles a Party City Halloween mask.

"May I help you, Ma'am?"

Leaning on her cane, the elderly woman says in a creaky voice, "All day long, I've been watching you walk up and down the other side of the street delivering mail, and you act like you're in no hurry to deliver to this side of the block and I've been waiting patiently for my social security check so I can get it cashed. Where is Marc, anyway?"

"He fell sick today, so he stayed home."

"And *you're* his replacement?" the snaggletooth woman snarls, as she pointed a finger that displayed a seashell-thick fingernail. "You better start getting here a little earlier or I'm gonna call your station and report you!"

Trembling with frustration, Cadina says, "Look Ma'am, I'm not the only person that's going to be covering this route—"

"Find my fuckin' check so I can cash it, please!"

The elderly woman plants a wad of Big Red tobacco inside the cheek of her mouth and begins chewing on it like a bulldog.

"What's your name and address?" Cadina asks.

The elderly woman spits out some of the chewed tobacco juice on the sidewalk and says, "Agatha Concepcion. I live right across the street, in the garden apartment. Here's my identification."

"Thank you, but I can't just hand you the mail out in the open. I have to deliver it to your mailbox, or I'd get in trouble—"

"Well, then stop your fuckin' babbling and meet me across the street, *now*! The check-cashing place closes in five minutes!"

She spits out some more tobacco juice before hobbling back across the street.

Searching for the relay bag with Agatha's mail in it, Cadina wishes for her help to arrive soon before she winds up spraying a few curse words of her own towards the tobacco-chewing hag.

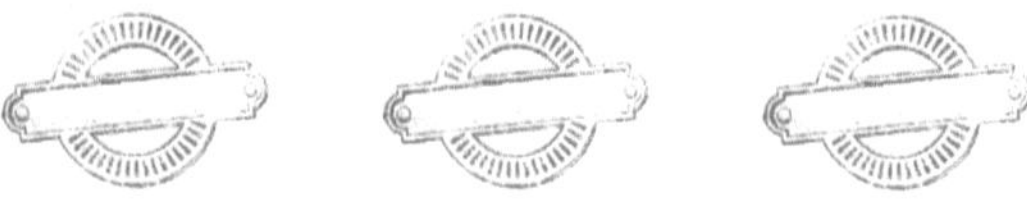

SIX-THIRTY IN THE EVENING; HER USUAL CLOCKING OUT PERIOD.

After promising James for the fourth time that she will be at his housewarming tomorrow evening, she exits the station and drags her dog-tired body down Eleventh Street en route to the subway station.

Still upset over the afternoon's events, it did, however, cement her decision to take tomorrow off. She has so much to do and so little time to do it in. She is used to cooking under stressful situations, but the playing field is much different this time around. Her body is exhausted from a week of driving trucks and slinging heavy bags all over town. She reminds herself to get at least a couple of hours of sleep after she food-shops with her mother, or else she will be dead on her feet come tomorrow morning. The challenge is on.

Cadina turns the corner of Fourth Avenue and spots Velour, dressed in a cream-colored biker jacket over a cream-colored jumpsuit, conversing on her phone. The postal diva leans on a sparkling pearl-white Porsche.

They trade smiles.

"I'll talk to you later, okay, bye." Velour slides the phone in her Gucci pocketbook. "Hey, Boo."

"Hey." Cadina's eyes are glued to the gleaming vehicle. "Is this you?"

"Two thousand sixteen Porsche Cayenne Turbo S–premium package," Velour boasts. "A gift to *moi*."

"An expensive gift, at that."

"Price tags don't scare me." Velour presses a remote button to roll down the Porsche's windows. She places her purse in the passenger seat. "Once I claim something, it's already mine, trust. I see you had another long day."

Cadina sighs, "I don't even wanna talk about it."

Velour chuckles. "You're going to have plenty of days like this, Boo, so my advice to you is to take it with a grain of salt and make that money. And, just maybe, in a few years, you can have yourself one of these."

Velour pats her shiny vehicle to emphasize her point.

"Yeah, right. Heading home?"

"Nope. I'm going to buy this fierce outfit I saw on Broadway for James' housewarming. Best believe I'm going to shut that party down tomorrow, you watch."

Cadina laughs. "It's just a housewarming party, Velour."

"Honey, I have standards to uphold. I just can't be looking any old kind of way out in public. I have to present myself accordingly."

"See, that's what I admire about you."

"What do you admire about me, girl?"

"I don't know, you seem to have this fearless attitude towards life. It can be very contagious."

Velour blushes at this admiration. She moves in closer to Cadina. "Like my brother always told me when we were young; if you're willing to work hard in life, you should be able to play twice as hard. And as of right now, life is a playground."

Cadina nods. "I heard that."

"See you tomorrow, Cadina."

Velour backpedals to her Porsche, slides behind the wheel, cranks up Lil' Kim's, *No Time For Fake Ones,* and peels off in dramatic fashion.

Cadina begins walking down the street while taking mental notes.

*She's definitely raking in the dough…*

Her phone rings.

It's her mother.

*Ah, man…*

She swipes her phone and says, "I know, Ma-"

"You said you'd be home two hours ago. What happened?"

"I'm sorry I didn't call you back, but I'll explain everything when we go shopping."

"Well, I'ma head out now, because you need to get some rest as soon as you get home."

"I'll be fine, Ma. But make sure you grab the list that I put on the fridge and I will meet you at the supermarket…"

Cadina heads down the subway stairs.

# TWENTY-THREE

## TUCKER

Something is not right. She feels it in her bones.

Saturday morning and the assistant manager, with her briefcase in one hand and coffee in the other, rides the elevator to the work floor. While taking a sip, her brain tries to decipher the situation involving Lexington's postponed enrollment. The timing of the whole matter is what disturbs her the most. Why didn't Davenport inform her about the added second class prior to the celebration dinner, so she would not have appeared just as surprised as Lexington when the subject was brought up? Or was it his intention to withhold that bit of information from her until the dinner? If so, *why*? They never operated under those conditions before.

Davenport has never given her a reason to doubt his credibility on any subject and up until now, he has always been sincere about his straightforwardness. Still, she has never been one to push a nagging feeling over to the sidelines. Tackling the bull by its horns is in her genetic structure, so she intends to find out whether this matter is legit, even if it means going over his head to do it.

She arrives on the work floor, greets the mail clerks, and checks the call-in sheet to see if anyone has called in absent.

One name sticks out like a sore thumb.

She cannot believe her eyes.

She *refuses* to believe her eyes.

Tucker turns to the clerk supervisor. "Excuse me, Barry, do you know who took Cadina's phone call?"

"Oh, she called right before you came in," he answers while condensing a letter tray.

"And what did she say?"

Barry shrugs. "Well, she told me she was coming down with the twenty-four-hour flu bug and she couldn't make it in."

*No, she didn't!* "Thanks."

She tosses her empty cup in a nearby wastebasket and storms back downstairs to her office.

She manages to jolt herself out of a nap and race into the kitchen. She snatches the oven door open, pulls out two pans to inspect her Creole honey barbeque ribs, and breathes a huge sigh of relief. She curses herself for nodding off after she called the station, but her body was on the brink of shutting down hours ago. She pushes the pan back into the oven to let it brown some more.

She plops down in a dinette chair and gradually browses over all the prepared dishes made within the past sixteen hours. It was on pure adrenaline alone that she accomplished her mission without a wink of sleep. She grabs the house phone to call her sister, who answers on one ring.

"Girl, I was just about to call you," Camille says.

"I hope you didn't make any plans today because I'ma need you to transport a lot of this food to the function, so you can start making space in the back of your Yukon and what time are you gonna try to make it over here because— "

"Whoa, whoa, whoa! Good God! Mom did say you were up all night, so I'm going to excuse the tone in your voice."

"I'm sorry. Just a little burnt out."

"Just a little, huh? What time is the party?"

"At three o'clock, in Bed-Stuy. You know where Cornerstone Baptist Church is, right? Right on Lewis and Madison?"

"Yes, Cadina, I do. Another question: did you remember to get the disposable chafing kits to keep the food warm?"

"*Shit!* I knew I forgot something!"

"Wow, okay. But did you design menus?"

"They didn't ask me to provide menus, Cammy, they just wanted me to prepare the food. That was it."

"Girl, they didn't have to ask you, this is about *your* presentation. Ms. Pauline is a wealthy angel investor, am I correct?"

Cadina rolls her eyes. "Yes, you are. And?"

"*And*, you're about to cater to a group of upper-class people who will be taking mental notes of you and your services. *And*, I'm quite sure there's going to be networking opportunities so everything has to be top-notch in order to attract future clients, come on now, girl."

This is the one thing their father adores about Camille; her entrepreneurial spirit.

Cadina hears a beep on the line. "Hold on for a sec, someone's beeping in." She presses the flash button. "Hello?"

"Good morning, my name is Denise Tucker, the assistant manager of Mid…Is this Cadina?"

She drops the phone.

Fear has frozen her body solid.

*Oh, my God!*

Tucker called her bluff big time.

She did not think her boss was even allowed, or bold enough for that matter, to call the house to check up on her. She thought wrong.

In slow motion, she retrieves the handset from the floor and nearly jumps to the ceiling when the phone rings in her hand. She checks the Caller I.D. before answering. It's her sister.

Cadina blows out relief. "Hey."

"What happened?"

"Uh, somehow we got disconnected when I switched over. Listen, could you be a doll and buy the kits and I reimburse you? I finally finished cooking and right now, I need to shut it all the way down."

"I gotcha. And before you do that, text me a list of the food you made, and I'll print out a batch of fancy menus. Shoot, my sister is not going out like no punk!"

"What will I ever do without you?"

"Hey, you need someone in your corner that's going to help mold you into that future entrepreneur."

"Now, you already know I have a full-time job."

"Yes, I do and it's the *wrong* full-time job. Get some rest, Boo."

Camille hangs up.

Cadina checks on her ribs. Pleased with the taste, she takes both pans out of the oven and wraps foil over them.

The phone rings.

She checks the number.

It's Tucker again.

She quickly turns the answering machine off.

She does not want Tucker leaving any messages she might not want to hear later. The phone continues to ring. And ring. And ring four more times before stopping altogether. Cadina's mind begins to play its customary tricks again.

*But she doesn't really know it was me, it could've been my sister answering the phone in her sleep. Yeah, that's it!*

Gradually coming to terms with her future alibi, she places both pans of ribs in the box marked MEAT and then teeters to her bedroom for some much-needed shut-eye.

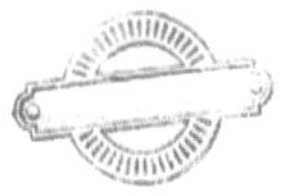 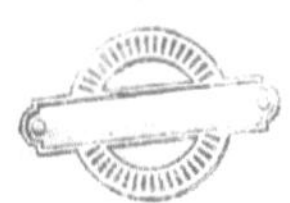 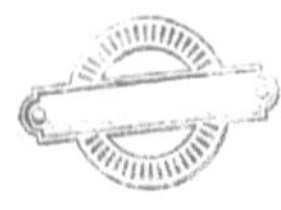

FIVE O'CLOCK IN THE AFTERNOON AND THE CORNERSTONE BAPTIST Church Center is thunderously raising the roof in gospel jubilee. After stomping along with Kirk Franklin's music, Cadina and Camille slither their way through the praising and worshipping crowd to a pair of vacant folding chairs along the side of the wall.

Camille fans the top of her black dress to allow her bosom to get some air. "Girl, if one more person asks for a plate of food, I'm going to cuss, you hear me?"

Cadina, also dressed in black, playfully grabs her sister's chin. "And after you finish cursing, you're going to serve that guest with that beautiful smile of yours."

"You better be glad I closed up my shop to help you out. Everything turned out great!"

"Didn't it?"

Cadina cannot help but smile.

Everyone who attended the event, young and old, devoured practically everything they placed on the dinner tables. Even with the requested second helpings, she and Camille found themselves rushing back and forth from the kitchen to the patiently, yet eagerly awaiting, attendees who left no bones or crumbs to be desired. From the zesty beef ribs dipped in her own secret Creole barbeque sauce to her baked ziti—*Gone.* Grilled salmon, baked catfish, baked and fried chicken—*Bye-Bye.* Yams, potato salad, collard greens, sweet onion and sweet pea mixed vegetable dish, tossed salad, deviled eggs—*See ya!* Even the 'Wah-co' taco salad dish she'd been experimenting with and perfected the past week—*Peace!*

But what really touched her heart was when people would pass her their business cards or pull her to the side to discuss employing her for future affairs. And it had as much to do with the added extras as it did the food. People loved the menus her sister designed which honored the birthday lady, the small bags of miniature chocolates, and the other festive trinkets which were placed at each table. Prior to the event, Cadina caught the brainstorm bug and jetted to Party City to buy a top hat and horn for the birthday lady. All and all, she was extremely pleased with the way things turned out.

Camille suddenly stands. "Here comes Bianca with the birthday girl."

Cadina rises to her feet as well.

Dressed in a gold blazer, a black medium-length skirt, and a joyful expression is Bianca, who works her way over to the sisters. By her side, wearing the top hat that Cadina bought and blowing the horn is Bianca's mother, Pauline. Everyone embraces one another.

"Ma'am, all I want to say is you're my role model," Camille says, holding Pauline's bracelet-adorned arm. "You look fabulous!"

Laced in a two-piece leopard-printed pants suit, with gold high-heels to match her short, blond hair, the brown-skinned birthday diva strikes an 'en vogue' pose.

"Child, tell me something I don't know!" Pauline blows her horn and laughs a deep, baritone laugh. She then turns to Cadina. "Cadina, Cadina, Cadina. I have one question to ask you, my dear…"

"Yes, Ma'am."

"Where did you learn how to prepare so many wonderful dishes? Child, I'm still farting out those collard greens you made, they were so *tasty*—"

"Motherrrr…" Bianca covers her face in embarrassment. "Too much information!"

"Oh, hush," Pauline waves her off. "I'm just letting her know she did an amazing job. Now, how long have you been in the catering business?"

Cadina feels giddy. "To answer your first question, our mother taught us how to cook at an early age, and I just kind of gravitated towards it. As for catering, I don't do this for a living, but once Bianca asked if I could cater your birthday, I felt honored to do so."

Pauline studies Cadina's face. "Hmmm. I see we're going to have to do something about that in the future, my dear."

Cadina grabs Camille's arm. "And my beautiful sister helped me with the decorative features and menus; so, it was a collaborative effort."

Pauline cups both hands together and points at the sisters. "Both of you, for making my day so extravagant, I will be forever grateful. Now, if y'all will excuse me, I must get my boogie on. Ain't God good?"

The birthday diva once again blows her horn, tips her top hat at everyone, and sashays across the thumping dance floor.

Bianca turns around and gives the sisters a hug. "Thank you both *so* much! I'll call you when it's time to cut the cake!"

Bianca leaves to entertain the other guests.

The sisters return to their seats.

Cadina checks her watch. "I hope the party ends on time so I can get ready for my next event."

"Yes! This housewarming gathering you've been invited to," Camille smirks. "What's his name and why does he get to have a big pan of oxtails when I've been begging you for the past three months to make me some?"

Cadina holds back a big grin. "Well, his name is James Richards. He works at my station. He and his mother just moved into their first home. He seems really cool."

"Any kids?"

"A daughter. I met his family the other day."

Cadina catches the worrisome expression on her sister's face.

"Now, you know how Pops feel about you fraternizing and you just started the job-"

"What, now I can't have any friends? I didn't say I was going to marry the guy-"

"I'm just saying. Don't let Pop find out."

"And if he did, he'd be alright. He can't run my life forever, I'm a grown woman-"

"You're just as stubborn as the day is long. And you're going to give me some of those oxtails before you take them to that party."

Cadina laughs. "Okay, okay. But just one scoop."

"Uh, uh. You are not monitoring my scoops, girl!"

Two gentlemen walk up to the ladies. They both appear to be in their fifties. And they both have that look of lust in their eyes.

"Excuse us, but, uh, we know you two have been busy all day serving folks," the taller gentleman says, quickly glancing at his friend. "But we were wondering if we can squeeze just one dance out of y'all before the evening is over with?"

"Yes, *Lord*," His friend adds, eyeballing Camille's bosom.

The sisters stare at the men before turning to each other, trying hard not to laugh.

Camille takes the lead as she stands.

"Okay, but I'm letting you both know right now that's the only thing you two are *squeezing* out of us, I hope I'm making myself clear-"

"Oh, yes, Ma'am!" the taller gentleman offers his hand to Cadina.

Cadina respectfully smiles as she takes the gentleman's hand and allows him to take her to the packed dance floor.

Davenport strolls inside of the nearly vacant station and heads straight to his office. Tucker had called him earlier while he was shopping in the SoHo district nearby. She was still scalding-hot about Cadina calling in sick earlier that morning. Mentioning that she wanted to fire the new sub on the spot once she arrives Monday morning, prompted him to now have to make an urgent trip to the station on what would have been his day off.

His assistant manager, as well as his dear friend, is known for using her energy to help employees keep their jobs rather than terminating them. And he does not see anything remotely different in Cadina's case, especially since her work performance has proved beyond exceptional since her first day on the job.

No, he senses something more…*Much* more.

Tucker has been somewhat distant toward him ever since that celebration dinner at the Sugar Bar. Her eyes threw silent darts at him all day yesterday and she never once said what was on her mind.

*She's on to him.*

They know each other like a book, footnotes and all. But if she were to skim through some of the additional pages he has recently tacked on, she would be surprised at what she would find. And if she has uncovered them already, well, he hopes she is willing to ride along with the current waves, instead of trying to confront them, as things could get a bit ugly.

He enters his office and sees Tucker in the corner, clicking away on the computer. Quietly, he removes his jacket and hat, hanging them on the coat stand. He then clears his throat for no reason and sits behind his desk to look over the numbers for the day. Not a word is spoken between the two of them.

"What time did the last carrier clock out?" he asks, breaking the silence.

"Around four-thirty."

He glances at the clock—5:15 pm. "You had yourself a good day then."

She continues tapping on the keyboard buttons without saying a word.

"So…are you attending James' party tonight?"

"Planning on it."

Her answers are short and to the point.

That's not her style at all.

He strolls over to sit on a short file cabinet right next to where she is working.

"I see Cadina got you all riled up to the point where you want to fire her? This doesn't sound like the Denise I know."

Tucker stops typing. She swivels her chair in his direction.

He gazes into her skeptical eyes.

She wears them like reading glasses.

He braces himself.

"Apparently, you don't know anything about the little prelude we had earlier in the week which led to her calling in sick this morning, so let me fill you in."

"By all means."

She stands and begins pacing the floor. "This past Tuesday, Cadina asked to have today off and I told her we couldn't do it because she's on probation, plus she was scheduled on a truck assignment. She *told* me she understood. But why do I come in this morning and see her name at the top of the call-in sheet? I knew damn well she wasn't sick, so I called her home, and do you know she had the audacity to hang up on me? I mean, who does that?"

Davenport grunts, now understanding the true nature of her fury.

"Do you know what she's saying to me by pulling this stunt, Michael? *The hell with you, Mrs. Tucker! I'm takin' the day off, regardless of your orders!* I swear, I could just—ugh!"

He chuckles. "You know, this is the first time I've ever seen you this upset over an employee's insubordination."

"Well, maybe if I were a little more dogmatic, people would think twice about testing my authority. I mean, am I wrong, Michael?"

"No, no. I'll back you one hundred percent if you feel there's no other way to resolve this matter."

Tucker sighs as she drops down in her seat. "I spoke to her father this afternoon."

"You have?" He raises an eyebrow. "How did that go?"

"I told him what happened and what I was planning to do about it. Michael, this man begged and pleaded his daughter's case, saying she'll never do it again. Long story short—"

"You gave in."

"She gets one more chance, Michael. I told her father if she doesn't get her act together, she's outta here, no third chances."

She swivels her chair back around to the computer.

Davenport chuckles as he walks across the office to retrieve his trench coat and hat.

"I would love to be a fly on James' wall when you two meet up tonight."

"Well, it's a risk she's going to have to take. I'm going to enjoy myself tonight."

"I heard that. Give my regards to James and his family."

"Where are you going?"

He opens the door. "To pick up Brenda from the nail salon and grab something to eat. You want to join us?"

"Close the door. We need to talk."

"Everything okay?"

Tucker swivels her chair back around. She crosses her arms. "I spoke to Elgin this afternoon, Michael."

His smile vanishes.

He calmly closes the door and takes off his hat and coat. He circles back behind his desk, only for the added authority that may be required during the debate that they are about to dive into. He sits down, crosses his legs, and says in a very calm manner, "I'm listening."

"We had a very interesting discussion regarding Lexington's situation. I brought it to his attention because it was gnawing at my own curiosity."

He taps his fingers on the desk. "And?"

"Did you have *anything* to do with switching Lexington's classes?"

He directs his devious grin down toward the desk.

She shakes her head in disgust. "Michael, how *could* you?"

"I would've told you soon enough-"

"You know, between you, Freeman and Cadina…the three of you must think I'm some new type of fool in this station-"

"On the contrary, Denise; I value you, completely." He leans back in his chair. "That's why I selected you as my assistant manager. But as far as this situation goes, you can spare me the dramatics, especially when there is no need for it."

"Who the hell gave *you* the authority to play chess with that man's career? And please don't tell me this has something to do with Sterling leaving the station, either."

Davenport stands. "Think about it, Denise. Having Lexington here will benefit him and the station long term. He's excellent with our computer system, he knows the logistics of all the routes, plus he has the kind of temperament that's necessary for dealing with some of the more rebellious carriers in the station-"

"But you're making it *his* problem to shoulder and that's not fair at all! That man has earned the right to move on to his next location-"

"And he *will*, Denise. Later this year."

"If you're so gung-ho about this pet project of yours, why not share it with the man who idolizes you instead of lying to his face as if you had absolutely nothing to do with this?"

Davenport felt the sting of that comeback.

But he plays it off coolly.

"What he doesn't know won't hurt him."

"Oh, really?" Tucker stands. "Well, *I* know. And it can be easily undone when the E. E. O. Commissions *and* the Carriers' Union Delegates catch wind of your little self-serving project."

"You're threatening *me*, Denise?" He laughs out loud. "In my office? Wow."

"I don't dish out threats, Michael, those are promises I'm making."

"You know what? Since you're so adamant about what *I'm* doing behind closed doors, let's talk about a particular situation you tried to keep from me a few weeks back."

"What situation?"

"You know exactly what I'm referring to, Denise; Freeman's accident."

Her bravado melts away, instantly.

He anticipated this happening.

He did not want to pull out the big guns on her just yet, but he had no choice in the matter since she went behind his back and pulled one of his cards.

He pours it on.

"Now, did I come to you and say you were being self-serving by withholding Freeman's true condition the day of the accident? Come to think of it, were you ever going to fill me in on that negligence?"

Tightlipped, she manages to squeeze out, "Freeman is not the issue here—"

"See! You weren't going to tell me! Why? Because you took it upon yourself to deal with the situation privately! You didn't need for me to worry about it, just like I don't need you badgering me about Lexington's situation-"

"But the difference here is I was helping Freeman with his dilemma! You, on the other hand, are hindering Lexington's forward progress and that's outright cruel and thoughtless on your part—"

"Bullshit. You were more worried about covering your own ass than helping Freeman—who do you think you're fooling here? You *knew* you were in the wrong for letting that man drive in his condition, but you did it anyway!"

"I-I know what I did, Michael. And for the record, he was not drunk-"

"He was *hungover*, Denise! Which is just as bad, you know this! And suppose that accident was his fault, what do you think would've happened next? Huh? The Postmaster would've held *you* responsible and you'd be fighting for your job as we speak! And *had* that happened, I would've fought for you because that's what we managers do. You, my dear, better get used to how the game is played at this level or you're going to find yourself fighting losing battles, *alone.*"

His penetrating speech leaves her vocally impaired and visibly stunned.

She breaks out of that spell by shutting down the computer, throwing her coat on, and wrapping her scarf around her dreads. All in humiliated silence.

"Denise, all I'm asking is for your support as a manager of this station because you know I'd do the same for you."

Tucker swings the door open. "Have a good afternoon, Michael."

"Denise-"

*SLAM!*

The portraits on the wall rattle in response to Tucker's anger.

*Damn.*

He was victorious in their battle, but there is no cause for celebrating. Relief would be his only reward. Never in his life could he imagine hurting one of his closest friends. But no one is going to change the way he runs Midway. Not even one who is as kind and generous as Denise.

His phone vibrates in his pocket.

It's his wife, Brenda.

He swipes his phone and says, "Hey, are you ready? Yes, I'm leaving the office now…But we already had seafood yesterday…My taste buds are calling for barbeque…No, I'm not being selfish."

He laughs as he slides on his coat. He turns off the lights and closes the door behind him.

# TWENTY-SIX

## JAMES

"HOT WINGS OVER HERE!" James shouts, entering the festive living room of his new home, carrying a steaming platter of wings that his mother prepared.

His cousin Sabrina dances over to him and takes the platter from his hands. She yells out over the music, "IS THE LASAGNA READY?"

"I'MA BRING IT OUT IN A MINUTE!"

"YOU BETTER HURRY UP! PEOPLE HUNGRY UP IN HERE!"

"I KNOW, I KNOW!"

Hands from every direction snatch up a wing or two as Sabrina dances the platter over to the food table.

James stands in the middle of the swinging doorway. He takes in the moment.

*Now, this is what I'm talkin' about.*

His dream home, finally a reality. Three spacious bedrooms–an eat-in kitchen; huge living and dining room areas; no more waiting in line to use one bathroom—they now possess two full bathrooms and a half; a sizable basement which he furnished as a man cave; a two-car garage; a wide front porch, and a decent-size backyard just screaming for summertime grilling.

Nineteen hundred square feet of pure bliss.

His eyes moisten.

Surveying the living room, it fills his heart to see family and friends enjoy themselves at his housewarming. On one side of the room, his cousin Sabrina, her female companions, and his aunts engage in loud girl-talk over appetizers. Across from them, Divine and Tucker's husband, Elliott, battle another couple in spades. James' male cousins, uncles, and the postal crew congregate in the dining room to watch the Knicks on his seventy-five-inch flat-screen. Some folks are eating, others are dancing and some doing both.

Life couldn't get any better.

Apart from Cadina showing up.

He hears commotion at the deejay table.

Both Shabbazz, the evening's deejay, and his Uncle Skillet, the family's honorary drunk, frantically wave him over.

*Jeezus, what now?*

He makes his way over to the disruption.

"Nephuw," his uncle slurs, pointing his callused finger toward Shabbazz. "Tell yo' deejay pal over here dat he don't wanna mess wit' me! *Buuurp!* Hell, I wear draws older dan his youn' ass!"

"What's wrong?"

"I tell you whas wong, nephuwww. Yo' Moooslim pal is wong! I asked him to plah my song over an hour 'go and he refooses to play it! He hatin' on my song, nephuw!"

"Yo, Jay, no disrespect…" Shabbazz says while focusing on his laptop. "but could you take him somewhere else, he's messing with my flow-"

"You ain' *got* no dam flo', *BOY*!"

Uncle Skillet stumbles backward as Shabbazz mixes in GQ's dance hit, *Disco Nights*, and the crowd sings along–

*"THE FEELIN'S RIGHT AND THE MUSIC'S TIGHT, ON A DISCO NII-II-IIIIIIGHT!"*

The middle of the living room becomes swarmed with fresh old-school dancers.

James grabs his slouching uncle and guides him to the kitchen.

"He had nooo righ' talkin' to meeeee like that, *nephuwwww*!"

"It'll be alright. Let's get you somewhere where you can cool off."

They stumble into the kitchen where Tucker is helping Grace prep the lasagna and collard greens.

"B-But how the hell I-I'ma coo' off in dis hot-ass kitchen—?"

Skillet drops in a chair and passes out with his mouth wide open and arms spread downward.

"Oh my God!" Tucker covers her mouth in shock. "Is he alright?"

"He's fine." Grace ties her apron straps behind her body. "Give him fifteen minutes and he'll be up again, dancing and harassing somebody. Have you heard anything from your coworker, James?"

He lifts his uncle to a more comfortable position in the seat. "Not yet. I called her apartment this afternoon because she called in sick today and I didn't get an answer. I hope she's okay."

Tucker almost chokes on her drink.

"Are you alright?" Grace asks.

"Girl, I had one of those days which calls for a couple of shots of this right here." She raises her cup to Grace and takes another hefty gulp of her drink.

"Well, you'd better slow down before you wind up sitting right next to my brother with your mouth open like his."

"Y'ALL READY FOR THE CHA-CHA SLIDE!" blares out from the speakers in the other room.

Tucker's husband, Elliott, wearing a pair of Isaac Hayes glasses and a toothy grin, peeks inside of the kitchen.

"Let's cha-cha, baby!"

Tucker stands. "Y'all excuse me while I get my dance on."

"We're right behind you."

Elliott grabs his wife's hand and pulls her into the room.

James and Grace grab the rest of the food and they enter the living room.

*"...SLIIIIIIDE TO THE LEFT! NOW SLIIIIIDE TO THE RIGHT! HANDS ON YOUR KNEES! HANDS ON YOUR KNEES!*

*HOW LOW CAN YOU GO? CAN YOU GO DOWN LOW?"*

"HOOOOOO!" the party people yell out, as they clumsily dance themselves into a delightful frenzy.

James sits the lasagna down, maneuvers his way through the dancers and onto the front porch where the postal crew is gulping down beers in the relaxing winter evening.

"What's up with the Knicks?" James asks.

"They lost," Roy deadpans. "Again."

"We need Ewing, Oakley, and Starks back, I don't care how old they are," grumbles Lou, sitting on the railing.

James points at the front door. "Man, y'all better get back in there before the food is all gone."

"What we need to do is make a beer run, like right now. I think I got the last one."

"You sure? We should have more in the garage cooler. I'll go check."

"Yo, is Cadina coming through?" Roy asks.

James checks his watch. "I texted her earlier, but didn't get any response, so I dunno."

Neville grins. "You didn't waste any time getting them digits, ain't that right, Playboy?"

"How else is she going to know how to get here? I told you about reaching, bruh."

"Get the fuck outta here," Lou smirks. You know you want that ass, Jay!"

"See, that's where your mind's at–"

"YOURS, TOO!" the crew laughs.

Roy points out into the street. "Yo, who's that pulling up?"

The crew turns their attention to the Porsche parking in James' driveway. A dapper-looking Freeman slides out of the passenger's seat and struts around to the driver's side to let Velour out.

She yells out to James, "You don't mind if I park here, do you? I don't want anyone bumping into my ride by accident."

"Nah, you good."

"Thanks." She turns her conceited grin to the rest of the crew. "Hey, y'all."

"Hey."

"James, now this is *nice.*" Velour walks through the gate, admiring the building's brick exterior. As she walks up the porch steps, she purposely pulls off her beige chinchilla fur coat to reveal her voluptuous physique in a form-fitting, cream-colored, velvet mock-neck mini-dress, with the matching Manolo Blahnik pumps and purse.

She nods in approval. "You deserve this, man."

"Appreciate it. The food is ready, drinks are in the fridge, and don't forget to say 'Hey' to my moms."

"I won't." She turns to Freeman, excited. "I'm so ready to get our dance on!"

James greets Freeman and the smell of liquor hits him immediately. "I see you already got the party started."

"Man, I'm feeling nice right about now." Freeman laughs while unbuttoning his brown wool coat, exposing a cream-colored outfit that matches Velour's. "I'll be back out in a minute."

"No rush. We ain't going nowhere."

"Yo, Velour!" Lou circles around the gleaming Porsche. "Is this *you*?"

"Yes, Louis, it's my baby."

"How much did it set you back?"

She smiles. "It didn't set me back anything."

She sticks her hand out for Freeman to grab and they walk inside the house.

"Damn!" Roy stretches back onto the chair. "Velour looking kinda spicy tonight!"

"You saw the way she took off her fur so we could check out her assets, right?" Neville sits his empty beer bottle on the floor. "She knew what the hell she was doing."

"Yo, Jay!" Lou still walks around the Porsche. "Do you keep up with the overtime Velour be doing?"

"That's none of my business," James replies.

"I'm just asking because this right here ain't your everyday, run-of-the-mill Porsche."

"Like your ass is an expert on luxury cars," Neville jests.

"Actually, I am, Papa." Lou walks up to the porch. "That right there is the late model Porsche Cayenne Turbo S, with the twin-turbo engine that kicks out five hundred and fifty horsepower, *easy*. And those models *start* at a hundred and forty thousand. Google that shit, son."

"Maybe she's renting it for this weekend," Roy shrugs. "Because if it *is* hers, I can't imagine the car notes, especially with full insurance."

"I can't imagine affording something like that working at the post office, period," Neville burps. "*And* living in New York, too?"

"And *maybe* she has a budget plan." James turns to Neville. "None of us know her finances like that."

"True dat."

James' cousin, Garfield, sticks his head out the door. "Yo! We need to make a beer run, quick! Uncle Skillet is running through them!" Garfield closes the door.

James digs into his back pocket to fish out his wallet. "This don't make no damn sense."

"Man, put that away, we got this," Roy says.

"Can't do that. Y'all helped move all of my stuff, remember?"

"It's all good." Neville pulls out his truck keys. "We'll be back."

Lou points at James. "Tell 'Bazz I wanna hear some Biggie when we get back, not all of them damn line-dance songs."

James laughs. "Yeah, okay."

Lou and Roy pile into Neville's Jeep Cherokee, and they peel off down the street.

James pulls out his cell phone, searches for Cadina's number, and then dials it. As he waits for her to answer, the sudden thought of oxtails has him licking his lips.

# TWENTY-SEVEN

## CADINA

Camille backs her Yukon into their parents' driveway and automatically opens the cargo door. The sisters grab a couple of boxes containing the cooking ware and make their way towards the rear entrance of the house.

"Are you going straight to the party after you leave here?" Camille asks.

"Yes, Ma'am. I brought my outfit over the other night so I wouldn't have to go back to my apartment."

"Alright now." Camille unlocks the back door. "Got your little outfit ready, and the oxtails. My little sister is getting herself a man at this party!"

"Girl, I'm going to get my boogie on and have a good time."

"That's how it all starts, with a little bumpin' and grindin' on the dancefloor. Next thing you know, you're bringing home puppies!"

"You ain't right!"

The sisters laugh their way inside of the kitchen.

Cadina is surprised to find their parents sitting at the table in their nightclothes. "What's up?" she asks, placing the box on the countertop.

Camille retrieves a Tupperware bowl from the cabinet. "We have some good news to share with y'all!"

Vernon and Lorraine remain funeral quiet.

Camille scoops oxtails from the pan and into the bowl. "Well, let me be the first to say your daughter right here was the *bomb-diggy* at the birthday bash! She left such an impression on those rich folks that she has already established a clientele for future events! Now, tell me, how you like Cadina *now*?!?"

Cadina grins at her sister while rinsing out a pot.

"Why are y'all looking like that?" Camille asks their parents.

Cadina turns around.

She immediately cuts off the water.

Drying her hands, she analyzes her parents' vibe.

Vernon slouches in his chair while nursing a drink. His eyes remain glued to the table.

Meanwhile, Lorraine burns a hole right through Cadina's skull with laser red glare.

Something is not right.

Cadina tentatively asks, "Is there something wrong?"

"When it comes to you, Cadina, yes, there always seems to be something *wrong*." Lorraine pushes herself from the table. "But you don't seem to give a damn about anyone it affects, now do you?"

The sisters turn to each other, baffled.

"Wh-What is going on-?"

"You're such a project, young lady, that I wonder why we even devote our time and energy into making you a responsible woman!" Lorraine slowly marches right up to Cadina's face. Everything we build for you, you wind up tearing it down because you're just too damn selfish! Is this how we raised you, Cadina? To lie to us, to lie to your own *mother*? You better answer me when I ask you a question-"

"*Why are you coming at me like that? What did I do?*" Cadina shrieks, backpedaling.

"Didn't I say I was going to handle this?" Vernon calmly asks.

"She's my headache as well as yours, and she's making it painfully clear that your way is not working at all!"

"Everything will change, starting tonight. I promise you."

"Can somebody *please* tell me what's going on?" Cadina begs.

"I said what I had to say, now you have to deal with your father." Lorraine throws her hands in the air. "You've got me so burnt out, I can't even look at you right now." Lorraine storms toward the kitchen door, and then turns around to yell, "*CAMILLE*?"

"Huh?"

"Leave," Vernon orders.

"Holla if you need me, girl."

Camille grabs her bowl and scurries from the kitchen.

Cadina is now alone with a man who habitually starts off all disputes with a glass of scotch.

"What did I do *this* time?"

Vernon finally lifts his head up from the table.

Bloodshot eyes narrowed in on her.

"You're really going to stand there and act oblivious to your mindless decisions?"

"Maybe if you tell me what I did or did not do, I can defend my actions-"

"Your assistant manager called me today."

Her body goes completely numb.

"She called…*you*."

"Denise Tucker, I believe her name was." He pauses for a moment. "And she had some rather disturbing news to share with me regarding your response to her station's policies."

She rolls her eyes and sighs. "Look, Dad, I know what I did was wrong—"

"Do you, *really*?" He raises his voice as he stands. "See, that's part of your problem right there! You seem to think that you can waltz into any environment with your own little set of rules and think everybody's supposed to abide by them? Little girl, you are so delusional-"

"Look, I asked this lady for the day off, in advance, mind you, so I could do this party. I even told her how important it was for me to attend, and she still told me no. So, yes, I took it upon myself to make a crucial decision. But like Cammy said; I was a *huge* success at this event!" Cadina pulls out an envelope from her dress coat to show her father. "A four-thousand-dollar *success*! And I'm sorry that I lied to Mommy, but I guarantee you this will never happen again—"

"There won't be a next time, Cadina…she fired you!"

Her face goes blank.

"What?"

"You heard me! You've been released!"

She hesitantly chuckles. "She's not gonna fire me for calling in sick, that's crazy—"

"What part are you not getting? She knew you weren't sick, that's why she called you directly, and then you had the audacity to hang up on her? What do you think was going to happen to you?"

His line of questioning has her unable to gather her thoughts.

"I really hate to say this about my own daughter, but you are becoming one bad investment! No matter what we do, or how many jobs we line up for you, you ruin every opportunity! You haven't been at the post office two weeks! Now, look what's happened!"

Her ringing cell phone halts Vernon's fury.

She fumbles in her coat pocket and answers the incoming call.

"H-Hello?"

*"How you doing, Cadina? It's James."*

"Oh, hey."

*"Saw your name on the call-in sheet this morning and felt the need to reach out to see how you were doing—"*

"TELL WHOEVER THAT IS, THAT THIS IS A BAD TIME FOR YOU TO TALK, CADINA!" Vernon yells out at the top of his lungs.

Darting her eyes to her father, she whispers, "James, I have to call you back, okay?"

*"Is everything alright?"*

"HANG UP, NOW!"

"I'll call you back." She ends the call. "Was that really necessary?"

"What is necessary, Cadina, is for you to tell me how you're going to support yourself, moving forward." Vernon tightens the belt on his bathrobe. "Do you have a business plan laid out? Any future investors ready to back your so-called catering services? You must have something lined up for you to keep pulling stupid stunts like this! And you'd better figure out something real quick because the bills don't stop for anybody. Like your car I had to cosign for, your apartment I also had to cosign for. I cosigned my life away for you and this is how you repay me? So, I'll ask again; what are your *plans*?"

He doesn't wait for a response.

He walks over to the kitchen counter to pour himself another drink.

This bit of news cripple her all the way down on a nearby stool.

Her eyes begin to swell.

Just when she thought she was making great strides in redeeming her father's faith in her, she gives him another reason to distance himself even further because of her hollow promises. Her cavalier ways have finally run their course and she does not have a clue on how to reverse this agonizing misfortune.

He returns to the table with scotch and interrogation on the breath. "So, did you come up with a way to pay your bills legally or what?"

She snaps back into reality. "D-Did she really fire me?"

"I don't have time for games, Cadina; You have four grand to play with, but do you have an idea to build on?"

She lowers her head. "No."

"She fired you, alright, but I had to convince her to reconsider."

Her head springs up. "What?"

"To be more precise, after five minutes of listening to me *beg*, she found it in her heart to give you another chance. But this time around, you will have no room for error or bullshit. You have a lot of ground to cover as far as regaining your manager's trust, and the same goes for me, as well. Understood?"

Cadina wipes her eyes and nods her head in agreement.

"I can't hear you-"

"Yes, Sir."

He stands to his feet and then points down on the table. "Now is the time for you to start behaving like an adult or you will find yourself without a job or *me* to fall back on. It's time to grow the hell up, Cadina."

He downs the rest of his drink, slams the glass on the table, and staggers out of the kitchen.

Gravity has her pinned solidly to her stool.

At a sloth-like pace, she musters up enough strength to rise to her feet, gather her belongings, including the oxtails, and head out quietly through the back door and onto the driveway where she finds Camille sitting idly in her running truck.

Cadina slides the pan of oxtails in the backseat. She then squirms around to the passenger side of the Yukon. She sits there, staring through the windshield.

Staring through newly formed tears.

Camille rubs her sister's arm. "It's going to be okay."

"Could you do me a huge favor? Drop off the oxtails at James' place for me, please? I know it's out your way, but I'll pay for the gas expense-"

"Don't worry about that, girl, I got you." Camille backs out of the driveway and roars down the street. "But are sure you don't want to go? The atmosphere might do you a world of good."

"I can't. I-I totally forgot that my manager might be there and the last thing I need is to bump heads with her, you know what I mean?"

"Mmm-hmm," Camille double-takes her sister while driving. "Caddy…"

"I know, I know," Cadina chokes up. *"I just need to go home. Why do I keep fuckin' up like this, Cammy? I…I just can't-"*

The rest of her words never come.

She plants her face in her hands and her tear ducts release waves of guilt that have been nestled inside of her conscience for as long as she remembers.

Camille grabs her hand in comfort for the duration of the drive.

James stares at his phone.

*Who in the world was screaming in the background like that?*

He texts Cadina telling her to give him a call and then heads back into the house. He makes his way into the kitchen, checks on his wasted uncle who is now snoring, grabs a new garbage bag and returns to the living room to collect the trash. He trades a couple of jokes with his cousin Sabrina's attractive girl crew.

They laugh.

And flirt.

On any other occasion, he would have hollered at one of his cousin's friends without hesitation. Cadina, unknowingly, put an end to that.

Shabbazz gets the crowd buzzing again by mixing in the song, *Love Thang,* by First Choice, which causes James to turn around and shout out, "YEAH, BABY!" in approval. He dances over to the area where Divine and Elliott rule the spades table.

"BAM!" Divine shouts, slamming her big joker card down to win the last book of the game. As the losing team shake their heads and trot to the dance floor, another couple quickly fills their seats for a new game. James laughs as he drops their plates into the bag.

"You got next, James?" Divine begins shuffling the cards. "Or you don't want to be embarrassed in your new home? Which is it?"

"He doesn't want any of this, Dee." Elliott smiles while bouncing to the music.

"I got next, then," James says. "And I don't care who my partner is!"

"That's what I like! A man with confidence!"

Elliott fist bumps James.

"I'll be back. I'ma check on 'Nae."

"I forgot she was upstairs." Divine spreads her cards out in her hand. "Why isn't she down here partying with us?"

"Good question. I'll ask her."

James walks into the hallway and places the bag near the banister. He then trots up the staircase and knocks on Janae's bedroom door.

"Come in!" she yells.

Crossing the threshold, he pauses to soak in his daughter's customized new room. Posters of Beyonce and Destiny's Child hang on walls that are dominated by New York Knicks colors–blue, orange, and white. Basketball trophies, big and small, stand out everywhere. A smiling teddy bear the size of his daughter sits on a huge bean bag tucked away in the corner. On her computer desk are more championship medallions hanging from her LED-lighted vanity mirror. Lava lamps, a laptop, and a beautiful picture of Janae's mother, LaToya, in a standing glass frame, also accompany the sports medals.

James mentally pats himself on the back, pleased with the results.

But when he turns his head, his heart sinks.

Lying on her bed, dressed in a purple Nike jumpsuit with both legs and arms crossed, Janae watches a music video on the wall-mounted flat screen. In the video, a rapper is squatting on top of a Mercedes Maybach with a cigar in one hand while flashing money with the other. Right beside the car is her mother, LaToya, dressed in a skimpy outfit and positioning herself in sexy poses.

His daughter must have watched this same video a hundred times.

And each time, it produces the same outcome.

More inquiries about a person Janae hardly knows.

"What other videos has Mommy been in?" she asks.

*Here we go.*

James walks over and cops a squat at the end of the bed. His eyes scroll her face.

No signs of happiness anywhere in her inquiry. Only curiosity.

"Now, that's a good question. I know of only three off the top of my head. You want to call her and ask-"

"I tried…went straight to voicemail."

Her response was as cold as it was distant.

Just like her mother's presence in her life.

Then, out of the blue, a smile appears on her face. Her eyes land on him. "Mommy said one day she will be the star of her own videos."

For the past two years, something as simple as a smile has been a rare commodity for his daughter to express. And she possesses such a beautiful one. He hopes it stays for a while.

"Yep. That's always been her priority." He puts on a happy face and asks, "You wanna swing by her place tomorrow after church? I'll drop you off and pick you up later in the evening?"

"Why bother? She'll only drop me off at Aunt Tasha's afterward like she did the last three times."

Her empty expression returns twofold.

She points the remote toward the flat screen and switches to a basketball game.

James remains upbeat. "Why don't you come down to the party and show everybody how to do the real Stanky Leg dance. And we could do it together, like this…"

James shoots up from the bed and clumsily performs the dance routine. She finally belts out a sincere laugh.

"Dad, that dance is so old. And you're doing it wrong."

"Whatever. Come downstairs with me."

"I don't feel like being sociable tonight, I'm sorry."

"No, no, that's fine."

"But can I eat up here while I watch tv? I promise I won't mess up my new room."

"I'll bring you up a plate and a food tray."

"Thanks, Daddy."

The doorbell rings.

*About time, Cadina.*

"Love you."

"Love you more."

Janae smiles while turning to the game.

James leaves the room and whistles down the staircase. The music pounding from the living room increases his nervousness. He checks himself in the mirror while trying to tame the butterflies circling around in his stomach.

*Calm your ass down, Soldier, Cadina's just another woman.*

But she is so pretty, though.

And cool as hell.

He takes a deep breath, opens the door…

…and receives one helluva surprise.

Standing in front of him, in a slimmer version of her former self, is Lovelle, who sports a thick, tan poncho that works perfectly with her black Chico jeans and black knee-high Milano boots. In front of her, she holds a gift bag with both hands.

"Hey, James!" she says, brimming with excitement.

He does a couple of fast double-takes inside the crowded living room to see if Freeman and Velour are visible. Lovelle steps inside the foyer and gives him a hug.

"What a surprise!" he says, meaning every word. "How are you?"

"I'm doing well, and it's good to see you! It's been a minute."

"I know." James maintains an exaggerated smile as his eyes ping-pong from Lovelle to the living room, then back to Lovelle. "I must say you're looking very nice tonight."

"Why, thank you!"

"I see you still hitting the gym. Arms all toned and everything..."

"Man, you made my day!" Her full bob hairdo bounces as she laughs. "I can't go back to old habits, my spirit won't allow it, so yes, hitting the gym every day is my new therapy and I feel great. Very proud of myself."

"That's good, that's good." James continues to stall, unsure what to do.

She extends the gift bag toward him. "I got you a little something for the house."

"Awww, thanks, but you didn't have to."

"Now, you know I wasn't coming over here empty-handed."

Suddenly, it dawned on him.

*How did she know about the housewarming? Because I know damn well Freeman didn't invite her over here-*

Divine rushes into the foyer with arms spread wide to hug Lovelle.

"Hey, girl!" she screams over the music. "I thought you'd never get here!"

James cuts his eyes at the instigator–Divine.

She returns a *yeah-I-invited-her* smile right back at him.

"You know I wasn't going to miss out on this!" Lovelle begins to wiggle her body to Sean Paul's song, *Like Glue.* "It sure is live up in here!"

"Well, let's get it in!"

Lovelle begins to two-step into the noisy living room. She cheeses at James. "I can't wait to see the rest of the house, James!"

*No you don't, Lovelle.*

"You're going to love it, trust me!" assures Divine.

They enter the packed living room.

Lovelle stops dead in her tracks.

"What's wrong?" Divine asks.

*Don't act stupid, Dee.*

James knows exactly what is wrong and so does she.

He follows Lovelle's gaze through the dancing couples, to the speaker by the wall. They all witness Freeman and Velour erotically slow-grinding against the wall as if it was a horizontal bed. But the ultimate stab is when Freeman deep-throats Velour with his tongue and she sucks on it as if it was an icicle pop.

From the corner of his eye, James sees Lovelle's bottom lip quivering from hurt.

She spins around, grabs Divine by the arm, and drags her back into the foyer.

He reluctantly follows them.

"Is this your idea of a sick joke, Dee?" Lovelle growls as she maintains a firm hold onto Divine's arm. "You told me your brother was looking forward to seeing *me* tonight! Who the hell is *she*?"

"Her name is Velour. She's our coworker."

"*Coworker?* She *works* with y'all?" Lovelle spins around. "Y'all knew about her all this time and then gonna smile in my face like everything is cool? *James*?"

His mouth opens but nothing comes out.

Instead, Divine does all the talking.

"Look, Lovelle, I'm sorry I lied to you, but I'm sick and tired of him playing you for a fool! Y'all are supposed to be getting married in six months. Does that look like someone who's ready to tie the knot in six months–"

"First of all, Dee, I do not appreciate you inviting me over here to be embarrassed-"

"That was never my intention, and you know this! I'm trying to help you see the light-"

"I am very capable of handling my own affairs, okay?" Lovelle lowers her tone. "You're my girl and all, Dee, but at this moment, you're about as full of shit as your brother in there."

"Come on now–"

"Enjoy your party, *James*."

Lovelle storms out the front door.

Right on her heels is Divine, vehemently trying to further explain her bold decision.

He walks out on the porch to get some air.

Instinctively, he pulls out his phone and dials Cadina's number.

It goes straight to voicemail.

*Maybe she is not coming after all.*

James pockets his phone while witnessing Lovelle slamming her car door in Divine's face and peeling off into the night.

Divine marches up the steps with an attitude.

"That wasn't cool what you did, Dee. And you made me look like a fool on top of it."

"Why is Freeman throwing away his relationship with Lovelle, just for a jump-off?" Divine stuffs her hands inside the pouch of her sweatshirt. "Because that's all Velour really is. I don't understand how it even got to this point."

"Maybe it's not for you to understand. What you need to do is fall back and let them handle their problems… and not become one. Ever thought of that?"

"Well, when the both of them stop coming to me like I'm their mediator, then I might just do that."

She walks past James and heads back into the house.

James inhales the cold air and blows out heated frustration. What was supposed to be an evening filled with joy and happiness has now taken a sour detour and the one person who he was hoping would swing through to brighten his mood won't even bother to return his phone call.

The postal crew return from the beer run, with each person carrying two twenty-four packs through the gate.

"You can never have enough, baby!" Neville walks inside the house.

"Any lasagna left? A brother is *starving*!" Roy asks.

"I don't know, man," James responds, "Look on the table in there."

James and the rest of the crew make their way inside and is loudly welcomed in by the classic oldie, *You're Gonna Miss My Lovin'*.

Lou almost drops his beer. "Oh, *HELLS* no! I wanna hear some Biggie, like right now!"

The fed-up Latino sits his case of beer down to have a word with his deejay friend.

Meanwhile, Uncle Skillet blasts from out of the kitchen, singing along with Lou Rawls, "*WHEN IT'S COLD OUTSIIIIIDE! TURN THAT SHIT UP, MOOOSLIM!*", at the top of his lungs while grabbing Tucker's hand to dance.

Grace walks up to James with a food plate. "This is for 'Nae. Try to get her to come downstairs and see her family."

"I tried earlier." James takes the plate and grabs a food tray from the rack. "But she's in her missing-her-mommy mood."

"I hate that this woman has scarred her like that." Grace shakes her head. "But we're going to have our day in court, mark my word."

"The countdown has already begun."

Grace nods. She returns to the living room and starts to dance along with Tucker and Skillet.

James heads up the staircase, wondering if he should make one last call to Cadina–

*Crash!*

*What the hell…*

James quickly sits the plate and tray down on the top of the staircase and rushes into Janae's room.

His eyes zig-zag around the area until they land on his daughter.

Tears race down her face as she stares downward.

His eyes continue traveling toward the hardwood floor.

He now sees the source of the noise.

LaToya's picture, which was neatly framed in a standing holder, now lay underneath shards of glass that can puncture deeply if Janae was to make one wrong step.

"I don't want her staring at me anymore!"

She begins trembling and breathing uncontrollably.

Her voice crackles when she attempts to speak again.

"*I-I…don't…want..h-her…looking…at…*"

James tiptoes around the shattered glass and scoops up Janae who continues to sob on his shoulders.

He collapses down on the bed.

They both hold onto each other tightly.

"*Why doesn't she like me, Daddy?*" Janae squeals. "*I didn't do anything to her! I didn't do NOTHING to her!*"

"Now, don't say that." He tightens his hug on her. "You know your mother loves you-"

*"She doesn't act like it! She never acts like it! How am I supposed to love her back? How, Daddy?"*

This hurts him to the core.

He lets her vent. She needs this time to purge.

It has been long overdue.

He rocks her back and forth and stares at the shattered image of LaToya laying on the floor while Lou Rawls' timeless oath seeps into his daughter's sanctuary.

*"I know, I know, I know, that you are gonna miss my lovin'…"*

# TWENTY-NINE

## FREEMAN

Stephanie Mills' quiet storm classic, *Secret Lady*, along with burning lemon lavender Yankee Candles, enhance the cozy atmosphere swirling around Freeman's living room.

Velour pours pineapple Ciroc in both glasses. They toast the evening, take sips, and she lays her head on Freeman's lap.

She suddenly cracks up. "Now, what was up with James' uncle? What's his name, Skeeter or something?"

"Skillet…" Freeman laughs. "They call him Skillet."

"Yo, when he spilled beer on Shabbazz's equipment, I just knew it was about to go down!"

"Skillet's mission was sabotage. He wanted Lou Rawls in heavy rotation."

"Yes, he did!" She winces while rubbing her feet. "I don't know how I left home without my flats, knowing I was going to be dancing. Now, my feet are paying for it."

"Corns screaming, huh?"

"Please. I do not possess any corns on my feet, okay?"

"I'll be the judge of that. Swing them bad boys over here."

She turns her body around and places her feet on his lap. He grabs the Jergens lotion from the nearby corner table, applies a small amount in his hands, and rubs them vigorously before going to work on her feet.

His massaging conjures soft moans from the diva.

She leans her head straight back.

Perky nipples indent the top of her dress.

Blond hair dangles in elation.

His manhood awakens.

She props her head on her hand and smiles at him through inebriated eyes. "You know, if you ever get tired of working at the p.o., this could definitely be your primary gig."

He grins. "I see the Ciroc got you talking crazy."

"Honey, I am not that drunk. You do have amazing hands."

"Then I will accept the compliment."

"As you should."

She takes another sip from the glass. She never lifts her eyes off him.

His manhood wants to stand at attention so badly.

*At ease, Soldier.*

"Can I ask you a personal question?"

"What's up?"

"Did you give up on church altogether because of your mother's passing?"

He reads her expression. She is sincere with her query.

Still, he shrugs while tending to her feet.

"I can understand if you don't want to talk about it—"

"No, no, it's cool." He realizes she is right. "I mean, other factors contributed as well, but that was a huge part of it, you know?"

She nods.

"My moms was one of God's true soldiers, for real. She helped our pastor build the church to the successful ministry it has become today. She sang in the choir, taught Sunday school, she was a deaconess, you name it, she did it and with pure intentions. It wasn't until recently that I had to face the fact that God relieved her from her duties here on earth." His words came out more somber than he intended. "You know, besides James, I really haven't had another person to share this whole crazy ordeal with."

"Wow. I feel honored." She rubs his hands. "I know it was hard."

"Time heals all wounds, right? I'ma be alright."

He stares at her, unsure about bringing up a particular topic, but decides to ask her, anyway.

"That night, when I dropped you off at your place after the show, things got a little heated with you and your brother as I was leaving."

She immediately grabs her drink.

She does not sip, this time. She gulps it all the way down.

Obviously, he had struck a nerve.

She smiles defensively. "I was wondering if you were going to bring that up."

"The way he was yelling at you, how could I not."

"It was just a brother and sister misunderstanding. No big deal."

"Let me guess. He wasn't exactly thrilled about you bringing company over to his humble abode."

Velour does not answer quickly.

Instead, she pours another round for them both.

She goes back to nursing her drink. "You can say that."

"I figured as much."

"Don't get me wrong, Vincent is very out-going and loves company. We just caught him at a bad time, but he was cool afterward."

"Any thoughts about getting your own place?"

Freeman caught it.

It was very subliminal, but she disguised it quickly with a drunken cackle.

Apparently, he touched another nerve when she flashed a dark look that lasted about a nano-second before the chuckling began.

Maybe he should not have brought it up.

But he is glad he did.

Velour brings the glass to her lips. "I don't see that happening any time soon."

"Oh, my bad. We're living in mansions and shit."

She almost spits out her drink in laughter. "*Noooo*, that's not the reason…"

He raises an eyebrow at her while massaging.

She sighs. "Well, it's not the *only* reason, okay? I love the quiet neighborhood we live in. We're not that far from Manhattan and we're like two minutes from City Island and you *know* how I love my seafood, so I like my situation. Is that a crime?"

"But it's not *your* place. No matter how big and fancy it may be, you have limitations placed on you if the owner is not in the mood… like, for example, inviting your friends over."

"I can always come here."

"Is that right?"

"Unless your fiancée has a say so in the matter."

He stops rubbing her feet.

"I like how you spun this whole conversation around, you ain't slick–"

She laughs. "I'm just saying! She may have reservations about my presence here."

"See, now, that's where you're wrong. *I'm* the master of this here domain."

"*Really*?"

"Yes, *really*. I pay the rent in this mofo."

She places her drink on the table and leans toward him.

"Well, the master has to make a decision tonight on what he really wants."

"Excuse me?"

She leans in closer.

Alcohol and sex on the tongue.

"My time is valuable, Freeman. And I play second fiddle to no one. So, what's up?"

She frees a foot from his hand and uses it to massage his manhood.

A huge bulge appears in his pants.

She means what she says.

"And what makes you think I haven't made my decision already?"

"I don't go by a person's word, Freeman. I need receipts."

"It's like that, huh…"

"Yep."

Freeman leisurely moves his hands up her legs.

She accommodates him by inching up her mini dress just enough for her cream thong to be exposed. His left-hand stays on course towards her love canal. Then, using two of his fingers, he slides the thong to the side while allowing the other fingers to enter her moistened tunnel.

"How is *this* for receipts?"

She grins wickedly. "Sliding your fingers inside my coochie hardly qualifies, Boo."

Yet, she widens her legs for easy access.

The gentle rubbing and probing with his fingers produce waterfalls of pure ecstasy.

Her head falls back onto the edge of the couch.

She closes her eyes and bites her bottom lip.

She moans and squirms in delight.

His manhood is now officially rock-hard.

"You did say my hands were amazing."

"*Oh, God*, I did say that, right?"

She lunges herself on top of him. He hurries to unbutton his dress shirt. She aggressively throws her tongue down his mouth as they begin rolling around on the living room rug. She spreads his shirt apart so she can suck on his hairy nipples. From there, her tongue slopes down to his belly button. Freeman fights with his belt buckle until it comes apart. As soon as he pulls his pants down, he hears the front door unlocking and opening, only to be stopped by the door chain.

*"SHIT!"*

He jumps to his feet, yanks his pants back up, and fastens his belt buckle.

Velour calmly pulls her dress back down. She then sits on the couch with her legs crossed, while retrieving her drink.

"Expecting company?" She giggles between sips.

BOOM! BOOM! BOOM! BOOM! BOOM!

"*I KNOW YOU'RE IN THERE! OPEN THE DAMN DOOR!*"

BOOM! BOOM! BOOM! BOOM! BOOM!

"Do you want me to leave?"

Freeman wipes his face with both hands. "No."

He takes a deep breath, and then clumsily advances to the front entrance.

He cracks the door open with the chain still attached.

The anger scorches from Lovelle's glare.

"Oh, so we're leaving chains on the door now, Freeman?"

"Look, this is not a good time—"

"When is it ever a good time, you tell me?" Her tone is more hurtful than angry. "I saw you at the party with your *coworker* and I really don't care if she's in there. *WE* need to talk, so open this damn door! Now!"

He has been avoiding this moment for months.

The moment of transparency.

He closes the door, slides off the chain, and then re-opens it.

Lovelle barges inside of the small entrance. She then makes her way into the living room and embarrassingly soaks in all the venereal stimulation that has been left lingering in the air.

Velour places her glass down on the table and stands.

Lovelle eyeballs her from head to toe.

The quiet tension hangs like a London fog.

Freeman clears his throat. "Uh, Lovelle, Velour. Velour, Lovelle-"

"What *part* of me even suggests that I wanted to know her fuckin' name, Freeman?" Lovelle tightens up on her purse handle. "I came here to talk to *you*! Not to get to know *her*! Let's be clear!"

Freeman and Velour trade glances.

Velour then picks up a Vibe magazine from the table. "I'ma, uh, go in the other room and let you two talk."

Velour shuffles barefoot to the back room.

Freeman swings around to Lovelle.

"First of all, coming in here all swoll and yelling at everybody is gonna get your ass out that door that much quicker, a'ight? So, bring it all the way down-"

"Was it *her* you took to the show, Freeman?" She points towards the back room. "With the tickets *I* bought you?"

"Yes! And if I remember correctly, you gave me the tickets to do whatever *I* wanted to do with them—"

"I bought those tickets for *us*, fool! Not for you to escort some high-yellow heffa! You think I'm that simple?"

"You never made it clear to me, so whose fault is that?"

"This is pathetic, man!"

She plops down on his couch and buries her face in her hands.

Tears leak between her fingers.

His breathing calms down. He takes a seat next to her.

"How long have you two been involved?" she asks, speaking through her hands.

He had to think about it for a second. "Just happened recently."

The silence is dense between the two.

She brings her wet face around to his. "So, is this temporary, permanent, which is it?"

He takes a deep breath. "I don't know."

"Are you breaking up with me, Freeman?"

Her eyes are filled with dreaded anticipation.

"You really want me to answer that?"

"The *answer* just jiggled her behind into your bedroom!" she points. "But I'm giving you the opportunity to be a man and tell me where the hell this relationship is going!"

He stands and points his finger directly in her face.

"Oh, just like I should've given you the opportunity to tell me where you were the day my mother got killed, right? We're talking about that kind of opportunity?"

The power of speech is snatched from her throat.

She turns away from him.

He could not keep it bottled in any longer.

Now it was his time to vent.

She faces him. Voice shaking in guilt. "So, this is your way of getting back at me for what I did? We went over this a thousand times-"

"And I'm *still* bringing the shit up!" he roars. "You shed some pounds and then you lose your fuckin' mind, in the process? I'm calling you about my mom's passing and where were you? Huh?

WHERE WERE YOU? And you had the nerve to let that nigga answer your *phone*? How am I supposed to forget that shit? And then you try to put the blame on me for not spending enough time with you, yet I'm busting my ass at work doing overtime just to buy that damn ring? I bet you didn't tell the Pastor that part, did you? Trying to be faithful to you and then you decide to get brand new on *me*? You played your own self, big time!"

She tries her best to contain her emotions.

He does a good job controlling his.

"Do you want another apology from me, Freeman? Fine. I'm *sorry*. I'm so sorry for messing up everything between us! I'm owning up to my mistake because I love you so much and want us to continue moving forward with our lives-"

"Oh, we're gonna move forward alright, but it won't be together."

"Why you *say* that?"

"Because after my moms' funeral, we still carried on as if nothing ever happened and that wasn't fair for either of us." He sits down next to her. "Now, I owe it to myself to figure out what I really want in my life. And that requires some space from you. I'm sorry."

An avalanche of tears rolls down her cheeks.

She grabs his hand. "I don't wanna lose you-"

"You're saying that out of guilt, Lovelle." He pulls his hand away. "You need this time yourself to figure out if you're really ready to settle down with someone. And I just don't see that happening."

"But I'm *telling* you right now-"

"Lovelle…let's not be redundant. I said my piece. Now, do us both a favor and go home."

"Go *home*? As much money as I've invested decorating this apartment, this *is* my home! *She* needs to go!"

"I'm not going back and forth with you, Lovelle. Leave… right now!"

They glare at each other for a hot five seconds.

In a low spiteful voice, Lovelle says, "Okay…that's how you wanna do this? Fine."

She pulls off the ring. She shoves it, along with the apartment key, into his hand.

She stands, grabs her purse, and points at him. "Have fun with your little coworker, if that's what you really want, I *know* the shit is temporary…because what we've built together over the years, Freeman, you just don't throw away over a piece of ass."

"But that's exactly what you did when you took 'ole boy to the hotel. Now, get the fuck out of my apartment!"

She stares him down before wiping her face and stomping down the hallway. She slams the door with enough authority to wake up the entire Co-op City area.

Freeman drops back down on the sofa.

He grabs the Ciroc bottle from the table and sucks it dry.

For months, he has tried to mask his hurt by either drinking his sorrows away or by absorbing all the overtime he could muster from his job. But the gut-wrenching pain of his fiancée admitting she was having an affair with another guy still reeked in his memory bank like fresh dog shit on a hot summer day. And with his mother passing around the same time, the emotional effort he put into working things out with Lovelle was about as mechanical as an assembly line. His clouded mind no longer needs the aggravation from her. What he needs now is instant healing from those painful memories.

The sound of Velour's footsteps breaks his chain of thoughts.

With her heels on, purse in hand, and fur underneath her arm, she smiles sympathetically while gently combing through his afro with her soft fingers.

The instant healing process begins.

"You alright?" she softly asks.

"Had better moments. Where are you off to?"

"Anywhere but here," she chuckles. "No offense, Freeman, but she might come back with a shotgun to take care of some unfinished business. *And* reclaim that ring. May I see it?"

He hands it to her.

She holds it up in the air. "I see you know your diamonds…I'm impressed."

"I stayed within my budget."

She gives the ring back to him. "It's beautiful."

"Thanks." He twirls the ring between his fingers before placing it next to the lamp. "But I seriously doubt she's coming back here." He grabs and holds her hand. "Stay. Please."

She mulls for a moment. "Okay. But if she comes back acting crazy, I will jump out that window, Bionic Woman-style."

His laughter triggers a sharp pain that shoots through his already swirling head. He rubs his head and eyes.

"What's wrong?"

"Ohhhh, nothing. Just my head trying to explode, that's all. Too much drama, too much of that pineapple shit…" he laughs, causing another sharp attack.

She throws her fur and purse on the couch and rubs his forehead. "Do you have any aspirin?"

"Motrins in the bathroom cabinet."

"Two Motrins coming right up." She hurries to the bathroom.

The migraine subsides, mercifully. He walks over to gaze out the window. Looking through the blinds, he notices Lovelle's Honda Accord still parked outside. He glances around the area, wondering where she is.

"Do you think this will cure that headache?"

Freeman turns around. "Well, I hope it does—"

Those were the only words that left his mouth.

Posing near the entertainment system is Velour, now dressed in a cream-colored, two-piece velvet lingerie set that shows off her butter-toned, hourglass figure.

"Are you ready to take your medicine now?"

Her velvet thong flosses between her golden round buttocks as she saunters towards him. She grabs a hold of his hand and guides him back to the sofa. She makes him sit down and then places two Motrin pills in his palm.

His manhood is ready to pop out of his pants.

"You know I'm going to need something to wash these down with."

She smiles ever so lovely while pushing her breasts in his face. "Not when you have *these* to suck on to create your own juices."

"You're just full of surprises tonight, aren't you?"

Velour straddles his lap. She places her finger on his mouth, telling him to, "*Shhhh.*"

She pops out one bouncy breast. She takes one of the pills from his hand and balances it on her bite-sized nipple.

She whispers, "Now open wide."

Freeman hungrily attacks the medicated tit and sucks it like a newborn child.

"*Ooooooh, yessssss...*"

She pulls out the other breast and repeats the performance. He continues tongue-kissing both throbbing nipples until her tongue meets him halfway and together, they embrace one another with unbridled passion and desire. He grabs both of her butt cheeks and begins to dry-hump Velour, who in return, cradles his head for ample support. The power of his hammer desperately tries to bust out of his zipper each time she breathes and moans in his face. As both sets of hands begin to rip off his pants, he suddenly stops.

"What's wrong, Baby?" she asks, sucking feverishly on his neck.

"My blinds."

Velour turns around and notices the window blinds are wide open. She turns back around and says, "What about 'em?"

Freeman laughs. "So, you don't mind if somebody from the building across the street decides to videotape us?"

Kissing his lips, she coos, "Wouldn't that be exciting…"

"I see you're the adventurous type." He sucks on her lips. "But tonight, I just want it to be me and you, not the whole boogie-down Bronx, a'ight?"

She laughs. "Fine with me. I'll get the blinds; *you* just take those pants off."

Her cat-like stroll toward the window has him snatching off the rest of his clothes and flinging them every which way in the living room. He then leans butt-naked on the couch and wrestles with the condom package. He notices her peering out the window for a mighty long time.

"Something caught your eye out there, or you just like the idea of having the moon shine on your ass?"

She folds the blinds and then flicks the lights off.

Traces of the moon's afterglow spotlights half of her glossy-toned body as she catwalks back over to him. She then slips out of her thong and bra set, fully exposing the delicious set of twins that stand firm and round on their very own. She kneels in front of his stiff soldier, snatches the condom package from his hand, and says, "I was thinking about how happy I am in your company right now."

He reads the genuineness deep within her eyes.

Feels it with her delicate touches.

She rips the condom bag open with her teeth and then pulls out its contents.

"*Very* happy," she softly repeats, with Gladys Knight's, *If I Were Your Woman*, chiming in the background.

As she deep-throats her way into a world of happiness, Freeman lay back, closes his eyes, and tells himself how happy *he* is that the two headaches he was suffering from, (the one beating inside his head and the other named Lovelle), are nullified by Velour's very presence.

This is the moment they have been craving for the past two months.

They sex each other to the break of dawn.

"Are you alright, young lady?"

Lovelle sits at the bottom of the building's staircase, head hanging, shoulders slumped, lost in a world filled with despair. She turns around to the voice of an old man carrying a garbage bag, staring down at her. Apparently, she is blocking traffic. She pushes herself from the steps.

"I'm fine, Sir."

"You don't look it."

The old man bristles before heading out the front entrance.

She pulls out her compact mirror. *Damn.* She stares at raccoon-looking eyes that washed away make-up and eyeliner hours ago with the last of her tears.

The old man was right. She looks like a hot mess.

She sighs before grabbing her purse and heading out the front door.

She manages to walk to her car with her head held high, only to conceal a heart that has become a wounded beneficiary ever since she stormed out of Freeman's apartment. She can still feel the harsh effects of his flaming anger. And she has nobody to blame but herself.

She wanted so badly to receive validation from him about her recent weight loss, but she never received it the way she envisioned. He was always tired from working many hours at the post office. So, her ego found someone else to fill that void. A dude at the gym, who was all too willing to show her how much he admires a woman "who takes care of herself."

The affair lasted only two sessions.

But it was the last session when she would receive that fateful phone call.

She was devastated by the horrific news about Freeman's mother.

But also embarrassed by getting caught.

And she was supposed to be a saved woman.

Truth be told, Freeman had always loved her, despite the weight. *She* was the one with the insecurity issues, so she expected him to over-compensate for her lack of self-love. Now stuck with the reality of losing the man once deemed by her parents "a godsend", she has no other choice but to leave her burdens with God because she got caught up in her own low-carb hype.

Opening the car door, her instincts prompt her to look up at the second-floor window to Freeman's apartment.

And when she does, she receives the mother of all surprises.

Sneering through the cracked blinds is Velour, watching *her* with hawk-like precision, all the while, exposing her bare essence.

Lovelle stands paralyzed, with her mouth wide open.

Velour squeezes her breasts and blows a kiss directly her way.

*No, that bitch didn't!*

And just like that, the blinds close shut, and the lights go off in the background.

Lovelle must have blinked twenty times in humiliation.

"Are you sure you're okay, young lady?"

She spins around.

The old man again.

This time, she shoots a hostile glare at him before collapsing into her Honda. Mashing the gas pedal, she makes a promise to herself to never step foot on this block for as long as she lives.

# EPIGRAPH

"The post office is not as laid back as people may think. Very strenuous, and very demanding of your time. I've seen my share of people who fell by the wayside because of either aggressive management, or the workload itself, and sometimes, both."

**–James Richards**

# JUNE 2016

# SUMMER MADNESS

# THIRTY-ONE

## LEXINGTON

"Yes, that's what I asked for…I understand the repairman is coming tomorrow to fix the a/c unit, but I need those fans on the work floor asap, it's ninety-plus degrees outside and people are burning up in here…just do as I say, alright? *Thank* you."

He slams the handset down.

*Damn maintenance.*

Lexington looks up and squints at the colorful rays of sunlight that beam through the tall work floor windows. Another scorching day in the latter part of June. He rolls up his dress shirt sleeves, grabs his clipboard from the podium, and begins walking toward the center of the section.

*Oh, I almost forgot...*

Lexington doubles back to the podium to retrieve an envelope.

He then grins devilishly as he yells out, "BREAK-TIME IS OVER, FOLKS! TIME FOR A SERVICE TALK, SO GATHER AROUND! LET'S GO!"

A chorus of boos rings out as carriers drag their stools to the middle of the section.

He superiorly peers over his section, who are dressed in postal shorts and "Stamp Out Hunger" t-shirts for the nation's largest one-day food drive. He clears his throat before proceeding.

"Alright, I want to make this meeting short so we can get back to work. But first, does everybody have enough bags to give out to customers for their non-perishable items? If not, see me before you leave the station-"

"And let's acknowledge our brother Marty Grace for making these nice red t-shirts for the annual food drive," Divine interjects, displaying her shirt. "Let's give it up for him!"

The carriers loudly celebrate, giving Marty hi-fives.

Lexington shoots Divine a thinly veiled look.

He despises being interrupted by foolish behavior.

"LET'S MOVE ON TO THE NEXT TOPIC, SHALL WE?"

The carriers stop celebrating. They glare in unison at Lexington.

*That's more like it.*

"ROUTE-27. YOU HAVE A CALL ONE LINE ONE!" blares from the intercom. "ROUTE-27, LINE ONE!"

Freeman excuses himself from the meeting to answer the phone.

Lexington now holds up the envelope he retrieved from the podium.

"Now, yesterday, it just so happened I found this piece of bulk mail behind someone's letter case." He waves the envelope in the air for three long seconds. "Had this been first-class mail that was found behind that very same case, the responsible carrier would've been giving a verbal warning. Ladies and gentlemen, I don't want to find any more mail left in your cases after you leave, understood?"

Carriers not only grumble because of his vile threat but also at the demeaning tone behind it.

"Another issue I need to address is carriers deviating from their assigned areas to assist other carriers and without authorization to do so. I'd strongly advise you to curtail that behavior. And all this hanging out with your boys or your significant other at the restaurant while still on the clock will not be tolerated, as well."

A sea of hands fills the air to challenge his authority.

But James sounds off immediately.

"Excuse me, Lexington-"

"That's Mr. VanGuard to you-"

"*Lexington*," James ignores him while taking a stand. "You need to start speaking more in general with these "issues" you're having because it seems as if they're directed towards the very same people you have a personal gripe with. Nobody is stupid around here."

Lexington feels pity for James, who is a particularly good employee, in his own regard.

*But not on my caliber, whatsoever.*

For if James were, he would have at least tried to advance his career within the ten years he's been in the postal system. But he hasn't. And now he wants to stand and voice his menial opinion to a person who's making power moves and with a fraction of James' postal tenure.

*It sucks to be you, boy.*

"I'm not here to insult your intelligence, Mr. Richards," Lexington replies. "But there are times when I must get my point across to those who fail to heed the rules. That's all I'm doing."

"Yeah, okay. But just remember before you started wearing that shirt and tie, you used to do the same things you're telling us not to do, so don't start developing amnesia."

"Didn't mean to step on your toes, Mr. Richards." He glances around at the other carriers. "Any more questions for me?"

Lou yells out, "Yo, when are you leaving? We need a real supervisor up in this piece."

"YEAH!" the carriers shout, loudly. "BRING BACK CHAPMAN! BRING BACK CHAPMAN! BRING BACK CHAPMAN!"

Lexington stands before them with his arms crossed, unfazed by their ridiculous exploitations.

"Are you through?" he calmly asks. "Now, again, does anyone have anything else for me?"

Evil glares from the carriers are his only response.

He holds back from laughing in their faces.

"Good. We have mail to deliver…let's get at it."

Carriers grumble under their breaths as they slide their stools back to their workstations.

He returns to the podium, followed by a few carriers in need of the perishable bags. He opens the bottom cabinet drawer and hands some out. As the carriers leave, his mind plays back to Lou's sarcastic question.

*When are you leaving?*

He turns around and studies his personal calendar, thumb-tacked next to the time clock. February, March, April, and May. All crossed out. June is the month he anticipates leaving Midway, altogether.

But he has yet to receive any news from the manager about his expected departure.

He wanted to ask Davenport whether he'd heard anything about the scheduled date for the next supervisor's class but has been reluctant to do so. The manager has been somewhat moody, as of late. But he needs to know something soon. That scheduled class could take place any day now, and the last thing he wants to hear is that he missed out on it. That would be the death of him.

He chuckles to himself for allowing even an ounce of anxiety to attack his self-assurance.

*I have faith in Michael.*

*He won't let me down.*

And until that glorious day arrives, he has a section to supervise at Midway.

*His* section.

And he will not allow James, Lou, or any of their non-driven minions to undermine his authority, in any form or fashion.

He impatiently waits for Freeman to finish up his phone conversation so he can call the maintenance people once again about those fans.

# THIRTY-TWO

## FREEMAN

Suddenly, the phone feels heavy inside of Freeman's hand as he passes it to an impatient Lexington. He returns to his workstation and grabs a tray of letters to sort.

"Lexington is a trip," laughs Velour, while working. "Trying to call people out! I'm glad James and Lou brought his ass back to reality."

Freeman glances her way but doesn't join in on the conversation.

Velour stops casing. She turns to him. "What's wrong, Baby?"

"Nothing, I hope."

He begins casing the letters but then turns to her. "You know Ms. Phillips in the 200 building, apartment 6D…little old lady with the poodle?"

"You know I know that crazy lady. Why?"

"That was her on the phone. Apparently, someone has been tampering with her mail."

"What?"

"She said this is the third time someone has ordered items using her credit card. This time it happened to be a bunch of weird electronic devices called shimmers."

"Wow." Her expression bears concern. That's crazy."

"But then she's gonna come out and say she's never had this kind of problem when Dante was on the route, insinuating that I may have had something to do with it. So, I politely told her to call the credit card company and dispute her case, but then she hung up on me."

"Maybe she had a thing for Dante and was upset that he didn't say goodbye to her."

She winks, letting him know it was a joke.

As the months roll along, Velour remains a fascinating enigma to him. They both agreed on keeping the relationship simple–no pressure, no commitment, just hook up and enjoy each other's company when time allows. And it has been working.

Somewhat.

Almost five months have passed, and he's barely scratched the surface of getting to know her personally. Besides being a beast in bed, she relentlessly showers him with gifts for no apparent reason–expensive clothes and jewelry he has no business wearing because they're not his style, but he wears them when they're together to keep her from pouting. And they can talk about everything under the sun, but when it pertains to her past or her family, she changes subjects completely, so he no longer bothers.

He still cannot shake the feeling that there is something unsettling about the relationship between Velour and her brother, Vincent. He barked at his sister when Freeman first met him in front of the post office. Then he barbarically lashed out at her in front of their precious mansion on their first night out together. Their relationship is about as nurturing as a demolition derby. He can imagine what goes on behind closed doors, which probably explains why they don't meet up at her home anymore.

Which is fine by him.

*Or maybe I'm over-exaggerating. Maybe Vincent is really a cool guy who just enjoys an intensely private life, who knows.*

Either way, he hopes to learn more about Velour, in the days to come. But in the meantime, he must deal with Ms. Phillips and her credit card situation.

"Ha, ha, hell," he quips. "I'm the one who has to see this lady every day and I don't want her nagging me with these accusations."

"Look at it this way, Boo; some people hate change. This was Dante's route for many years, even before I came aboard, so any wrongdoing, you're going to be the number one suspect. But this will all blow over, trust me."

"I pray it does. And fast."

"Awww, my baby is upset."

She hugs him from behind. And whispers in his ear.

"I know what could put a smile on your face."

"Besides you hugging me at the job?"

"In addition to that."

"And what's that?"

"Finishing our delivery and going somewhere to "deviate" from our route, just to get on Lexington's nerves."

She kisses the back of his neck and giggles as she returns to casing the magazines.

She always has a way of making light of any situation.

Even if it's in a joking manner.

A trait he can live with for the time being.

He laughs along with her while returning to the mail.

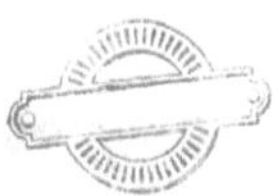 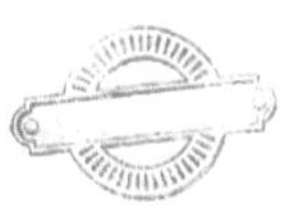 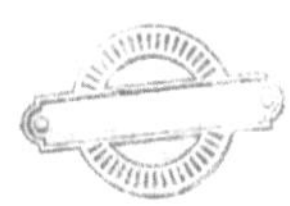

"I AM OFFICIALLY DONE FOR THE WEEKEND!"

Freeman and James guzzle down bottled water in front of the station while watching in amusement as Cadina hops out of the postal truck and dances up to them in dramatic fashion.

"I'm about to be done for the weekend *and* I'm about to be off Tucker's "extended" probation, now what!"

The men look at each other.

"Some people get their uniform allowance and don't know how to act," James jokes to Freeman.

"I beg your pardon?" She does a model twirl, displaying her crispy new postal summer uniform. "I earned all of this, Sweetheart, plus the weekend off, *thank* you."

"Your probation period may be over, but you're still a newbie in my eyes."

She walks right up to James' face. "Well, this newbie expects you to be at my parents' house at six pm, sharp, you got that?"

"Oh, I hear you loud and clear."

"You better."

"Miss Wilson?"

Tucker throws her briefcase in the backseat of her Lexus and turns to Cadina.

"The garage called. Your truck is scheduled for maintenance in about an hour."

"Yes, Ma'am, they informed me this morning, thanks." Cadina swings back around to James. "Now, you make sure you and Janae wear something nice, okay, because I'm treating y'all to dinner, end of discussion-"

"I suggest you get a move on, now, Miss Wilson. Yours is the last truck that needs to be serviced and nobody should have to wait on you before they can go home."

Tucker keeps her no-nonsense stare on Cadina.

"Uh, yes, Ma'am." Cadina meekly turns back around. "Six o'clock, James. Enjoy your weekend, Freeman."

Cadina peeks at the assistant manager before climbing into her truck and pulling off from the curb.

Tucker dips into her vehicle and peels off down the street, right behind Cadina.

"Wow." Freeman turns to James. "I see Tucker's still busting Cadina's chops over the smallest things. What did she do to piss her off?"

"Man, I asked her the very same thing about a month ago and she just laughed it off, saying it's a woman thing, so I don't know."

"Well, I'm not gonna hold you up. First time meeting the parents?"

"Yep." James gives him the half-hug pound. "And it won't be the last, either. I'll holler at you."

Freeman chuckles. "A'ight, peace."

James rushes down the block to catch up with the station's shop steward.

Freeman downs his water as another postal truck pulls up and parks in the vacant spot where Cadina's truck had been. Bouncing out of the passenger's side is a person he has not seen since the early part of the year.

Freeman shouts, "You know you can't park there, that's for working people!"

Dante welcomes him with a bear hug. "What's good, Playboy?" He slaps Freeman's back as hard as he can.

"Chillin', chillin'. I haven't seen you in a minute! How's parcel post treating you?"

"Man, everything's gravy." Dante uses a damp rag to wipe over a bald head that once sported a short fade. "Those Amazon packages got a brother humping all around Manhattan, you know what I'm saying? But I'm lovin' it, though. How's everything going between you and Velour?"

Freeman can't help but smile. "Man, she's been spoiling a brother *rotten*. I mean, she practically insists on handling all the tedious work, like the return to sender mail, the forwardable mail, she breaks down the parcels, plus all the mail sweeps! I'm surprised you wanted to leave with that kind of support."

"I know, but it was time to move on, that's how the universe works. I got what I wanted, you got what you needed, and she got *you*, in more ways than one."

"Don't start that mess. I hear enough of that upstairs."

"I bet you do!" Dante playfully taps Freeman's chest. "But yo, let me handle my business so I can get out of this heat! It's hotter than *twelve* muthafuckas out here."

"Who you telling? I'm out. Peace!"

Dante opens the back of his truck and pulls out a tub filled with parcels.

Freeman throws his backpack over his shoulder, takes a couple of steps, and then turns back around. "Yo, Dante…"

Dante closes his cargo door, and then pushes his tub of parcels over to him. "What's up?"

"You remember Ms. Phillips; she lives in the 200 building?"

"Apartment 6D, yeah. Why, what's up?"

"Has she ever complained to you about someone using her credit cards?"

"Nah, man, can't say that she has." Dante ponders for a moment. "Someone messing with her mail like that?"

"She said it happened three times in the past two months. Velour says she's not playing with a full deck and just to ignore her."

"Well, if that's what Velour said, then you don't have anything to worry about, right?"

"I guess not. Yo, be good."

Freeman heads down the block, wondering whether he should grab a hotdog from the street vendor.

"Yo, Free!"

He turns around.

His heart skips a major beat.

Just a minute ago, Dante's energy was bigger than life itself.

The expression he currently bears is the polar opposite.

Absolute fear.

"What's up?" *What's wrong with you?* is the question Freeman really wants to ask.

For what seems an eternity, Dante finally answers. "Ah, nothing. Just be careful."

Freeman squints not only from the sun but also from curiosity. "Careful about what?"

Another long, drawn-out pause controls Dante's speech. "Home. Just be careful going home, that's all. I'll holla at you later."

And just like that, the toothy grin reappears on Dante's face as he pushes the tub of parcels up the loading dock ramp.

Freeman stands idle, trying to digest what just happened.

*Just be careful.*

*Did he really mean to be careful going home?*

*Or something else?*

Freeman lets it go. The next time he bumps into Dante, maybe he will inquire more about it. He stops at the vendor to purchase two icy bottled drinks of water instead of the hotdog he was craving. He guzzles down one of the bottles until it's empty and takes his sticky body down the subway stairs.

# THIRTY-THREE

## VERNON

Cadina rushes into the living room and places her father's dinner on the folding table.

"Appreciate it." Vernon mumbles a quick grace, points the remote toward the flat screen, and begins to devour his food.

*Invasion of the Body Snatchers*, the 1956 version, fills the wall-mounted television.

"Yes!" His eyes light up as he motions toward the screen. "This movie never gets old."

"You won't allow it to."

He studies his daughter's appearance as she sits on the sofa. She is all dolled up.

"Going out?"

"Yes. With my friends for a little while in Brooklyn."

He nods. "How's it going at work?"

"Everything is falling into place. I've settled into my position; I'm cool with my coworkers…and I'm keeping my eyes on the prize."

"Good. Just make sure you keep doing what you're supposed to, that's all I ask of you, okay?"

Father and daughter trade smiles.

The doorbell rings.

She pops up like a jack-in-the-box. "Could you get that for me, please, Daddy? Thank you very much!"

"Hold up, where are you going—"

She dashes out of the room.

*"Now, she sees me eating..."*

He shakes his head and shuffles to the door.

He peeks through the peephole, then steps back and pauses. He peeks again and tries to recall where he has seen this young man, who is accompanied by a little girl holding a gift bag.

He opens the door. "Can I help you?"

"Mr. Wilson?"

He cautiously stares at the young man. "And who is asking?"

"My name is James Richards, and this is my daughter, Janae. I work at the post office with Cadina. She said we could meet her here at this address."

He thoroughly sizes them up before extending his hand.

"Vernon. Vernon Wilson."

James firmly shakes his hand. "A pleasure meeting you, Sir."

"Likewise. Come on in."

Vernon leads them into the living room.

"Cadina will be down in a minute. Make yourselves comfortable."

He returns to his food while keeping an eye on the father and daughter duo, who quietly soak in the breathtaking interior decor that surrounds them.

"Woooow," Janae marvels. "You have a beautiful home, Sir."

"Why, thank you, little lady."

He furthers his visual summation of James. A good-looking guy, in a rugged sort of way. Facial features are neatly groomed. Black slacks tapered over a nice pair of black shoes. A burgundy short-sleeved casual shirt covers his medium build. And no blinged-out accessories anywhere on his body. The man is unknowingly off to a good start with putting in the first impression.

"So, James, how long have you been working at the post office?"

"A little over ten years, as a letter carrier, Sir."

"Cadina told me she never realized how much work was involved in that position."

"It's not as laid back as people may think," James asserts. "Very strenuous, and very demanding of your time. I've seen my share of people who fell by the wayside because of either aggressive management, or the workload itself, and sometimes, both."

"I see..."

"But your daughter has been an incredible worker." James suddenly chuckles. "I don't know if she was aware of it, but there were actual bets placed on whether or not she'd quit. Needless to say, a few people lost a lot of money."

Vernon grins. "That's good to hear."

"Daddy, can I give this to him now?" Janae asks.

"Go right ahead."

She speed-walks over to hand Vernon a silver gift bag.

Taken aback, he says, "This for me?"

"Yep."

"It took me a while to pick Cadina's brain without her knowing what I was up to, so we hope you like it," James says.

Vernon stares at the bag and then at the smiling father/daughter duo.

He reaches inside the bag and pulls out a gift that tugs at his heartstrings.

A DVD box collection containing all of the Twilight Zone classic episodes.

His insides bubble with child-like joy.

Cadina's coworker/friend truly did his homework and found one way to win his heart. But it still does not make up for her purposely disregarding his visitation policy.

"Wow. My all-time favorite sci-fi series. I don't know what to say but thank you very much. It's greatly appreciated." Vernon returns the gift back into the bag.

"Cadina!"

Janae sprints over to hug Cadina, who steps into the middle of the living room flourishing in a form-fitting burgundy summer dress and burgundy ankle-strap sandals.

He has not seen his daughter dress this way since...well, he simply can't remember.

"You look *nice.*" James respectfully kisses her cheek.

"Thanks. You do, too." She smiles at her father. "I see the three of you've met."

He returns a fake smile. "Yeah, we were having good conversation."

"And he *loved* the present we gave him!" Janae declares.

"What present?"

Vernon hands the gift bag to her.

When she pulls out the DVD collection, she punches a laughing James on the arm.

"I *knew* you were up to something when you were asking me all those questions about what he likes!"

"But wasn't I *smooth* with it, though?" James chuckles.

"Excuse me…" Vernon interrupts. "but before you leave, dear, I need you to help me look for something real quick."

"Okay." She faces James. "I'll meet you at your truck, okay?"

"Not a problem." James shakes Vernon's hand. It was a pleasure meeting you, Sir—*finally.*"

"Yes, *finally.*"

"Enjoy your gift, Sir."

Janae surprises Vernon with a hug.

He winds up embracing the little girl.

"I look forward to it."

Cadina escorts them both out the front door.

Vernon's grin soon disappears.

She returns to the room.

"Soooo," her voice anxiously rises. "What did you think?"

"Have you lost your damn mind, Cadina?"

She rolls her eyes. "Here we go…"

"Do you have *any* idea what position you're putting me in? Do you?"

"Trust me, I do, Daddy. But you know I would never bring anyone over here without your permission…unless I knew for sure he was the absolute one."

Vernon cocks his head in confusion. "He's the absolute one for *what*?"

She grabs him by the arms.

Face glowing with euphoria.

"We've been seeing each other for the past five months and I can't even describe to you how incredible it's been. He has such a beautiful spirit. He's goal-oriented, he's a great father to his daughter, kind of reminds me of you. That's why I felt you needed to meet him."

"I really hope you're putting in half the effort in your duties at work as you are in a relationship you have no idea how long will last-"

"Wait a minute, Daddy." She let loose his arms. "That's your reaction? After everything I just expressed to you about this man?"

"I'm surprised you expected anything different! And since when did you feel you were ready to become someone's mother?"

He punctured his daughter deeply with that remark.

He wishes he could take it back.

"Wow." She throws her hands in the air. "I can't seem to do anything right in your eyes. I thought by bringing James and his daughter here, I was showing you how responsible I've become by being upfront with you, *while* I'm busting my butt to make things right at work. Is this your way of making it harder for me to earn your respect? I mean, what more do you need for me to do? You tell me."

He closes the gap between them.

"Don't bring any more of your coworkers around here. *Ever*. Am I clear on that?"

Her eyes are filled with hurt.

The damage has been done.

"Enjoy your gift."

She grabs her purse from the table and marches out the front door.

Vernon walks over to the window. He draws the curtains back.

She stands on the porch with her hands over her eyes.

Damn.

He gives in to the thought of going out there to console her.

But then James pops out of his vehicle to see what's troubling her. She plays it off like the trooper she is by grabbing his hand and walking to the SUV. They drive off. Vernon releases the curtains.

He returns to the living room and sits behind the tray, but he does not touch his food.

Instead, he rubs his face, questioning the lack of empathy he has for his youngest daughter.

*Am I really that hard on her?*

He stares at a family portrait that hangs over the fireplace.

He zooms in on Cadina's face.

So innocently happy and beautiful.

She may have had good intentions by bringing James over, but his home comes with guidelines. Guidelines that were drawn up way before she was even old enough to get a job. But this still does not soothe the hurt he feels, slighting his daughter the way he just did, when he knows she has been doing an exceptional job at the post office and not taking her position lightly.

She is just in *love.*

He stands and heads for the kitchen to reheat the dinner which was prepared by the one he just emotionally slaughtered.

# THIRTY-FOUR

## VELOUR

Foxy Brown's, *Ill Na Na*, has Velour humming the rap tune to herself as she grabs the Louis Vuitton and Prada bags, plus an overnight bag from the backseat of her Porsche. She struts merrily down the cobblestone walkway to the front entrance while pulling out the house keys from her purse. She sticks the key in to unlock the door. It does not turn. She checks to make sure it is the correct key, which it is, so she tries again. No luck. She jiggles the key a few more times before pressing the doorbell.

A wide-bodied, brown-skinned dude in denim shorts, a white T-shirt, and a fitted Yankee cap, opens the door. He appears to be shocked by her presence. "H-Hey, Velour-"

"What's wrong with the lock?" She brushes past him as if he were nothing more than a personal servant. "I tried my key but it wouldn't turn."

"Vin had the locks changed."

"What, he lost his key?"

He avoids eye contact. "You gotta ask him that, I don't know."

She does not make it past the foyer when she slows to a complete stop.

All her shopping bags fall from her hands.

Lined up along the hallway walls are suitcases. *Her* suitcases. Along with her garment bags, her painted portraits, mountains of shoe boxes, liquor boxes filled with her perfumes, and other small accessories. Further down the hallway are her entertainment system, her dressers, armoire, and vanity set. And before she can even close her mouth, she watches in horror as a couple of Vincent's workers struggle to bring her headboard down the staircase, and yell at one another about not breaking it.

"*Bunions*!" Velour screams as she spins around to face him, fidgeting. "*Explain this*!"

"Well, uh, you see…"

"I don't need you stuttering, you fat bastard! What is my stuff doing downstairs in the hallway?!?"

Bunions suck his teeth. "Yo, why you always gotta call me out my name—"

*"FUCK YOU AND YOUR NAME! WHERE'S MY BROTHER?"*

"*WHERE HE ALWAYS IS! IN HIS DAMN OFFICE*! Shoot, yelling at me for…"

She storms down the hallway, screaming and cursing at the thug-movers about not breaking any of her expensive belongings.

She stops in her tracks.

Something dawns on her.

It was the quietness.

Besides the noisy thug-movers struggling with her headboard, the house is abnormally calm.

She re-routes to the basement entry.

Before she can turn the knob, the door flings open.

More of Vincent's henchmen stumbling out, carrying boxes and computer equipment.

They greet her.

She ignores them.

They continue out the back of the house with the equipment.

Velour creeps down the staircase into the place deemed by her brother as the Activity Basement. She searches for the light switch because the place is dark. This is her first red flag. The basement is never dark. It is always bright and bustling with four five-man crews working eight-hour shifts, day and night, seven days a week.

She scans the entire basement, which is nearly empty, except for a few tables and chairs.

Second red flag.

All the computer equipment, the credit card scanners, and the boxes filled with the shimmer devices used for credit card hacking…gone.

*What the hell?*

She figures there must be a valid reason for this. But that is a concern for another time. She marches back up the stairs and down to the office to deal with her immediate problem.

With enough sense not to bust into her brother's office like a raging madwoman, she closes her eyes and exhales before walking calmly into the relatively tranquil room.

Vincent's right-hand man and muscle-bound enforcer, Wise, sits behind a currency counter machine, wrapping stacks of bills. He quickly peeks at her, nods, and continues with his work.

Bending over on the loveseat painting her toenails while nodding her head to Super Cat's, *Dolly Me Baby*, is Vincent's girlfriend, Joy. She peeks up at Velour, displays a misleading smirk, and resumes her pedicure.

Velour would love to drop-kick her dead in her face.

She has a laundry list of reasons why she cannot stomach the light-skinned Trinidadian from Flatbush. The main reason is that Joy poses a serious threat to the strong bond Velour once shared with her brother. She wonders if this skinny gold-digger is the reason her stuff is in the hallway.

Her eyes finally land on her brother, at his desk, tapping away on his laptop. A desk that is now minus his main computer. Velour senses something very serious going on.

"I hope you enjoyed your weekend with your coworker," Vincent mutters. He pops his head up. "We have urgent matters to discuss."

"What's going on around here, Vincent? And why the hell are all my belongings in the hallway?"

"Hold up a sec."

He continues punching away on the laptop.

"Could you stop typing for one minute and talk to me!"

Joy snickers loudly.

Velour swings around and approaches the smirking Trinidadian. "Why don't you make yourself useful, Bitch, and take your ass outside while I talk to my brother, alright?"

Joy stops polishing. "I beg your pardon?"

"You heard what the fuck I said—"

"Hey!" Vincent closes the laptop and stands. He does some stretching in his black workout clothes. "You both know I don't tolerate that nonsense in my office—"

"WHY IS MY SHIT IN THE HALLWAY, VINCENT?"

He hands out the car keys and money to Joy. "Be a doll and get me a gallon of orange juice and cherry Black and Milds for me, please? Thank you."

Joy springs up and grabs the car keys only. "Put that away, Babe, I got you."

She gives him a kiss, slips on her flip-flops, and sashays past Velour wearing a tiny black shirt and tight denim shorts.

Velour wants to trip her, so badly.

Vincent sits behind his desk. "Have a seat, Velour-"

"Uh-uh, Vince, you're not going to treat me like I'm one of your little flunkies around here-"

He pops out of his chair. "Do you need me to show you how to take a seat? Sit your ass down."

She falls into the chair in quiet frustration.

He returns to his seat. "Now, while you were away on your little *rendezvous*, our operation had to undergo some unexpected changes."

"Yeah, like changing the lock on the door and placing all of *MY* shit downstairs-"

"Trust me, I know how this looks—"

"It looks like you're kicking me out! Did I do something to you, Vin? Or did that skinny tramp put you up to this?"

Knowing exactly what she said, she waits for her brother to flip out on her.

But he remains uncannily cool.

"Let this be the last time you call Joy out her name, you got that?"

Velour rolls her eyes and turns her head the other way.

"Now, as I was saying; a lot has happened while you were gone." He slips his weight gloves on and then flexes his arms back and forth. "Seven of our employees from the Bronx were arrested Friday. And another four were bagged up yesterday, this time from Brooklyn."

Her mouth hangs open. "Are you serious?"

"As a heart attack." He struts bare-footed over to the other side of the room to stand in front of a spectacular in-wall aquarium. "But here's the kicker; They were all released today. *All* of them. Coincidence, don't you think?"

Velour now understands the nature of his worries.

Twelve years ago, her brother left the slow-paced atmosphere in Rock Hill, South Carolina, and moved to New York City, where he turned his small bootlegging hustle into a formidable money-making enterprise. CDs and DVDs were his original cash cows. But they both took a backseat to high-end auto and credit card theft. Four childhood friends whom he trusted moved to the city along with him, and collectively, they formed a pact known as the Phantom Adversary Circle (P.A.C. MEN for short). Each member assembled his own mobile unit which spread throughout the five boroughs and within a ten-year period, amassed over twenty million dollars combined, from all illegal activities.

Now the operation has finally been scarred by this current dilemma and knowing her cautious brother, he will not overlook anything that could be detrimental to him or his business, no matter how small or coincidental it may appear.

"Have you reached out to any of them?" she asks.

"Antonio got in contact with the Bronx crew and they all said the exact thing." Vincent spins his head around to her. "They were all interrogated about the stolen vehicles."

"Whoa."

She glances at Wise, who is oblivious to their conversation as he jots down numbers in the accounting ledger.

She turns to her brother. “So, what’s our next move?”

He removes himself from the aquarium and returns to his desk. “This reeks of something bad and I’ma nip it in the bud before it ever has a chance of nipping me.”

“What do you mean by that?”

“I’m shutting down the entire operation until further notice. We’ve already sold the remaining cars from our inventory, and I also sent out a message to everyone to refrain from any credit card transactions.”

“This doesn’t include me, right?”

“HA!”

Wise pauses from his routine. He smiles in amazement. “You’re a trip, girl.”

She peeks at Wise, confused.

She turns back to Vincent.

His whole demeanor darkens.

“Are you deaf or what, Velour?” he asks. “This includes everybody!”

“I literally have the world at my fingertips through my job, Vincent. How am I going to pass up on that kind of money?”

“That’s exactly my point! With everything we’re tied up in, what makes you think you won’t be the next target? You have been a central part of our operation by supplying credit cards from the post office and the last thing I need is for any detective questioning you to get to me!”

“Okay, so what you’re really saying is you’re kicking me out to save your own ass. Is that where this is leading to?”

“You still refuse to see the bigger picture. Here…”

He hands her a printed version of a craigslist classified advertisement.

She reads it in disgust. “Are you fuckin’ kidding me, Vincent?”

He walks around and sits on the edge of the desk with his arms folded.

"If I'm not mistaken, I vividly remember you telling me you were going to find yourself an apartment once you got on your feet. I knew it was all bullshit the minute it left your mouth, so I took the liberty of making that move for you." He snatches the paper from her and points to a specific ad. "This Brooklyn owner is renting out their upstairs floor. One bed and bath, fifteen hundred a month, utilities not included. I've already paid this month's rent and security for you."

She brushes the paper from her face. "You're so full of shit, Vincent. You know I can't afford that rent, plus utilities *and* a car note with full insurance without the use of those credit cards-!"

"Why not when you got a job, Miss Mail-Lady? Nobody told you to go out and buy that Porsche knowing you were supposed to be looking for an apartment–"

"Oh, so you and your crew can ride around in nice rides, except for me?"

"What postal worker *you* know owns a hundred-thousand-dollar car in New York? You stick out like a fuckin' sore thumb, but you act like you can't listen to me when I tell you to play your role-"

"Forget it, just forget it!" She pulls out her cell. "I'll ask Tanya if she wouldn't mind me staying with her for a little while. This is really fuckin' crazy, man."

"Welcome to the real world."

He walks over and lays his back down on the weight bench to do a couple of sets.

She does not know which hurts more, getting the boot from the mansion or not being able to make her lucrative side money. Too close to call. One thing she does know for sure is that cutting into her postal check to pay for rent is already making her lightheaded. There has to be another alternative and she won't rest until she finds it.

She ends her call. "Now, where am I supposed to stay tonight? Tanya's not picking up, and my bed is disassembled."

"You could—*whoo*—stay in one of the guest bedrooms," he grunts, in between bench presses. "I never—*whoo*—intended for you to leave tonight—*whoo*—but I had to get the ball rolling in order to plan my next move—*whoo*. You know what I mean?"

"What, moving your scalawag girlfriend's things into my room?"

Wise stops counting the money and pops his head up. "Awww, shit–"

CLANG!!!!

Vincent drops the barbell on the bar rack. He leaps off the bench and squats down right in front of her.

The blood rapidly drains from her face.

"You know, for all of the bitching and whining you seem to enjoy doing, you should be thankful you have a solid job to fall back on. Most of my employees do not have that option. They must rely on me, and for their commitment, I intend to support their means. Didn't I say to you before you moved up here to expect dry spells every now and then?"

She braces herself. "Y-You may have mentioned it—"

"It's called life, Velour, get that through your thick head. I've already put the house up for sale, so me and Joy will be staying downtown for a while until things cool down."

He gently places a hand on her neck.

She swallows a lump of fear.

"Now, instead of you worrying about what me and my lady are doing, get *your* affairs in order first, you got that?"

He gently squeezes her neck.

Tears begin rolling down her face.

"Start controlling your money and don't let it control you. That way, people will respect you and start taking you seriously."

She gags as he tightens up on his grip. "*V-V-Vin-s-s-stop!*"

"Don't bring any more credit cards to this address, I hope I don't have to repeat myself."

"*P-PLEASE-COUGH-VIN!*"

"Now, take heed to this final warning; the next time I hear you call my lady out of her name, I'ma knock your fucking teeth out of your mouth. You hear me? I said, do you *hear* me?"

Wise stands. "Vincent…enough! You made your point."

Vincent pushes her neck back, letting her go.

She collapses to the floor while coughing up spit and broken oxygen. She does not dare look up, in fear that he might grab her neck again. Or worse.

Joy glides into the room from her bodega run. She walks around Velour while holding up a bottle of vodka. "I figured you'd want something to go with the juice."

Vincent laughs as he grabs Joy and tongues her down. He then smiles at Velour. "One of the many attributes Joy and I have in common–being proactive."

Joy hands him a plastic cup. She turns to Velour. "You care for a drink?"

Velour cuts her eyes at the Trinidadian. She gathers herself before heading to the door.

"Hey, Sis!"

Velour turns around. She catches him lighting up a Black and Mild cigar.

"How does Freeman feel about your side ventures?"

He's fishing to see if she's being faithful to the organization.

And she is…for the time being.

"He doesn't know anything about them, alright?"

He exhales cherry-scented smoke that rises above his suspicious eyes. "That's good. And I'ma need you to reimburse me for the security deposit I laid out for that apartment. Unlike you, I don't have money to squander. Ain't that right, Baby?"

Joy giggles as she mixes the drinks.

A fresh set of tears form in Velour's eyes.

She turns back around and storms out of the room, slamming the door in the process.

This is the first time Cadina has seen Velour this vulnerable. Sitting on her work stool, barely eating her mixed fruit. Staring blankly into the empty case.

Sulking.

Moments before, Velour confided in Freeman and her about her brother's decision to put his house up for sale and it seemed like that bit of news has snatched the life out of the diva.

"So, what happens now?" Freeman asks.

Velour sighs. "Well, he wants the place empty so he can prep it for an open house. In the meantime, I have to put all of my stuff in storage until I find my own place."

"Seems like this came out of nowhere," Cadina says.

"I know. But he's had it for about eight years…says he doesn't need the extra space anymore."

"You know you're more than welcome to stay with me until you get on your feet," Freeman offers.

"You're so sweet." Velour rubs his hand. "But I've already made arrangements to stay with my cousin. But I'll keep you in mind if anything changes."

"You do that."

Lou joins the group, along with a new male employee.

"Freeman, Velour, Cadina; meet our new sub, Emmanuel DeBest."

"Welcome aboard!"

They all shake the hand of the lanky newcomer with the cornrows and big grin. His eyes happily bounce from Velour to Cadina.

"Man, I'm diggin' this station already!" the youngster announces. "Y'all have all the cuties up in here!"

"Why, thank you!" Cadina cheeses.

"But I think he has his eyes on your sis, Free," Lou laughs.

"Oh, really?"

"Divine is *your* sister?" Emmanuel glances around at everybody. "Hey, I was just admiring her beauty, no disrespect."

Cadina laughs. "I see this is going to be fun to watch-"

"MISS WILSON, ARE YOU THROUGH SOCIALIZING?" Lexington barks from the podium. "YOU NEED TO MOVE YOUR TRUCK FROM THE LOADING DOCK, NOW, PLEASE!"

Cadina twitches in anger.

Lexington has been using her as a verbal punching bag ever since she declined his dinner offer, many months ago. Normally, she would ignore the bastard.

But enough is enough.

"Do you want me to go talk to him?" Freeman asks.

"Nope. I'm about to handle this, right now. I'm getting sick of his shit."

She walks over to the podium where Lexington is positioning a fan in his direction.

"Lexington, may I have a word with you by the time-clock, please?"

"I have a ton of paperwork to do, plus I have to count this in-coming mail, and didn't I tell *everyone* to address me as Mr. VanGuard—"

"Over by the time-clock, *now*."

He huffs before following her to the clock.

"What is it, Miss Wilson?"

"Do you have a problem with me?"

He folds his arms and sneers at her. "*Personally*, no. But I do have an issue with your total disregard for route maintenance?"

"What are you talking about?"

"I gave you label strips to put on the route-case this morning, but you haven't felt the urgency to complete that task yet-"

"That's because you wanted me to pick up a truck from the garage and I'm just now getting back."

He clenches his jaw. "What about updating the names inside your residential mailboxes?"

She crosses her arms. "It was all done last week. We can walk the route whenever you have the time."

She watches him struggle to control the conversation.

"You may be off probation, Miss Wilson, but you still have a long way to go before you reach my level of proficiency when I was a letter carrier-"

"You mean overrated."

"Excuse me?"

"I'm every bit as good as you were, Lexington. In fact, better."

Lexington scoffs. "Clearly, you're joking-"

"You see me laughing?" she questions with a straight face. "And let me make this one thing clear to you; the next time you single me out in front of everybody over some petty nonsense, I will file harassment charges against you and try me if you think I'm kidding."

"Whatever gave you the idea that I've been harassing you, Miss Wilson?"

"I see you enjoy playing dumb and that's okay. Come at me wrong again, that's all I'm saying."

James strolls over to the argument, carrying a mail bucket.

"What's the problem over here?" he asks Cadina.

"Keep walking, James," Lexington responds. "This matter doesn't concern you."

"Nah, see, that's where you're wrong, Lex. Anything that pertains to *this* lady right here, concerns me-"

"And I'm telling you to go case up your mail and learn how to follow a direct order-"

"And I will. As soon as you learn how to start showing respect to the people you're supervising."

"Is that so?"

"Hey…HEY!"

Chapman hurries over to the quarrel. "What's going on over here?"

"Nothing, Sir." Lexington quickly adjusts his attitude. "Just making sure people understand the core values of the business. I have it under control."

James scoffs. "That's what you call yourself doing?"

Cadina points her finger toward Lexington. "You have one more chance, Lex."

Chapman eyeballs the trio. "I trust whatever is going on between you three will be corrected after I leave." He turns to the section. "Breaktime is over, folks! Let's get back to work! Lou, show Emmanuel how to hand out the mail." He turns back to Lexington. "Come with me downstairs, I want to have a word with you."

Lexington grills both Cadina and James before following Chapman down the work floor.

"I think I got the message across to that nitwit," she says. "What about you?"

James pulls out a small brown bag from his mail bucket and hands it to her.

"Got the banana and yogurt you wanted."

She studies his flat demeanor.

"Are you okay?"

"Yeah…yeah, I'm good. I'll see you before you leave."

He returns to his workstation.

His smile was empty. And the eyes never lie, either.

Something is bothering him.

But she will probe him later about it.

She hears clapping sounds from behind.

She turns around. The entire section is giving her a round of applause.

"We're proud of you, girl," Velour says.

"And you maintained your integrity, too," Freeman adds.

"It's about time you stood up for yourself," Lou yells out from his workstation. "We thought you were gonna punk out like you usually do."

"I got your punk right here, Lou," Cadina counters.

Lou laughs as he resumes training the new sub.

She takes a bow in front of the section before racing to the stairwell to move her truck.

# THIRTY-SIX

## JAMES

The humidity continues its firm hold on the evening as he pulls up to Cadina's parents' home. He turns the car off and then digs into his pants pocket for a folded sheet of paper. He hands it to her.

"Give this to Lou, he's covering my route tomorrow. It's a list of people whose mail is on hold."

Cadina stuffs the paper in her shirt pocket. She turns to him. "Okay, James, out with it. You've been moping around the station like something's bothering you. Talk to me, Babe, what's up?"

He wipes his face and slouches in his seat. "Tomorrow morning, me and Moms are going to court for custody of Janae."

A moment passes between them.

"And you weren't planning on telling me?"

"Boo, I tried keeping a low profile on this, I didn't want anyone knowing."

"But why-"

"Because I'm scared out of my ass, that's why." He gazes out the front windshield. "You gotta understand, Cadina, for the past two years, I've been waiting for this day and now that it's finally here, I'm a nervous wreck. I just don't want the judge to overlook the significance of my presence in my child's life, that's all I'm saying."

She grabs his hand. "And the judge won't–trust me. Look at what Janae has accomplished because of you; honor roll student, captain of her basketball team, she loves theater. All of this was because of the structure you built around her and no court can take that away from you."

"Yeah, but I've heard of too many cases where the good fathers get the short end of the stick in court–way too many. Why should mine be any different?"

"Well, I have a feeling everything's going to work out in Janae's best interest. So, come tomorrow morning, I want you to remember that when you walk into that courtroom, okay? Look at me, James–okay?"

She pulls his chin closer. They share a kiss.

"Call me later," she says.

"I will. And thanks."

"For what."

"Reassurance."

"That's what I'm here for."

Cadina gives him the thumbs up, exits the vehicle, and strolls up the brick walkway to her parents' home.

He has never laid eyes on any other lady that looked so damn sexy in a pair of summer postal shorts.

But he jumps when someone knocks on his window.

*What the hell…*

Vernon parks his car right behind James' Suburban.

He cuts his engine off. He watches Cadina walk the pathway towards the front door. He grabs his briefcase and steps out of his vehicle.

The sticky temperature has him loosening his tie as he makes his way over to the SUV's driver's side. He notices James keeping his eyes on his daughter.

Vernon shakes his head.

*Always be aware of your surroundings, young man.*

He raps on the window.

James jumps in his seat, then swivels his head. He rolls down the window.

"James, right?" Vernon asks.

"Yes. How's it going, Sir?"

"It's going. I see you dropped my daughter off."

"Ah, yes, Sir. And I'm about to head on home."

Vernon nods and then leans in closer to him. "Listen, James, I'm going to be straightforward with you. Normally I don't allow my daughters to bring their friends over to my house. Cadina caught me off-guard when she invited you and your daughter the other day and I confronted her on it. I want you to know that."

He watches James straighten up in the seat, ready to plead his case.

"Sir, I hope I didn't disrespect you or your family in any way-"

"May I finish?"

James sighs. "Yes, Sir."

"I also want you to know that I pride myself on having a good judge of character." He sticks his hand out to him. "Do right by my baby, that's all I ask of you."

James shakes his hand. "I'm going to be the same way with my daughter, so I do understand."

Vernon grins. "Get home safe."

"I will and thank you for your honesty."

Vernon nods and then moves out of the way as James pulls off down the street.

Cadina steps outside and stands idly by the front door with her arms folded.

He walks up the front steps, equipped with a smile. "Hey, doll—"

"What did you say to James?"

The tone in her voice tells him she is ready to defend her boyfriend's honor by any means necessary.

And he is going to allow her that platform.

It's the least he can do to atone for the other day.

He takes a seat on the steps and pulls out his pipe. "Nothing much. Just small talk."

"I know your idea of *small talk*, Daddy."

"I'm sure you do."

"Look, the man just dropped me off from work, that was it. He has a big day ahead of him tomorrow and he doesn't need any distractions, okay? Enough with the mind games."

He loads his pipe with tobacco and then lights it. "What's for dinner?"

He stumped her for a second.

"I'm not cooking *anything* tonight. We're ordering Chinese food."

"Then I'll have General Tso's Chicken, fried rice with vegetables, steamed broccoli, and a sweet tea, thank you."

Again, awkward silence on her end.

"Okay, but you're paying!"

She storms back into the house.

He almost chokes on his smoke from his hearty laughter.

# THIRTY-EIGHT

## DIVINE

"Are you going to be nice to our guest this evening, Dee?"

Divine fake-smiles her older sister, Majestic, while intentionally slamming the fork and spoon down next to the plate. "Aren't I *always* nice?"

"You need to let it go." Majestic places a chair at the dinner table. "Neither you, me, nor anyone else can control who Freeman wants to spend his time with. It's his life."

"Well, I'm not going to sit up here and pretend I'm buddy-buddy with Velour. Especially after the way she ruined my relationship with Lovelle."

"It seems to me that you're angrier at Freeman and the choices *he's* making rather than his new lady friend."

"Trust me, Sis, Velour is very persuasive when it comes to Freeman. If you worked at my job, you'd see that firsthand."

"So, you're telling me you can't find one positive thing to say about this lady?"

Divine mulls for a moment. "I'm positive she's not right for our knucklehead brother. How about that?"

Majestic laughs and shakes her head. "I give up with you."

Entering the dining room with a hot pot roast in his hands, their father, Foster, hurries to place the casserole dish on the table. "They're on their way up," he announces in his baritone voice. "Get the door for me, Dee?"

Divine turns to her sister. "Can you *please* get the door for—"

"Cabbage coming right up!" Majestic moves quickly to the kitchen.

Divine drags herself down the hallway. She opens the front door and sizes up Freeman and Velour, who are both dressed in pink. And he is wearing jewelry. She remembers a time when he said he would not be caught dead in bling. Now he stands before her, dripping in platinum on his neck and wrist. Divine rolls her eyes and heads back into the dining room.

"And *hi* to you, too, Dee," Freeman retorts, leading Velour into the apartment.

"Whatever."

Freeman hugs his father. "Sorry we're late, traffic was crazy. Velour, I want you to meet my handsome father, Foster. Pop, this is Velour."

Foster shakes her hand. "Nice to meet you, Velour."

"Likewise," Velour replies.

Majestic saunters into the room and places the cabbage bowl down to hug Freeman.

"Heeeey, little big brother!"

"Whassup! When did you get into town?"

"This morning. Wanted to spend time with my family before I fly out to New Orleans with my girls." She smiles and shakes Velour's hand. "I'm Majestic and it's a pleasure meeting you."

"Nice to meet you, too. Where can I wash my hands?"

"Down the hall, to the left."

"Thanks."

Velour smiles at everyone before heading to the bathroom.

"My stomach's grumbling, which means it's time to eat. Shall we?" Foster invites everyone to take a seat.

Freeman whispers in Divine's ear. "Let me talk to you, right quick."

"Excuse me?"

He scoops her up by the arm and pulls her into the kitchen.

"What's wrong with you, fool?" Divine yelps.

"I don't have to worry about your mouth this evening, do I?"

She folds her arms and shoots him a cynical look. "How's that old saying goes? 'If you don't have anything nice to say, don't say anything at all?'"

"Don't show your ass, you got that?"

"First of all, you don't tell me how to act. This is *my* home-"

"You heard what I said."

"Just move out my way."

She grabs the lemon meringue pie she made from the kitchen counter and they both return to the dining room. She places the pie down and takes her seat.

"I just want to say thank you for inviting me over to dinner." Velour glances around the table. "I'm truly grateful."

"It's no problem. In our home, we welcome everybody with open arms. Isn't that right, family?"

Divine cuts her eyes at her smiling father.

"And on that note...Dee, would you do the honors?"

Divine grabs Freeman and Majestic's hands. Everyone follows her lead except Velour, who is already helping herself to the cabbage. She finally realizes what is about to take place and embarrassingly places the bowl of cabbage back down.

"Oh, I'm sorry." She quickly grabs Freeman and Foster's hands.

Divine shakes her head and then blesses the food.

"And this time, we're staying at my favorite hotel, Springhill Suites," Majestic says, between bites. "They make their grits to perfection, hands down."

"You haven't missed an Essence Festival yet, have you?" Foster asks.

"Not one. As long as Mary J. Blige is on the bill, *I'm* there," she laughs. "That's my girl!"

"Now, that's an understatement." Freeman pours himself some juice. "Pop, she saw Mary so many times, she got her entire dance routine down pat." He points at Majestic. "Come on, get on up and show them the Mary Dance-"

"You stupid," Majestic laughs. "And no, I'm not getting up to dance for you, either."

"Awww, come on, now…"

Velour listens and smiles at everyone while woofing down her second serving of food. Juicy pot roast. Sauteed cabbage. Lima beans. Lemon butter cornbread. She cannot recall the last time she's had a home-cook meal that tasted so delicious.

And she would enjoy it even more if Divine would quit staring down her throat.

"Forgive me for saying this," Velour wipes her mouth. "…but this food is the bomb. Everything tastes so incredible!"

"I'm glad you're enjoying it," Foster replies.

"Excuse me, Velour, but where are you from?" Majestic asks.

"I live in New Rochelle."

"No, originally."

"Originally, I'm from Rock Hill, South Carolina."

"I knew it!" Majestic yells. "I knew I heard some southern twang in your voice. What made you decide to move to the Big Apple?"

"Everything! There's no other place like it in the world! When I was little, I would visit my cousin Tanya in Brooklyn and I would always tell myself this would be my permanent home when I got older. So, when my brother moved to New Rochelle ten years ago, that provided the perfect opportunity."

"How often do you go back to your hometown?"

"I don't."

"I know your family must miss you and your brother."

"My parents passed away when we were young."

Majestic cups her mouth. "I'm sorry, I didn't mean to pry like that."

Velour waves her off. "It's okay. It was so long ago. I think I was eight years old when Alfred was murdered in some bar. Or that's how the story went, anyway."

"Alfred was your father?" Foster asks.

"Our biological, yes, but that's how far it went, you know? But when our mother died two years later from a stroke, that's when everything went downhill. So, it was kind of rough growing up."

Everyone falls silent.

Velour finishes her plate.

"Man, how unfortunate," Foster expresses. "May I ask who raised you two after she passed?"

"Can I have a piece of pie first?" she happily asks.

"Sure!" Majestic slices a piece on a saucer and hands it to Velour. "Divine always have a lemon meringue ready for me on my visits."

Velour gulps down the first bite. “Mmmm.” She gives Divine the thumbs up. “Delish.”

“Thanks,” Divine stubbornly replies.

“Well, our aunt and uncle on my momma’s side were pressured into adopting us because they had some money, but that became a total nightmare.”

“Really…” Foster asks.

“They were bougie *and* evil.” She takes another spoonful before resuming. “Imagine living in a big ole fancy house where you couldn’t touch anything without getting your butt whupped. On top of that, they would always go on these family outings without us but expected me and my brother to do all the chores while they were away. But what bothered me most was the fact that we were actually frowned upon because of our skin complexion. We were called piss-colored so often, I really thought it was a crayon color! We were never welcomed in that house, so when my brother got his first apartment, we were outta there and never looked back.” Velour glances at everyone. “I’m sorry, I didn’t mean to ramble on like-”

“Nooo, it’s okay,” Majestic assures, grabbing Velour’s hand. “To me, it sounded like you’ve needed to get that off your chest for the longest.”

“Maybe. But you know what? I always remind myself that other children are less fortunate than we were, so I try not to waddle in self-pity.”

“Amen to putting a positive spin on it,” Foster acknowledges.

“Do you mind if I have another piece of pie? It is so good and today’s my cheat day for sweets.”

Majestic begins slicing the pie. “Girl, you help yourself!”

“Would you care for some milk to go along with your pie, Velour?” Divine asks.

The entire table gasps at her.

“A half glass would be fine.” Velour responds. “Thank you.”

Divine glares at everyone else at the table. “And why are y’all looking at me all crazy?”

“YOU KNOW WHY!”

They all burst into laughter.

Except for Velour.

She glances around the table at the close-knit family.

And suddenly feels depressed.

"Excuse me." She stands. "I have to use the bathroom."

"Freeman grabs her hand. "Everything okay?"

"Yes, everything is fine."

Velour walks down the hallway, enters the bathroom, and closes the door behind her.

She checks out her facial appearance in the mirror.

She smiles to make sure nothing is stuck between her teeth.

She looks at the right side of her face and then the left.

"*Ha, Ha, Ha, Ha, Ha…*" is all she hears from the dining room.

She stares at herself in the mirror.

She let her guard down.

Big time.

She has never done that before.

She places the lid down on the toilet and takes a seat.

She tries to pinpoint the origin of her vulnerability.

Was it the home-cooked meal?

Maybe the pie?

Or was it the genuine love she received from Freeman's family which compelled her to unearth that buried coffin of the past?

All the above.

She never planned on telling anyone about the way she was raised, in an attempt to keep her personal life well intact. There were plenty of men she has been with since moving to the big city that could care less about her upbringing. They got what they wanted from her and left. And most of them were married.

Not Freeman.

She can tell he is falling for her real fast and exposing her afflicted childhood would only have him wanting to do more for her.

But she will not allow that to happen.

In due time, she will have to find a way to dissolve their romantic attachments to a mere platonic relationship so she can carry out her own private mission she has been mulling over the past week. But judging by his romantic flair and spiritual benevolence towards her, it will not be an easy feat to accomplish.

"*Oh, see, now look at Dee! She's doing the Mary Dance*!"

"*Who do you think taught her? Go'head, Dee! Bring it down for Pops*!"

"*Y'all are a mess! Mary be dancing like that*?"

"*I'm trying to tell ya! Go, Dee! Go, Dee*!"

Velour stares at the wall as she listens to the lively activity in the other room.

She wishes she'd experienced that kind of love growing up.

# FORTY

## JAMES

Outside of the courtroom, James sits impatiently. He glances at Grace and Janae and notices he is the only one fidgeting. He decides to pace the floor again. The added stress makes his white dress shirt sweatier by the second.

"You want some more juice?" Grace asks him, shading her eyes from the bright sunbeams cascading through the floor-to-ceiling courthouse windows in the hallway.

"I'm good." He checks his watch again and then blows. "They told us in thirty minutes they would start; it's almost an hour. What's up with that?"

"James, sit back down before you make a ditch in the floor." Grace nibbles on a cracker and quickly wipe the crumbs from her navy blue, two-piece dress suit. "They'll call us in when they're ready."

He grumbles as he takes a seat on the wooden bench. Soon after, a lady court officer opens the courtroom door.

"We're ready to begin," she confirms with a cordial smile.

Grace stands and turns to her son. "You ready?"

James bolts up from the bench. "I'm ready." He takes a couple of deep breaths before extending his hand out to his daughter. "Ready?"

Wearing a sunny yellow dress that does not match her mood, Janae continues to gaze out of the gigantic windows.

"Janae?"

She pushes herself from the bench and grabs his hand. They enter the courtroom and take a designated seat in the front.

A minute later, Janae's other grandmother, Leslie Brooks, rushes into the courtroom and takes a seat opposite the Richards family. The well-dressed, heavyset woman nervously waves at them. They wave back at her.

Creeping inside the room wearing a medium-length pink raincoat, clear-heeled stiletto boots, and a huge pair of pink Christian Dior sunglasses underneath a wildly cropped brown weave, is Janae's mother, LaToya Brooks.

"Lord have mercy," Grace murmurs under her breath.

"Mommy!" Janae yells. She leaves her seat to approach her mother.

LaToya takes off her sunglasses and hugs Janae firmly. Then she releases Janae and whispers for her to return to her seat. Janae plops next to James with tears swelling in her eyes.

James and LaToya make eye contact and he instantly feels sorry for her. Behind all the thick make-up and glassy-eyed stare, lies a beautiful woman who is still holding onto fading dreams of becoming famous in the entertainment industry, but it is taking a toll on her physically and emotionally. She cracks a crooked smile at him. He does not return one.

"ALL RISE!" the bailiff commands.

As the judge walks in, James frowns.

An older white woman in a black robe takes a seat behind the bench.

He studies her stoic expression behind a pair of glasses, which to him, wears enough experience to render a decision in a matter of seconds.

But Cadina's voice enters his spirit, putting him at ease.

She is right.

All the positives are in his favor.

LaToya has had plenty of chances to redeem herself but has blown them.

Now, the bottom line is Janae's well-being.

Still, his heart races like a horse at a Kentucky Derby. He grabs his daughter's hand and braces himself for a long, drawn-out afternoon.

The bailiff announces, "COURT IS NOW IN SESSION!"

# FORTY-ONE

## CADINA

The doorbell rings.

Cadina rushes from the kitchen while wiping her hands with a towel. She peeks through the peephole and then opens the door. James crosses the threshold, and they embrace in a hug. She then leads the way to the living room where he falls back on the loveseat, exhausted. She sits beside him and begins playing in his hair.

"Hungry?" she asks him.

"I could eat."

He takes off his wrinkled dress shirt and tosses it to the side. He repositions his body so that he can lay his head on her lap.

She continues messing with his hair. "I tried calling you about an hour ago, to make sure everyone was alright."

He pulls his phone from his pocket. "My bad. I forgot to turn it back on after I left the courthouse."

"Oh." She begins rubbing his eyebrows. "Soooo…"

"I was awarded full custody of Janae."

She allows the statement to digest for a moment.

"How is she?"

He stares at the ceiling. "Sad. Confused. Hurt."

She nods. "I know it must've been rough in that courtroom. How do you feel?"

He gives her question some thought. "Hmmm. Played? Yeah. That's the best way to describe it. I felt played."

"Why do you say that?"

"LaToya voluntarily relinquished all rights to Janae."

"Really..."

"Yep. And you know what really pissed me off? She was rushing the process so she could catch a flight out to Miami for a video shoot."

"Nooo..."

"And then she was about to leave without saying anything to Janae, but her mother had to force her to talk to her own child."

"Whoa."

He kicks off his shoes and socks. He cuddles his head back on her lap and plants his eyes on the ceiling.

"I gotta hand it to LaToya. She is very clever." He lets out a condescending snicker. "I believe she had this planned from the jump. She probably figured if she kept doing dumb shit, that eventually I'd take her to court. But she waited until I initiated the first move so it wouldn't have appeared obvious that she never wanted to raise Janae to begin with. She flipped the script, lovely."

"Well, this still should be a victorious day for you and Janae-"

"There're no winners in this, Cadina." His eyes finally latch onto hers. "LaToya's delusional ass gets to travel the world and not be held accountable for anything. Meanwhile, I'll be at home, explaining to Janae why her mother chose to chase a fleeting dream over parenting her own daughter."

"I'm sorry. I didn't mean for it to sound the way it came out."

He grabs her hand. "I know."

She finds herself analyzing the situation.

Would she alienate her child to pursue a dream?

No, that would leave a major complex on that child's psyche. She would figure out a way to balance raising a family and achieving personal goals. But some people are just built differently.

"I smell steak," he says.

"You want me to make your plate?"

"If you don't mind."

"Sure." She pushes herself from the loveseat. "I made you a rib-eye, loaded potato, and spinach. The spaghetti and meatballs you can take home to Janae."

"Thanks, Babe."

She shuffles to the kitchen.

"How was work?" he yells out.

"Work was cool." She begins preparing his food. "I see Lexington likes to talk to me in a civil manner when you're not around."

"Yeah, I bet."

"And check this out; Divine was actually having a *conversation* with Velour!"

"Really…"

"It bugged everybody out. People were low-key taking pictures of them together, it was too funny!" She grabs his plate from the counter. "What are you drinking? James, you hear me?"

She enters the living room with his food.

James is snoring as loudly as he can.

She makes a U-turn back to the kitchen to wrap his food. She then returns to the living room and places a pillow underneath his head. She lies opposite him and surfs the television channels to see what is worth watching. Nothing. She settles on the smooth R&B music channel, softly playing Angela Bofill's, *Let Me Be The One.* The haunting melody in the songstress' voice causes her eyelids to grow heavy.

Before succumbing to her own drowsiness, she brainstorms an idea to wipe away some of James and Janae's courthouse drama. She hopes it does the trick, if only for a temporary moment in their lives.

The song puts her out for the rest of the evening.

It has not been a full two days and she already has zero tolerance for her cousin Tanya and her substandard living arrangements inside of a less than desirable tenement building, located in East New York, Brooklyn. The bedroom she sleeps in should be considered a walk-in closet. The water in the bathtub drains extremely slow, even though she poured two quarts of Drano Max Gel down the drainpipe the prior afternoon. Last night, she heard squeaking and scurrying sounds inside of the walls, causing her to sleep with one eye open and a pipe in her hand. No central air unit or air conditioner available, just cheap dusty fans placed in each room of the raggedy apartment.

And the place reeks of a cat-piss smell.

This is not the way she envisioned herself living.

Or any human being.

A text notification pops up on her phone. She reads the message. Instantly her mood brightens.

While responding to the text, Tanya rumbles into the living room dressed in her MTA Train Conductor uniform, digging inside her purse.

Velour positions the fan in the direction of the couch where she is sitting. "I don't know if you're aware of this, but Walmart does sell plenty of inexpensive air conditioners you can put in the window–"

"And you're more than welcome to buy one for yourself, Velour," Tanya retorts. "As long as you know you'll be paying the electric bill. *Capish*?"

Velour rolls her eyes at her cousin.

Tanya pulls out a small piece of paper and hands it to her.

"What's this?"

"Grocery list." Tanya pulls her hair back and ties it in a knot. "And don't go to that nasty ass bodega on the corner, either. There's a Pathmark two blocks past that."

Velour places the list on the couch. "I, uh, appreciate you letting me stay here until my place is ready for me to move into–"

"That's what family do for one another, right? Help each other in a time of need?"

Tanya stares at her with a straight face.

Velour feels so unwelcomed here.

"Look, Tanya, I know you feel some type of way about Vincent, but he's really not what you think he is–"

"FUCK Vincent, okay? He showed his true colors by never inviting me over to his high-priced palace. Even after I let his country ass stay with me when he didn't have a pot to piss in nor a window to throw it out of? The day is coming when someone humbles his drug-selling ass and I hope it's the Feds–"

"How many times do I have to tell you he's not a drug dealer–"

"Then you explain to me how's he able to afford that big ass mansion and the lifestyle he's living? That nigga ain't got no degree! He moves here to New York and suddenly he's this big-time millionaire? Please…"

Velour hesitates before replying, "Like I told you before, he details and fixes–"

"Cars, riiiight." Tanya nods her head in mockery. "I see you still on that bullshit. I'll be so glad when you move into your little *condo* because the last thing I need is your shiesty ass bringing any unwanted guests to my apartment, you follow me?"

Tanya slides her purse over her shoulders. She keeps her distrustful glare on Velour.

"Two peas in a fuckin' pod, I tell ya. Don't forget about the groceries…at Pathmark."

Tanya snatches her keys from the stand and rushes out the door.

*Fuck you, too.*

In one swift motion, Velour does a roundhouse kick, knocking the fan to the floor. She mumbles more choice words for her cousin before reluctantly picking up the fan.

She hears a ping from her phone. A response to her text.

Her heart now flutters with titillating joy.

She responds with a thumbs-up emoji while hurrying into the bedroom to change her outfit. For this occasion, it requires only her pink cut-off Baby Phat tank-top, a matching thong, and a pink, silk headscarf. She sprays perfume over her entire body and then returns to the living room couch.

As she waits for his arrival, her eyes embarrassingly scrutinize the dreadful apartment.

A pregnant roach scales the wall opposite of her.

She snatches her sneaker from the matted rug and races over to smash the nasty critter. She drops back on the couch and rubs her arms from the creepy-crawling sensation she now possesses.

*I can't wait to get the fuck up outta here.*

Her new place will be ready in another two weeks. She had to withdraw a good chunk of money from the bank to secure the type of condo that would suit her vanity and she already feels as though her savings account is steadily dwindling. She hates to admit it, but Vincent was right; she has done a piss poor job with managing her money.

But all of that is about to change soon enough.

She is about to take matters into her own hands so she can maintain the extravagant lifestyle she's accustomed to living. The finer things are all she craves, and she has no desire to backtrack from them, either.

Even if it means going behind her brother's back.

Another text message pops up. She reads it.

Her smile cannot get any bigger.

He is here.

She checks her sexy appearance.

She then glances around the room, primarily at the walls. No creepy crawlies in sight.

She saunters toward the front door and swings it open.

Standing before her is a six feet four inches, well-built, smoldering-eyed stud, decked out in a pair of gym shorts and a t-shirt. He casts a dimpled-wide smile as he crosses the doorway and places his bag down on the hallway floor.

Her thong is moistened just by the smell of his cologne alone.

She met Ahmed about two months ago at a car show. They exchanged numbers. They enjoyed conversations over the phone and while in bed. His profession revolves around real estate investments, and he is the one responsible for showing her the impressive condo she's about to move into.

She wastes no time leaping into his arms and showering him with lustful gratitude.

# FORTY-THREE

## FREEMAN

"To Jay…" Roy leads the toast with drinks hoisted. "… representing for all the good fathers across the globe. Salute!"

"Salute!"

Freeman guzzles down his water and then moseys over to the breakroom's recyclable bin to throw away the bottle. He returns to the table and pulls out a royal blue and gold softball jersey from a plastic bag. He displays the jersey with the DEMOODAY imprint in front of James. "Jay, not to sound unappreciative because God knows we needed new softball jerseys…but what the hell is a DEMOODAY?"

Roy and Marc laugh.

"I've been meaning to ask you the very same question," questions the old-timer.

James stands, eager to reply. "Say the word backward."

They study the name for a moment.

"Yadoomed?" questions Marc.

"Exactly!" James points at the old-timer. "When our competition sees us out on the field and says DeMooday, we hit 'em back with Yadoomed! Get it? Like y'all are *doomed* when they play against us!"

Blank stares fall on James.

Roy shakes his head. "They're gonna think it's Swahili for a bunch of assholes."

"Well, I think it's unique."

"Of course you're gonna feel that way, you made that shit up!"

"C'mon, y'all. We *needed* a new identity, especially after getting our asses whooped by the Boriqua squad the past two years–"

"And you think the name *DeMooday* helps our cause? The Boriquas are going to laugh at us!"

"I see the logic behind it, James." Marc scratches his chin. "And the name is kind of growing on me."

"Oh my God, Marc, tell me you're not buying into his madness?" laughs Roy.

Window Clerk Claudell Washington enters the breakroom. He slides a Tupperware bowl inside of a microwave.

Roy yells out, "Yo, Claude! You're gonna be ready to pitch on Opening Day?"

"Ready as I'll ever be," answers the broad shoulder clerk.

"I got your shirt in my locker," replies James.

Claudell laughs while checking on his food. "Yeah, I heard about our new name."

"Kinda fly, right?"

James proudly displays the shirt for Claudell, who quickly winces.

Everyone laughs.

"See, I told you, Jay!" shouts Roy.

"But the blue and gold combination is dope." Claudell purchases a Pepsi from the vending machine. "Yo, Free, you're on Route Twenty-Seven, right?"

"Yeah, what's up?"

"A lady by the name of Havana Blunt is outside waiting to speak to a carrier from your route." Claudell grabs his food from the microwave and heads to the stairwell. "You can't miss her; she's wearing all white."

"Thanks."

Freeman stands and then swings back around to the fellas. "Okay, trial run–DEMOODAY!"

James and Marc shout, "YA DOOMED!!!!"

"Man, I am not yelling that shit," bristles Roy.

Freeman laughs as he makes his way down the staircase.

He opens the exit door and swallows enough hot afternoon air to inflate his lungs. Standing in the far corner, near the collection mail bins, is an elegant figure in a breezy, sleeveless white summer outfit. Her long, silver mane is covered by a straw hat, and her gaze onto the street exhibits the inner peace of someone looking across the Mediterranean Sea. In her arms, she cuddles a package as if it was a newborn baby.

Freeman assumes the parcel is the reason for her visit.

He clears his throat for a more professional tone. "Good afternoon, Ma'am. Can I help you?"

The lady turns around. She flaunts teeth as white as her attire. "I'm fine, Dah-ling. I'm waiting on Dante, thank you."

"Dante doesn't work at this station anymore. I'm assigned to his route now."

The lady's cheerful demeanor vanishes.

"Oh, *really*?"

She rudely sizes him up. "And when did this happen, young man?"

He soon realizes he is no longer a *dah-ling*.

He precedes the conversation with extreme caution. "Around six months ago. Is there something I can help you with or do you need to speak to him directly?"

"No, I think I came to the right person." The callousness in her voice grows as she thrusts the box into his chest. "Explain this."

He catches the package before it hits the ground. "Excuse me?"

"*Someone's* been purchasing items from a credit card I never activated! That package is the third package in the past two weeks that contained DVDs and CDs I would've never considered ordering!"

"Well, have you called the credit card company to file a complaint–"

"That was the first step I took, Mr.–"

"Souls. Freeman Souls."

"Well, Mr. Souls, they're in the process of canceling that card and while they're investigating this matter, I may have a pretty good idea who's behind this."

The accusation from her glare looms heavily from underneath her straw hat.

She has already prosecuted him.

His body tenses up.

"With all due respect, Ms. Blunt, I am not responsible for this–"

"Who else has access to my mail and mailbox besides you, Mr. Souls? Thirty years living in the same building, and I've never encountered an issue with Dante or the mailman before him! Now, you come along, and I have to deal with this every week?!?"

It takes every morsel of strength in him to keep his emotions in check.

"I understand your plight, Ma'am, I really do, but I don't know what else to tell you other than I'm not doing anything with your mail–"

"Have it your way, Mr. Souls." She rips the package from his hands. "I would like to speak to your manager at once, so we can get to the bottom of this, thank you."

Havana turns her back to him and stares out into the populated street.

Freeman sighs heavily and then storms back inside of the building. He curses under his breath at the lady for challenging his integrity. But this is the second time this month he has been accused of the same uncanny dilemma.

His memory drifts back to the day he questioned Dante about the first occurrence, which Dante coolly told him he did not know anything about. But then seconds later, Dante had that strange look on his face, telling him to be careful.

He wonders if Dante was being honest with him.

Quickening his pace, he searches the first floor for Chapman instead of Davenport to get to the bottom of this.

Just like the angry lady in white.

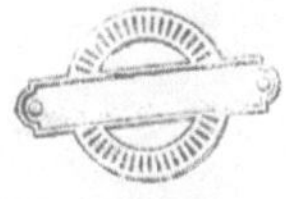 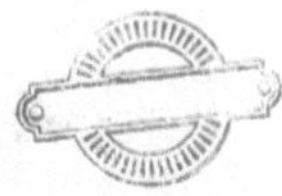 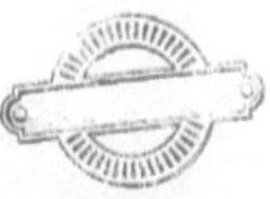

FREEMAN LEANS BACK ON HIS ROUTE-CASE LEDGE AND STARES AT Lexington, who moves from one workstation to the next inspecting route books. With his eyes on the temporary supervisor, his mind reels around to Havana Blunt's accusations. Earlier in the month, another lady probed him with the exact same concern. Too much of a coincidence.

Lou approaches him, unbuttoning his postal shirt. "Yo, you're still playing ball with us after work, right?"

Freeman snaps out of his funk. "Uh, yeah. I'm going to switch out the label strips on my route-case, then I'll be on my way."

"A'ight, I'ma change and be right back."

Lou be-bops away and waves at the remaining carriers as they leave the work floor.

Freeman pulls out his cell and speed-dials Velour to update her on the rising problem occurring on their route while he looks for the updated label strips.

Her phone rings for a long time.

Ahmed snatches the tank top from Velour's body before flipping her over on her stomach. He follows that by laying his solid frame on top of her back. He then generates a series of slow grinds. She moans in delight. Afterward, he rubs his horse-sized tool between her legs. He gnaws on her ears, jaw, neck, anything he can possibly sink his teeth into, while his fingers travel underneath to dig into her soaking wet love canal. A relaxed Velour willingly spreads her legs wide enough for him to probe in. And just when his stiff tool begins to penetrate the outer layers of her dripping love canal—

Her cell rings.

*FUCK!*

"Hold up, Baby." Velour reaches for her phone and screens the number.

She rolls her eyes.

She presses the talk button and calmly says to Freeman, "Hey."

"*Hey, Beautiful. How's your day off treating you?*"

"Good. Just relaxing in my cousin's humble abode, that's all." Ahmed nibbles on her neck. She struggles to maintain her composure. "How's work?"

*"I was having a good day until someone else accused me of tampering with her mail."*

Velour immediately sits up. "Who this time?"

*"Havana Blunt, who owns the brownstone on Tenth Street. Told me someone used a credit card that she never activated to buy DVDs and other merchandise."*

"Sooo, what happened?"

*"I had to get Chapman to vouch for me and to calm her ass down."*

Velour shushes Ahmed so she can listen carefully to Freeman. "And what did she say?"

*"That we haven't heard the last of her and then she left. Man, I don't know what is going on, but answer this question for me…"*

She holds her breath. "What?"

*"You know Dante better than most of the people here. Do you think he would pull off something like this? When I asked him about the situation with Ms. Phillips earlier this month, he seemed a bit too nonchalant about it."*

"And what did Dante say about Ms. Phillips?"

*"He told me not to worry about her, but I'm like–"*

"And I couldn't agree more, Freeman. Personally, I think Havana Blunt is having financial trouble. You know her husband died a year ago…"

*"I didn't know that."*

"Yeah, and she's been crying a river to anybody within earshot about their bankruptcy situation. So, if I were you, I wouldn't put too much stock into what she's babbling about."

*"It's easy for you to say. You're not the one being accused of anything."*

"Ohhhh…my…God…"

*"Velour? You still there?"*

Freeman's words fall on deaf ears as her riveting body falls prey to Ahmed's wicked foreplay action. The momentum of his tongue increases as it slopes down the crease of her arched back, and then wedges between the inner regions of her derriere, straight down to the depths of her soaked love canal where the oral pleasures he is creating change the entire dynamics of their phone conversation.

"*Velour? Did you hear what I said?*"

"H-Huh?"

"*Is everything alright?*"

Trembling with dizzy sensation, Velour grips the couch. "I–I p-pulled a m-muscle e-earlier while w-w-working out–"

"*Awww, man. I wish I was there to use my magic hands and make it go away.*"

"Yeeeah…m-m-magic h-hands…"

Ahmed strong-arms her wobbly legs and tongue-teases her fluctuating love canal, causing her bottom to Harlem Shake all up in his face. She sinks her teeth into her tank top.

"Oooooo…"

"*Listen, I'ma let you go so you can deal with that, alright? They can be no joke.*"

"Yeah, uh, I-I'll call youuuu, l-later, okay? Sm-Smooches."

The phone slides out of her hand and onto the floor.

She does not need to hear any more stress-inducing issues concerning her partner, the route, the stink-ass apartment, or anything else, for that matter.

Ahmed could not have arrived at a better time.

He grips both sides of her hips, and then slides his horse tool inside of her hungry canal as she lay face down on the pillow. She closes her eyes and smiles, knowing that her Indian sugar daddy is going to pound the rest of her worries straight into oblivion.

# FORTY-FIVE

## FREEMAN

A disturbing thought enters his mind, but he brushes off the crazy notion.

*Nah. It was her pulled muscle making her moan like that.*

Freeman cradles his phone on his hip. He looks up and observes his fellow crew members dressed in basketball gear approaching the section. He joins them over by the time clock.

Shabbazz tosses the basketball to him. "We're thinking about hitting the club this Saturday to celebrate James' victory—you down?"

"Sounds like a plan." Freeman bounces the ball. "It's been a minute since we've been to the club, anyway."

"Word," Roy agrees. "It gives me a reason to get out of the house. Wifey be getting on my damn nerves."

"You finished with the labels?" asks Lou.

Freeman ponders. He decides he will deal with the label strips first thing in the morning.

"Yeah, I'm done."

Carriers are lined up to clock out for the day.

Freeman joins the crew en route to the stairwell.

"Mr. Souls!" Lexington calls out.

"Freeman turns around. "What's up?"

"I thought you were going to switch out the label strips?"

"I'm coming in early tomorrow morning. It shouldn't take that long."

"It's been almost three days and I find it hard to believe you and Velour still haven't found the time to put those strips up." Lexington staples a couple of forms together. "If it's not done by tomorrow, I'll have no choice but to report it to Davenport for failure to comply."

*This mutha–*

Freeman is probably the only employee at Midway who tries to give him the benefit of the doubt while others doubted his leadership abilities long before he stepped to the podium. But Lexington does not see that. He would rather take offense to anything that people do or say, thinking they are out to discredit him. Now, this nitwit feels the need to include *him* on the bandwagon.

But that's where Freeman draws the line.

"Actually, Lex, we do have choices to make." He moves in closer to him. "Like which battles are deemed worthy of fighting, or the ones we let go simply because they're not worth the time nor energy. You want to go down that road with me?"

He squares off into Lexington's beady eyes.

He believes the temporary supervisor gets the message.

"Just make sure it gets done in the morning."

Lexington returns to his paperwork.

Freeman shakes his head before catching up with the crew.

"Fucking moron, man," mutters Lou.

"I don't see him lasting as a supervisor," quips Neville. "He's gonna say the wrong thing to somebody and get his head knocked off."

"Yeah, and it'll probably be by your sister, Free."

"I can see Dee smacking him across the face with her bible, saying 'LEAD US NOT…*SMACK*…INTO TEMPTATION… *SMACK, SMACK*…BUT DELIVER US FROM THE EVIL OF LEXINGTON VANGUARD…*SMACK*!"

They laugh hard.

He cannot help but chuckle.

He also cannot help but think about Havana slamming that package into his chest, either.

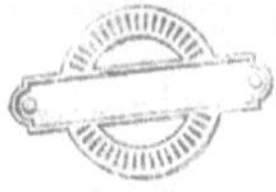 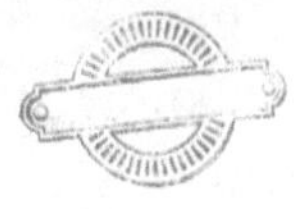 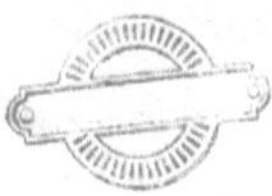

DARKENED SKIES RELEASE A SERIES OF RAINDROPS OVER A CITY IN GREAT need of some relief from the sun's scorching activities.

James switches on his windshield wipers and low beams. "So, what's this I hear about you and Lex having words before you clocked out?"

Freeman shrugs. "It was nothing."

He returns his stare out the window.

"It must've been something for him to bring out the monster from your mellow ass."

He turns to James. "How well do you know Dante?"

James looks at him and then ponders the question. "Honestly, I really don't. He's always kept to himself. Put it this way; I know as much as you do. Now, why are you asking?"

He takes a wearisome breath. "Check this out, man. Twice this month, I've been accused of breaking into somebody's mail."

James double-takes him. "Word? But how, who—?"

"These two ladies on my route. One over the phone and the other one was this lady who was waiting on me in the bay area."

"What happened?"

"This lady named Havana…man, she called me everything but a child of God."

"Get out…"

"She swore up and down that not only was I tampering with her mail, but I also used her credit cards to *buy* the actual DVDs that I was supposed to be breaking into!"

"You serious?"

"Very serious." He gazes out at the steady rain. "The first lady who accused me, I kind of pushed it to the side, you know, thinking it was nothing. But then this Havana lady steps to me at the station with the same gripe? Too much of a coincidence if you ask me. That's why I wanted to know how well you knew Dante."

"You think he has something to do with this?"

"I don't know, man, I'm just trying to put two and two together." He picks at his shorts before turning to James. "I'm wondering if this was planned all along, you know? Like I'm being set up to take the fall for somebody, but why?" He sighs again. "Not to sound paranoid or anything, but I have a feeling this is just the beginning of something big, you know, and it's eating at me because I don't know which direction it's coming from. Now, tell me if I'm sounding crazy for feeling this way."

"I wouldn't worry too much about it, because whoever it is that's doing this will eventually get caught, so don't sweat it." James exits off on Baychester Road and stops at a red light. "It generally takes time for some customers to get used to seeing someone new delivering their mail, so naturally, they're going to put a new face to a new crime, even when they have no proof. This will blow over, that's all I'm saying, you watch."

Freeman nods and stares out into the dark skies.

They drive in silence until James' phone rings. He checks the number. His face lights up. "Hey...Yeah. I'm dropping off Freeman, then I'm going home to change, and we'll be over there in about an hour." James turns to him. "Cadina says, 'Whazzup!'"

He waves without turning his head.

"He said, 'Hey'. And don't forget your overnight bag. A'ight, later." James turns to him. "Cadina's taking me and 'Nae out somewhere as a surprise. You know, to cheer 'Nae up."

"That's cool of her."

James pulls up to Freeman's building.

He digs into his bag for his wallet and pulls out a twenty. He hands it to James. "Give this to 'Nae. Tell her Uncle Free loves her."

James takes the money and they bump fists.

He exits the vehicle and walks to his building, with serious intentions of getting in contact with Dante.

"S*torming…outside, rain, she keeps me home…'* Your verse is coming up, Princess."

Buckled up in the passenger seat, Janae does not waiver from her melancholy state. If anything, she finds herself slipping deeper into a mode of solitude while staring straight through the front windshield at the heavy rainstorm.

She hates the way she feels.

She would rather join her father in their off-beat, duet version of the Carl Thomas tune, *Summer Rain*, but her heart doesn't capture the melody. Instead, she blames herself for not being a good child, because if she had, then maybe things would have been different within her family structure. Maybe her mother would not have walked out of her life the way that she did.

Exiting the Throgs Neck Bridge into Queens, she continues to gaze beyond the steady downpour while tugging on her braids. Long ago, she recognized the fact that her parents did not care for each other too much. She was mature enough to accept that. But what she does not understand is why she is not the center of her mother's universe the way she is in her father's. She thought it was because of her falling grades at one point. But, when she surprised her parents by jumping from a C- average to becoming an A- student, it did not faze her mother one bit. Still, she tried to put in more of an effort by making breakfast for her mother and learning how to bake pork chops and cornbread for dinner. Flowers, cards, and candy were also added for acceptance in her mother's world.

A poem was even constructed to get her point across:

*Roses are Red,*
*Violets are Blue,*
*I love my Mommy with all my heart,*
*And I hope she loves me, too.*

Her acts of devotion, in turn, brought her all kinds of tangible items: Expensive clothing, video games, a shiny new bike…but, never closer to her mother's heart. She realized that inside the courtroom.

Her daddy pulls up to a corner. Dressed in a red buttoned-up blouse, denim capris, and white Nikes stands Cadina underneath her umbrella.

Janae cannot help but feel better when she is around her.

She watches her dad's girlfriend pause directly in front of her window to make a goofy face. Even in her depressed state, she cracks a goofy smile right back at her.

Cadina quickly closes the umbrella, slides in the backseat, and slams the door, all in one motion. She leans forward and plants a kiss on Janae's cheek, and then one on James.

James smiles. "Where are we going?"

"New Roc City! You know how to get there, right?"

James gives her the side-eye. "I can't believe you're even asking me that."

"I don't know, Boo. The last time I asked you if you knew how to get to Flushing Meadow Park in Queens, you said *yeah*, and blew right past it, heading straight to Long Island. You remember, 'Nae?"

"Yes, I do!" Janae says. "We had to turn all the way around, and then he almost passed it again!"

"Both of y'all can do me a favor and be quiet…next stop, New Rochelle!"

They all belly-laugh.

Janae feels Cadina fingers slipping between hers to hold her hand. Suddenly, she feels alive again. So much so, that she begins singing the Carl Thomas song out loud. James and Cadina collectively sing the background vocals, making the rest of the trip even more soothing.

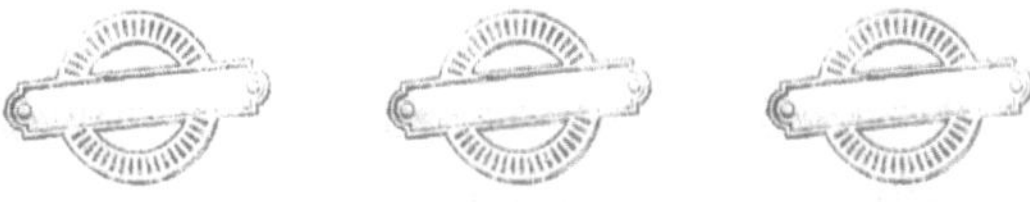

New Roc City, the entertainment epicenter of fun and excitement for people of all ages, exposes something to Janae she rarely sees at places like these—no crowds. No crowds mean no waiting in long lines. Not waiting in long lines means she gets to play all the games she desires, at *least* four or five times. She thanks God for the rain.

With starry-eyed excitement, she asks Cadina, "Can I play some video games first?"

"Whatever you want!" Cadina hands her a game card. "Today's *your* day!"

She races off and swipes her card into every game she lays her hands on. She then jumps in a racing car booth and notices a Stephen Curry-jersey-wearing, blow-pop-sucking Puerto Rican boy with a Caesar haircut in the next car.

He stares at the orange-denim Knicks skirt set she's wearing.

The boy pulls out his blow-pop, and then plainly announces, "The Knicks *suck*."

"That's why I'ma beat you with my red car!" She fires back, with an attitude.

"Yeah, right!"

*Challenge!*

They simultaneously swipe their cards and race against one another with juvenile intensity. After blow-pop boy wins hands down, the two tykes sprint their competitive spirits over to the air-hockey table where Janae dusts him off two games straight. Then the wonder twins activate their true powers on the basketball shoot-out arcade, which ends in a high-scoring draw.

Enjoying her newfound friend's company, they trot over to the bumper cars where they meet up with some other high-strung kids eager to smash one another's car with raging enthusiasm.

She had no idea this silver lining surprise would clear up her overcast disposition.

Cadina also promised to take her to her favorite restaurant of all time—Friday's!

And after spending five months with Cadina, she knows she will not break her promise, either–unlike her biological "stranger".

Driving around in circles, she observes blow-pop boy waving to his mother and father, who smiles at him while enjoying their ice cream.

She spots her daddy and Cadina watching her as they hold hands. She waves at them and Cadina joyfully waves back.

Like a real parent would.

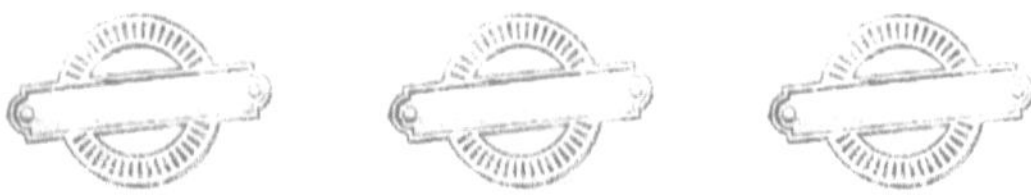

JAMES TIPTOES OUT OF JANAE'S ROOM AND CLOSES THE DOOR. SHUFFLING downstairs to the basement, he stops halfway to admire Cadina, in her shirt and panties, on the sofa. She picks up a framed picture of the two of them which he recently placed on the end table. She smiles and then places it back down on the table. As she stretches her arms to release a yawn, she jumps when she spots him on the staircase, causing her to stifle her yawn. They both giggle as Cadina shakes a clenched fist at him. He heads down the rest of the stairs.

"Don't you ever scare me like that again, you hear me, Mr. Richards?"

James drops himself right next to her and she throws her legs across his lap. "Or what are you gonna do?"

"I don't know. What would you like for me to do?"

Her response was two-fold. She rubs on his inner thigh.

"I hope I'm not talking foreign to you, James."

Her eyes are telling.

The tone in her voice is suggestive as hell.

His hormones scream at him to act accordingly.

Still, he pushes the sexual urges to the side.

He rubs the hand that rubs his thigh.

"Thanks."

"For what?"

"For putting a smile on Janae's face."

She pauses her actions. "It was the least I could do, you know?"

"This is for you. From Janae."

He hands her a piece of paper.

She looks at him, and then reads the note out loud:

> *Thank you for taking time out of your day to make me feel special. You didn't have to, but you did. I am so blessed to have you in my life.*
>
> *Hug and Kisses,*
> *Nae-Nae*

"Ohhhhh!" She cups her mouth. "That was so sweet of her! Is she still up? I want to tell her it was my pleasure."

"She's asleep now, but I will. You, uh, ready for me to take you home?"

She takes his hand and guides it down toward her private area.

"But I thought I was already home?"

He slides his hand underneath her panties to get a better feel of her wetness and then rubs gently to produce even more waterfalls between her squirming legs.

"I mean, *oooooo yeah,* I can get ready to go, if that's what you want me to do. It's totally up to you*…ooooo, right there…sssss.*"

"You might not be able to get a good night's rest if I allow you to stay."

"That's your main concern? *Please.*" She quickly straddles him. Her lustful stare pours deep into his own. "What I *do* want is to show my appreciation to *you*. But I can't if you're going to continue being a gentleman around me."

"Hold up…" He gives her a cock-eyed look. "You mean to tell me all this time I could've hit it with no problem?"

"The man I love, yeah." She repeatedly kisses his neck. "He could've smashed this, months ago."

His entire world just became surreal to him. He gazes into her tempting eyes and finds truth behind those words. He should know; he feels the exact same way about her, too.

Soul mate confirmation.

"The man you love, huh?"

"You heard what I said." She loosens his belt buckle and pants to grab his rock-hard manhood.

He becomes the aggressor at this point. He pulls her shirt over her head and gobbles on boobs round and perky enough to stand without the aid of a bra.

"Whatever you have in mind is fine by me, Miss Wilson."

"What I have in store for you, *oooo, yeah, suck on that titty*, doesn't involve the gentleman side of you tonight–so get rid of him."

"I think I can make that happen."

"Please do."

They snicker in each other's faces.

He pushes himself off the couch with her legs still wrapped around his torso. They both chuckle and rub noses before he says, "Girl, had I seen this side of you earlier, I would've hung up that gentleman's hat a long time ago."

Kissing his nose and playing with his hair, she whispers, "Then I wouldn't have built up this massive attraction I have for you, right now."

Her smile is worth a thousand sunshines.

"I love you," James confirms.

"I know."

Their tongues intertwine for good.

He carries his better half over the threshold of his bedroom door. Even the streaks of lightning, along with the barrels of thunder that bottom out from the evening sky, cannot deny the love they display for one another throughout the wee hours of the morning.

# FORTY-SEVEN

## FREEMAN

Freeman pushes his empty cart down Fifth Street towards his coworker Marc, who is loading his pushcart with bags from the relay box.

"I just got here myself," Marc gripes. He wipes his sweaty brow with a hand towel. "Your buddy, Lexington? He's an asshole. Did your sister tell you what he did or failed to do?"

"He forgot to assign someone to case her mail while they walked her route." Freeman grabs the remaining two bags from the box. "Then he caught an attitude when she called him out on it."

"But then I had to go to Chapman and tell him she was going to need help delivering her route because that nitwit wasn't going to assign anybody."

"I know."

Marc pulls out a Newport, lights it, takes a drag, and blows out heated steam. "You know, I've seen his kind come and go. They get a new position, forget where they come from, and start smelling themselves. Kissing Davenport's ass is only going to take him but so far, he's going to learn the hard way, trust me."

Freeman laughs as he locks the relay box. "Are you going to miss any of this when you make that final swipe into retirement?"

Marc scratches his square jaw while pondering. "Truth be told, Freeman, you might see me in this uniform for another couple of years."

"Can't get enough of the postal life, huh…"

"Both of my sons live in Nebraska with their families now. Their mother and I have been separated for about ten years. This job keeps me going, you know?"

Freeman nods. "Well, if you're still here next year, we're gonna treat you to a white-water rafting outing as a retirement gift. How does that sound?"

The old-timer's eyes glow with glee. "Ahh, yes! Class Five Expert Level, I hope!"

"Try the Beginner's Level, okay? We're not trying to drown out there!"

"You wuss! Where're your balls?"

"Right where they need to be! We're trying to retire, too, if that's okay with you?"

"C'mon, Free! The adrenaline alone will have you yearning for more!" Marc flicks the cigarette butt in the street. He quickly pulls out another Newport and lights it. "And I will train you all! What do you say?"

"We're going to take your ass bowling. You're just a little too excited about this event!"

They laugh as they push their loaded carts down the block.

 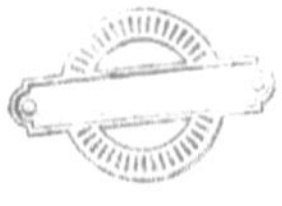 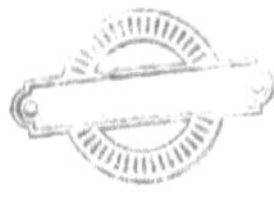

FREEMAN LEANS HIS BACK AGAINST A BROWNSTONE FRONT STOOP AND waits for Marc to finish delivering the mail inside of the building. He pulls out a towel to dry his face from the beating it took from the day's brutal heat index.

He also pulls out his cell to call Dante about those recent accusations.

An automated message cheerfully responds.

*We're sorry, you have reached a number that is no longer in service…Bye."*

*Huh?*

He tries to curtail a sour emotion bubbling up within him.

*Why is this motherfucker's phone all of a sudden disconnected?*

*Is he trying to avoid me now?*

*Is he the one behind all this nonsense?*

His blood now boils in internal rage.

The only thing that prevents him from cursing out loud is seeing Cadina park her postal truck in front of the brownstone and hopping out with a brown paper bag in hand.

"I hope you have something in that bag to drink," he says.

She whips out an icy Aquafina bottled water from the bag and hands it to him.

"Thanks."

"No, I'm thanking *you* and Marc for coming out here to give us a hand." She sits next to him and takes a swig of water from her own bottle. "I don't know why that fool Lexington thought I could do any of your sister's buildings and make it in time to do my afternoon collection. He be trippin'."

He finishes his bottle and burps. "It's your fault."

"What's my fault?"

"You could've at least had dinner with the man when you got hired. Now you're permanently on his shit-list."

She scoffs in laughter. "That was *NOT* going to happen. When is he supposed to leave for the Supervisor's Academy, anyway?"

"Your guess is as good as everyone else's. But I think you'd be the perfect person to throw him a going-away party."

"I might just do that. And I won't invite his ass, either."

He laughs. "Now that sounds like a plan. Have you heard from Dee?"

She stands to her feet and wipes off her butt. "She and the new guy Emmanuel were heading back to the station."

He checks his watch and turns around to the front of the brownstone. "Marc should've been finished already."

"He's probably flirting with the owner of this building."

"Well, he can do that on his own time. We have places to be."

"You got that right. I'll check on the old playa."

She climbs the stairs and enters the building.

The thought of getting more info from Velour about Dante's personal life crosses his mind but decides not to get her involved. He might just take a trip to Dante's new postal station to confront him on this matter–

"FREEMAN!"

He swings his head around to the top of the staircase.

Cadina's face is pale white.

"IT'S MARC!"

She disappears back inside.

With his heartbeat doubling with each stride, Freeman dashes up the staircase to see what has happened to the veteran carrier.

 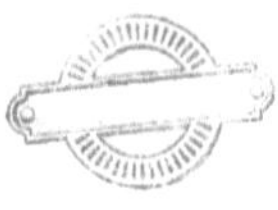 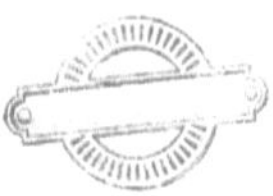

FREEMAN HOLDS ON TO DEAR LIFE AS CADINA MUSCLES THROUGH THE congested traffic on First Avenue and then swerves the truck onto Eleventh Street. He then peeks into the cargo area where Marc is recuperating on a pile of empty collection bags. The old-timer holds his head down between his legs with his mouth gaped open and a line of spit traveling down to the floor.

"We should've called an ambulance for you," Freeman asserts.

"Why?" Marc slurs. "Because she panicked for no reason?"

Cadina peeks in the back. "Marc, your head was hanging down to your knees like it is right now and you were gagging uncontrollably–"

"I was catching my breath–"

"You look like you were on the verge of passing out and I agree with Freeman–"

"And I would've kicked the both of you in the head."

"You're not kicking anybody in your condition."

"Whatever." Marc raises his head and props it against the wall. "Look, I had taken my pills and was resting when you walked in and saw me that way. I'm feeling much better now– trust me on this."

Freeman and Cadina wait for the other to give a final decision.

Neither says anything as she pulls up to the station's curb. They both hop out and walk around to the back of the truck.

She blows out frustration. "We should've called the ambulance–"

"I know." He looks around for postal employees. The area is vacant, at the moment. He turns back to her. "Let's see how this plays out. If he so much as stumbles out of the truck, I'm dialing nine-one-one."

"Agreed."

She unlocks the cargo door and allows it to roll all the way up.

Marc, now full of energy, smiles while positioning both pushcarts to the edge of the cargo opening.

They both stare at the old-timer, dumbfounded.

"Help me with these, Freeman."

Freeman quickly grabs the carts and sits them both down on the street. Marc then jumps off the back of the truck and lands on his feet as if he were a gymnast receiving a perfect ten for execution.

The old-timer pushes his cart towards them. "Nobody needs to know about this incident, okay? Not Tucker, Davenport, anyone."

"Would it kill you to at least get yourself checked out to see what you're dealing with?"

"I think you know the answer to that, my friend."

"Jesus Christ, why are you so stubborn?" Cadina shakes her head. "God forbid if this happens again and there's nobody around to look after you! Then what?"

Marc rolls his eyes and then sighs. "You two are worse than my ex-wife. Fine, I'll make an appointment tomorrow, if that will make the two of you happy."

"It's not about our happiness, Marc," Freeman states. "And you need to cut back on the cancer sticks, too. I'm quite sure that's contributing to your health issues."

Marc's eyes stay on him. "*Nobody* needs to know about this, okay?"

"You're asking a lot, you know that, right?" Cadina counters.

The old-timer pats her on the shoulder. "And it's greatly appreciated, my dear. Freeman, I'll hold you to that white-water event next year." Marc winks at him before racing his pushcart up the ramp and onto an elevator lift.

Cadina turns to him. "Do you think we did the right thing?"

He grabs the pushcart handle and turns it around. "Do you?"

She sighs before boarding her truck and pulling off down the street.

Freeman pushes his cart up the ramp and waits on the arriving elevator lift. He boards the lift and presses the second-floor button. His mind returns to his first mission and that is dealing with Dante.

But he cannot shake the notion that staring at Marc earlier was like staring death in the face.

# FORTY-EIGHT

## VELOUR

The clicking sounds of her stiletto heels pacing back and forth are getting on her own nerves. She glances up and down Pitkin Avenue before checking her Michael Kors watch. It reads 9:38 pm.

*The fuck is he at?*

Her plans for the Saturday evening involve setting up shop in front of Ahmed's storefront in Manhattan and having Bunions run the operation while she hangs out with her coworkers at the Twilight nightclub. But she must find a way to secretly send customers from the club to the nearby operation without her friends' knowledge.

She is so ready for the challenge.

A black Hyundai screeches up and parks in front of a fire hydrant. Out pops Bunions, clothed in his trademark white tee, denim shorts, Air Force Ones, and fitted Yankee cap. The brown-skinned behemoth nervously scans the surroundings while gritting his teeth on a chew stick. He stomps his way towards her.

"You're late," she scolds.

He stops chewing on the stick. "And you look very nice in your white dress–"

"Just shut up and follow me."

She struts over to the back of her Porsche and presses her remote button. The back door opens upward, displaying six boxes, two folding tables, and a folding chair in the cargo area. She removes the box covers for Bunions to view. He squints in confusion.

"The boxes with the blue tape have the DVDs movies and Blu-Ray movies. The ones with the red tape are filled with music CDs. The boxes with the green tape are–"

"Is *this* why you called me out here? To sell fuckin' DVDs and shit?"

She folds her arms and glares at him.

"It's two thousand sixteen, Velour. Nobody is buying DVDs and CDs like that anymore–"

"It's really embarrassing how stupid you sound, Bunions. But I guess that's part of your stupidity, right?"

He pulls the chew stick out of his mouth and points it at her. "First of all, you gonna stop calling me out of my name and like I just said–"

"Like I was *about* to say…" She uncovers a box with the green tape. "…the boxes with the green tape are filled with the loaded firesticks." She covers the box, closes the back door, and faces the buffoon. "Stop thinking small, Bunions, not everyone wants a firestick, I don't care what year it is."

He returns the stick to his mouth. "So, you want me to be a part of your little operation, huh…"

"Nigga, don't act like we're not in a crisis right now–"

"But you know I can't do this, right?"

"Dude, I told you over the phone that I had a plan to make us some money and now you're gonna act funny about it?"

"Our peoples are getting bagged up left and right by po-po because of this! I don't know about you, but I don't look too good in handcuffs."

"And that's where you're wrong again! They're getting bagged up because of the credit cards and the cars. Vincent never said we couldn't go back to selling *these*, so we're good–"

"Still can't do it, Vee."

"I can't believe this shit." She throws her hands in the air. "This is coming from a person who would jack a car simply because he was bored. And the police were never a concern. What's the real problem?"

He peeks around the area. Fear grips his expression. "It's your brother."

"What about him?"

"C'mon, girl, you know how he is and the way he deals with people he feels has betrayed him in some way…I don't want any parts of that."

"Why, I'm ashamed of you, Bunions." Her fists embrace her hips. "While you're standing in front of my face questioning your manhood, my brother and his crew are sitting back chillin' off the money we made for them; through the chop shops, these DVDs and not to mention the credit cards–*you* were the mastermind behind that! That's why he kept you close! But do you really feel that you've been fully compensated for all of your contributions?"

He shifts his eyes down the block. He never responds.

"That's what I thought. It's only right we make ourselves a priority moving forward."

She pulls out a thick wad of cash, wrapped tightly in a rubber band, from her purse. She dangles it in front of his face.

"Scared money don't make none, Boo."

His chew stick falls to the ground.

"And I want the rest of the equipment I asked for by next week–do I make myself clear?"

He snatches the money and lumbers to his car. "I'll follow you."

She smiles, struts around to the driver's side of her vehicle, and pulls off down the street.

"Follow me, please!"

A pretty hostess leads the postal crew, along with their mates, through the crowded Twilight nightclub and to their reserved booth.

The hostess whips out a pad and pen. She begins taking orders.

James yells out, "A virgin cranberry and pineapple mix for me!"

His homies stare at him.

"I'm driving, remember?"

"Give him a Corona, please, thank you!" Freeman shouts.

The hostess laughs. "I'll be right back!"

She rushes to another booth.

Neville stands and points across the club.

"Yo, Roy, you see those two over there at the bar, right?" he asks.

Roy staggers to his feet, already tipsy. "I'm way ahead of you, son!"

They both swagger over to the ladies at the bar and pull them to the dance floor.

The crew engages in lively conversation and laughter as the energetic crowd on the dance floor move their bodies to the Donell Jones dance hit, *U Know What's Up*, featuring the late Left Eye.

The hostess returns and hands everyone their drinks.

James pulls out his wallet.

"Uh-uh…" Shabbazz grunts. "Your money isn't good here, tonight!"

James' eyes widen. He pockets his wallet.

After paying and tipping the hostess, Freeman holds his rum and coke up high. Everyone follows suit.

"To Jay and 'Nae!"

"Jay and 'Nae!"

*CLINK!*

"Appreciate the love," James expresses.

Returning to the booth are Roy and Neville, exhausted from dancing.

Neville grabs his towel to wipe his forehead and then points at Roy. "You can't take this flat-footed cat nowhere."

"What are you talking about?" Roy drops down in the booth next to Lou's wife, Marisol. "I was tearing it up out there."

"Is he embarrassing you, Neville?" giggles the curly hair, glasses-wearing Puerto Rican.

"He knows his drunk ass is too big to be doing the Cabbage Patch!" Neville laughs while sipping his drink. "Bumping into people, looking straight crazy…his own dance partner left him alone out on the floor!"

"I was like this, y'all, killing it!" Roy does the Cabbage Patch dance where he sits.

The deejay mixes in a new jack swing classic, Wreckx-N-Effect's *Rump Shaker*.

*"All I Wanna Do Is Zooma, Zoom, Zoom, Zoom, In The Boom, Boom… Just Shake Your Rump!"*

"Aww, hell, they done fucked up now!" Roy struggles to his feet. "You're my wingman, Nev, let's go!"

Neville shakes his head as he stands. "Nah, this way, Playboy…I don't think we're welcomed over there anymore!"

Roy and Neville work their way to the opposite side of the room.

Marisol turns to James. "So, word around town is you have a new Boo. Congratulations!"

James cocks his eyes at Lou, who cheeses at him while chugging his beer.

"Please, he tells me everything that goes on at the post office," Marisol confides.

"She's just nosy, Papa," Lou concedes.

Shabbazz points to the front entrance. "I believe your *Boo* just arrived, Jay…"

With her silky black mane flowing freely down the back of her peach sundress, Cadina struts her sexiness across the room with the grace of a seasoned runway model. She flashes a Malibu smile at James before shimmying into his welcoming arms.

"Sorry I'm late," she says. "I had to take care of some business at my parents' home."

"It's all good." James turns to the crew. "Cadina, this is Lou's wife, Marisol, and Shabbazz' wife, Najya."

Cadina extends her hand toward the ladies. "Nice to meet the both of you!"

"Nah, Mommy," Marisol responds, with her arms open. "I give out hugs!"

"I was going to say the same thing!" Najya laughs, in her matching turquoise dress and headwrap. "Come here, girl…"

Cadina hugs both ladies.

"I love that name, '*Najya*'", Cadina says. "What does it mean?"

"It's Arabic for 'Victorious'," Najya beams.

"And that you are!"

Marisol playfully hits James on the arm. "You didn't tell me Cadina was a model…she's gorgeous!"

Cadina blushes. "Look at *you*, Marisol! Rocking that beautiful yellow dress!"

Marisol starts posing, "Ain't it cute?"

"Okay, enough gassing each other up." Lou stands and grabs his wife's hand. "Let's go get our boogie on."

"We're following y'all…let's go, King!" Najya says as she and Shabbazz follow the Puerto Rican couple to the dance floor.

James turns to Cadina. "What are you drinking?"

"Baby, I came here to dance, I can drink later!"

"Well, lead the way!"

Cadina hands Freeman her purse. "Velour called me and said she had to stop by her uncle's store…she should be here any minute."

"Yeah, she just texted me. Thanks!"

The rumbling drums of Marshall Jefferson's house music anthem, *Move Your Body*, has Cadina hopping in her heels.

"That's my jam!"

She yanks James to the middle of the dance crowd.

Freeman laughs as he motions to the hostess for another round of drinks.

# FIFTY

## VELOUR

Ahmed directed two of his employees to move their vehicles in order for Velour and Bunions to park and set up shop right in front of his establishment, *Ahmed's Beauty Supply Store.*

He blows a kiss at her.

She returns the gesture.

Bunions bangs on her window.

She quickly swings open her door and growls, "Must you bang on my window like a damn lunatic?"

"Then pop the trunk! Shoot…"

She presses the cargo button before sliding out of the vehicle. She grabs her purse, smooths out her white mini-dress, and saunters over to Ahmed, who stands handsomely in front of his store.

Bunions, setting up the tables, yells out, "How about giving me a hand with all of this?"

"Do I look like I want to get dirty?"

Bunions mutters under his breath as he continues to unload the items.

She turns around and embraces Ahmed.

The kisses he plants on her neck send ripples of passion throughout her being.

"Now Ahmed, behave." She releases him before succumbing to his charisma. "I'm with company tonight. Around the corner at Twilight."

Decked out in a black casual outfit with black dress shoes, Ahmed pinches her chin. "Then I'll behave…*tonight.* How's my favorite girl?"

"Outstanding, thanks to you and your considerable generosity. Now, when can I move into my condo?"

"Hopefully by the end of next week. We've just upgraded the place with high-end appliances and cherry hardwood flooring and once the balcony renovations are complete, you'll be good to go."

"Oh, my God! I get a balcony, too?"

"Overlooking the Hudson River."

"Is that going to be an extra cost?"

"Like I told you before, I can always work around your budget." He kisses the back of her hand. "As long as you're accessible to meet my needs, we'll be fine. Deal?"

She places her hand on his chest. "I'm always a phone call away, you know that."

"Good." He motions towards Bunions. "I don't believe I've met your friend."

She rolls her eyes. "His name is Bernard. We call him Bunions."

"Oh…he has a foot disorder?"

"Just a nickname. Now, I don't have to worry about the police around here, do I?"

"Around here, we're all friends."

"It's good to have friends in all occupations."

"Indeed. Now, may I ask you a personal question?"

"Shoot."

"This peddling DVDs for nickels and dimes…is this really long-term? Because I don't see a future in it for you."

His inquiry just bruised her confidence.

Of all people, she thought he would understand and champion her hustler's mentality, being that they are both cut from the same cloth.

Nevertheless, she rebounds from the slight. "My brother amassed a great fortune from *peddling* these DVDs, so I don't see why I can't mimic his success–"

"And why didn't he take care of you financially so you wouldn't have to be out here late at night doing...*this*?"

Another stab.

Had it been anyone else questioning her moves, she would have been jumped down their throat. But this is her lover. And on top of that, he is asking the same questions she has been asking herself.

"I'm my own entity, Ahmed. I answer to no one–not even him."

"Fair enough. Then I wish you nothing but success with your venture."

"*Really*?" Her chuckle is condescending. "Seems like you're mocking what I'm trying to accomplish–"

Ahmed swallows her tongue whole.

She melts in his arms.

Ten seconds of rapture end with her staring at the ground.

He gently nudges her head upward. His smoldering eyes connect with hers. "I would never do that to you and if it came off that way, I apologize. I *want* to see you win. How else are you going to pay for the condo?"

She smiles. "Good comeback."

"I thought it was."

She picks at his black shirt.

Enjoying their moment together.

But duty calls.

"I, uh, gotta go." She slowly backpedals, but still holds his hand. "My coworkers are probably wondering where I'm at."

"Enjoy your evening."

"I'll call you tomorrow."

"You do that."

She releases his hand and moseys over to Bunions, who is surrounded by potential customers who are either pulling out their money or flipping through the stacks of DVDs and CDs.

"See, what I told you?" she gleams. "You should be able to sell out in no time."

Bunions side-eyes her as he bags up CDs for a customer. "So, I take it you won't be relieving me anytime tonight?"

"Nope."

"See, I knew it! You got me doing all the fuckin' work!"

She opens her purse to pull out a stack of flyers. "What I will be doing is passing these out to potential customers at the club. That's my role, Bunions. We need to stay focused and make this money, not bump heads–"

"Okay, okay! Do what you do best…damn."

"Thank you."

She proceeds to walk away.

"I see you like cupcaking with them curry-smelling niggas–what's up with that?"

Her spin around was so fast, that it caught him totally off-guard.

"Mind your fuckin' business and sell the merchandise–you got that?"

He fumes before returning to customers, who laugh at him as they complete their transactions.

She struts around Twenty-Eighth Street and measures the people in line waiting to enter Club Twilight. She hands out flyers to those interested before approaching the bouncer.

She smiles.

He waves her in.

The contagious energy permeating the entrance hall has her already two-stepping. She discreetly hands out more flyers while surveying the crowd. She spots her coworkers having a good time on the dance floor.

Her eyes graze the bar area.

Freeman mingles with his bratty sister and the new employee.

She wonders how long she can keep the charade going with him.

He is beginning to bore her.

*Oh, well…might as well enjoy the night with him.*

*But after tonight, the countdown begins.*

She conjures up a winning smile and maneuvers through the crowd towards her soon-to-be ex-boo.

# FIFTY-ONE

## FREEMAN

"*Girl, I'll House You…Girl, I'll House you…You're In My Hut Now…My Hut!*"

The sheer force of the Jungle Brothers' signature jam ignites a stampede to the dance floor.

Freeman downs his drink and casually scans through the flashing spotlights and gyrating couples in search of Velour.

Instead, he spots someone else, sitting at the bar.

Someone familiar.

Pushing himself from the booth, he side-steps swinging elbows and legs to focus on the petite, dark-skinned lady dressed in a form-fitting lilac dress, purple high-heel evening sandals, and a sparkling Halle Berry haircut.

He comes to a complete stop.

*Oh, hells no...*

He marches up to Divine and taps her on the shoulder.

She swings her happiness his way. "Hey, Freeman! I just saw some of the others on the dance floor and I was wondering where you were!"

He immediately notices her eyes.

They are *twinkling*!

"Why are you here?" he probes.

"Wait a minute! They don't allow church folk up in the club?" She laughs at her own sarcasm. "I surely didn't get the memo, Big Brother–"

"You're the one who told me the club scene wasn't your thing."

"Trust me, I'm not making this a habit. I'm here with a mutual friend to have fun–just like *you*."

"And who that might be?"

As if on cue, Emmanuel two-steps over to them with two drinks and hands one to her. The lanky youngblood's smile is about as loud as his tropical red shirt.

"What's good, Free?" he asks. "I see the crew getting busy on the floor. Where's Velour?"

He ignores the youngblood while snatching the cup from his sister's hand and sniffing it.

She snatches it right back. "It's ginger ale, fool!"

"Mine, too!" Emmanuel yells. "Gotta stay alert! Dudes be out here on the prowl, for real!"

The youngblood winks at him.

The deejay blends in a house music crowd-pleaser, Soho's *Hot Music*, making everyone bounce up and down with their hands in the air as if they were on a thumping trampoline.

"Ooooh, that's my song!" Divine hops off the stool and reaches out her glass toward him. "Hold my drink, Big Brother!"

He takes her drink as Emmanuel leads her to the dance floor.

For a minute, he stares in amazement at some of his younger sister's slightly provocative dance moves. But his thoughts are interrupted by a pair of smooth, gold-bangled arms sliding up from underneath his armpits and gently hugging him. This is followed by a spine-tingling kiss that spikes the hairs on the back of his neck. He turns around and is strongly aroused by Velour's slinky white mini-dress, complete with gem-encrusted, stiletto heels, showing off her perfectly pedicured toes.

"Whoa," he manages to say while kissing her lips. "I see you're trying to show out."

She models for him. "I take it, you like?"

"Hell, we can roll up outta here, right now, it's up to you!"

"You're so silly. Now, were my eyes deceiving me, or was that your sister looking all sexy with *Emmanuel*?"

"Yep. And that's why we're dancing right next to them. C'mon."

"I'm right behind you!"

The earthquake-pounding bass from the surrounding speakers provides the very platform for the body-rocking partygoers to lay everything they have on the pulsating dance floor.

Freeman Souls is having the time of his life. He twirls Velour around in a couple of breathtaking, ice-skating circles…

# FIFTY-TWO

## VELOUR

. . . And when she stops spinning, she does her best salsa impersonation to the song's percussion-heavy, chaotic freestyle cadence. But as she attempts to do the bump with Cadina, an imposing figure blocks her movement, causing her entire complexion to turn whiter than the Ku Klux Klan.

Right in front of her frightening eyes, decked out in a white Versace silk outfit and a matching white Panamanian Bailey Thurston hat with a burning cigar nestled in the corner of his mouth, is her brother Vincent, accompanied by Joy and four of his equally dapper comrades.

All wrapping their opposing eyes around her.

Vincent turns to a surprised Freeman and whispers in his ear, "I need to borrow my sister for a moment, you don't mind, do you?"

He vice-grips her arm and pulls her off the dance floor, with two of his henchmen parting the way through the lively dance floor.

"You've been a very busy girl, haven't you?" he whispers in her ear.

"V-Vincent—"

"Shut your ass up!"

The longer he pulls on her arm, the more painful his grip becomes. He winds up pulling her into the men's bathroom and flinging her against the wall, near the automatic hand dryer.

"OUCH!" she screams, rubbing her arm as she slides halfway down the wall.

With his platinum-ringed finger pressed on the top of her forehead, Vincent barks, "Do you have a fuckin' problem listening or what, Velour?"

"Wh-What are you talking about?"

"Playing stupid is going to get your head smashed right against this wall, so you better choose your words carefully!" He presses his finger even harder onto her forehead. "Before you do that, ask yourself…out of all the clubs in Manhattan, how did my brother know I was *here*?"

*Huh*?

"You really thought you had Bunions in your pocket like that? I thanked him by doubling what you gave him to be a part of your shitty operation!"

*Why, that fat fuck! Took my goddamn money!*

That transforms her fright into fury.

"Now, I reiterate, do you have a problem listening or what?" he impatiently asks.

She slowly rises, nursing her arm. "I wouldn't be doing any of this if you were taking care of me the way you're supposed to."

"Taking care of you? What the hell are you talking about? You're a grown-ass woman, Velour–"

"I'm your goddamn *sister*, you keep forgetting that?" she barks in his face. "You wanted me to bring in legitimate income for the mansion, so I did, by working at the post office for the past six years. I did my part, Vincent, but I've yet to see a fraction of my worth deposited into my account!"

"Are you still making this about *you*?" He points in her face. "Well, let me update you on our latest crisis! Detectives just happened to drop by my Jersey shop yesterday, questioning my mechanics about me…ME, VELOUR! Do you not understand the urgency of this matter?"

She attempts to say something but stifles it and looks the other way.

He lets out a cynical chuckle. "You know, all day I was feeling depressed, Velour, to the point where the fellas suggested we go hang out tonight, just to clear our heads. Then I get a call from Bunions. And I'm glad he called because it's clear to me that I have to continue cutting the dead weight that's jeopardizing my empire!"

Velour does not like the way that sounds.

She is nobody's dead weight.

But, she is not in the mood to argue anymore tonight.

*Just apologize and get it over with.*

She downsizes her temper. "It won't happen again, okay?"

"I know it won't because I'm confiscating your truck until you decide to get your head out of your ass!"

Her anger rebirths instantly. "But that's *MY* truck, Vincent! I paid for that vehicle!"

"By using *whose* credit card?" he reminds her. "Continue doing this independent shit and trust me, that truck will be the least of your worries!" He checks himself out in the mirror. "Enjoy your night."

He storms out of the bathroom, with his crew following behind him.

Joy faces her, disgusted. "And you wonder why he stays on your ass all the time?"

The Trinidadian leaves that question for Velour to mull over as she struts out the door.

She is all alone now.

Drowning in a sea of animosity.

She kicks the nearby trash can clear across the bathroom floor, causing it to topple over.

Two men enter the bathroom, deep in conversation.

They stop talking when they realize she is in the wrong bathroom.

"The fuck are y'all looking at?" she shouts, stomping towards the door.

As she enters the hallway, she sees her coworkers making their way into the enclosed area, towards her.

"*Fuck…not now…*" she mutters.

Freeman is leading the group and the concerned expression on his face tells her he is going to expect a valid explanation of the reason Vincent yanked her off the dance floor. She understands this immensely.

Too bad he will not receive one, though.

Crystal Waters' blazing hit, *Gypsy Woman,* explodes from the speakers, causing Velour to have dizzy spells filled with hatred and embarrassment.

So, she just stands there.

"*She's just like you and me, but she's homeless…*
*She's homeless,*
*And she stands there…singing for moneyyyy…*"

# FIFTY-THREE

## FREEMAN

*"La da dee, la dee da, la da dee, la dee da…"*

James pulls Freeman close to him and asks, "What was that all about?"

"Don't know," Freeman responds as the rest of the crew gathers around. "Said he needed to talk to Velour."

"But why did he pull her off the floor like that?" Najya questions.

"I guess we're going to find out, right now."

He leads the crew through the maze of dancers. From afar, he catches Vincent and his entourage leaving the club altogether.

Lou shouts, "Yo, there goes her brother and his crew!"

"But where is she at?" Roy asks.

They continue towards the area where the bathrooms are located. They turn down the hallway and there they find Velour.

Just standing there.

Brewing in rage.

Cautiously, he asks, "Are you alright?"

"Not now, Freeman…"

She bolts past him and the rest of the crew, toward the exit.

They all stand around looking at one another, confused.

"So…" Divine sarcastically smiles at him. "…are you going to see what's up with your girlfriend?"

He side-eyes his sister before leading the crew outside of the club.

They plod through the murmuring crowd to witness Velour screaming at Vincent as he climbs into the passenger seat of her Porsche with a woman behind the wheel, who then pulls off down the street. They are followed by a black Escalade. And if that was not painful enough to watch, Velour begins yelling at the departing trucks while stomping around in a tight circle. She abruptly stops, but the damage has been done.

"What the hell?" James utters, under his breath.

That same question whirls around in Freeman's mind. He initially thought Vincent felt some type of way with his involvement with Velour, but now he has the discomforting feeling that this may not be the case at all. It must be something way bigger for them to keep having these types of falling outs.

But that's a conversation for another time.

*Right now, she needs me.*

He turns to his crew. "Y'all give me a minute with her."

He walks over to her where Velour stands, blocking traffic.

"FUCK YOU!", she screams at the cars honking their horns.

"Hey, let's get you out of the street–"

She brushes past him and marches to the sidewalk.

He follows Velour and starts caressing her arms. "Are you alright?"

She swings around and snaps, "That's a stupid question. Does it *look* like I'm okay?"

Her stare is so blank.

Worse, it has a coldness to it he has never experienced from her. Like he was a complete stranger to her. And she holds onto the stare without even trying to conceal it.

"Flag me down a taxi, right now," she demands.

"Why?"

"*Why*? Because I'm not in the mood for any more socializing. *That's* why!"

He takes a deep breath. He tries to lower the volume of their conversation. "You want to talk about what's going on?"

"Are you deaf or what, Freeman?" she raises her voice even higher. "Flag me down a cab, NOW!"

"So, your brother shows up, kills your vibe and now you want to go home? Even when we were just having a good time on the dance floor?" He gently holds onto her arm. "C'mon, let's go back inside, get you a drink, and be amongst your peoples–"

She rips her arm from his grip. "Get your *fuckin'* hands off me! Damn!"

He stands there, surprised.

And embarrassed.

He peeks at his people.

They are just as stunned as he is.

Velour also notices her coworkers' reactions.

"I'm sorry for sounding nasty, but yes, my brother did fuck my mood up," she confesses, softening her wrath. "See, I have to go out of my way and beg for my own truck back like I'm some damn child! Now, how does that sound to you, Freeman? Not good, right? All I want to do is go home and get my mind right if that's okay with you?"

He buys her story and then pulls out his car keys. "Alright. But you're not going home alone. I'ma tell them that we're done for the night–"

"I don't *want* your company, Freeman…not tonight, okay?"

She quickly cops an attitude when an empty taxi whizzes by them down the street.

"I gave you one task…" she snarls. "And you couldn't even do that right!"

She steps into the street and flags down the next taxi. She slides into the back seat.

Cadina rushes over to hand Velour her purse through the window.

"Thank you, Boo," she smiles. "I'll call you tomorrow."

The taxi pulls off down the street.

The crew joins Freeman where he stands.

Divine attempts to say something, but he cuts her off immediately.

"I don't wanna hear not one, '*I told you so*', out of you, alright?" he warns.

"I was going to ask if you were okay?"

He sighs. "Yeah, I guess. Sorry."

"Apology accepted…now you need to toss her to the curb for the way she treated you–"

"Knock it off, Dee…" James interjects.

"Nooo, let Dee speak her mind," Marisol says, siding with Divine. "Velour could've handled herself better than that."

"Why don't we take this back inside." Shabbazz and Najya begin walking toward the club. "I think we had enough drama for tonight."

"I second that!" burps Roy. "Another round on me!"

"Man, get your drunk ass inside somewhere and sit down!" laughs Neville.

The crew returns to the club.

Freeman does not budge from his spot near the curb.

James holds the door for Cadina to enter, but double-takes Freeman. He returns to him.

"The party is this way, my brother." James points toward the club.

He turns to James. "How did it go from sugar to shit in less than ten minutes? And then I get screamed on like I did something to her."

James nods sympathetically. "Well, how do you think Velour feels? She was just humiliated in front of the entire club by her own brother. Would *you* want to hang around here?"

Wow.

He never considered Velour's feelings, not one time, only his. Now, he understands why she felt the need to lash out at him.

But still…

*Let it go, Free. She'll be okay by tomorrow.*

*I pray.*

He turns around and heads for the club's entrance. "I'ma need two bottles after this crazy episode."

"You know what? I'll join you."

James hugs him by the neck as they walk inside the club.

# FIFTY-FOUR

## FREEMAN

Monday morning, Fourth of July, casually dressed letter carriers celebrate their overtime patriotism by blasting personal radios to earth-shattering decibels while casing mail for the next day's regular mail delivery.

Walking into his section, Freeman shows Lexington his bucket of mail to record before he heads over to his route where Velour has begun casing the letters. Ever since he clocked in, they've barely said two words to each other. Not even a simple kiss, which she usually greets him with every morning, no matter how she is feeling. Freeman throws his bucket on the magazine ledge and reaches out a handful of letters to her.

"Here."

She pauses for a moment to redo the knot on her multi-colored head bandanna. She then extends her hand out for the mail, all the while avoiding direct eye contact.

"Did you read the text message I sent you yesterday?"

"Yeah, I read it." She returns to casing the letters.

"*And*?"

She pauses working. "I'm getting my truck back this afternoon. Does that answer your question?"

Her words are like icicles dangling off his earlobes.

He places his magazines on the ledge and then sits down on a stool, next to her. He rubs his fingers on her arm. "You want to talk about whatever is on your mind? You know I'm a good listener and it won't go any further than right here–"

"I know where this is heading, Freeman." She finally makes eye contact with him, even though they appear dull. "Believe me when I say, my brother and I are just fine."

"You say that, yet he drags you through the club and into the men's bathroom to have a conversation. I mean, not for nothing, but every time I see you two together, he always seems to enjoy barking in your face–"

"And I've seen you and your sister go at it on several occasions, but am I all up in y'all business like that? No. and I don't need for you to be all up in mine, okay?"

"How long has he been abusing you?"

She pauses for a moment before laughing as she places the letters on the ledge. "Really, Freeman? Have you *seen* a bruise anywhere on my body? No, and you never will–"

"I'm not talking physical, Velour. I'm talking mental abuse–"

"Just, just stop it, Freeman, okay?" She accidentally knocks the pile of letters onto the floor. "You're not a psychologist, so case up the mail so I can go home."

She scoops up the letters from the floor and continues sorting.

He touched a serious nerve.

But with a defensive wall built around her, it is pointless to keep probing until she is ready to talk.

Marching into the section is a visibly upset Davenport. He stands in the middle of the section, and in a commanding voice, shouts, "IF YOU'RE HAVING TROUBLE HEARING MY VOICE AT THIS VERY MOMENT, IT MEANS YOUR RADIO IS WAY TOO LOUD! LOWER YOUR MUSIC OR I'LL HAVE THAT PRIVILEGE TAKEN AWAY FROM YOU!"

Snickering carriers lower their radios.

Davenport then marches straight to Freeman and Velour's work area.

In a straightforward manner, he says, "Miss Patterns, Mr. Souls, I need to see you two in my office. It won't take long."

"Excuse me, Michael?"

Davenport whips around to see Lexington behind him, vying for his attention.

"What?" the manager asks.

"I wanted to inform you that Marc called out today and he was scheduled to work this holiday."

Davenport grunts. "Make a notation concerning this matter so I won't forget."

Lexington eagerly jots it down on his yellow legal pad. "You got it, Mike."

"I didn't know we were on a first-name basis, Mr. VanGuard."

Lexington peeks up from his legal pad. "Well, I thought since all the other supervisors called you by your first name that I—"

"They are my colleagues, son," Davenport points out. "*And* very dear friends of mine. You haven't reached either plateau, have you?"

Lexington glances at Freeman and Velour before mumbling, "No, Sir."

"Now, the next time I come up here and I have to discipline your section, I'm going to start with *you*. Understood?"

"Uh, yes...Mr. Davenport."

Lexington meekly returns to the podium.

Davenport turns back around to Freeman and Velour. "Let's go."

Velour places her letters down and follows the speed-walking manager.

Freeman follows them, with the uncanny feeling that bad news is waiting for them at the end of their destination.

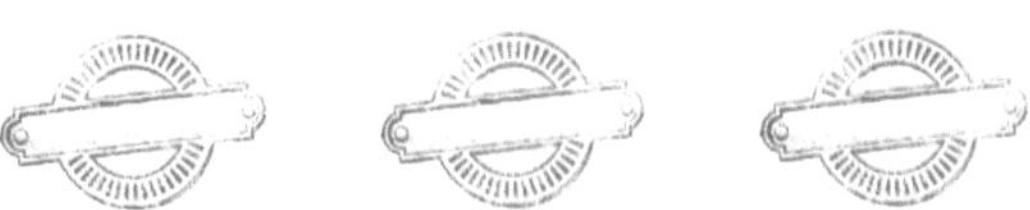

THE LAST TIME HE SAT IN DAVENPORT'S OFFICE, TUCKER WAS BEHIND the desk, giving him a stern lecture involving brutal ultimatums concerning his career. There has been no need for him to return.

Until now.

He feels that same level of uneasiness encircling his head, already. It does not help matters when the manager, dressed down in a white polo shirt and beige slacks, positions his body into a thinking position. Freeman gulps down some of his tension.

Davenport leans forward on his desk with his hands clasped. "Has either of you noticed any unusual activity on your route as of late?"

*Uh-oh.*

"Like what?" Freeman cautiously asks.

"A tenant from one of your buildings named Havana Blunt called and spoke to me extensively about someone allegedly using her credit cards as well as her deceased husband's credit cards for their own personal use. She said she spoke to you last week about this matter."

"She did, Sir, " Freeman admits. "She came to the station to speak to Dante, but when I told her he moved to another station and that I replaced him, she became very skeptical and in a roundabout way, accused me of messing with her mail."

"Really?" The manager sits upward in his chair, fully attentive. "Why didn't you tell me about this conversation?"

"I told Chapman about it that day and he told me not to worry, that he'd look into it."

Freeman turns to Velour.

"You remember when I called and spoke to you about her accusing me of this, right?"

"I don't remember you talking to me about her at all."

Freeman double-takes her so hard, that he almost stumbles out of his chair.

"What are you talking about? It was on your day off when I called you, remember? You were the one who *told* me she was off her rocker!"

She shakes her head. "I would've remembered, Freeman. Maybe you were juiced that day and assumed you had a conversation with me."

His mouth hangs wide open.

"*Juiced?* What are you talking–"

"You were drinking, Freeman?" Davenport leans back in his chair, with his eyes firmly on him.

Freeman sits on the edge of his seat. "I was at work when we spoke, Velour, and I damn sure wasn't juiced!" He whips his head around to Davenport. "Look, Sir, I don't want you thinking I'm hiding something because I'm not and I definitely don't want you thinking I'm messing with someone's mail–"

"I'm not accusing you of anything, Freeman," Davenport cuts in. "It just so happens that another route is going through a similar ordeal. So, tomorrow I will hold a special meeting concerning this very matter. I assume you didn't make out a statement about this incident."

Freeman shakes his head. He then glares at Velour. She stares straight ahead at their manager while demonstrating an uncannily cool demeanor.

"Then go ahead and prepare one so I can have it on file just in case this incident grows wings. Moving forward, I want you both to be aware of your surroundings on your route, check mailboxes for vandalism, ask the doorman about suspicious-looking characters hanging around in the mailroom or lobby area this past year and notify me, okay?"

They both replied, "Yes, Sir."

"Thank you. That will be all."

Freeman and Velour prepare to leave.

"Freeman?"

As Velour heads out the door, he turns around.

And stares into Davenport's interrogative eyes.

"No more surprises, okay?"

Seething, Freeman turns back around and storms out of the office.

He spots Velour heading outside to the loading dock.

He beelines towards the exit and pushes the door open before it closes.

"Velour…"

She turns around and rudely responds, "What?"

"What the hell was that back there?"

"What was what, Freeman?"

"'*Maybe you were juiced that day*'? Why would you tell a lie like that around that man?"

"Key word, Freeman–*maybe.* I didn't say you actually were–"

"But you *do* remember the conversation we had about Ms. Blunt, right?"

She sucks her teeth. "You know what? I can't deal with you being so damn paranoid–"

"Paranoid? While you were in there throwing me under the bus, *I'm* being paranoid?"

"Did the man accuse you of anything? No, he didn't. And he just told you it happened on another route, so you need to relax."

Employees pour out of the building during break-time.

Velour places a hand on her hip. "Now, is there anything else I can help you with?"

"Did your brother jack you up so badly that you gotta have an attitude with me?"

She looks around at the coworkers before inching closer to his ear and whispers, "I'm going to say this one time, Freeman. You don't know anything about my brother and what he's going through, so my advice to you from this point on is to leave his name off your fuckin' tongue–you got that?"

The threatening tone in her voice.

Her nasty disposition.

He finally concludes that this is the dark side of Velour.

And he is not feeling it at all.

Cadina pops up and suddenly, Velour is all smiles.

"James and I are about to get some breakfast," Cadina says. "Y'all wanna come? My treat!"

"Alright now, I won't be turning down that invitation!" Velour laughs.

Cadina turns to him. "You coming?"

"Uh, Davenport needs him to finish up a report." Velour states. "Right, Freeman?"

It takes everything in his power to keep from slapping that shit-eating grin from her face.

"I'll bring you back something."

Velour winks at him while holding onto Cadina's arm as they walk down the ramp and onto the sidewalk.

Freeman marches back inside the building.

Ready to punch a hole in a wall.

# FIFTY-FIVE

## VELOUR

Velour giggles while leafing through the pages of a high school graduation book Cadina had left on her route-case ledge earlier that day. She then takes a breather from the book to look around the work floor, observing as a few more carriers clock out to end their overtime workday.

Cadina and James enter her line of sight. They stand next to the time clock, in private conversation, and playfully pinch each other's butts. Velour blushes at their kinky behavior.

She admires their relationship–so innocent; so genuine. Their whole vibe screams, *it's all about us!*

Velour hopes to one day reach a point in her life where she, too, can commit to a relationship grounded in complete sincerity, rather than sexual propaganda. But until that day arrives, it's all about the Benjamins.

She listens as Cadina tells James she was heading over to spend some time with her.

Velour straightens up, slaps on her *I'm-having-problems-but-I'll-be-alright* smile, and waves goodbye to James as he leaves. Cadina makes her way over to Velour's workstation, bringing love and happiness along the way.

At the same time, a gentleman dressed in white painter's coveralls carrying a ladder follows Cadina. He then ventures to the workstation next to Velour's and spreads out his ladder.

He nods and smiles at her.

She smiles back.

*He's cute.*

"It's about time they brought someone in to brighten up these walls," Velour says to Cadina. "But I'm surprised Davenport didn't inform us in advance about a paint job on this floor."

"I know, right?" Cadina pulls up a stool to sit next to her. "So, is everything okay with you and Freeman?"

She glances at her while turning a book page. "I hope I didn't make a mistake with him."

"In what way?"

"Persuading him to bid for my route, I don't know… everything." Velour closes the book and places it on the ledge. "I just feel that our relationship is slowly coming to a close, at least on my end, anyway, and it's been nagging the hell out of me."

"How does he feel about it?"

"Girl, when I tell you that brother is in it for the long haul…I wish it was the same for me, but I'm not in that space yet."

"Yeah, well, you sure fooled everyone around here the way you two carried on. We all thought y'all were an item."

"That's on me, I led him to believe that. Truth is, I never had a guy treat me the way Freeman has–*ever*. I don't know how to break it off with him without hurting his feelings–"

The sooner, the better. You don't need the bitterness hanging over this workstation you two share."

She is grateful to Cadina for keeping her company. No one else would have even bothered. However, she finds it more and more difficult to lie to someone she considers a true friend. But lying comes so easy for her that she doesn't know how to shut it off, even when she needs to.

"It might be a little too late for that," Velour says. "We're not on speaking terms at the moment."

"Like I said—the sooner the better. Prolonging will only make matters worse. And please don't be nasty about it. Talk to him like you're talking to me now. Show him that respect."

Velour nods in appreciation. She stands and zips up her shoulder bag. "I'll heed your advice, Miss Glee Club Member, freshman year, rocking the MC Lyte hairstyle with the door-knocker earrings with your name in the middle…"

She holds up the yearbook.

Cadina laughs. "You know I bought this book because Lou and I graduated from the same high school, and I wanted to show him."

"Lou is in this book!" Velour flips through the pages. "I gotta see this! Where is he?"

Cadina finds the page and points him out.

Velour howls in laughter. "Oh, my God! He looks like one of those Menudo kids from back in the day!"

"See, now that is not nice!"

"Have the other guys seen this?"

"Not yet."

"Girl, they're going to clown him something awful when they see this picture!"

"Awww, he doesn't look that bad."

"I didn't say he did…but that ducktail, though, c'mon now."

They gather their belongings to clock out.

"Take care, Frank," states Cadina, waving at the painter.

The painter stares at her and then gives a hesitant smile. "Have a good afternoon."

As they swipe their badges, Velour slyly grins at her. "Okay, I see you..."

Cadina shakes her head. "Don't play yourself, alright? He told me his name downstairs."

"Mmm-hmm." Velour pokes her lips out. "As tight as his ass looks in his outfit, I wouldn't blame you one bit."

"Alright now, Velour—"

"Girlfriend, you are not married or blind, you can admire from a distance, damn!"

Cadina blushes. "His chest ain't bad-looking, either…"

"Thank you! Don't you be playing Miss Goodie Two Shoes around me, shoo, I will call you out!"

"You are a mess!"

Velour begins singing, "*You mind if I stroke you up? I don't minddddddd…*"

"STOP!"

The ladies laugh their way down the stairwell.

*"Don't let the small frame fool you, son,*
*I tear a nigga out the membrane, and that includes you, dun,*
*Claiming to the masses you believe to be my equal,*
*But I'ma dominate the game by not refraining on my sequel,*
*I spit so much fire, so consider me an arsonist,*
*A true narcissist, I'm a neighborhood's*
*pharmacist,*
*You name it, I cooked it, then pushed it, too hot to handle,*
*A Black Sox Scandal, niggaz can't even hold a candle,*
*Ridiculous with the words, I send shivers up my own spine,*
*Quick to slap a nigga if he gets the fuck out of line,*
*I'm an asset to any label; I amount to big checks,*
*If I roll up on any crew's cypher,*
*Guess who's gonna rock it DeBest,*
*Holla at your boy…"*

"That's what I'm talking about…off the top of the dome!" Lou yells, jumping out of his seat to give Emmanuel his freestyling kudos. Lou then turns to the Midway Station softball team. "Any comments? Thoughts?"

"I have a comment…" Neville replies, raising his hand.

Soft giggles escape from the softball squad.

Neville stands up, clears his throat, and with a straight face says, "His lyrics made me feel good about myself as a grown-ass man. Especially the part, '*He's quick to slap a nigga if he gets the fuck out of line…*'. It sent *chills* through my soul! That's my comment for today."

The entire breakroom erupts with laughter.

A beet-red Emmanuel turns to Lou. "You see what I mean? I told you this was a bad idea from the jump! They can't connect with my genre, nor my generation, and I'm not in the mood to be getting clowned–"

"Well, you better get used to it if you're going to keep rapping about bullshit." Roy stands up. "And have you ever sold drugs in your entire life, that's what I want to know?"

Emmanuel sheepishly avoids eye contact. "Well, no, not directly–"

"Man, sit your punk ass down." Roy turns to Lou. "And you! You call yourself mentoring this young cat?"

"Mentoring him to getting his ass shot." Neville laughs. "He ain't about that life!"

"Man, ain't nobody gonna do *jack* to me–"

"SIT YOUR PUNK ASS DOWN!" the entire team shouts.

"Pay them no mind, Manny," Lou boasts as he takes off his postal shirt. "Two years from now, we're going to be signing autographs and traveling the world while they'll still be loading dusty relay bags inside the back of hot ass postal trucks."

"And it's an honest living, my dude, don't get it twisted," Roy counters while oiling down his catcher's mitt.

"Yeah, okay."

James and the shop steward/softball coach Martinez hurry into the breakroom carrying oversized boxes and sitting them on the table.

"Alright, squad, listen up…" the chubby coach opens one of the boxes and hands out the shirts. "Brand new jerseys with your names on the back and fitted hats. Courtesy of James."

"That's what's up!" the squad cheers, giving him his accolades.

Neville holds up the authentic royal blue jersey with the name DEMOODAY boldly embroidered in gold letters with navy blue trim. He stares at it in confusion. “Coach, what the hell is a *DEMOODAY*?”

“James will answer that question on the way to the field. The game starts in one hour.”

As the softball squad gathers their equipment, Freeman, already dressed in his softball attire, enters the breakroom and approaches James, Lou, and the Coach.

“Bad news, y’all.” Freeman sits on the edge of the table. “Claudell can’t play today. His wife surprised him with a trip to Hawaii.”

“You mean to tell me he chose *Hawaii* over our first game?” Lou says, in disgust. “Is he crazy?”

“It’s their anniversary, what do you think he was going to do?”

“This is straight cah-cah, Bro. How’re we going to matchup against the Boriquas without our starting pitcher.”

“We might as well put Marc on the mound to keep from forfeiting the game,” James suggests.

“But if we do that, who’s going to cover first base?”

Freeman mulls over a thought. “What about the man who wanted to be on the team from day one?”

Lou and James glance at one another. They both shake their heads in disapproval.

“Not that cat…” Lou says. “Anybody but him.”

“We don’t have any other options at this point.”

“But can he play? That’s the question,” the Coach asks.

“He told me he won a gold glove by playing first base back in the day.”

“It’s your call, Coach,” Lou huffs as he grabs his duffle bag. “This is fucked up, man.”

Lou and James leave the breakroom.

The Coach turns to Freeman. “Let me know asap if he wants to play. I might have to suit up myself.”

The Coach speed-walks toward the locker room.

Freeman grabs his duffle bag before heading to the stairwell.

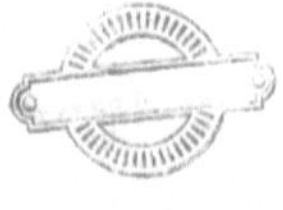 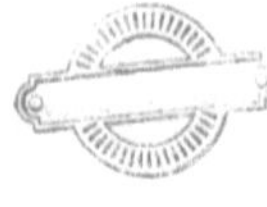 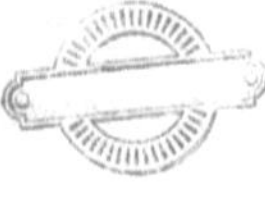

He arrives at the work floor.

A lopsided back-and-forth session coming from his section slows his pace down to a stutter-step.

*Sounds like an argument.*

He quickly moves behind a letter-case which places him out of the view of Lexington, who is getting chastised by Davenport at the podium. The manager holds a form in front of Lexington's face.

Freeman has never seen or heard the manager lash out at anyone in the way that he is lashing out at his so-called protégé.

He listens carefully:

*"Do you have any idea what's going on in your section? Davenport asks. "Apparently not! Look at these numbers, boy…LOOK AT THEM! Overtime jumped eight percent in your section just these past few months. What is the number one goal of a supervisor?"*

*"To reduce the overtime numbers, Sir, but you don't understand—"*

*"No, YOU don't understand, son! You're allowing these overtime hungry carriers to walk all over you and the net result is this eight percent increase! You better get it together and in a hurry or there won't be a trip to the supervisor's academy, no matter what you received on your written exam—am I getting through to you, boy?"*

*"I'm on it, Sir."*

*"For your sake, I hope so."*

The boiling manager storms out of the section.

Freeman pretends he had just arrived on the floor. Davenport stops right in front of him with a deranged grin and his hand extended.

"My *main* man," Davenport shouts while checking out his softball uniform. "Opening Day, I see…"

"Uh, yeah." He shakes the manager's hand. "Oh, did you get a chance to go over the statements I left on your desk earlier, concerning the two ladies and their accusations?"

"I have and thank you for your cooperation." The manager pauses, and then in a booming voice, he adds, "You know, Freeman,

I wish you were on *my* team. We sure could benefit from the type of diligence you display…it is sorely lacking in your section."

Freeman peeks at Lexington's demoralized reaction to the manager's statement.

His message was received loud and clear.

Freeman quickly changes subjects. "Hey, we'll try to bring back a win for the station."

"As far as I'm concerned, Freeman, you're ALWAYS a winner by my standards!"

Davenport marches toward the stairwell.

Freeman hurries over to the podium where he finds Lexington picking up forms that have fallen to the floor. Freeman quietly waits for him to pick up the paper as if they were the pieces of his manhood Davenport ripped apart moments ago.

Lexington eyeballs him. "Aren't you going to be late for your game?"

"You alright?"

"Why wouldn't I be, Freeman?" he responds surly. "Because of what just happened? The man is obviously making the necessary adjustments needed to equip me for the academy, that's all."

Lexington tosses the paperwork on the podium and without saying another word, slouches on his stool with his head hanging down the way a defeated boxer does after his camp throws in the towel. Freeman has never seen him this fragile. Lexington is now realizing his armored-plated arrogance is no match for Davenport who is causing enough mental damage to make Lexington a shell of the man he was six months ago.

"You sure that's all he was doing?" Freeman asks.

"Why are you so concerned? Like I told you before, I am built for this. So whatever constructive criticism comes my way, I have to adapt and move on."

"Whatever, man. Look, I just came to see if you wanted to play with us today."

"Excuse me?"

"Do you want to play softball with us today?"

A hint of gleam controls Lexington's beady eyes. "You're asking me if I want to play–"

"Yes, first base."

Lexington boasts the kind of grin that would make Hannibal Lecter uneasy.

"So, the guys *do* need me on the team after all, huh?"

"It's either yay or nay, the game starts in less than an hour."

Lexington crouches down, pulls out the bottom cabinet drawer, and retrieves his worn Wilson baseball glove and sneakers. He slides his hand into the glove and pounds it with a fist. "I kept my equipment here just for this occasion. Needs a little oil, but it's more than capable of handling the job."

Lexington then sticks his glove under his armpit, grabs his sneakers, and struts toward the stairwell.

"Well, let me at least give you the address–"

"East River Park, which is next to the FDR Drive–I know where it's located. You did your part, Freeman, thank you."

Lexington practically sprints to the stairwell.

Freeman grabs a cup to get water from the cooler. He downs the water in one gulp and then trots toward the exit, with plans of revitalizing what's left of his maligned relationship with Velour, plus breaking a four-year losing streak against the defending champions, the Boriquas.

A generous gust of afternoon wind blows onto the East River Ballfields where the Bogart Postal Station's Boriquas, sporting candy-apple red jerseys with white lettering and red trimming, practice mightily on one of the dark green, manicured baseball diamonds.

Near the picnic area, Cadina and Marisol are placing small Bunsen burners under aluminum pans to keep some of the food Cadina prepared nice and warm until after the game.

"Seriously, I don't know how you find the energy…" Marisol lights a Bunsen burner. "I mean, look at all of this; burgers, hot dogs, fried chicken, barbeque chicken, baked beans, black beans and yellow rice, roast chicken and white rice mix, potato salad, apple *and* cherry pies, and what's those over there, next to the tossed salad?"

"Chicken enchiladas."

"What!" Marisol grabs a take-out container and a spatula. "I'm putting two to the side for me and Papa right now."

Cadina laughs. "You are a mess!"

"I'm just amazed at how you took it upon yourself to cook all of this."

"Well, since I was off today, I felt like making a little extra for the team's first game."

"Girl, I am not mad at you." Marisol woofs down a forkful of enchilada. "But you watch, they're going to expect a feast like this every game, so be ready."

"I will."

Cadina peeks over at the Boriquas' dugout where Velour is boldly engrossed in close conversation with one of the opposing players, a muscular Puerto Rican pretty boy. Her suggestive body language, along with her white spandex shorts, tells Cadina that their conversation is more flirtatious than casual.

"I see Velour is all chummy with the Boriqua players," Cadina says.

Marisol pours ice over the beer in the coolers before standing. "I'ma be honest with you, Chica; ever since Papa introduced me to Velour a few years back, I made it my business to say as little as humanly possible to her."

"Really? Why?"

"I don't know…it's just the way she carries herself. Right before you were hired, I dropped by the station and asked if Papa had already left to deliver the mail. Don't you know she had the nerve to look me up and down like I stole something from her? *And* she ignored me on top of that? You don't forget shit like that."

"Maybe you caught her on a bad day." Cadina tears off a piece of aluminum foil. "I mean, she embraced me with open arms when I first arrived at the station."

"Yeah. And she also embraced Freeman with her open legs and now she's cursing him out in public. What does that tell you about her character?"

Cadina glances back at Velour as she saunters away from the handsome ballplayer, who licks his lips, all the while, staring at her bootylicious biker shorts.

"Time for me to go. Just watch yourself around her; she's not who you think she is." Marisol glares at Velour. "Skank…"

"Shhh!" warns Cadina.

Velour joins the women with a glow on her face that resembles a person who has just been laid. She whistles, "Hey, Cadina!.. Marisol…"

"Velour." Marisol places the lids on the coolers and then faces Cadina. "I'ma head to the bodega to get some more bags of ice. Do you need anything?"

Cadina browses the table. "Plastic forks, spoons, and paper towels."

"Gotcha."

Marisol cuts her eyes at Velour before grabbing her food container and walking towards the DeMooday dugout.

"She stays with a bug up her ass, I swear." Velour chuckles as she reaches for a container. "You know, Cadina, right now I'm in the process of getting my finances in order, and when I do, I'm thinking about investing in a food truck for you. Make us both some money."

"Really?" Cadina raises her brow at the diva. "Where did this idea come from? Better yet, why would you want to do that for me?"

Velour shrugs while filling the container with food. "Maybe because I believe you're a good investment and this is what you enjoy doing. It's not that complicated, girl."

"Wow. You made me feel special."

"You're different than most." Velour grabs some napkins. "I'm sure you noticed that people are either intimidated by me or they just tolerate me. You do neither. When we talk, it's genuine and I value that."

Cadina smiles while throwing some burger patties on the grill. "I don't know what else to say but thanks."

"Thank me when the food truck comes to fruition."

"I will."

Cadina sees the handsome Boriqua player still watching Velour from a distance.

"I, uh, see you were very friendly over there with the competition."

Velour peeks up at her. "There're no secrets surrounding my relationship with the Boriquas. I was assigned to their station for about a year before I transferred to Midway. Those are my peoples."

"Have you spoken to Freeman yet?"

"Haven't had the time."

Cadina wipes her hands with a cloth. "Well, it seems like there's no better time, being that the weekend is here, the weather is gorgeous…you're smiling and hugging up on other men without a care in the world…"

"Oh, I see," Velour chuckles sarcastically. "You and big mouth Marisol were over here pre-judging me, like what you're doing at this very moment–"

"Freeman is going to arrive here any minute and you know if he sees you all up in some other guy's face, he's going to flip out. Do you really want to invite that kind of energy out here?"

"Well, maybe it's none of your business how I decide to handle my situation, Cadina."

Strutting over to the picnic area with last year's trophy held over their heads, are Miguel and Jose, filled with championship vigor.

"Don't tell me, Velour," Miguel jokes, rubbing his chubby belly. "Y'all going to honor the defending champions with a feast after the game, right?"

"You wish," Velour replies. "Allow me to introduce my dear coworker and reigning Midway chef, Cadina. Cadina, meet Miguel and Jose. Soon to be ex-champions."

"Yeah, right!"

Cadina politely shakes their hands.

"I guess we have something to look forward to after we lay the smackdown on—" Jose bends down to read Cadina's jersey. "How do you pronounce that, anyway?"

"It's Demooday, baby!" shouts Velour. "Get it right!"

"What the hell does that mean?" laughs Jose.

"It means you won't be winning today's game, now what?"

"Maaaan, we're gonna whoop that ass—"

"*HOOOO-DE-HOOOOOO!*"

Arriving through the front gate, dipped in a sea of royal blue and gold, and full of softball swagger is the boisterous DeMooday squad, led by a chanting Lou. Once on the baseball field, they exchange proper greetings and friendly mudslinging with their arch-rivals, the Boriquas.

"Ah, yeah, it's *on* now, Papo!" Jose declares to Miguel.

"Let's go whip up on some DeMooday ass!"

The two opponents raise their huge trophy up in the air for everyone to view. Miguel then turns around and says, "Yo, Cadina, we'll be back for some of that grub–"

"Five dollars per opposing player!" Velour yells and then winks at Cadina. "Make that money, girl, you've worked too hard."

Cadina tunes her out to cheer on their team as they run onto the field to get in their fifteen minutes of pre-game practice. She waves and blows a kiss toward James, who returns the gesture before he trots out to left field. Neville belts out some vicious grounders to slick-fielding, third baseman Lou, who, in return, scoops them up and rockets them to second baseman Shabbazz. He completes the practice double play by firing them to an awkward catching Lexington at first, an unexpected addition to her eyes. She closely monitors the physical condition of old-timer Marc, as he winds up and whips his pitches to the catcher, Roy. Divine plays lover's toss with Emmanuel near the sidelines, which Cadina finds so cute.

Then her eyes land on Freeman, who is marching towards the picnic area.

His entire focus is on Velour.

"Handle your business," Cadina tells Velour.

Velour side-eyes her as Freeman walks up and grabs her arm.

"I need to holler at you for a sec," he says, pulling her to the side.

Velour yanks her arm from his grip. "I don't appreciate you trying to cause a scene, Freeman."

"You don't talk to me all day at work, yet you come out here and run your mouth to everybody you see." Steam escapes from his nostrils. "If you have a problem with me, just say so–"

"Haven't I said enough to you already?"

He takes a step back to analyze Velour.

Cadina feels so awful for him.

Finally, he points at Velour. "So, you thought the relationship was going to die on its own without any kind of communication?

Was *that* the mature way to go about it, Velour? Playing all these mind games instead of being straight up with me–"

"When did I ever give you the impression that what we had was long-term, huh?" Velour sneers in his face. "I would never commit to a momma's boy who is so annoying, his ex cheated on him because she needed a break from his ass. Why would I want that for me? If anything, you should've been honest with your damn self!"

Velour walks away from him to retrieve her food from the table.

Freeman nods his head in anger before returning to the field.

Cadina glares at the diva. "That was really foul, Velour."

"Nobody said it was going to be pretty, Boo." Velour grabs a beer from the cooler. "By the way; think about what color food truck you envision yourself owning."

The diva waves over to the rest of the Boriqua players before gliding over to her own team's bench with her biker booty shorts bouncing to the beat of her own drum.

Cadina suppresses her frustration as she douses out the grill. She then follows her superficial coworker to cheer on their fired-up squad as they prepare for their first game of the season.

# FIFTY-EIGHT

## PLAY BALL!

*From the opening pitch, the Bogart Boriquas show Midway why they are the four-time reigning champions, as they bash off to a torrid start by jumping to a 5-0 lead in the very first inning. However, the new, improved DeMooday squad stormed right back in the next two innings to even the score. Both teams make their share of sparkling defensive plays as well as their share of top ten bloopers. Roy, the Albino Rhino, belts his second homer of the game in the sixth inning for a 7-5 DeMooday lead, but Miguel, Jose, and Carlos blast consecutive dingers to regain the lead once again. The score flip-flops back and forth until the Boriquas withstand a Demooday surge in the ninth, ultimately winning the game, 15-14.*

# FIFTY-NINE

## LOU

Lou swallows the last bite of his enchilada, leans his bare tattooed back onto the gate behind the dugout bench, and finally washes his meal down with a cold Heineken. He finds himself feeling extremely optimistic about the team's future, despite the outcome. After giving their rivals everything they had, without the contribution of their star pitcher, they still could've won the game.

*We had them!*

He takes another swig from his brew and then frowns upon their pathetic replacement at first base, Lexington, who dries himself off with a towel before putting his dress attire back on. Lou is very tempted to throw his bottle at him.

Carrying take-out containers filled with Cadina's food, the Boriquas stroll over to show their respect before leaving the park.

"Good game, fellas," Miguel says, shaking Lou's hand.

"For y'all, it was," Neville grumbles, munching over his plate.

"Can't wait to play y'all next time," Jose yells out.

"Because you know we're gonna whoop that ass, right?"

"Hell no, Papo, we're not worrying about y'all." Miguel raises his food container. "It's these chicken enchiladas, son! These joints are off the *hook*! One love, baby!"

The Bogart Boriquas resume their championship swagger toward the front gate, hoisting last year's trophy high in the sky for the masses to see.

"Man, we *had* this game," Roy shouts in frustration as he takes off his jersey. "But their centerfielder snagged what could've been my third homer which could've won it for us!"

"Yo, bottom line; we made a statement out there." Lou finishes his bottle. "I mean, look, we didn't have our star pitcher, yet we *still* almost won. So, you know what that means, right?"

"No, Lou, what does that mean?" Shabbazz asks.

"We're gonna whoop their ass the next time around because by *then,* we'll be at full strength, you know what I'm saying? And now we know we have a deep bench with Manny and Divine—Yoooo! What about that diving catch she made out there?"

"*And* she gunned it back to Shabbazz to catch Miguel's fat ass trying to dive back into second!" Neville adds.

"Yo, but did you see their faces in the dugout?"

They erupt with hand-slapping and laughter in honor of Divine's solid defensive skills.

"See, that's what I'm talking about!" Lou jumps up, feeling rejuvenated. "She's a *ballplayer*!" He then glances over at Lexington. "But this *pendejo* over here, man..."

Lexington lifts his head up and looks at Lou. "If you're thinking about pinning this loss on me, you can go somewhere else with that."

"You're supposed to be Mr. Gold Glove! Had I known you were going to be a brick on first, I would've let my son Hector play that position!"

"If you would've thrown the ball with just a little accuracy, then maybe I would've completed all of the plays at my position!"

The dugout bursts into laughter.

"I know this cat didn't question my arm?"

"I believe he did, Lou," Neville smirks.

"And the fact that you ignored the Coach's signal to stop at third and got thrown out at home plate, hell, that cost us the game right there!" Lexington slips on his pair of slacks. "If it wasn't for me carrying the team into the ninth inning, we would've lost by a lot more than just one, I tell you that much!"

The dugout erupts into more heckling at their disillusioned supervisor.

"What you need to do is carry your ass into Davenport's office and ask him what's the hold up for your next class."

Lexington furiously fights to wrestle his foot into his shoe. He gives Lou the side-eye. "And that's none of your business."

"That's because you're afraid to face the truth."

"And what truth would that be, Lou?"

"That you're not going anywhere, Playboy." Lou pops the top off another beer. "You're stuck at Midway for the rest of your career or until Davenport is through using your non-supervising ass."

"You don't even know what the hell you're talking about–"

"You wanna put some money on it, Lex, because we could do this, you know." Lou grabs his wallet from his bag and pulls out five twenty-dollar bills. He flashes them in front of Lexington's face. "I got a hundred right here, easy money. What's up?"

"You talk a whole lot of shit for a person who don't know shit." Lexington thrusts his arms into his shirt sleeves with so much force, he almost rips open a stitch. "You walk around the station with your pants hanging off your ass, looking like a wack nineties rapper, reciting childish rhymes, sounding like a complete idiot. Why don't you try growing up for once, you may like it and stay the hell out of my business."

"Ooooooooo…" chants the dugout.

"He done told your ass, son!" laughs Roy.

Lou finds himself chuckling, as well. "Okay, I see you wanna take it there." He then turns to Neville. "You remember I told you about my cousin, Eduardo Fernandez?"

Neville lifts his head up from the bench. "You told me he took the supervisor exam right along with Lexington and passed."

"That's right, and I told you he passed with an eighty-six." Lou turns his speech around to Lexington and repeats loudly, "AN *EIGHTY-SIX*, *PAPA*! And guess what? He didn't have to wait for a second class, either! He's already supervising at his new station uptown! Now, look at you, Mr. Ninety-Eight. Got your hopes pinned on going to the academy yet refuses to accept the fact that your mentor is preventing you from moving on."

"Like I said before..." Lexington reiterates, but with less confidence, as he crams his equipment inside his backpack. "You don't know what the hell you're talking about."

"Prove me wrong and I'll drop the whole subject!"

Lou teases Lexington by waving the money in his face.

"Fuck you, Lou."

Lexington grabs his bag, throws it over his shoulder, and storms from the dugout.

"Yeah, that's right!" Lou shouts. "Go walk that shit off and figure out why your ass is being pimped!"

Lexington whips around and gives Lou a long, hateful glare before leaving the park.

Roy turns to Lou. "Damn, bruh, you done hurt the man's feelings."

"Man, fuck him *and* his feelings, to be honest with you." Lou puts his money back inside his wallet. "He had this shit coming—y'all know that! If he's gonna manage people, then he needs to adjust his way of thinking, but later for his stupid ass." He holds his beer in the air. "For a good game that we should've won. DEMOODAY!"

"YADOOMED!"

"Yo, where did James get that damn name from?"

"I've been trying to tell y'all!" Roy laughs.

Lou glances over at Marc, who's leaning back with his eyes closed and mouth hanging at the end of the bench.

The old-timer appears exhausted.

"Yo, Marc! You a'ight over there?"

The old-timer doesn't say anything.

"Yo, Marc–"

"I'm good, I'm good," the old-timer finally replies, cracking his eyes open. "Still just catching my breath from all that running."

Lou squints his eyes at Marc.

For some reason, he doesn't sound good.

"You sure you–?"

"Yes, Lou…" Marc smiles, wearily. "But I could go for a water bottle, right now."

"We'll get it for you, just hang tight. YO, CADINA! ANY MORE OF THOSE ENCHILADAS LEFT?" He turns back to the team. "Those joints were the truth! She needs to teach Marisol how to make them bad boys."

Everyone laughs as they stroll over to the picnic area.

Davenport, along with Tucker, marches toward his office carrying a briefcase in hand, and a ton of thoughts rambling through his mind. He pulls out a handkerchief from his shirt pocket to wipe the sweat from his shaven head and face. He doesn't know if his perspiration is due to the morning humidity or the fact that he's thinking too hard. He assumes both.

Digging into his pants pocket for his office key, he suddenly pauses. On the other side of the door, he hears the copier machine running and becomes confused because no one has received authorization to be in his office. Disturbed, he pushes the door open and finds Lexington standing patiently in front of the copier, with his arms folded, waiting for the print job to complete.

"Good morning, Mr. Davenport, Mrs. Tucker."

"I thought I locked this door yesterday." Davenport glares at Lexington as if he has broken into his house.

"I, uh, noticed it was unlocked, so I came in to make copies."

"What's wrong with the copier upstairs?"

"Broke, remember?"

Davenport bristles as he sits behind his desk.

Tucker powers the computer and then smiles at Lexington. "How did the game go yesterday?"

"We lost. But I had a couple of hits and scored two runs—"

"Did you give Marc the letter I gave you?" Davenport asks.

"Lexington turns to his manager. He calmly replies, "I did, and he wants his shop-steward present before he signs anything."

Davenport leans back in his chair. "I figured he would."

"Do you mind if *I* ask you something, Sir?"

Davenport lowers his eyes at Lexington. "What is it?"

The front door burst open.

Marc bum-rushes inside and slams the letter down on the desk, right in front of Davenport. "The next time you want to hand me a write-up, I'd prefer it come straight from the source instead of your flunky over there!"

Davenport stands. "If you give me a minute to explain to you why I did what I felt—"

"*This* is self-explanatory, Michael, what are you talking about?" Marc plants his finger on the letter. "And what makes it even worse is that you failed to give me a verbal warning before handing me this crap!"

"Oh, let me correct you right there, Marc…I'd given you several verbal warnings about this common occurrence of yours, and no matter how many times, *you* chose to ignore me, but I can't ignore it any longer!"

"I was sick, for crying out loud! What did you want me to do? Come in, barf on the floor, and leave?"

"How long did you think I was going to tolerate your shoddy attendance, Marc? You're fine one week, but then you're out the next! You signed up to work overtime this past holiday but failed to show up! If you put your name on the overtime list, I expect you to come in and work, just like the rest of your coworkers; it's as simple as that."

Marc shakes his head at Davenport in disappointment. "This is coming from a man that has *personally* asked me to assist other carriers so they could be back before nightfall because he knew I didn't mind working through my lunch breaks–"

"I don't want to waste this morning going tit for tat with you, Marc…" Davenport swipes the form and reaches it out to Marc. "Either sign this now or take it to your shop steward to have it grieved–those are your options."

Marc snatches the form, scribbles his name, and then flings the pen, causing it to ricochet across the desk. "Do me a favor and scratch my name from the overtime list immediately."

The disgruntled veteran darts his eyes at a stunned Tucker, and then at an unfazed Lexington before saving his best glare for Davenport.

"You may have grown in ranks, Michael, but you damn sure haven't grown in character, I can assure you that!" Marc bolts out of the office and slams the door behind him.

Davenport collapses in his chair and loosens his tie. "Uh, Denise, could you omit Marc from the overtime—?"

"Already on it," Tucker confirms, clicking away on the computer.

"Mr. Davenport?"

He turns Lexington's way. "What?"

"I know this may be bad timing, but have you heard anything regarding the scheduled date of the next class?"

Davenport rubs his chin, sizing up the young man's concern. He peeks at Tucker. She swivels her chair around, in eager anticipation of an answer, as well. The morning hasn't been kind to him, at all.

"Let me, uh, make a phone call uptown and I'll get back with you later today," Davenport replies, with a strained smile.

"Wow," Lexington half-chuckles. "You usually stay on top of things of this nature. Especially since it's already been five months."

That statement rubs Davenport the wrong way.

"You think your situation is the only item on my to-do list, Lexington? I have customers calling my station complaining about their mail being tampered with–a serious matter, I might add. This morning, I couldn't get out of my car before two carriers approached me with issues with their clothing allowance. And now I must call a repairman about the upstairs copier machine. You're still my top priority, so don't you ever question it, understood?"

Lexington's stare oozes with skepticism, making Davenport extremely uncomfortable.

"You have a problem with what I just said, son?"

"No, Sir." Lexington grabs his copies and heads for the door. "I'm just ready to move on, that's all." He quietly leaves the office.

Tucker scurries toward the front door. She peeks out in the hallway before closing the door shut. She turns to Davenport, suppressing her frustration. "Michael…please tell me you're not trying to hold him back again? His class starts next month, and he needs to start preparing himself for it–"

"Lexington's lack of social skills is preventing him from being an effective leader, Denise." He leans forward on his desk. "That's why I intend to remove him from the academy altogether in order to mentor him properly–and on my timetable."

"Do you even hear yourself? You don't have the authority to make such a move–"

"I can make anything happen, Denise, you know that. And I don't want that man going anywhere bringing embarrassment to my good name because of his clueless disposition."

"You get off on humiliating him in front of his peers, don't you? That's what this is all about–"

"He will remain *here*, Denise, and receive the proper training."

"Not on my watch, he won't." She gathers a couple of folders before squaring off into his eyes. "He will make it to the next class. It's just a matter of who he's going to hear it from–you or Equal Employment Opportunity. Your power-tripping days are over."

She leaves the office.

All alone, Davenport is bound by lurid silence and his own bitterness.

Marc.

Lexington.

Now, Denise.

Three swings, three misses.

There's certainly no rest for the weary.

He picks up the phone and calls his friend uptown notifying him to scratch Lexington's name from the list until further notice. While waiting, he wonders if he should deal with Denise's threat immediately. He'll let it go for the time being. Too close to retirement to allow any more of his prestigious numbers slip away, even if it means riding Lexington's back for the time being.

No one answers, so he leaves a message. He sits back and listens to the quietness enclosing around him. It tells him to forget everything and everybody.

This is *his* world.

And he intends to go out with a bang.

The pain is unbearable.

As he pushes his mailcart down the sidewalk, old-timer Marc Speid is finding this feat to be an excruciating stop-and-go session. Each time the pain shoots up in his chest and around his heart, the veteran carrier whips out one of his many water bottles and sucks it dry. He tries to appear calm to avoid drawing attention from pedestrians, unaware of his failing condition. The humidity doesn't help much, either, as it continues to wear him down with its brick-oven heat.

But he doesn't let up.

One more building to go.

Too much showing off at the softball game, he figures. Trying to add more speed to his pitches. Trying to stretch singles into doubles, doubles into triples, almost giving himself a triple bypass in the process.

As the latest attack subsides, Marc takes a couple of heavy breaths before arriving at his final building of the day. He digs inside of the cart, pulls out a bundle of mail, and labors up the steps into the quiet brownstone building hallway. He places the magazines and small parcels on the table and then opens the mailbox panel. While delivering the letters, he reflects on the feud he had with his long-time friend/manager earlier that morning.

Bad move.

He understands Davenport's position and he knows he hasn't been as reliable as he used to be of late. But the mere thought of receiving a write-up, the first one he's received in his entire career, not only blemishes his impeccable record but also tarnishes the friendship he and Davenport once shared.

Frustrated, Marc slams the panel so hard that it causes another pain to rupture within his chest. Only this one cripples him straight to the floor. With his eyes tightly shut and teeth clenched, he balls up in a fetal position in front of the staircase, hoping the pain will go away as quickly as it came.

It doesn't.

What takes place next is a series of internal explosions within his chest cavity, which leads to him frantically reaching in his shirt pocket for pills he seldom uses. *Shit!* He left them back at the station.

Panic starts to sink in as the profound attacks disperse throughout his body, causing spastic convulsions. His glasses fall as he struggles to stand up, but he crashes back down to the floor, knocking over the table stand with the parcels and magazines. Gasping for air like a person who's about to drown, he now realizes how it feels to have the Grim Reaper bang on your front door, ready to snatch your soul away from the living.

If he ever needed his pills, this was the time to have them. He grabs for his phone to call the station. Even though he's suffering the worst attack he's ever experienced, he still feels that if he can somehow weather this vicious storm and get his medication, everything will be okay.

*God, help me…please!*

Another sharp pain rips through his bones, making him squeal, "*AAGHHH!*" He speed-dials the station and waits for what seems an eternity for someone to answer his emergency phone call.

# SIXTY-TWO

## LEXINGTON

Chewing on his pen cap, Lexington sits at the podium with his eyes fixated on James and Cadina rubber-stamping letters at James' workstation. The couple is also demonstrating a ton of affection toward one another, to the point where it's become rather annoying.

Normally, their lewd behavior would pull at his jealous chords.

But his mind lay elsewhere.

It travels back to that day at the park after their loss against the Boriquas.

He could give a damn about the game.

It was the verbal sparring he had with Lou which has his mind in a stupor. That loudmouth Puerto Rican had the audacity to insinuate Davenport is merely using him for his own personal experimentation.

That's not the manager he knows and is being mentored by.

Davenport is a standup guy, a man of integrity–

*"You're not going anywhere, Playboy."* Lou had stated. *"You're stuck at Midway for the rest of your career or until Davenport is through using your non-supervising ass."*

Now, that's absurd.

He knows full well Davenport has his best interest at heart–

"*My cousin passed with an EIGHTY-SIX, PAPA! He's already supervising at his new station uptown! Now, look at you, Mr. Ninety-Eight. Got your hopes pinned on going to the academy yet refuses to accept the fact that your mentor is preventing you from moving on.*"

*"You're stuck at Midway."*

*"Your mentor doesn't want you to leave."*

*"Your ass is being pimped, Playboy!"*

"No!"

Lexington's sudden outburst sparks James and Cadina to look up at him, surprised. He shoots them the evil eye.

*The fuck y'all looking at–*

The phone rings.

Lexington snatches the handset from its base. "Midway Station, Supervisor VanGuard speaking, May I help you?...Chapman went home for the day, Marc...You need help? For what? You should've been finished, it's going on four o'clock…No, no, no, you listen to me, I don't have anyone to help you, but this is what I'm going to do. I'm giving you an hour to finish up and be back here to clock out…Yes, I do understand, Marc...Look, I must take another call, so please hurry back before we both get in trouble." Lexington presses line two to receive the other call. "Midway Station, Supervisor VanGuard speaking, may I help you? Hello?"

Lexington places the phone on the base. He pulls out his wallet from his back pocket and searches for singles to use in the upstairs vending machine–

*"I have a hundred right here, Papa, easy money…prove me wrong!"*

He quickly shuts his eyes. He won't allow Lou, of all people, to become the voice of reason inside his head.

*Davenport is a good man…he wouldn't stoop that low to block my advancement to the academy…*

*…would he?*

"OH MY GOD, OH MY GOD! DID YOU HEAR WHAT HAPPENED?"

Pandemonium at the other end of the floor interrupts his thoughts. He turns his attention towards the hysterical letter carrier running out of the stairwell yelling out something to the other coworkers.

"SOMETHING HAPPENED TO MARC!" the lady carrier shouts at the top of her lungs. "THE AMBULANCE IS ON ITS WAY TO MARC'S ROUTE!" She diverts her attention to James and Cadina. "DID YOU HEAR ABOUT MARC?"

They look at each other with startling bewilderment.

"WHAT HAPPENED?" James yells back.

"SOMEBODY CALLED FROM ONE OF MARC'S BUILDINGS AND SAID HE WAS HAVING A HEART ATTACK!"

"Oh my God!" cries Cadina, covering her mouth. She stares at James and asks, "B-But wasn't Lex just talking to him like five minutes ago?"

Lexington stares at Cadina.

His own heart begins beating loudly.

Tucker rushes from the stairwell and heads straight to Marc's workstation. She frantically searches through his desk until she spots his medication and snatches them from the drawer.

The assistant manager swings around and shouts, "Marc called here about five minutes ago. Who spoke to him?"

James and Cadina turn to Lexington.

"Well, what did he say to you?" Tucker demands as she backpedals out of the section.

"I-I can't remember," Lexington stutters. "He mumbled something, then hung up on me—"

"Why are you lying?" shouts James. "Y'all were having a conversation, and you told him you had another call and you hung up on *him*!"

"How are you going to tell me what I said to the man?"

"Because you were talking loud enough for us to hear you—that's how!" Cadina retorts.

"You need to mind your damn business!"

"Not if you're going to lie about somebody's health! Are you crazy?"

"HEY!" Tucker yells, pointing at James and Cadina. "You two, clock out and ride with me to the hospital." She takes off toward the exit.

James and Cadina snatch their discs from the rack and race to the time clock to swipe out. When they return their discs, James eyeballs him.

"You ain't shit, you know that? You're going to sit up here and lie about a *telephone* conversation?"

"We don't have time for that, Boo; we gotta go before she leaves!"

Cadina pulls James' arm and they both rush toward the stairwell.

Lexington continues to stand in his spot and stare down the work floor–

Speechless.

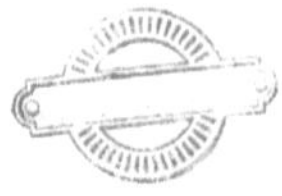 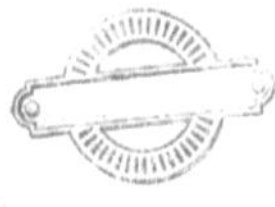 

SIX O'CLOCK IN THE EVENING AND THE NUMBNESS THAT EMPOWERED Lexington's body two hours ago still has him glued to his podium seat. He's the only person left on the work floor. Left to muddle in his own stench of uncertainty. He replays the phone conversation over and over in his head, in a frail attempt to find a glitch that could work in his favor.

> *Supervisor VanGuard speaking. May I help you?*
> *—Th-This Marc, where's Ch-Chapman?*
> *Chapman went home for the day, Marc, what's up?*
> *—I-I (cough) need help b-bad—*
> *Need help? For what? You should've been finished; it's going on four o'clock.*
> *—LISTEN TO ME, LEX! (cough)*
> *No, you listen to me; I don't have anyone here to help you so this is what I'm*
> *going to do. I'm giving you one more hour to finish up and be back here to*

*clock out.*
*— (Wheezing, coughing up spit) Y-You don't understand, m-my pills—*
*I do understand, Marc. Look, I must take another call, so please hurry back*
*before we both get in trouble.*
*Click.*

The more it recycles in his brain, the more nauseating he feels.

*How did I fuck up like that?*

Rubbing his forehead, it doesn't take long for the answers to come crashing down on him like construction debris. The eye-opening story Lou revealed to him about his cousin's immediate entry into the supervisor's academy with a score lower than his. The crude, evasive response he received from Davenport regarding *his* scheduled departure date. Two isolated occurrences tangled together to heighten his suspicions of everyone and everything surrounding him at Midway. Suspicions so high that he inadvertently botches up an emergency phone call.

"LEXINGTON! IF YOU'RE STILL IN THE BUILDING, REPORT TO MY OFFICE THIS INSTANT!"

The blistering command jolts him from the stool. Yet, numbness continues to rule his legs as he treads to the stairwell. When he reaches the first floor, he stares at the painted picture before him; letter carriers, clerks, supervisors, and custodians, all sitting around, grieving in their own world. They don't seem to notice him at all.

From the corner of his eye, he catches the sight of James escorting a weeping Cadina from the manager's office. His heart beats at a triple cadence.

Marc Euro Speid was pronounced dead at exactly 5:45 pm at Beth Israel Hospital, and to some extent, he feels his fate as a supervisor at Midway has expired, as well.

Davenport holds the door for him to enter his office.

Lexington avoids all eye contact as he takes a seat in front of the manager's desk. He has a lot of explaining to do about the final conversation he had with Midway's most beloved carrier.

# SIXTY-THREE

## JAMES

*"LET'S HAVE A MOMENT OF SILENCE FOR OUR FELLOW COWORKER AND FAMILY MEMBER, MARC SPEID," Tucker expresses over the intercom. "MAY HE ALWAYS BE REMEMBERED AS A PERSON WHO WAS EXTREMELY DEDICATED TO HIS PROFESSION, A WAR VETERAN WHO SERVED HIS COUNTRY, AND ONE WHO POSSESSED A HEART OF GOLD. MAY HE REST IN PEACE."*

The overcast weather reflects the somber mood spread throughout Midway Station. Employees, who were unaware of the news until that morning, whisper amongst themselves in total shock. Others bore the heavy burden of carrying the devastating news home with them the previous afternoon, only to bring the pain back to the station, as James does. After reading the R.I.P. banner enshrined over Marc's workstation—

*"After Thirty Years of Continuous Postal Delivery,*
*Marc Will Help God Deliver Many Blessings*
*In Holy Victory!*
*1956-2016*
*His Spirit Lives On Forever!"*

—James watches Cadina stand underneath the banner, with her head lowered. She has the honor of upholding his route now. He knows those are big shoes to fill, but he's quite sure she's up for the challenge. Out of respect for Marc, anyway.

He glances around to examine other coworkers' displays of grief. Senior carriers wipe the tears that mourn a man they've known forever. Divine murmurs a silent prayer to herself. Lou crosses himself Catholic style. James notices Freeman and Velour unknowingly standing in the same exact stance; arms folded and leaning back against their route-cases. He doesn't want to imagine the kind of thoughts rambling inside of their heads.

Finally, his eyes land on Lexington.

He stands by his workstation, fully dressed in a carrier uniform about as raggedy as his persona. And Lex has the nerve to be eyeballing *him* like he's responsible for his demotion back to the letter carrier position.

*Fuck you.*

James is not trying to hear any of that. He can give a rat's ass about whether Lexington saw him and Cadina walking out of the manager's office. They told Davenport what they overheard, and it was all true. He returns the glare right back at the ex-supervisor: *Fuck....youuuuuuu.*

"THANK YOU," Tucker concludes. "YOU MAY TAKE YOUR BREAK NOW."

James strolls over to Cadina. She still has her eyes planted on the floor.

"You okay?" he asks.

Slowly, she faces him and takes a deep breath. "About two weeks ago, Freeman and I caught Marc having trouble breathing and he didn't want either of us to tell anyone about his condition. And I'm kicking myself now because I knew we should've said something to Davenport–"

"Hey…don't do that to yourself, alright? Marc was a great man, but unfortunately, he was stubborn as hell. You know how many people he told to mind their own business when it pertained to his health? Don't put this on your shoulders, okay?"

Tears develop in her eyes. She quickly wipes them. "I miss him, already."

"We all do." He rubs her arm in comfort. "I'ma go grab my earbuds from the locker room. I'll be back."

"Okay."

James jogs to the stairwell, takes the steps by threes up to the second floor, and speed-walks to his locker. He unlocks the door and grabs his earbuds from the top shelf. A photo taped to the inside locker door brings a smile to his face—him with Cadina, on the night they went clubbing with the crew.

Something causes his nose to suddenly twitch.

James sniffs the air and then frowns. He sniffs himself to make sure the foul odor is not coming from him. Finally, he glances around his locker door…

…and ducks just in the nick of time as the Crown Royal bottle whizzes past his head and crashes against another locker.

James screams out, "*WHAT THE—*"

He is met with a thunderous impact as Lexington pins him solid against his locker. James quickly takes advantage of the sluggish coworker by picking him up, body-slamming him onto the floor, and punishing Lexington's face.

Kicking and screaming out of control, Lexington catches James off-guard by kneeing him in the testicles, causing him to double over in pain. This gives Lexington ample opportunity to return some firepower of his own. Blocking half of the punches thrown at his head, James swings blindly and connects with Lexington's jaw a couple of times. Using his legs to thrust Lexington off him, James quickly wraps him in a chokehold.

Carriers spring out from every corner of the locker room to grab James and pry his arm from Lexington's neck, preventing the ex-supervisor from becoming the second carrier to be sent to the hospital in a span of two days.

Parking his Volvo inside the loading dock bay area, Davenport bolts out of his car and throws his briefcase strap callously over his shoulder. He grabs his and Tucker's coffee, and then storms into the station. As quickly as he moves across the first floor, his angry eyes rove around just as fast, causing employees to clear the path as he enters his office. He loops behind his desk, not even acknowledging the company that awaits his arrival. He hands Tucker her coffee and then leans back in his chair. He quietly analyzes both battle-scarred carriers, who sit on opposite sides of the room.

On his left, with shop steward Martinez hovering over him, is James, who huffs and puffs in his seat, ready to finish off a job undone.

On Davenport's right, with shop steward Willameena Jenkins by his side is Lexington, who, with a severely bruised face, appears abnormally calm.

Davenport leans his body forward on the desk and folds his hands together, as he directly eyeballs each carrier. "You do realize this doesn't look good for either one of you, right?"

James launches from his chair. "With all due respect, Sir, this asshole attacked me from behind while I was at my locker, so I had no choice but to defend myself!"

"Was there anyone else around to witness this altercation?" Davenport asks the shop stewards before turning his attention back to James. "Because as far as I can tell, you did some serious damage to Lexington's face–"

"What was I supposed to do? Just let the man hit me upside my head with a bottle as proof that he initiated the fight? That wasn't going to happen!"

Davenport turns to Lexington. "Do you have anything you want to share with us?"

Lexington sits back in his seat and stares at the manager.

Tucker leans on the desk. "He just asked you a question, Lexington–"

"I started the fight," Lexington confesses. "You happy now?"

The room falls silent at his admission.

"But you stated in your report that James instigated the confrontation," Jenkins says.

Lexington shrugs. "I lied. Sorry."

"BOOM! There's your confession!" James stands. "Now, can I go and do my job?"

Davenport nods for James to leave.

James bends down in front of Lexington's face. "Don't you ever in your life take my quietness for weakness again, you feel me?"

Lexington coolly replies, "Your momma."

"Don't think I won't beat your ass in front of these people in here–"

"Somebody get James out of here before I do suspend him!" Davenport roars.

"Be quiet, James, and let's go…" Martinez orders, pushing him out of the office and closing the door behind him.

Davenport, Tucker, and Jenkins rest their eyes on Lexington, who lounges in his seat as if unfazed by any of his recent actions.

Davenport circles around the desk and leans on its edge, right in front of him. He examines his facial wounds, from his swollen eye to his busted lip. But nothing curdles the manager's blood more than the smirk growing on his former protégé's face.

"I guess you haven't fully grasped the seriousness of your situation, son, because if you did, you would wipe that smile off your face as of right now."

Lexington increases his grin to a full-blown smile.

Davenport didn't expect any of this. He assumed Lexington would fall on his hands and knees, begging for mercy at this stage of the game. He doesn't know what Lexington's angle is, but he sure as hell is not going to allow him to upstage this discussion with his carefree antics.

"You know what you're doing, right?" Davenport stands, with his finger pointed down on his desk. "You're forcing me to make a crucial decision on your future with this company."

Lexington inspects his fingernails, completely ignoring him.

"Do you *not* understand the severity of this situation, son–"

"Ohhhh, you're talking about the fight, right?" Lexington nods. "Yeah, it's right up there with the excessive overtime caused by me, Marc's death caused by me, and the piss stains I left on the toilet seat earlier–"

"What's gotten into you? Are you looking to get fired? Is that why you're putting on this pitiful act?"

"Tell me something, Michael; why the hell are you so concerned?"

"Lexington!" yells both Tucker and Jenkins.

Davenport leans in closer to Lexington. "Who do you think you're talking to like that, son?"

"I'm talking to *you*, Michael!" Lexington seethes. "And for the record, I'm not your damn son–"

"I think you better lower your voice before I lower it for you, young man–"

"Michael, stop it!" Tucker jumps in. "Lexington, I don't know what's gotten into you, but you owe this man an apology. You're completely out of order!"

Lexington laughs sarcastically. "Out of order? Riiiiight! BAM!!!"

He slams a miniature cassette recorder on the manager's desk and presses the PLAY button. "Let's go to the audiotape, shall we? "Let me know if these voices sound familiar to you."

The conversation streaming out of the tiny recorder blows a hole right through Davenport's Kevlar ego:

> *"Michael…please tell me you're not trying to hold him back again? His class starts next month, and he needs to start preparing himself for it–"*
> *"Lexington's lack of social skills is preventing him from being an effective leader, Denise. That's why I intend to remove him from the academy altogether so I can mentor him properly, and on my timetable–"*
> *"Do you even hear yourself? You don't have the authority to make such a move–"*
> *"I can make anything happen, Denise, you know that. And I don't want that man going anywhere bringing embarrassment to my good name because of his clueless disposition."*
> *"You get off on humiliating him in front of his peers, don't you? That's what this is all about–"*
> *"He will remain here, Denise, and that's all there is to it."*

Lexington presses the stop button. He taunts his incensed manager. "Now, do you want to hear the part where Marc insulted your character, or have you heard enough already–"

"You want to mock me, boy?" Davenport reaches out to grab a handful of Lexington. "You want to play those types of games with me—"

"Michael, stop it now!" Tucker and Jenkins strain to hold him back.

"Is this true, Michael?" Jenkins asks.

"They both know it's true and the truth hurts, right?" shouts Lexington. "I can call you Michael now, right? You said I had to be on your fucked up level to call you by your first name, so there it is!"

"You disappoint me, you know that right?" Davenport wrestles to get Tucker out of his way. "After all the time and energy spent helping you become a better supervisor, a better man! You weren't anything until I put you under my wing–"

"UNDER YOUR WING? I SUFFERED UNDER YOUR WING, WHAT THE HELL ARE YOU TALKING ABOUT?" Lexington stands to his feet. "I WORSHIPED YOU, MICHAEL! I BASICALLY PATTERNED MY WHOLE LIFE AFTER YOURS! BUT YOU TURNED ME INTO THE LAUGHINGSTOCK OF THIS WHOLE STATION! AND YOU CALL YOURSELF HELPING ME? THE HELL WITH YOU!"

"OKAY, LEXINGTON, THAT'S IT!" Tucker shouts back. "YOU'VE SAID ENOUGH AS IT IS, ALREADY!"

"Don't you ever get tired of kissing his ass, Denise?"

Tucker catches herself before she responds to Lexington and instead, turns to the speechless union delegate. "Willameena, could you get Martinez and have him escort Lexington off the premises, please?"

Lexington ejects the tape from the recorder and tosses it on the manager's desk. "You can keep that tape, Michael, as a constant reminder of the kind of man you really are."

Davenport finally pushes Tucker off him and gets right in Lexington's face. "You think that tape holds any weight against me, boy?"

"When this goes to arbitration, you're going to wish I went on with my life, you selfish bastard—"

"GET THE HELL OUT OF MY STATION BEFORE I THROW YOU OUT MYSELF!"

Lexington backpedals toward the door. "If I were you, Michael, I'd check this whole office to see if I left any more of my gadgets lying around."

"You son-of-a-"

"Let's go, Lexington," orders Jenkins.

Lexington shares a disturbing grin with everyone before marching out of the office.

Jenkins glares at Davenport. "I'll be back to get to the bottom of this, Michael." She leaves, closing the door behind her.

"He's got some damn nerve, threatening me in my own office?" He picks up the handset and begins dialing. "Coming in my house drunk! And almost causing bodily harm to another employee! Let's see how smart his mouth gets when I terminate his behind altogether–"

"No, you're not." Tucker snatches the phone away from his hand. "You've done enough already."

He tries to grab the phone, but Tucker denies him.

"Hand me the phone, Denise."

"Everything that just happened in this office is because of your misdoings, Michael." Tucker slams the handset down on the base. "All of it! I sat back and allowed you to have your way, now I have no choice but to clean up your mess."

"You're doing no such thing–!"

"Or do you want me to start making calls of my own? Which is it, Michael?"

She doesn't bat an eye.

His anger wants to lash out at her, but his common sense puts a halt to that.

Deniece is too strong of an individual to be intimidated by his presence, so he circles around his desk and falls back into his chair.

"*Thank* you. Now, if you'd excuse me, I'm going to have a talk with Lexington." She walks to the door and then turns around. "I don't know where it all went wrong, Michael, but you used to be better than this."

She allows that statement to resonate before leaving the office.

Davenport wipes the beads of sweat from his face. He never envisioned his scheme collapsing the way it did. And Lexington has him pinned against the ropes with a recording of his conversation.

A recording that has enough incriminating info to tarnish his brilliant legacy as a manager.

Time to make some serious phone calls.

But before he does, he rises from his seat, pushes the small, yet convicting tape to the floor, and crushes it with one stomp of his foot.

*Crash!*

The darkest day of his life draws to a merciful end as he sits inside his apartment in Flatbush, Brooklyn. With a freezer bag of ice pressed against his face, he drags himself into the kitchen to retrieve the broom and the dustpan. He returns to the living room to sweep up the broken glass resulting from him smashing a picture of his deceitful ex-manager grinning, onto the hardwood floor.

After disposing the glass in the garbage can, he grabs his ice pack, walks back into the room, and sits behind his computer. He picks up a typed letter, addressed to the Postmaster herself. He reads it for the hundredth time, and then he tosses it to the side for the hundredth time.

*I had his ass!*

He had Davenport right in the palm of his hand. Yet, that same hand defeated his own purpose by flinging a Royal Crown bottle at James' head. No matter how much resentment he harbored for his coworker, he still couldn't justify his actions in that locker room. It was totally uncalled for; and to walk up in there drunk as a skunk, too?

*Damn.*

He could've simply given the tape to the shop steward, nailed the cocksure manager, and been well on his way to the academy.

But he ends up going postal for no reason at all.

His only glimmer of hope lies in the fact that it's inevitably the Postmaster's decision. If she could just find it in her heart to understand why he pulled such an insane act, then he might have a chance to continue working in the postal system. It sucks, but it would be a start at amending his wrongdoings.

After cracking his knuckles, he begins tapping away on the keyboard. Despite having a horrendous day, something else has been troubling him and now he feels compelled to investigate, using his trusty computer.

That something was located on Velour's workstation ledge.

As he types away, he stumbles across an immediate roadblock to something that would ordinarily be so simple to open.

Odd.

*But why?*

Lexington straightens up and decides to put his exceptional hacking skills to work using every illegal back door entry available to access the necessary files he needs. Whatever they are.

After forty minutes of vigorous probing, he arrives at an unusual port the entity's network left open. He enters the connection and continues with his mission until he inadvertently discovers a strange-looking file that begins to unveil in front of him.

*What the—?*

His mouth crashes to the floor harder than Davenport's picture.

Pushing himself from the computer, he stands up and begins pacing the floor. But his scattering thoughts outpace him. He struggles to put two and two together, but it finally dawns on him.

A devilish grin has never felt so rewarding on his swollen face.

He quickly downloads the information before someone on the other end has time to realize what's occurring and closes the file on him. He then turns on his laser printer.

He doesn't know whether his chest is swelling with long-forgotten confidence or newfound retribution. Either way, he feels elated.

As the printer works its magic, he stares out the window at the dark skies. A falling star disappears behind a community of faraway project buildings.

An ominous sign of a person who is about to have their entire world exposed.

He kicks his feet up on the desk and hums along to the sound of his speedy laser printer.

The squealing brakes from the 5-train snap his head back into the upright position. He rubs his eyes, then reads the outside sign–Gun Hill Road Station.

The conductor opens the doors, and the morning crowd trickles in, filling vacant seats throughout the air-conditioned car.

Freeman purposely props his leg up on the seat next to him, making sure no one gets any ideas.

"WATCH THE CLOSING DOORS!"

The train pulls out of the station.

The subway advertisements embracing the walls hold his attention, if only for the moment. His thoughts casually segue to the continuous drama which has plagued Midway Station as of late. When he heard about the locker room altercation involving James and Lexington, it didn't shock him as much as hearing about Lex cursing out Davenport afterward.

And Freeman thought *he* had problems.

The elevated train rumbles into its next stop and a handful of commuters board the ice-cold car.

"WATCH THE CLOSING–"

*"YO, HOLD UP!"*

That voice.

Sounds starkly familiar.

Freeman lifts his head and peers through the window.

Dante races up the steps and squeezes his stocky frame through the closing doors. He then locates a corner seat on the opposite end of the car. With headphones strapped over his ears, the parcel post driver nods his head while thumbing his cellphone, tuning out the rest of the transit world.

*Oh, no you don't.*

Freeman pops out of his seat, grabs his backpack, and maneuvers his way over to sit next to Velour's ex-partner.

Dante nonchalantly glances to his left and a smile fills his fat cheeks. He snatches off his headphones and sticks out his hand. "What's up, Playboy?"

Freeman ignores his hand, completely. "I don't normally see you on this train. You live out here?"

Dante eases up on the bloated grin. He half chuckles. "Yeah, uh, my in-laws stay on Boston Road. But yo! What in the world is going on over at your station? All I keep hearing about is Lex got into a fight with James and then he cursed out Davenport—"

"Are you messing with people's credit cards and having them thinking I'm doing it?"

Dante's gossipy enthusiasm deflates like air escaping a balloon. His fat face shifts to his phone and stays there.

Freeman glances around his immediate area, primed to back Dante up against a wall if need be. "Dude, I know you hear me–"

"It was all Velour's idea."

Freeman squints, trying to comprehend what just came out of Dante's mouth. "What do you mean it was all Velour's idea? *What* was Velour's idea?"

The train bullets full speed into the underground tunnel.

The uneasiness spewing from Dante heightens his anticipation.

"Look, Freeman; what I'm about to share with you does not need to have my name attached to it, alright?"

"BRUH!" Freeman shifts his eyes around the car before lowering his tone. "If my ass gets into any more trouble behind this, you're my cosigner–bottom line!"

Dante takes a deep breath. "Velour is the one messing around with other people's mail."

The train arrives at its next stop.

More passengers load the car.

But Freeman is oblivious to them.

He maintains his confused look on Dante. "What did you just say–"

"Velour has been tampering with customers' mail for a hot minute and not just on your route, either."

That declaration was a bucket of cold water thrown in Freeman's face and his entire world is now drenched in a realm of incomprehension.

"Freeman?"

He turns and glares at Dante. "All the shit I've been going through is because of *her*?"

"I'm quite sure you've met her brother by now…Vincent?"

The mere mention of that bastard's name curdles his blood. "Yeah, I met him. But why are you bringing him up?"

"I don't know what she told you about him, but he's involved in a slew of illegal activities–bootlegging, grand auto theft, but his main cash cow has been credit card fraud."

"Jesus Christ." Freeman rubs his face while staring at the floor. "What…why…how–"

"Vincent has Velour doing all kinds of shit, but she feels she's not being compensated fairly, so she started making plans on branching out and forming her own group, again, relying on other people's credit information."

Freeman soaks in the alarming information like a dirty sponge. Her precious Porsche. Her minks. Countless jewelry. The expensive clothes she bought for him on numerous occasions…and he thought it was because of all the overtime she was doing.

"You set me up." Freeman faces Dante. "You knew about all this and yet, you convinced me to bid on that damn assignment."

Dante leans his head back on the wall. He side-glances Freeman. "My bad, dawg."

"So, you were in on it, too."

"Not at all."

"Bullshit. That's *way* too much information for her to be sharing with somebody who's not directly involved with her–"

The answer slams against his head like a swinging wrecking ball.

He reads into Dante's shamefaced expression.

It all makes sense now.

"You were sleeping with Velour, weren't you?"

Dante doesn't bother to look his way. He just stares into space.

Freeman grits his teeth. "Ain't this a bitch…"

Dante whispers, "Do you know what kind of person she is?"

"I do, now! No thanks to your lying ass!"

"You wanted to hear the whole story, right? So let me finish it." Dante peeks around as if someone may be watching him. "She's the type of person that doesn't take the word *no* too kindly."

Freeman doesn't say anything, only listens.

"One morning, she confided everything to me that I just told you. That's when she asked if I wanted to be down with her nonsense. It shocked the hell out of me that she was bold enough to even share this. So, of course, I told her no and I advised her not to go through with it. That was the last time she ever bought up the subject."

"And you didn't think to tell anybody about this?"

"No, because I never caught her in the act. Plus, at the time, we never received calls from customers complaining about their mail. So, in my mind, I'm thinking everything was cool–but later, I realized how I underestimated her motives."

Freeman visualizes Dante taking Velour to the St. Marks Hotel to bang her brains out but quickly disposes of the image.

"The week following that conversation, she handed me a DVD." Dante's voice becomes increasingly shaky. "She told me it was a gift that my wife would really get a kick out of. *'A great family movie!'*, she said. And like a dumbass, I took that DVD to my house."

Freeman hangs onto his every word, knowing exactly where this is heading.

"Free, I took that DVD home, popped it in my entertainment system, and played it to make sure it was good quality..." Dante pauses as if conjuring that memory serves as an ongoing punishment for his unfaithfulness. "And there I was, standing in my own living room, watching myself have relations with Velour at every hotel we'd meet up at."

Freeman feels sick to his stomach. "Where was your family?"

"At Pathmark, thank God. I approached Velour the next day about the DVD, and I swear to you, she just laughed in my face! Told me she had more copies just in case I ran my mouth about her *business*. That's when I started to believe how corrupt she really was and I knew it was time for me to leave Midway for good."

"But yet, you had no problem recruiting me to take your place."

"And I apologize for that, but I had no other choice–"

"I don't need your apologies, bruh! I need for you to come back to the station and tell Davenport everything you just got finished telling me–"

"Can't do that–"

"Oh, I think you can. I didn't ask for any of this shit, man! You *put* me in this position–"

"And that bitch has me on *videotape,* Free!" Dante's whispering tone begs for mercy. "You don't know how it feels to go home every day, shittin' bricks thinking my wife checked the mailbox and found a package mailed specifically to her from that damn lunatic! That's what I have to deal with, Freeman—every single day!"

"That sounds like a personal problem to me," Freeman replies, with no remorse. "Either you do the right thing or I'ma do the right thing *for* you. Feel me?"

The train barrels into 59th Street.

Dante snatches his bag from the floor and stands. He peers down at Freeman. "Look, do what you have to do, alright, but I'm going to do whatever it takes to protect my family."

"Oh, so *now* it's all about family, huh? How considerate."

A mixture of anger and guilt outlines Dante's expression. He throws his bag over his shoulder, straps his headphones over his ears, and disappears through the boarding crowd.

Either the conductor turned off the air-conditioner or Freeman has succumbed to his own volcanic temper which is ready to erupt at any second. With two more stops until he arrives at his destination, he struggles mightily to harbor his anger until he reaches Midway.

And God forbid anyone who steps in his way.

# SIXTY-SEVEN

## VELOUR

The reflection from the ladies' bathroom mirror tells Velour something is missing from her face. She then sighs before digging into her make-up kit.

She pulls out a tube of lipstick.

Metallic Blue–to coordinate with her postal uniform and her bleak mood.

While coloring her lips, she grimaces at the thought of Vincent reprimanding her for trying to color outside his uber-strict guidelines. And sending his goons out to follow her to make sure she doesn't step out of line is total bullshit and a waste of his time and manpower.

She never was a caged bird and doesn't plan on becoming one now.

She puckers her blue lips slightly to make sure the color is even.

Perfect.

She places the lipstick back in her make-up kit and examines her overall appearance.

*I still got it going on.*

Loud conversations from the ladies' locker room pour into the bathroom.

Discussions about the James and Lexington altercation.

Velour grins.

She sees this as the perfect opportunity to persuade Freeman to put his bid in for Lexington's vacant assignment. She is tired of his goody two-shoe ass. Plus, he was never a good fit for her insidious program, just as Dante never was.

Her phone rings.

It's Ahmed.

She smiles.

Somewhat dispiritedly.

She grabs the phone and answers. "What's up?"

"You tell me," Ahmed responds. "I'm standing outside on your balcony, soaking in this breathtaking view without your company. Everything okay?"

Velour stares into the mirror, picturing the pristine condo at the Riviera Towers located in West New York, New Jersey. A fantastic one-bedroom residence equipped with high-end stainless steel amenities, a two-sided white marble fireplace, and a spectacular balcony boasting a staggering panoramic view of the Hudson River and the Manhattan skyline. As soon as she stepped inside of the condo's expansive living room bathed in glorious sunlight, she was sold. Now that reality seems to be fading away from her.

"I don't think I'll be moving anytime soon."

"Oh? And why not?"

"I can't afford it. Even with your discounted offer, it'll still be a stretch for me, so…"

"Is this decision based on your brother shutting down your operation in front of my store the other weekend?"

"Possibly."

"Velour…you don't strike me as a person who throws in the towel so quickly."

"There's a lot going on with my brother's business you don't know about, and yes, it has put me in a financial bind."

She could hear Ahmed thinking on the other end.

"Say no more. I want you to come work with me."

She stares at herself in the mirror before responding, "Run that by me again?"

"If I recall, you mentioned to me that you have a certain *knack* for repairing people's credit accounts."

Velour glances around the empty bathroom. She quickly moves into an open stall and closes the door, for this conversation has now taken an interesting turn.

In a low but clear tone, she asks, "What are you proposing?"

"Your skill set would prove valuable to a particular company I'm in the process of setting up. It'll be part-time, of course, but I can easily match what you're currently earning at the post office. And I guarantee, within three to six months, you won't need to remain at the post office, or work anywhere else, for that matter."

An orgasm was almost created by this unexpected offer.

She bites down hard on her hand to contain her excitement before regaining composure. "Wow. I definitely didn't see this coming. Thank you for the opportunity, first and foremost, but we need to talk more in-depth about this proposition in person."

"Tomorrow evening, at your new condo. And I'm not taking no for an answer, either."

Velour quickly weighs her options.

Tanya's roach-infested dump or the condo with a doorman and swimming pool access.

*Fuck it…you only live once.*

"I'll see you then. Smooches."

She presses the END button and does a silent celebration in the bathroom stall.

*There IS light at the end of the tunnel!*

Velour gathers her bubbling emotions before walking out of the stall…

…and almost jumps when she sees Tucker checking her appearance in the mirror.

"Oh my God, you scared me, Mrs. Tucker." Velour holds her chest in a dramatic fashion. "I didn't hear you come in."

"I didn't mean to startle you, Miss Patterns."

Velour doesn't exactly hear any sincerity in the manager's words.

And she can't recall Tucker ever using the upstairs ladies' bathroom.

Velour fakes a smile as she washes her hands. "I've been meaning to talk to you, Ma'am. It's about Freeman."

Tucker pulls away from the mirror. "I'm not busy now. Let's take this to my office where we can talk in private."

"Okay."

Something is not right.

Velour can't put her finger on it, but the vibes she's receiving from Tucker are off.

Way off.

But it doesn't matter.

Six months from now she can kiss the entire postal system goodbye.

She follows Tucker out of the bathroom and down the stairwell.

"Now, I want to make it clear that this doesn't have anything to do with Freeman's work ethic, but we recently had a huge falling out and he's been sort of combative with me ever since."

Tucker turns to Velour, surprised. "Combative? *Freeman*?"

"You never know about a person until you start working with them. Anyway, I figured if you could somehow persuade him to bid for Lexington's route since it's open, we could at least maintain a cordial relationship."

"Now, I can't make him do anything, that's entirely up to Freeman–"

"I know, but he listens to you. Maybe you can make him see the benefits of operating a one-man route."

"I see you've put some thought into this."

"I just don't want the tension to keep building and spill over into our work performance."

They arrive at the office and stand in front of the door.

Tucker smiles at Velour. "Tell you what. Let's run this by Davenport, maybe we can speed up the process of moving Freeman to another route. Fair enough?"

The day just keeps getting better for Velour.

She didn't think throwing Freeman under the bus would be this easy.

"I appreciate it."

Tucker turns the knob and pushes the door open. "After you."

Before Velour can step one foot inside the office, she senses something terribly wrong.

Slouching in his chair behind the desk is Davenport. He has that sedated look as if someone has shot him with an elephant tranquilizer gun.

He doesn't bother to look her way.

Because his gaze is aimed at the four individuals sitting across from him.

Three distinguished-looking men and one woman.

Dressed in bold, dark suits.

Suits with badges.

They drop their idle chatter and stand to their feet. The sight of these individuals with interrogating eyes and broad-shouldered authority does not mesh with her vibe.

"Velour Patterns?"

She shifts her eyes toward the gentleman who spoke her name—the eldest-looking individual of the group. "Uh, yes. Can I help you?"

The tall elder, with streaks of gray dominating his low haircut, slowly approaches Velour.

"I am William Harris, Postal Inspector-in-Charge of the New York Metro Division. That's my assistant over there, Inspector Moses."

She peeks at his huge partner. He doesn't utter a word. His intense expression says it all.

The elder points at the remaining two personnel. "That's Detective Strait and Special Agent Whitaker and we came to see you, Miss Patterns. Do I need to explain the urgency of our visitation?"

She cannot move.

Her first impulse is to spin around and run for dear life.

But Tucker squashes those thoughts by pushing her clear across the office threshold.

"Grab a seat, young lady," the assistant manager orders, through tight lips.

Nearly collapsing into the nearest chair, Velour asks, "Sh-Should I have my shop steward present with me?"

"One is on the way, my dear," Inspector Harris assures. "…but it's not going to help you any. This matter goes *way* beyond the postal jurisdiction. You see, you disrupted quite a few lives during your time here, Miss Patterns–but it ends today." He motions to his partner. "Larry, if you will, please..."

Moses reaches into his briefcase and pulls out a videotape. He slides it into the nearby VCR and turns on the television.

Velour's heart rate quadruples.

She connects with Inspector Harris' eyes.

He studies her the way an eagle studies his prey right before the planned attack.

But she knows what this matter is about.

That's why she begins to cry, even before Moses can press the play button.

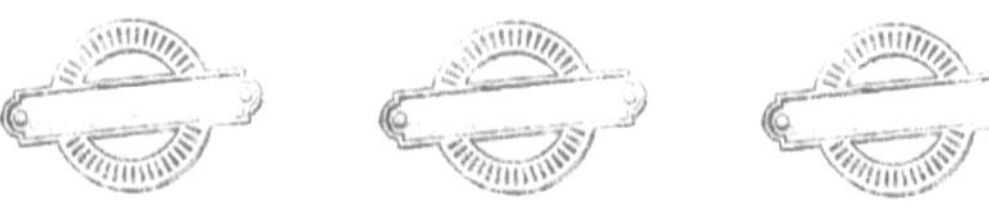

TEN MINUTES OF SHAME CAUGHT ON TAPE.

In a quiet office filled with high-ranking officials and speechless managers, Velour sits alone in her misery. Even shop steward Willameena has tears in her eyes. Velour ran out of tears minutes ago, so she sits motionless, the way Davenport sits as he pops a pill in his mouth. She would need an aspirin, too, if she was forced into having to watch one of her employees steal mail from different workstations. Ten minutes worth of non-stop flagrancy.

"In a ten-month span, we've received numerous complaints about tampered mail within this station's delivery radius," explains Inspector Moses, while turning off the television. "Over sixty percent of those complaints stemmed from your route, Miss Patterns, so we narrowed down our surveillance to your activities the past six months, as you can see for yourself."

Her bottom blue lip quivers.

Velour doesn't need to listen to any more of this but has no other choice.

"You were very selective with your victims' profiles, weren't you, Miss Patterns?" Inspector Harris crosses his legs. "The elderly, the mentally impaired, the widows dealing with their deceased husbands' credit accounts–all whom would have a difficult time recovering from the hole you put them in."

Inspector Moses leans into Velour's face so close that she can tell him exactly how his eggs were cooked earlier. "We acted on the notion that you had accomplices, like your ex-partner or your current partner, but our sources confirmed you were riding solo on this venture."

"Is there anything you would like to say before we go any further, Miss Patterns?" Inspector Harris asks.

Velour's voice crackles, "A-Are y'all going to f-fire me?"

"Jesus Christ," mutters Tucker.

"I'm afraid termination is the least of your worries, my dear," Inspector Harris continues. "As it stands now, you're facing thirty counts of identity theft, thirty counts of mail tampering, thirty counts of mail theft, thirty counts of mail fraud, thirty counts of destruction of mail–we're looking at a minimum of forty-five years on those charges alone."

"*Oh, my God…*" Velour buries her face in her hands.

"How long did you think this was going to last, young lady?" Inspector Harris' voice finally adds some weight. "Damaging people's credit reports, all for the sake of your personal gratification? Were you *that* oblivious to such a vile offense?"

New tears stream down her cheeks as she wipes her face with a handkerchief provided by the elder inspector. A half-hour ago, she was mentally furnishing her newly acquired upscale residence. Her reality now entails correction officers, prison uniforms, and a claustrophobic jail cell that bans you from the rest of the outside world. She can't even think straight. This was not in her cards of life.

She blows her nose into the handkerchief. "I can't go to jail, Sir, I-I just can't…"

"You should've thought about the consequences before committing these crimes, young lady. The only way your victims would ever feel vindicated is to see you behind bars."

*"But I can't go to jail, I just can't! I'll do anything...please..."*

Inspector Harris and Inspector Moses trade uncomfortable glances.

Inspector Harris then straightens up in his seat. His eyes home in on Velour's mascara-smeared face. "However, there is an alternative to your present dilemma, Miss Patterns."

Velour pops her head up. "What?"

"If you agree to our terms, you can avoid sentencing, altogether."

"Y-You're saying no jail time?"

"You will serve an eight-year probationary period. During that time, we will volunteer your services at nursing homes, rehab centers, as well as obligating your time at college campuses to discuss the repercussions of committing identity theft. This is how you will repay your debt to society. Does this interest you, Miss Patterns?"

Her eyes bounce from one official to the other.

This is too good to be true.

Her road to freedom consists of wiping old folks' asses and leading a *'Just Say No to Piracy!'* campaign to ignorant students.

There must be a catch.

She turns to Inspector Harris. "I-Is that all I have to do?"

"Not quite." The elder inspector turns his attention toward the detective. "Detective Strait, you have the floor."

Detective Charles Strait leans on Davenport's desk. His square jaw and rectangular glasses exude a certain confidence in his disposition. "Miss Patterns, I lead a special unit that cracks down on the pirating of counterfeit merchandise throughout this city. Now, when we examined the items you purchased from those credit accounts you hijacked, we noted that the majority of your purchases were items such as computers, high-tech camcorders, burners, a shrink-wrap machine, plastic jewel cases, firesticks, boxes of blank CDs, and DVDs. Now, would it be safe to say that you purchased these items to generate counterfeit CDs and DVDs for the sole purpose of profit, Miss Patterns?"

Velour doesn't bother to answer. She assumes they know but wonders where this line of questioning is leading to.

"I'll answer that for you," he continues. "You see, the inspectors and I are often involved in joint investigations when dealing with high-profile crimes that are somehow related. Now, our unit is in the process of busting one of the biggest crime syndicates this side of the continent."

A chill runs down her spine.

She doesn't like where this is going at all.

"Not only is this organization highly sophisticated, but they also have their hands in other illegal practices. Just yesterday, we raided four so-called custom shops, one in Queens, the other three in Jersey, and were able to confiscate dozens of boxes filled with credit card scanners and shimmer devices used for credit card hacking. But that wasn't all we discovered at these chop shops, which led me to reach out to my colleague, a Special Operations Supervisor from the Border Patrol Enforcement. Agent Whitaker…"

Supervisory Border Patrol Agent Helen Whitaker–tall, pretty, short blond haircut–strolls over with her hands folded behind her. She firmly peers down at Velour.

"When Detective Straits notified me of their recent findings, we had to take over the investigation from there," Agent Whitaker states, now with her arms folded. "Our organization deals with perpetrators smuggling goods in and out of this country and this crew has been able to pull off an insanely profitable racket by shipping stolen vehicles to their foreign customers. Now, the owner of one of the Jersey shops, Jimmy Littles, is being charged with car theft as well as warehousing counterfeit and stolen merchandise, but he's telling us he had no knowledge of the overseas transactions–but, for minimum jail time, he was more than willing to give us the names of those who *are* involved. We believe you know these people."

The chill down Velour's back becomes arctic-cold.

Detective Straits kneels in front of her, eagerly flipping through a small notepad.

He begins running off names with conviction.

"Kaution, a.k.a. Kevin Savage. Hyper, a.k.a. Harold Simmons. Wise, a.k.a. William Griffin, and the mastermind himself–Mr. Invincible, a.k.a. Vincent Patterns. You both vacated the mansion in New Rochelle not too long ago, knowing the dots were strongly connecting against you two." He pockets the notepad inside of his jacket. His blue eyes penetrate through her empty stare. "You want your get-out-of-jail card, Miss Patterns? Then I suggest you hand over your brother and his crew's current location on the very same platter we're delivering you your gift-wrapped probation package."

"And we will assure you...," Inspector Harris adds, "That everything you say to us will be placed under strict confidentiality. It won't go any further than this room."

The walls appear to be closing around her.

Making it impossible for her to even breathe.

These officials backed her in a corner with hardcore evidence and revelations.

And dangling a dangerous ultimatum in front of her face as her only source of light.

But she's not going to take the bait.

"I'm afraid I can't do that, Sir."

"Let me broaden the scope for you, young lady," Agent Whitaker counters, with her fists mounted on her hips. "If you fail to take advantage of this unique opportunity, not only will you be facing the initial charges, but by withholding viable information, you will also be indicted on possession of stolen property, carjacking, and racketeering, which ultimately means a life sentence–is that what you want?"

*Girl, you better start lying to these people.*

"When he sold the house, he didn't want anyone to know where he was moving just in case something like this occurred. He was always cautious, in that way."

Inspector Moses barks out a laugh. "You really expect us to believe your brother would leave his own sister out of the loop and let you take the heat like the rest of his street-level workers, Miss Patterns?"

Velour turns to the inspector. "Right now, I live in a nasty ass one-bedroom apartment with my cousin Tanya out in East New York, Brooklyn. Do you think I would downgrade myself to that kind of living, on my own terms? No. The plan was that everyone would go their own separate way so nobody would know where the other is staying."

Agent Whitaker pitifully smiles at Velour. "Personally, I find it rather odd that you had to work, considering the amount of money your brother and his crew have been raking in over the years… or was that by design?" Her smile morphs into a full-blown sneer. "Move you from South Carolina to the Big City, just to push a mail cart, no offense, while he and his running mates sit back and relish in the fruits of *your* labor? Because that's who you're protecting."

Velour eyeballs the sneering agent for that coldhearted comment.

Her voice shivers, "I'm telling you the God's honest truth; I don't know where he is staying."

"The bottom line here, Miss Patterns, is that your brother and his crew are now listed as fugitives," Inspector Harris reveals. "They'll eventually slip up because they're running out of options. But with your cooperation, you can make this a lot easier, not only for us but for yourself, as well. Bear in mind, this rather *unique* little package we're offering you is due out of mere sympathy from our inspectors–the first of its kind."

Inspector Harris motions to his colleagues to wrap up the visit. He stands up, digs into his inside jacket pocket, and pulls out a laminated card. He hands it to a confused Velour, who thought for sure they would've been slapping cuffs on her wrists by now.

"But the deal expires in forty-eight hours. We expect a call from you at nine o'clock Monday morning, sharp. If we don't hear from you, you will be listed as a fugitive, as well. It behooves you to make the right decision, Miss Patterns."

The elder inspector follows the rest of the officials out the door.

The office is now saturated in silence.

Velour still can't believe she's not being escorted out of the building and thrown in the back of a police vehicle. But the temporary freedom the law-abiding officials are providing her is not something for her to rejoice in. The life of Letter Carrier Velour Patterns has now officially ended. Even if she was bold enough to hand her brother over to the authorities, the guilt would always loom over her like a quilted shadow.

What infuriates her is the way they portrayed her brother's character. Like he's some ruthless gangster. Vincent's a hustler and a damn good one. That's why nobody in this city can touch him, not his competitors, not even the law. And those cocky bastards are not going to use her dire circumstances for bait to fish out the one person she loves more than life itself. They gave the wrong person two days to pick her own poison. Two days is enough time for her and Vincent to slide on out of the city or maybe even the country for good.

*Gotta go out with a bang!*

Velour slowly rises from her seat and heads for the door. She turns around to make eye contact with her manager who hasn't said a word since she entered the office. Still slumped in his chair, he doesn't say anything now. The hurt in his expression says it all.

"I'm sorry, Mr. Davenport–"

Tucker pushes her out of the office and slams the door behind her. "I want you to get your belongings and leave. You got that?"

Velour stumbles after the push. But she turns to Tucker and says, "That's the second time you've pushed me, Mrs. Tucker—"

"And?"

"Don't put your hands on me no more. I'm not your property—understood?"

Tucker points straight ahead and growls at Velour in front of a group of shocked employees, "Go upstairs and gather your belongings, young lady! You're in no position to back-talk anyone around here!"

"Whatever."

Velour rolls her eyes at Tucker while trying to out-pace her at the same time.

They both stomp up the staircase and onto the work floor where Velour is instantly met with judgmental glares from carriers as if they know about her fate already. The disgruntled diva holds her shameful head up high as she marches toward her section.

Her eyes turn blood-red at the sight of her primary target—Freeman.

He, in return, shoots a venomous glare from afar before resuming to casing the letters.

With Tucker approaching Chapman at the podium, this gives Velour the perfect opportunity to deal with Freeman.

She gets right in his face and says, "What else did Dante say about me, huh? He had to run his mouth to somebody and that somebody had to be your bitch-ass–"

"Get the hell away from me, Velour."

She points in his face. "You're going to get what's coming to you, trust me on this."

"And when I have a talk with Davenport, that's exactly what's going to happen to you–now, back the fuck off–"

Velour slaps Freeman across the face, and then she desperately attempts to scratch his eyes out, but Freeman quickly grabs her swinging hands.

"*YO, WHAT THE HELL IS WRONG WITH YOU?*"

"You feel like talking? Let's see how much talking you'll do when my brother rolls up on you and bust a hole through your fucking chest!"

"YO, TUCKER! GET HER OFF ME BEFORE I HURT HER!"

Not trying to match strengths with him, Velour snatches her wrists away from his hands and kicks over his six-story column of letters, sending organized DPS mail sprawled out all over the floor.

"Are you out of your mind, Velour?" shouts Tucker, as she again grabs Velour's arm.

"Get your *fuckin'* hands off me!" She snatches her arm away from Tucker. "I told you about that already…AND FOR THOSE WHO HAVE BEEN HATING ON ME EVER SINCE I'VE BEEN HERE, Y'ALL CAN KISS MY ASS! EACH AND EVERY ONE OF Y'ALL!"

"GET YOUR BELONGINGS AND GET THE HELL OUT OF HERE–NOW!!!"

The entire work floor gasps in disbelief.

Velour sizes up every single employee's expression.

A few are scared shitless.

Some show remorse.

But the vast majority show great animosity towards her as if she is some evil seed. That will be the last expression etched in her memories of Midway Station.

Velour softens her tantrum and walks over to a spooked Cadina. "I'm quite sure you'll hear everything about me when I leave, but I'll call you later to tell you why I did what I did. And I'm sorry I let you down with everything." She hugs her only friend.

"I'm sorry, too," Cadina replies, embracing the unexpected hug.

Tucker muscles her way through the crowd. "Don't make me throw you out of this station, Velour—*LEAVE! RIGHT NOW!*"

Velour releases Cadina, readjusts her bags, and chaperones her hatred toward the exit. When she marches out into the humid morning air, fear begins to swell in her throat. She stares at the outer structure of the station. New tears develop. In some warped way, this building has represented a home away from home. Now both homes are gone.

The sound of the on-coming elevator lift breaks her chain of thoughts.

Carriers disperse from the elevator, in full gossip mode about her violent outburst.

She checks her watch and realizes it's break-time for them.

For *them*.

Damn.

She's already accepted the fact she's no longer a part of *them*, anymore.

Time to move on.

Velour holds onto her bags and whips around the corner to avoid her ex-coworkers. With each stride she makes, she grows suspicious of her immediate surroundings. She's not so sure whether to trust the inspector's two-day extension. For all she knows, they could be tailing her right now. She quickly scans every car that passes, every pedestrian that brushes against her, every unforgiving look from bottle-sipping vagrants.

She makes it around Twelfth Street and staggers to a nearby brownstone building to sit on their porch steps. She has never encountered a day more devastating than this one and that includes the tumultuous years with her legal guardians. Oblivious to the world around her, she shields her face with her hands and whimpers to herself. Through her fingers, she watches the shadows of pedestrians counter-cross each other on the sidewalk, heading to places unknown. One particular shadow stops right in front of her, causing her to look up.

The rage within her builds up again.

The last person she wants to see is Lexington. Looking unkempt in his baggy shorts, buttoned-down short-sleeved shirt, and worn New Balances, the stubbly ex-carrier/supervisor flashes an uneasy expression while holding a large manila envelope.

"What the–" She glares at Lexington. "Are you following me? Why are you even here?"

"Nobody's stalking you, Velour," Lexington responds, shifting his beady eyes up and down the street. "I saw you staggering down the block and I wanted to make sure you were alright."

"Are you trying to be funny? Because if you are, I suggest you get the fuck outta my face right now—"

"Whoa, now, what's with the hostility? I'm coming to you in good faith–"

"Good faith, my ass!" Velour stands to her feet. "I bet you knew about this all along, didn't you? And you're gonna smile in my face like everything is cool?"

"What in the hell are you talking—?" Lexington cuts himself off and then takes a deep breath. "First of all, I don't know why you're barking at me, and at this point, I really don't care, but I need you to take a look at this."

He holds out a large manila envelope in front of her.

From the corner of her eye, she spots Detectives Strait and Border Patrol Agent Whitaker, sitting in a silver Dodge Charger, sipping on coffee, and watching her from across the street. Even from afar, she can tell that they're talking about her.

Velour snatches the envelope from his hand and holds it in the air. "Did the agents give this to you to give to me?"

"Agents?" he repeats. "Nobody gave me this, but—"

WHAP! WHAP! WHAP! WHAP! WHAP!

Velour soundly wails on his bald head with the very same envelope he delivered to her. "BOY, TAKE YOUR LYING ASS SOMEWHERE ELSE AND STAY THE HELL OUT OF MY LIFE! I HOPE I'M MAKING MYSELF CLEAR!"

"*WHAT THE HELL IS WRONG WITH YOU?*" He helplessly blocks her blows. "You know what? I don't need this shit, I'm outta here! But do yourself a favor and look into that—I'm serious! It might be worth your while!" Lexington wipes his arms from the vicious attack while walking off. He then spins around and yells out, "You're fuckin' crazy!", before scurrying off down the street.

Velour turns to the officials across the street.

Detective Straits pulls his camera back in the car and rolls up the tinted window.

Velour stuffs the envelope inside of her bag. Then she contemplates on: *A*. How to visit her brother at his girlfriend's place without being tailed by these officials. And *B*. Whether or not Vincent is going to put a foot up her ass once she drops the unbearable news on him. The bowels of her pain don't seem to have a comfortable landing at this point.

Her forty-eight-hour grace period is ticking away.

Dizzy from the morning's emotional onslaught, she fumbles inside of her pocketbook for her keys, unlocks her Porsche, jumps in, and screeches down Twelfth Street.

She peeks into the rearview mirror.

The officials are right on her tail.

Velour's mind goes to work searching for a way out of this mess. For her brother's sake.

And hers.

Every postal employee works in stunned silence as they help Freeman gather the remaining letters from the floor and place them back into the plastic letter trays.

He thanks his coworkers for their assistance before copping a squat on his stool. He grabs a handful of mail to case up, but then, places the mail back in its tray.

His left ear still rings from Velour's attack.

But the humiliation he feels outweighs the assault by plenty.

Bell Biv Devoe's debut song pops into his mind and it couldn't have been more befitting.

*You can't trust a big butt and a smile…that girl is POISONNNN!*

Velour is more than just poison; she's a dark cloud looming over a holiday parade, a rusty nail buried deep in someone's foot, a calculating evil spirit disguised as a bodacious female specimen.

But the witch showed him a massive amount of attention when he was most vulnerable.

And he fell for the okey-doke…*hard.*

He slumps his head over the tray of mail and wonders. Wonders what else lies ahead in his unpredictable future. He wonders how much more he can take before he goes crazy himself. He wonders how long he will be viewed as the village idiot amongst his close peers, who tirelessly ride shotgun on his emotional rollercoaster… one that never seems to come to its final loop.

Tucker and Chapman join him at his workstation.

The assistant manager rubs his back and sighs, "I guess you heard the news by now."

He doesn't look at her. "What news?"

"Velour has been terminated."

He turns to her while slowly standing to his feet. "Really…"

"She was caught stealing mail and was charged with other fraudulent acts, as well."

Freeman cautiously eyeballs Tucker and Chapman. He whispers through clenched teeth, "I hope y'all don't think I was involved—"

Tucker silences him with a nod. "We know, Freeman, nor was Dante involved in any of her activities. This station has been under surveillance by the postal inspectors."

"Y'all *knew* she was doing this the whole time?"

"No, not until yesterday afternoon." Tucker whips around to make sure no one is eavesdropping on their conversation. She whispers, "The inspectors have been monitoring her affairs for quite a while."

"And you're sure these inspectors are not going to come back to bag me up for her mess?"

"I *promise* you; that's not going to happen. She's done enough damage to land herself in jail for good, but by the grace of God, they've given her somewhat of an opportunity to redeem herself."

"Why?"

"It's very complicated, Freeman; I can't divulge any more than I've shared with you already, but she's about to pay a heavy price for her misdoings."

Freeman reads her eyes. She wants to spill the beans but can't. He doesn't press the issue. He resumes casing his mail.

Chapman steps to Freeman. "I, uh, wish I had the manpower to help you case up your route, but as you already know, we're severely undermanned at this point, with Marc's passing and Lexington's suspension—"

"It's cool," Freeman monotones. "I can handle casing the route by myself."

Chapman understandably nods. "I will send out an army to help you later on, alright?"

"Just concentrate on her side of the route. I'll be fine on my end."

Tucker cracks a sympathetic grin before she and Chapman leave his work area.

Seconds go by before Divine, Cadina, and Lou creep over to his workstation.

"Are you okay?" Divine asks.

"Not really."

"Is it true that they fired Velour?"

"Yep. She was stealing people's mail and their identities."

"Whoa."

Divine, Cadina, and Lou stare at one another in complete shock.

Lou scratches his chin. "But they're just gonna let her walk out of here freely? That's how they do things now–"

"No disrespect, Lou, but now is not the time for me to start explaining shit. I have this whole route to case up by myself and I don't want to waste any more time…okay?"

"Okay…but you didn't know Velour was doing any of that, though, right?"

"What part of 'now is not the time…' don't you understand, Lou?"

"I got him, Freeman." Cadina grabs Lou by the arm. "Let's go, Louis."

"We're gonna talk later, a'ight?" states Lou as Cadina pulls him away from Freeman's workstation.

Divine rubs his shoulder. "You want me to get you anything from outside?"

"Nah, I'm good. Thanks, anyway."

She waves him off. "I'ma get you a bacon, egg and cheese on a roll, and an orange juice. You need something on your stomach."

"Thanks."

"I'm your little sister, I have to take care of you."

She sensed the evil side of Velour months ago, but he totally ignored her and embarrassed her in front of their friends. He feels like an asshole now. "And thanks again."

"For what?"

"For not rubbing it in my face."

Oh, the day is not over, trust me, I will be all on your case after we clock out."

She winks at him before walking down the work floor.

Freeman finally cracks a grin as he grabs for his phone. He searches his music playlist for his favorite gospel group, Take 6. He sticks his wireless buds in his ears and cranks the volume up as high as it can go.

Time to go to work.

For the next three hours, he cases up all the mixed Delivery Point Sequence letters that were supposed to be in order, cases up all the magazines and big envelopes, and then deals with the parcels. Today, he is in no hurry to beat the clock. No need for urgency.

Now, time to tie down his route.

It takes him another hour to do that.

Shabbazz arrives upstairs to take Freeman's relay bags down to his truck. The dreadlocked driver bumps fists with Freeman before pushing the skid toward the elevator. Freeman finishes loading his pushcart. He goes downstairs to retrieve his scanner, arrow key, valuable mail and then pushes his cart outside on the loading dock.

He is the last carrier to leave the station.

Building after building, he delivers the mail while soaking in the message Take 6 harmonizes in their uplifting single, *A Few More Miles*. Hours pass by, turning the afternoon to evening. Still, a couple of buildings left to do. He scans across the dark street at his coworkers darting in and out of buildings once assigned to Velour.

A briefcase-toting gentleman strolls up to him and makes it obvious that he's checking his watch. "Hmmm. It's funny, but I never thought I'd beat the mailman home at this time of the night. What…you're trying to break some sort of record?"

*How about if I break my foot off in your—*

*"SPREAD LOOOOOOOVE! DAH, DAAAH, DAH!"* wails his favorite gospel band through his earbuds.

"I'll be at your building in a minute," Freeman calmly replies.

"Maybe you should have one of your coworkers over on this side of the block to help you out. Sounds like a good idea to you?" The brash businessman heads to his building, jingling his keys.

Freeman grits his teeth and moves on.

He finishes his last building and then checks his watch.

9:30 pm.

He leads a crew of letter carriers back to the station where they end their long day with a swipe of their discs.

On his way home, Freeman stretches out on an empty seat as the speeding 5-train rockets upward and onto the elevated tracks, where the sky's darkness makes it appear as though they're still in the underground tunnel. He knows plenty about darkness. It's been his shroud ever since his mom's early departure from his life. No matter how hard he's tried to put a positive spin on an old situation, a new negative serves him an uppercut dead on his jaw. Velour really did a number on his psyche. So much so, he needs to dull his senses for the rest of the night.

He exits the next stop.

Even late at night, the intersection of Gun Hill Road and Eastchester Road stays bustling. In front of the Golden Krust Bakery, the older Jamaican owner blasts Cutty Ranks dancehall banger, *A Who Seh Me Dun*, while the youngsters in white tees and shorts across the street spit-shine their custom whips.

Freeman walks by the youngsters and heads inside Teddy's Joint, a local bar he occasionally frequents when he needs to escape the unfairness of the world.

He calls next on the pool table before he lands in a vacant bar seat and orders his usual, a rum and coke. He requests the bartender to go heavy on the rum. He spins around on his stool and leans back on the bar counter to view the older regulars engaged in lively chatter while others laugh and sing along to the O'Jays, *She Used To Be My Girl.*

At the other end of the bar, Freeman notices an elderly letter carrier, clothed in an old school postal uniform that is seriously in need of a thorough washing. The carrier looks as though he's had ten shots too many.

The bartender slides Freeman's drink to him, but he doesn't take notice.

He peeks at the pool players for a moment, but then his eyes creep back to the wasted mailman, who now becomes an embarrassing sideshow act. With his eyes matted shut, the dusty mailman sways from side to side until his head hits the back of a young lady, who turns and glares at him before returning to her male friend. Freeman watches the same scene repeat itself two more times until the annoyed lady elbows the drunken mailman in the face, causing him to crack open his crusty eyes and browse around the room as if he's unaware of where he is. The old mailman wipes his mouth, waves at the bartender, stumbles from the stool, and staggers his way out the door.

Freeman overhears the lady that elbowed the old mailman, saying to her friend, *"Now I see why I don't get my mail on time. Overpaid, drunk-ass messengers—that's all they are!"* She laughs before changing the subject.

Her harsh comment stays with him.

"Yo, Money, you're next!"

Freeman snaps out of his trance and tells the guys he's changed his mind.

He glances at the lady again.

She now cuts her sarcastic eyes at him while whispering in her friend's ear.

Apparently, she's talking about him.

Freeman realizes why. He still has on his postal uniform.

*Time to bounce.*

Freeman dips into his pockets and pays for a drink that never reaches his lips. He hears the lady's loud laughter as he walks out of the front door.

What the rum and coke were supposed to do for him in the next eight hours, the refreshing walk to his apartment complex has done in less than fifteen minutes—cleanse his mind. He can't tell if the old mailman had anything to do with it, but his mood feels about as light as the sudden cool breeze that cuts through the warmness of the night.

Freeman enters his apartment with the mailman still on his mind. As he turns on the shower and adjusts the temperature, he wonders if God was sending a message through the old drunk by showing him *his* future should he keep walking the path he's making for himself. His mother always said that if you drift away from the laid-out plans God has for you, it's going to be hell getting back on track, but He'll be there to guide you every step of the way. Freeman doesn't want to compare his hell with anyone else's, but he feels he's suffered way more of his share than the next person.

For ten relaxing minutes, he washes away the disastrous day from his body and then steps out of the shower to dry off. He slips on his tank top and boxers and drags his body into the living room to plop onto the sofa. Examining the quiet area, he reminds himself to fumigate any items that contain Velour's twisted brand on them. He'll do that tomorrow.

His thoughts dance around to Lovelle.

Why? He doesn't know.

The humming of the air conditioner lulls him into a woozy state, causing his eyelids to slowly close. Still, he wonders. Wonders what his ex is doing these days. *Who* she's been doing these days. He wonders. He drifts.

He dreams.

> *"I will always love you, Freeman," Lovelle declared, with a*
> *voice filled with*
> *angelic hope and desperation. "You hear me, Freeman? Always!"*
> *"Freeman?...Freeman...FREEMAN!"*
> *"You don't ignore me, Freeman, I ignore you!" Velour seethed,*
> *in a serpent's*
> *tongue.*
> *"You're getting waaaaaay too close to me, Freeman!"*
> *"Get your fuckin' hands off me, Freeman!"*

*"I'ma get my brother on you!"*
*"FREEEEEMAAAAAAAN!"*

He shoots up from the sofa in a cold, shivering sweat. His foggy eyes whip around his apartment, now occupied by streaks of bright Sunday morning sunshine and tranquility. He regains his vision to read the cable box clock. 10:10 am. As much as he likes to analyze the depth of a prior dream, he prefers to leave this one alone.

He yawns his way over to the window to open the blinds. A beautiful burst of sunlight warms his face. He squints down at the sight of parents loading up their three little children into a caravan. The family is dressed in all white and the kids are as hyper as they want to be.

*Baptism*, Freeman assumes.

The caravan pulls off from the curb.

Not giving it a second thought, he hops in and out of the shower, brushes his teeth, and picks his afro. He shaves and colognes his entire body before donning a comfortable blue and yellow summer church outfit. He grabs his bible and bolts out of his apartment.

Driving his Sentra down Boston Road, he catches himself speeding and slows down just a tad. He doesn't need to get a ticket on the Lord's Day, but he also doesn't want to be late and have the congregation stare and whisper about him as soon as he steps inside the building. That'll make him turn back and head for Teddy's.

He parks his car in a tight spot across the street from Piney Stone Baptist Church. Then, he hurries through the tall wooden doors and receives a program from a smiling usher.

The young people's choir is rocking from side to side, clapping their hands thunderously in unison, and sending the bouncing worshippers into a sanctified frenzy with their soul-stirring rendition of, *I Will Bless The Lord.*

Freeman sneaks around the rear benches looking for a seat and spots a familiar face in a nearby pew. He excuses himself as he squeezes by church members to stand next to his young coworker, Emmanuel, who is dressed in a neat blue and white outfit. The youngblood stops clapping to give Freeman a hearty hug.

The choir continues to sing while taking a seat behind the pulpit. The rest of the church shout out, *HALLELUJAH!*, all the way down to theirs.

Freeman turns to Emmanuel and whispers, "Why am I not surprised to see you here?"

"Your sister has a way of persuading me to see things her way."

"She had you in a headlock, didn't she?"

"Oh, yessir!" Emmanuel snickers. "But it's all good, though. I'm enjoying myself."

Freeman glances at the choir.

He sees Divine, sitting next to Lovelle.

His sister smiles directly at him.

He returns the gesture.

Lovelle's gaze is the exact opposite.

His smile begins to lose its luster.

Reverend Newark, a short but thick older man with a round, glowing face that sits behind a pair of reading glasses, wipes his forehead with a hand towel and then adjusts his black summer robe. Afterward, he rises to the pulpit and flips through his oversized bible.

"Let the church say amen."

"Amen!"

"Let the church say amen, again."

"AMEN!"

"Amen." He grins at his eager congregation. "I must tell you, I am so delighted by our visitors coming to fellowship with Piney Stone on this glorious day. Especially the young man Sister Souls extended an invitation to–Brother Emmanuel DeBest, I believe his name is." He turns to Divine. "He's your coworker, am I correct?"

Divine smiles suspiciously. "Yes, Reverend."

"Alright, now. That's usually how it begins...as coworkers."

"AMEN!!!" the congregation enthusiastically responds.

Divine blushes. "Alright, Rev…"

"I'm teasing, I'm teasing. Thank you for attending, young man. Our doors are always open and we look forward to more visits in the future. I'm quite sure Sister Souls will make that happen."

Divine shakes her head as the congregation laughs and chants, "AMEN!"

"I see you over there, Brother Souls."

That itchy feeling of nervousness crawls all over Freeman's body. He nods his head at the Reverend.

"It's so good to have you back home, Brother Souls," the Reverend proudly announces, before his voice turns a shade grave. "We do understand and sympathize with you, so don't you ever think you're alone in this matter. Deaconess Lucille was a pillar in our church for many years and her tireless work as the head of our bible school ministry continues to set the standard for those who have presided after her. She may not be physically present, but her legacy will live on at Piney Stone. I just wanted to share that with you, can I get an amen?"

"AMEN!"

Freeman's eyes glisten after receiving that heartfelt tribute to his mother from the Reverend.

"In fact, before I begin today's sermon, in commemoration of Deaconess Lucille Souls, I'm going to ask Sister Taylor to lead the choir in a song your mother used to love to sing–one of my favorites. Is that alright, Piney Stone?"

The congregation responds with a rousing, "AMEN!"

Reverend Newark turns to Lovelle. "You know which song I'm referring to, Sister Taylor?"

Lovelle peeks at Freeman before nodding to the Reverend. She cues the musicians and they dive into the slow tempo melody of Denise Williams' spiritual song, *God is Amazing*. The black-robed choir stands in unison and gently sways from side to side as Lovelle pulls the microphone from the stand.

She takes a deep breath, closes her eyes, and softly begins, "*Gooood is truly amaaaazing…Goooood is truly amaaaazing…*"

Lovelle is only on the song's chorus, yet church members are already popping up out of their seats, clapping and singing along.

Freeman nods to the music.

But then asks himself…

*Why am I here?*

*Did Velour and her bullshit motives chase me back to church?*

*Did I low-key miss this place of worship?*

*Or am I just faking the funk?*

Those questions never get answered.

Because it doesn't matter at this point.

All that matters now is the welcoming peace that quenched his soul as soon as he walked through those arched double doors.

So, he stands on his feet.

And clap along with the rest of the congregation while his ex-fiancée blows the roof off the building with her golden vocal cords, as if she is guided by the Holy Spirit Himself.

"Child, I could just listen to you sing all day, Sister Taylor. Your voice is truly a gift from God!"

Lovelle hears Sister Watkins talking, but her eyes follow Freeman's movement, from the Reverend at the pulpit, all the way to the other members who are about to leave the church grounds.

She slips out of her choir robe and then smiles at Piney Stone's secretary. "Yes, Ma'am, nothing but God."

Sister Watkins hugs Lovelle, gathers her purse and bible, and then waves at Reverend Newark before leaving.

Divine, along with Emmanuel, approaches Lovelle by the pews. "Now, this lady right *here*!" she laughs. "She's like a big sister to me. Meet Lovelle Taylor."

The youngblood eagerly shakes Lovelle's hand. "A pleasure meeting you. Man, I thought you were Whitney Houston for a hot minute, your vocals are crazy!"

Lovelle blushes. "Thank you, Emmanuel, and thanks for visiting our church today."

"I'll be back."

"Why, that's good to hear!"

He points at Divine. "She's forcing me to."

Divine slaps his finger down. "Boy, nobody's forcing you to do anything, and don't be lying up in church, either."

Lovelle laughs.

She quick-peeks Freeman, who is standing by the piano.

He's obviously waiting on her.

Looking handsome in his blue and yellow ensemble.

A little too handsome.

Downright sexy.

*Lord, give me strength.*

She curtails bedroom thoughts while standing on holy ground.

"I'm going to call you tomorrow about Freeman's birthday," Divine says, in a hushed tone.

"Wait by my car," Lovelle replies. "Give me about ten minutes."

Divine follows Lovelle's gaze toward her brother by the piano.

She grins at Lovelle.

"Good luck." Divine grabs Emmanuel's hand. "Let's go."

Divine yanks the youngblood toward the front entrance.

Lovelle folds her robe and places it in her bag. She turns around.

Freeman stares at her while waiting.

She wonders what kinds of thoughts are rambling behind that stare.

She strolls over to the piano and begins gathering the music sheets. "Hey."

"Hey."

Silence falls between them.

"You brought the house down, as usual," Freeman says, breaking the awkwardness.

She smiles. "I tried to do it justice, you know, like how your mother used to."

"I heard they made you Director of Music. It's about time."

"Actually, it was by default." She places the sheets to the side and takes a seat on the bench. "Nobody else wanted it, so I was offered the role, you know."

"You were destined for it, anyway. Congratulations."

"Appreciate that."

Silence returns.

Freeman looks around the church before saying, "I, uh, gotta get going. It's been one helluva–I mean–a crazy week at work, sooo… you take care of yourself."

He graces her with an uncomfortable grin before walking away.

*Don't let him leave, Lovelle!*

She quickly stands and says, "Dee told me about your route partner getting fired."

Freeman whips around, startled. He takes a couple of steps toward her. "Yeah, they let her go yesterday."

"How do you feel about it?"

"She got caught doing dirt and now has to pay the piper–"

"That's not what I asked."

She moves in on him and then stops.

Eyes flooded with anticipation.

"I asked, how do you *really* feel about the situation?"

He ponders the question before saying, "I don't have any feelings about it. None at all."

She plays it cool but her heart fills with hope.

"We're having our revival next week," she says. "Six o'clock. Food afterward, but only for that Monday, though."

"Yeah, Reverend Newark reminded me."

She nods. "Get home safe, Freeman."

He smiles before spinning around and walking out of the church altogether.

She returns to the bench.

With a grin bordering on the goofy side.

But she doesn't care, though.

Her fingers begin tickling the piano keys.

Followed by a melodic reaction from her golden vocal cords.

She finds herself softly crooning, "*God is truly amaaaazing…*"

# SEVENTY

## VELOUR

This was a bold move she was making.

Sunday afternoon was beyond adventurous for Velour. She had to unweave her blond extensions, throw on an afro wig and a pair of Jackie Onassis sunglasses before traveling through the murky basement of Tanya's rundown apartment building to get to the other grungy apartment building right beside it and sneaking through the backyard to the other side of the block. Too much Mission Impossible drama in her life right now.

After flagging down a cab, she tosses her bags, and then her body in the backseat. She gives the driver an address in Lower Manhattan's NoLita area and immediately calls Joy to make sure her brother stays put until she arrives. Joy asks her a ton of questions, but Velour lets her deal with the dial tone. Every now and then she swivels her head to see if the detectives were tailing her, and then ducks down in the seat. Paranoia chokeholds her equilibrium. She even purchased a prepaid phone for the sole purpose of telling Joy she was on her way over. The rest of the news will be told to Vincent face-to-face. News that had to be edited, fabricated, and slanted so that she won't be viewed as one of the many anchors bringing down her brother's sinking enterprise.

The cab driver parks at the crossing of Prince and Elizabeth Street, right in front of a regal seven-story, red-brick condominium. She hastily pays the driver before pushing herself out of the vehicle. She nervously darts her eyes around the area before scurrying inside the grand entrance's double doors.

As she rides the elevator to the top floor, it dawns on her that she has never been inside Joy's new apartment before.

Rather her *penthouse*.

The high-priced penthouse Vincent had the audacity to surprise Joy with on her birthday—

*Let it go, girl. You have other issues to deal with.*

As the elevator doors open, Velour walks to the penthouse's front entrance. A loud thumping sound seemingly comes out of nowhere. She realizes it's her own heart trying to bust out from under her blouse. She takes a few breaths before pressing the doorbell.

She waits impatiently for about ten seconds before ringing the doorbell again.

Before pressing for the third time, she hears shuffling on the other side of the door.

Joy cracks the door open. Her Trinidadian eyes confusingly land upon Velour's afro puff and large glasses.

"Is that *you,* Velour?"

"Is Vin still here?"

"Yeah, but is there anything I can help you with?"

Velour pushes the door open and invites herself into the penthouse.

She then stops dead in her Nikes.

Velour soaks in all of Joy's lavish decor with infinite jealousy.

Colorful eclectic furniture embellishes the expansive living room area. A state-of-the-art entertainment system. Thick wall-to-wall carpet dipped in hunter-green that blends well with the copper-painted walls. Tropical paintings and one-of-a-kind sculptures perfectly placed around Joy's sanctuary, accentuating her West Indian heritage.

And she has a *fucking* roof terrace.

*This* is how Velour is supposed to live.

Not in some rat-infested dump with her hating-ass cousin, Tanya–

*Let…it…go, Velour!*

She drops her bags and then drops herself onto the plush leather sofa. She notices sandalwood candles burning on the marble table, an unopened bottle of Red Berry Ciroc snug between two tall crystal glasses, and the hauntingly silky vocals of Sade serenading the background.

*Is It a Crime? That I still love you…*

Apparently, she's interrupting Vincent and Joy's version of Sunday brunch.

She can give a rat's ass.

Wrapping herself in her gold bathrobe, Joy growls, "If it wasn't painfully obvious to you, *Velour*, we were in the middle of something, so can you please state your business here–"

"Shut the fuck up and tell Vincent that I'm here."

"Let me tell you something, Velour," Joy points in her face. "What you're *not* going to do is come into my home and think you can start talking reckless to me…you got that?"

Velour rolls her eyes. "Go get my brother, right now, please?"

*"WHO DAT?"* Vincent yells from the bathroom.

"IT'S YOUR SISTER!"

Vincent strolls barefoot into the living room in his burgundy silk pajama set. Brushing his teeth vigorously, the hulky figure stands next to Joy as if they were about to pose for Playboy's evening wear catalog.

"What brings you over here?" he asks through Colgate foam. "And what's with that getup you have on?"

Velour shoots straight up from the sofa and snatches off her disguise. "W-We're in d-deep shit, Vin."

"What the hell you're talking about?"

She hesitates. Her eyes dart toward Joy and then back to her brother.

"Talk, Velour!"

"T-They released me from my job yesterday."

Vincent stops brushing. "For what reason?"

"They know about us, Vincent…"

"THEY? WHO THE FUCK IS *THEY*?"

"I-I was interrogated by the Feds at my station."

"You're joking, right?"

"I-I w-wish I was—"

Vincent's temper gradually becomes nuclear.

He drops his toothbrush.

Then marches toward Velour.

Rolling up his bathrobe sleeves.

And cracking his knuckles.

"You were interrogated by the Feds, huh…"

Joy yells out, "*BABY, NO!*"

Vincent grabs his backpedaling sister.

*"Vincent, please!"*

He slaps Velour so hard that she is sent sailing over the leather sofa, landing solidly on the plush rug. He then leaps over the sofa and grabs his crawling sister by the throat.

"DIDN'T I TELL YOU TO STOP MOVING PRODUCT, HUH? DIDN'T I?"

"*VINCENT, PLEASE! THAT'S YOUR SISTER!*"

"TALK TO ME, BITCH! IS THIS SOME SORT OF SICK JOKE? TALK!"

Velour gags, "*…let, mheee, explllllannnn!*"

*"SHE CAN'T SPEAK IF YOU'RE CHOKING HER HALF TO DEATH!"* Joy yells.

Vincent releases Velour's throat, pulls her up by her blouse and throws her on the sofa. He hops on her and pulls her face toward his. "What the fuck is up, Sis? You got them muthafuckas waiting for me outside—?"

*"Noooo, Vince! Please let me explain—OOOOOOOOOOOUCH!"*

Vincent punches her square in the eye and then hops off her chest.

Velour screams in pain as she holds her inflamed eye.

"TALK, DAMMIT! OR I'MA DEAD THAT OTHER EYE!"

Velour rolls off the couch and falls to the floor. As she struggles to stand up, she yells in desperation, *"I wasn't moving product or anything! They questioned me about our business and they wanted me to give you up! But I didn't tell them anything, I swear to you!"*

*"You really think I'm stupid, Velour!"* He readjusts his grip on her blouse. *"If you didn't tell them anything, you wouldn't be here talking to me! And they wouldn't just let you walk if they didn't plan on following your stupid ass!"*

*"Look outside if you don't believe me!"*

Vincent peeks at Joy before darting out the room and up the staircase to the terrace.

Joy immediately rushes over to aid Velour, who gasps for air.

Vincent storms back downstairs and marches straight to the ladies. He turns to Joy.

"Check the lobby area and be discreet about it."

Joy throws on her clothes right in front of them, grabs her keys, and rushes out the door.

Vincent squats down in front of Velour's terrified face. "So, I guess it didn't take long for them to figure out that I had a sister, right?"

She knows he is talking more to himself than to her. "I-I guess not."

"And the reason you're not in jail is because…?"

"Huh?"

"If you can *huh*, you can hear, Bitch. I assume they fired you because of your connection with me, but they didn't detain you. Why?"

"To get their message across that if I didn't hand you over to them by tomorrow morning, they'd throw *me* in jail."

"So in essence, they're using you as bait."

Her one good eye widens in horror. "Yeah, but that's not why I'm here—"

"Stand up."

"They didn't bug me, Vin—"

"STAND THE FUCK UP!"

Her brother cocks his fist back and she springs to her feet. He frantically frisks her down from her head to toe, plus the fake afro and the glasses.

"Take your clothes off."

She quickly loosens her blouse and her shorts and then hands them to her brother. He snatches her outfit from her hand to visually inspect them up close. Never in her life has she felt uneasy in her panties and bra. Vincent double-takes her twice.

"The fuck are you waiting on? Take them other shits off, too!"

"I-I can't." She embarrassingly whispers, "I'm on the rag—"

"TAKE THEM OFF NOW BEFORE I DO IT FOR YOU!"

Velour unhooks and slides off her bra, then fights her panties off and hands them to him. Vincent only snatches the bra.

"Lift that pad up so I can see what's under there."

Standing in butt-naked humiliation, Velour rips the bloody maxi pad off for her brother's inspection. "You should have a little more trust in me than this, Vincent."

"Trust you?" He flings the bra at her face. "My empire has crumbled right before my eyes and I'm supposed to trust you because you're my *sister*? Put your clothes back on right here and don't get any of that red shit on my sofa, either."

Velour stumbles toward her purse to retrieve a new pad. After she slips on the rest of her clothes, she bursts into more tears.

Joy returns to the penthouse and tosses her keys on the table. "Nothing. No cops, Feds, nobody. Even the doorman says the lobby area has been quiet all day."

Vincent grabs Velour by the blouse and pulls her toward him. In an even tone, he says, "You better start from the very beginning and don't leave out one fucking detail."

"It was Freeman," she sputters through heavy breathing.

*"Freeman?"* His squinty-eyed glare homes in on her statement. "What the fuck does Freeman have to do with my situation, huh? You've been telling that nigga my business, is that what you're telling me–"

"No, never! He wanted to know how you made your money and I told him through the customs shops, that was it!" She swallows down fear before continuing. "But for some reason, he tells my manager that I shouldn't be living in a mansion with what I make at the post office! Next thing I know, I'm in my manager's office being interrogated by postal inspectors…and then they tell me that Jimmy named you as the ringleader behind the vehicle shipments overseas and the bootlegging operation–"

"Hold the fuck up!" He slowly releases his grip on her shirt. "Let me get this straight; Postal inspectors told you *Jimmy* gave them my real name? *Our* Jimmy from my Jersey shop?"

She nods with pleading eyes. "They know *everything*, Vince. They've promised Jimmy a lesser sentence once they have you in custody and now, they're offering me a probation package, but I would never do that to you!"

Vincent studies her in every degree.

So does Joy.

"What does Freeman gain from any of this if he doesn't know of my dealings, Velour?"

"Freeman is an asshole. All he ever wanted to talk about was your house and finances. That's why when I told him I wanted to see other people…" Velour delivers an award-worthy sigh. "…he became very aggressive towards me."

"He put his hands on you?" he growls.

She nods. "After our softball game last week."

Vincent turns to Joy.

Joy stares at Velour, suspiciously.

He turns back to Velour. "And you expect me to believe you didn't flap your gums to him about my organization?"

"How do I look telling him about any of your business? Think about it, Vince; that's putting *my* ass on the line, as well! That's why I had to cut him loose."

Vincent finally stands and paces the living room. He turns around to Velour. "And the Feds told you *Jimmy* gave up my name…"

"And confiscated everything from four of our shops, I'm sure you heard about that."

"But me and Jimmy had an understanding..." Vincent blurts out to no one in particular. "A *financial* understanding, at that, to keep my name out of any conversation...Motherfucker..."

Velour retrieves her purse from the table. She pulls out a Delta Airlines envelope and hands it to Vincent.

"What the fuck is this?"

"First class tickets to London, leaving tonight. I even got one for Joy's goofy ass."

Joy glares at Velour but then stares at Vincent.

"I figure we can lay low over there for a while until we determine our next move."

Velour senses the uncertainty rising through his iron-clad anger.

He moves in on her.

But doesn't grab any of her clothing or her throat.

Just his perplexed face close to hers.

"I swear, Velour, if this is some clever setup you're involved in with these inspectors or feds, I guarantee it won't end well for you–"

"Look, Vince, I did not throw that wig on, climb a backyard fence, and buy these expensive plane tickets, just to come all the way here to set you up!" She doesn't back down from her brother's eyes. "I'm not like any of your so-called friends who've been diming you out just to save their own ass! I'm your *sister*! We're in this together! Hooking up with Freeman was bad judgment on my part, I own up to that. But if you go down, *I* go down–that's how family is supposed to roll!"

Five seconds later, Vincent breaks away from her and stands in front of Joy's small aquarium.

Velour can hear him muttering to himself. "Goddamn Jimmy gave them my name–?"

"That's why we gotta get the hell out of this city fast. It's only a matter of time before they find out about Joy. And who else knows about this place besides our immediate circle?"

Vincent ponders her question while staring at the fish swimming around the rocks.

Jimmy's situation is eating away at his conscience.

She anticipated this.

"They're expecting a call from me by tomorrow morning, Vince. If we're going to do something, we need to be doing it right now."

A moment of silence passes.

Vincent thinly asks, "What time does our flight leave?"

*Yes!*

"Eight-thirty tonight, out of JFK."

"Not tonight. Tomorrow afternoon is better for me. Too much housecleaning I need to do to prepare for this trip. Accounts need to be transferred, things of that nature."

"By that time, they may have the airport crawling with police waiting for our arrival–"

"Who says we're flying out of New York?"

She stares blankly at her brother.

He pulls away from the aquarium and wipes the remaining toothpaste from his mouth. "You forget we have friends who own private jets who can help us in our time of need? One so happens to live in Atlanta. That's our destination for tomorrow afternoon."

A smile attempts to bubble up on her face. She quickly masks it. "Gotcha."

"Get me your phone, Babe," Vincent motions to Joy. "Gotta alert the others about our recent dilemma so they can make the proper arrangements." He points at Velour. "As for you, you're staying here until we pull out tomorrow. Whatever shopping you need to do, needs to be done in this vicinity, don't go straying anywhere else. And definitely no debit or credit card transactions from here on out."

"All of my cards are cut up." She checks her eye in the compact mirror. "But I'm a little strapped for cash right now."

Vincent walks to the kitchen. He returns with his wallet. He pulls out a wad of cash and hands it to her.

"Thanks."

As she counts the money, she becomes overwhelmed by emotions.

Vincent bends down in front of her.

"I didn't mean to take my frustration out on you." He rubs her head while holding her hand. "I'm under a ton of stress and the last thing I ever want is to lash my anger out on my own sister. You do understand, don't you?"

"C'mon, Vince, we're cool." Her grin is unstable. The one good eye she has uncomfortably connects with his. "I mean, we've been through worse together and bounced back even harder, so, this too shall pass, right?"

"Come here…"

He motions for her to give him a hug.

And like a child seeking acceptance, she abides by giving him a tight bear hug.

Just being in her brother's arms is all the apology she needs.

"I love you," Vincent whispers. "You know that, right?"

"I love you, more," she whimpers.

She witnesses Joy staring at her.

Skeptically.

*Get used to this, Bitch.*

Vincent releases her and walks over to the bar to get another crystal glass. He returns to the sofa, cracks open the Ciroc, and pours into each glass. He then hands them out to the ladies.

"Who would've thought my final days in the good ole United States of America would end on a sour note?"

"New beginnings, Boo." Joy sits across from them in a recliner. "That's how I view it. Ain't that right, Velour?"

She fake-smiles Joy. "To new beginnings."

They all raise their glasses to the toast and take a sip.

Velour stands. "I'll be back shortly. Do y'all need anything while I'm out?"

"Only for you to bring your ass back, asap," Vincent responds with Joy's phone stuck to his ear. He grabs Velour's wig and shades from the rug and tosses them to her. "Put this shit back on, so nobody recognizes you."

Velour dons the disguise, slings her purse over her shoulder, and walks out the door.

The elevator couldn't have arrived at a better time. She climbs aboard and waits for the doors to close so she can let out a big '*WOO-WEE!*'.

Her brother believed her.

He believed her mixture of hardcore facts with straight bullshit and the only drawback was a swollen eye. A small price to pay for the ultimate jackpot down the road. She gurgles with excitement all the way down to the first floor.

The doors open and she skips out of the elevator like a little girl going to her first fair. The reconnection with the only blood relative in the world she cares about has been established. And to celebrate, Velour's going to venture around North of Little Italy's magnificent shopping area to do some serious spending before they leave the country altogether. She flashes her winning smile as she exits out of the double doors and gazes up toward the powder-puffed blue sky.

The sun has never shined brighter in her life.

# SEVENTY-ONE

## VINCENT

From the rooftop terrace, Vincent and Joy watch Velour slide inside a taxi and pull off down Elizabeth Street. They glance at each other before returning to the penthouse. He lights up a Brazilian Maduro cigar, falls back on the sofa, and props his feet upon the marble table. He takes a couple of puffs as he watches Joy pace around the living room area. Nervous and pissed.

He exhales smoke before grumbling, "Go ahead and say it."

"What else do you want me to say, Vincent? I've been saying it!" Joy snatches her glass from the table and downs the rest of her drink. She places her glass back on the table and sits across from him. She leans forward, in full panic mode. "I told you from the very beginning when you sold the mansion, do *not* let her know where we were going to stay. But you did it anyway, against my wishes–"

"Do you believe her story?"

She throws her hands in the air. "Which *part* of the story are you referring to?"

Her frustration is beginning to rub off on him. He leans in closer to her. "I asked you a simple question. Do you believe her story–?"

"When it comes to your sister, I don't know what to believe. But she came here in a fucking disguise, Vincent! She told you about Jimmy, now that part is a cause of concern because when was the last time you heard from him once the feds shut down our shops and warehouse? But the rest of her story sounds like some Velour bullshit. I mean, who is this Freeman dude who is supposedly telling inspectors about your business? Huh? That shit doesn't even sound right! I just don't trust her at this point, and neither do you. That's why you keep asking me the same question."

He leans back on the sofa and puffs mightily on the cigar.

He hates to admit it, but she speaks the truth.

And the truth about Velour's state of mind burns deep in his soul.

He loves his sister. He really does.

They survived a difficult childhood when they lost both of their parents. They overcame spiteful-ass relatives who didn't want anything to do with the Patterns children. It was always him and Velour against the world. Big brother protecting little sister. Big brother spoiling little sister.

But somewhere along the journey, their relationship took a harsh nosedive.

And it led to their current situation.

But how? What led to this bitter disconnect with Velour?

Worse, is his own sister becoming too heavy a burden to bear?

Joy pops up from the chair and kneels by his side. "Right now, you need to ask yourself what's going to happen next. And regardless of whether the whole story is true or not, do you want to risk it by staying here another second? We need to leave and don't ever look back. And we need to decipher who goes with us and who we leave behind–"

"The fuck is you saying, Joy?" He snarls. "You think I want to do that to my own kin–?"

"Your *kin* is a virus, Vincent, infecting everything and everyone she comes in to contact with, and I won't sit back and allow her to do that with our business." She grabs and holds his hand. "It's time to cut ties for good. Some people need to find their own way in life. I'm going to pack, and I suggest you do the same."

She rises to her feet and hurries to her bedroom.
Vincent continues to lounge back on the sofa.
He blows out more smoke into the air.
Again, she spoke the truth.
And for the first time in his adult life…the truth hurts.

*8:00am...tick...tock...*

Divine closely observes Freeman as he walks toward his workstation carrying a small brown bag. He plops himself on his stool, pulls out and opens the aluminum foil to get to his cream cheese sesame seed bagel.

She studies her brother's facial expression as he chews. A certain calmness claims his demeanor. He's been through a lot–with Lovelle; With his customers; And now Velour.

It's time to show him some sibling love on his special day.

She scoops up a blue gift bag from the floor, conceals it behind her back, and strolls over to her brother's work area.

He peeks up from his food and greets her with a nod.

And a smile.

She finds comfort in that smile.

Particularly, on his special day.

"How do you feel this morning?" she asks.

"Hungry." He licks the cream cheese from his thumb. "I was starving–"

"Let me rephrase the question; how does my brother feel on his thirty-fourth birthday? Still young at heart or has the mid-life crisis syndrome started settling in on ya?"

He takes a swig of orange juice before replying, "Aside from assessing the craziness I've experienced the past couple of weeks, I actually feel good."

"Cool."

She reveals the blue gift bag and then hands it over to him.

Freeman wipes his mouth. "Thanks. You know you didn't have to."

"I didn't. Compliments of Lovelle."

Surprised, he digs into the bag and pulls out a three-book soft-cover collection of The Wayward Pines Trilogy, by author Blake Crouch. His face lights up in approval. "She always knows what to get me. The tv series was incredible, so I know these novels are going to be off the chain."

"I know you can't wait to read them."

"I'm going to crack open part one tonight." He places the books back into the bag. "Tell her I said thanks."

"You tell her yourself."

She casually glances over at her workstation.

Cadina, Lou, and Emmanuel wait patiently for her to return.

Divine nods at them and then faces her brother.

She humbly says, "Lovelle told me she was to blame for you two breaking up and I'm so sorry for assuming the worst in you. I hope you can accept my apology."

She motions for a hug.

"Oh, now I know it's my birthday," he laughs as he hugs his sister. "Apology accepted."

"Lovelle really misses you."

Freeman releases her but doesn't add to the statement.

"You should read what she wrote in your card. That should remind you of how you two used to be."

"Oh, so now you're into reading other people's cards without permission, huh?"

"Oops! Gotta go case up some mail! I'll see you later, beloved brother of mine!"

She plants a big kiss on the side of his suspicious grill and hustles across the section to huddle up with the crew at her workstation.

"He's in a way better mood than he was the other day," she states.

"I still don't see why we can't have his surprise birthday upstairs in the swing room like we've been doing instead of this outside shit y'all planning," Lou grumbles.

"With everything that's happened the past week, nobody's in a festive mood around here."

"Well, maybe that's what this station needs! Something to boost people's spirits up!"

"True, but I'm not trying to feed everyone in here, either. This is for the crew *only.*"

"And then we can take him out this weekend and really get our party on!" Cadina adds.

Lou rolls his eyes. "Whatever. Just let me know what you need from me."

"Just sodas." Divine snatches up her notepad and a pen to start scribbling. "Neville and Roy are picking up the wings and fries and Cadina blessed us with a small cake. I will get the paper plates and forks and we should be good to go."

"BREAKTIME IS OVER, FOLKS!" Chapman yells. "WE HAVE MORE MAIL ON THE WAY, SO LET'S GET BACK TO OUR ASSIGNMENTS!"

"I'm working with your brother today," Emmanuel says. "…so, we should be done early. I'll call you." He winks at her before leaving her workstation.

Divine smiles at him. "Thanks, Boo."

She turns around.

Cadina and Lou stare at her in shock.

"*Boo?*" they both question.

"What?" Divine blushes. "I didn't say Boo. Did I?"

"Awww, yeah!" Lou smirks, rubbing his hands together. "My man finally cracked the code to that safe and got all of them jewels out, huh, Ma?"

Divine swings at a laughing Lou. "I'ma crack you if you keep flapping your gums–"

"YO, MANNY! YOU THE MAN! WE GOTTA TALK, SON!"

Lou bebops out of her workstation.

Cadina turns to Divine. "I wish I could be at the gathering this afternoon, but James is taking me out somewhere, it's a surprise, so…"

"Girl, I'm not stressing that. Just have your dancing shoes ready for this weekend. Freeman's going to have a party he'll never forget!"

"Oooo, I know it's going to be lit!"

"That's how we do it!"

Cadina hi-fives Divine before returning to her workstation.

Divine glances over at her brother.

He's reading his birthday card from Lovelle.

And he's *glowing*!

That made her day.

She grabs a handful of letters. She peeks at the clock on her portable desk radio.

It reads 8:20 am.

# SEVENTY-THREE

## VINCENT

The clock on the dashboard reads 11 am.

Vincent, along with Wise, Kaution, and Hyper, three of his partners-in-crime from his notorious P.A.C. Man Crew, sit idly in a limousine-tint Suburban SUV, which is parked across from Midway Postal Station. The cannabis smoke hazes the interior as they stare through the windows at each letter carrier pushing their loaded carts down the street.

"That's him, right there," Hyper states in a raspy voice.

The four men watch Freeman and his coworker push their carts down the ramp, and onto the sidewalk.

Vincent clenches his teeth in contempt.

Kaution turns his thick, bifocaled head around to face Vincent. "So, Vince, tell us again why we're here?"

"I'm tired of repeating myself, Kaution," Vincent huffs in the back seat. "I already told you what the deal was, and you didn't have any problems rolling with me before we left. Why all the questions now?"

"Because none of this makes any sense, that's why."

Vincent glares at his comrades.

"Look, all of y'all can go and catch up with Joy before she pulls out, it makes me no difference. Y'all want me to call her?"

"This is not you, Vin," Wise injects.

Vincent turns to his right-hand man. "What's not me?"

"Letting your emotions cloud your better judgment." Wise's baritone voice remains level as he takes a pull from the blunt. "And over some punk-ass mailman at that?"

"There's the door. I'm not twisting nobody's arm here if you're not comfortable with–"

"Vince, let's break down what you told us yesterday." Wise shifts his massive body around to face him. "Velour told you that Jimmy gave up all of our names to the feds, right? That may be true because I had someone call Jimmy last night and the person told me both of his phones are disconnected. So, I can see *that*. But this story about this Freeman cat giving up your address to his manager for no apparent reason? That don't sit well with me, at all–"

"So, you're saying Velour is lying about all of this?"

"I'm not saying that–"

"Well, that's how it's coming across! Why does her story have to be so far-fetched?"

"How can I say this without you getting all into your feelings?" Wise passes the blunt to Hyper. "Velour is not the snotty-nosed kid you raised back in Rock Hill anymore. Nooo, she's a grown woman who is extremely charming and manipulative and would go behind her brother's back to do the exact opposite of what you tell her! Now, I'm not saying she's lying about the conversation she had with these inspectors, feds, whoever, but I wouldn't put it past her to bend the truth to make herself look like the innocent victim. You, of all people, should know this."

"So, she's also lying about this clown putting his hands on her, too, right?"

Wise looks out the window at Freeman pushing his mailcart around the corner of Fourth Avenue. "By *that* nigga?"

"Hey, we've all seen Velour cut down many dudes with her tongue," Hyper adds while passing the blunt to Kaution. "This cat

Freeman probably snapped and went postal on her ass. And that's why we're really here, right, Vin?"

Wise cuts his red eyes at Vincent. "So that's the reason we're stalking him–?"

"Look, all I know is that certain people are going to pay for the collapse of our business, and I wish I could start with Jimmy's snitching ass." Vincent eyeballs his comrades. "But this thing with Freeman? Yes, I know it's personal, but fuck it, *nobody* put their hands on my sister and think there won't be any repercussions from it. And whoever has an issue with it can step, right now."

They all remain silent for a moment.

"It's been a while since we touched up someone," Hyper smirks. "I say we do this."

Vincent turns to Kaution, who sits behind the wheel.

"Whatever, man," Kaution says, gesturing with his hands.

Vincent then turns to Wise.

"I guess I can't be the odd man out, right?" Wise scoffs. "But tell me this, Vince; with everything that's been happening the past few months, I feel as though we need to streamline the operation and make sure whoever is still on our team, is on the same *page*. Now, don't get me wrong, Velour is like our sister, too, you know, but we gotta make sure–"

"She's not coming with us to Canada. Is that what you want to hear?" Vincent takes the remaining blunt from Kaution.

Wise leans back in his seat, satisfied with the response. "Let's make this quick and be ghost."

Vincent nods.

Kaution cranks the SUV and pulls off from the curb. "Question, Vince; how're we going to pull this off anyway, in broad daylight?"

"You let me worry about that. Just stay close to them."

Kaution makes a right on Fourth Avenue and begins their surveillance on Freeman.

Vincent cracks the window and flicks the small blunt stem into the street.

As they pass by the carriers, he catches Freeman smiling and laughing.

Vincent took great offense to that.

*Keep laughing, motherfucker.*

In his mind, Vincent visualizes how he's going to severely dot Freeman's eyes and cross his fucking tee—for the betterment of his conscience.

# SEVENTY-FOUR

## DIVINE

"What time do you have, Dee?"

Roy barrels the postal truck through every yellow light he approaches along First Avenue. Divine quietly prays for a safe commute.

She checks her watch. "It's three."

A red light forces Roy to slam the brakes.

She bucks back in the passenger seat. "And there's no reason for you to be speeding like this."

"You're the one who wants to beat your brother to his last delivery building, so that's what I'm trying to do."

"Are y'all alright back there?" she yells in the back of the truck.

Lou stumbles to the front cab. "Yeah, we're good."

The light turns green.

Roy mashes the gas pedal and the truck bolts off like a rocket.

Divine roars, "Roy!"

"My bad," he laughs.

She shakes her head. She happens to peek up at Lou.

He smiles mischievously at her as if he's up to something.

"What, Lou?"

He turns around to the cargo area and says, "Y'all know Dee and Manny are smashing on the low, right?"

Eating a piece of chicken, Neville blurts out, "Hell, I been knew that."

"Really?" Shabbazz peeks up from his phone, smiling. "Congratulations, Dee!"

Divine stares at them with her mouth open in complete shock.

"Ain't nobody smashing *this*, Louis!" She turns to a laughing Neville. "And what do you mean by, *I been knew that*? Who told you that?"

Neville points to Lou.

"And you believe that fool?"

Lou says, "Dee, you took my man to church yesterday, called him *Boo* earlier this morning–"

"And what does that have to do with anything?"

"So that's why youngblood be smiling at work all the time." Neville wipes his hands with a napkin. "You be percolating for him, Dee?" He begins singing, "*It's time for the percolator…*"

"Nobody's percolating anything–" Divine cuts off her own statement, admitting defeat. "You know what? I can't with y'all."

"C'mon, Dee, that's a beautiful thing!" says Lou. "Now you don't have to go on ChristianMingle.com anymore looking for righteous dudes!"

"You so stupid, Lou!" She busts out laughing. "Nobody is going online looking for no man and nobody is smashing this either, so stop with the narrative."

"If you say so."

She glances at Roy, who's grinning behind the wheel.

"And you need to concentrate on getting us to Freeman's route before he leaves and stop smiling like a Cheshire cat."

Roy begins chanting and drumming on the steering wheel, "*It's Time For the Percolator…It's Time For the Percolator…*"

The crew chants along, "*IT'S TIME FOR THE PERCOLATOR! IT'S TIME FOR THE PERCOLATOR*!"

Divine covers her mouth, trying her best not to laugh.

# SEVENTY-FIVE

## VINCENT

The Suburban double-parks in the middle of a one-way residential street.

They watch from a distance as Freeman grabs a bundle of mail from his pushcart and trots up a flight of brownstone steps.

Vincent checks his platinum watch.

It blings 3:05 pm.

He examines the connecting brownstones on both sides of the street.

Not a soul in sight.

"If we're going to do something, Vince, I suggest we do it now and get it over with," Wise impatiently states.

Vincent nods. "Park the truck in front of that building he went in."

Kaution slowly pulls off and then parks the truck right in front of the brownstone.

"We go in, *whap! whap!*, and then bounce, y'all got it?" Wise instructs.

Kaution shakes his head. "Yo, I still don't feel good about this, so I'ma wait here and keep a look-out until y'all come out."

"No problem." Vincent turns to Wise and Hyper. "Let's go."

The three men exit the truck.

Vincent's phone rings.

He pulls it out and screens the number.

It's Joy.

She informs him of several things. First, she is already waiting for them at a specified location in Midtown Manhattan. Second, she left the penthouse keys with Velour. Third, she didn't tell Velour about their recent change of plans. When his sister realizes what has happened, she'll be severely hurt, *pissed* to be more precise, but he hopes his message becomes clear to her; she needs to start fending for herself from this point on. And for starters, should she decide to stay in this country, she's welcome to live in Joy's penthouse, complete with a renewed lease in her name. That's the least he could do for his sister.

That's if the law doesn't catch her first.

After they finish handling their business with Freeman, the men will then meet up with Joy, along with the rest of their affiliates, and continue their travels across the George Washington Bridge and on I-95 South until they reach Dekalb/Peachtree Airport, based out in Chamblee, Georgia. They would board a private jet and fly off to Toronto, Canada, where they have established and maintained many high-profile relationships over the course of their corrupted years.

Vincent breathes in the excitement as the three men in casual black clothing boldly swagger up the steps toward the front entrance. He presses one of the apartment buzzers and then scans the block one more time. Still, no signs of life.

He smiles at this huge window of opportunity.

He presses the doorbell again.

# SEVENTY-SIX

## FREEMAN

Freeman sits the parcel on the small table and unlocks the mailbox panel. He checks his watch.

3:07 pm.

He then pulls the rubber band from the mail bundle to begin delivering to his last building for the day.

The door to apartment 1A swings open and out saunters Trevor, wearing a white bathrobe and flip-flops. He smiles and points at Freeman. “I thought I heard you out here, Birthday Boy.”

Freeman turns to him, surprised. “How do you know it’s my birthday, Trev?”

The gangly resident sporting a blond fade haircut purses his lips at him. “Please, I asked Velour about you last year. I’m kind of nosy like that.”

Freeman scoops up the parcel from the table and hands it to Trevor. “Here you go, Mr. Nosy, and the rest of your mail.”

“Thank you, Freeman.” Trevor takes the mail and points at him. “And when you see that heffa Velour, tell her I’ve been trying to reach her all weekend and she needs to call me asap. How're things between you two, anyway?"

Freeman side-eyes him while sliding the magazines into their appropriate boxes. "We're not together anymore."

"Had a falling out, huh?" Trevor shakes his head. "Oh well, shit does happen. Honestly, I thought she was too high maintenance for you, anyway. You should be dating someone within your budget, like a schoolteacher."

Freeman coughs up laughter. "A teacher, huh?"

"I have a gift for you, Freeman," Trevor purrs while tugging on his bathrobe belt.

Freeman eyeballs the flirting resident. "Uh, honestly, Trev, you didn't have to give me anything–"

Trevor motions with his hands for Freeman to stop talking. "My department store is forced to get rid of certain overstock, so I've been able to bless people with some really nice merchandise, okay? So, calm your ass down, Freeman, you ain't that cute!"

Freeman smiles in relief. "Well, I appreciate it."

"You better. Now, I'ma throw on some clothes and bring out your gift. In the meantime, I'ma dedicate a song to you. Here it goes… *Go Shawty, It's Your Birthday… We're gonna party like it's your birthday…"*

Trevor dances back inside his apartment and closes the door. The gangly resident then cranks up 50 Cent's, *In Da Club,* to the maximum volume.

Freeman shakes his head as he wraps up his delivery. His mind toys with the idea of setting up a date with Lovelle just to see where her head is these days. And to get a good idea of where his head is, as well.

Murmurs in the background break up his thought process as he slams the panel door shut and locks it. He turns around and is ruefully greeted with a perfect uppercut to his chin that sends his head crashing into the brass mailbox panel. Sprawling to the wall with his teeth and head still rattling, Freeman is snatched by the collar and is unmercifully hammered with fists flying from every direction, creating multiple bruises on his face and neck. A gigantic Stacy Adams shoe caves into his stomach, making him heave up the

Wendy's he had for lunch earlier. He then falls helplessly onto his own bloody vomit.

Struggling to move, he faintly hears one of the assailants say, *"Pick his punk-ass up*!"

Two sets of hands slide underneath his armpits and lift him up from the slippery floor and slam him hard into the wall. Breathing out bits of blood and food, his vision fights through its fogginess to make out the assailant's identity.

*"Vi-Vin...what...you..."*

Vincent grabs him by the neck.

"I hear you have trouble keeping your hands to yourself, Freeman." Vincent steadily chokes him with one hand. "We're gonna help you fix that little problem of yours, right quick!"

"*Blo....chssst...,"* Freeman weakly stutters. "*...Bloo...Christ—"*

"What did you say?"

"*...B-Blood...Christ...."*

"Y'all hear this? He's asking for the Lord to save his black ass!"

"*B-BLOOD OF CH-CHRIST!*"

"You're gonna wish I did send you to your Maker after I get finished with you, bitch-ass nigga!"

"*GO, SHAWTY...IT'S YOUR BIRTHDAY*!" is the last statement Freeman hears as Vincent takes the ferocious liberty of battering away at his face until one striking blow to the temple—*BAM!*—sends him into another faraway world completely.

# SEVENTY-SEVEN

## KAUTION

After adjusting the rear-view mirror, Kaution checks his watch again.

3:10 pm.

He then wipes the sweat from his glasses for the umpteenth time.

His nerves have gotten the best of him.

*Relax, take deep breaths, they'll be out soon.*

Before he can take his first breath, a young, lanky letter carrier pushes his cart past the front of the Suburban and onto the sidewalk. He parks his pushcart next to Freeman's.

Kaution tries not to panic.

But then something in the rear-view catches his attention.

His eyeballs almost pop out of their sockets.

*Awww, shit…*

Parking behind the Suburban is a postal truck.

A muscular albino driver jumps out of the truck, along with a young petite lady.

And three more dudes jump out from the back.

The lanky letter carrier joins the crew and they huddle up to talk next to the brownstone.

Kaution quickly calls Vincent's phone, to no avail.

Wasting no more time, he quickly slides out of the running SUV, discreetly walks past the postal group, and then hurries up the brownstone front steps.

He rings and bangs on the front door.

"Come on…come ON!"

# SEVENTY-EIGHT

## MAYHEM

"Vin. Vin! *VINCENT*!" Wise bear-hugs him. "He's out, man! Look at him!"

Vincent pushes his homeboy off him and staggers around in one place, breathing uncontrollably.

He must've blacked out.

*Had* to have blacked out.

For he wasn't just punishing Freeman's face. He was punishing Jimmy's snitching mouth for telling the feds about their identities. He even busted Velour's other eye. In this brutal, spellbinding moment, he unleashed all the pent-up fury he had for everyone who'd double-crossed him and contributed to his downfall onto a man who now lay next to his Stacy Adams shoes.

A man who is not moving at all.

Hyper bends down to turn Freeman's body upright.

Vincent's heart skips a beat.

He can't even recognize Freeman for the blood painted over his face. Vincent glances at Wise. His partner glances at him, as well, but says nothing. Vincent then stares at Hyper, who is looking right at him. The skinny thug sticks a piece of gum in his mouth and stands to his feet. He shoots Vincent a merciless smirk. Vincent doesn't return one.

"Let's dump him in the back, next to the garbage cans, and get the fuck out of here," Wise orders Hyper.

Vincent quietly watches his homeboys drag Freeman's blood-soaked body underneath the flight of stairs behind the recycling garbage cans. He scans up the staircase to see if anyone was witnessing the ugly scene. Not one soul. The loud music coming from the apartment across from them had muffled the violent sounds of the attack.

Wise and Hyper quickly shuffle from the back area. "Let's get the fuck out of here right now."

"*When I pull out up front, you see the Benz on dubs!*"

The door from apartment 1-A swings open and Trevor, wearing an all-white short ensemble, prances out into the hallway singing and holding a gift in his hand.

Trevor pauses and then smiles at Vincent. "Excuse me, but I thought you were the mailman—*Whoooooaaa*!" He slips but regains his balance. He checks the bottom of his white Vans sneakers. He drops the smile completely. "What the hell?"

Vincent watches Trevor follow the trail of blood and vomit to the back of the hallway. He feels a hand tugging his arm.

"*Let's go*," Level-Head insists.

Before they can take their first step, a frantic Kaution runs into the building and blocks the doorway. "I told you this wasn't a good idea, Vin!"

*"OOOH, MY GOD, FREEMAN!"* cries Trevor. *"HOO-HOOO, MY GOD! WHAT DID Y'ALL DO TO HIM? YOU FRIGGIN' ANIMALS! ALL OF YOU! OOOH MY GOD! FREEMAN! FREEMAN! HOOO-HOOOOOOO!"*

Vincent motions for them to leave.

But Kaution doesn't budge.

"The fuck's your problem, big man?" Vincent snaps. "Let's roll up outta here!"

"We can't!"

"Who says we can't?"

"We got company!"

Through the stained glass on the second door entrance, they observe the movement of people shuffling through the first door entrance and singing.

"*Happy Birthday, to youuuuuu, Happy Birthday, to youuuuuu–*"

"*That shit is corny, Ma. Let's do Stevie Wonder's version.*"

"*Okay, okay. HA-PPY BIRTHDAY TO YOU, HA-PPY BIRTHDAY TO YOU…*"

Vincent and crew backpedal to the staircase as the singing postal entourage make their grand entrance inside of the foyer area.

"HAPPY BIIIIIIRTHDAYYYYYY!"

The song trails off to dead silence.

The postal crew lock eyes with Vincent and his crew.

Not a creature stirs inside the small hallway.

Holding the candle-flaming birthday cake, Divine stares at Vincent and in an innocent tone, asks no one in particular, "Where's Freeman?"

"THESE NIGGAZ TRIED TO KILL FREEMAN, Y'ALL! HE'S BARELY BREATHING, HE NEEDS AN AMBULANCE, NOW! I'MA CALL THE POLICE, 'CAUSE THIS DON'T MAKE NO DAMN SENSE AT ALL!"

Divine drops the cake and dashes to the back area.

The blood-curdling cry from Divine's throat penetrates throughout the entire building.

"*FREEMAN! OH MY GOD, FREEMAN, NOOOOOOO!*"

"C'mon, y'all!" Hyper yells, walking towards the door. "Fuck these muthafuckas—"

WHAP!

An all-out riot jumps off so fast that the play-by-play action turns surreal in every form and fashion. Lou, screaming something in Spanish, chops Hyper in the throat and grabs him in a chokehold while Emmanuel pummels into the skinny goon's ribs. Wise punches Neville in his nose, causing it to bleed, but Shabbazz leads an elbow into Wise's mouth and the two postal truck drivers pounce on him with maddening force. Kaution escapes the building without ever looking back. Trevor and Divine carry Freeman into Trevor's apartment.

An anchor of a fist cold-cocks Vincent, sending him wobbling toward the staircase. He shakes it off quickly and narrowly avoids another haymaker by ducking his head and returning heavy firepower of his own. But his opponent, the muscular albino named Roy, counters with a flurry of accurate jabs and combinations that rock Vincent senseless, right into the apartment.

*"PO-PO IS ON THEIR WAY! PO-PO IS ON THEIR WAY!"* Trevor yells.

Roy grabs Vincent by the collar but Vincent collects enough strength to knee Roy in his private. Roy doubles over in pain, giving Vincent the perfect opportunity to rally his troops and head for the truck. He grabs Shabbazz by his dreads—*"AAGHH"*—and yanks him with both hands across the hallway. He yells out to Wise about heading to the SUV. Wise hears him and quickly takes care of Neville. With the hallway floor splattered with mashed-up cake, Vincent and Wise slip and slide their way over to Lou and Emmanuel to pry them away from Hyper. Then, they hurry out the front door, only to be met by a growing crowd of curious on-lookers whom they could do without. And to add insult to injury, sirens blare from afar.

"YOOOOO!" screams Kaution, behind the steering wheel. "GET THE FUCK IN! AWWW, SHIT—WATCH OUT!"

It was too late.

Like a pack of angry wolves, the postal crew, smothered in cake and blood, burst from the building and leap from the steps, nabbing Wise and Hyper from behind to continue the avenging assault. Following them is the flamboyant Trevor, wielding a baseball bat from the top of the stairs to the front of the Suburban.

"WHERE YOU THINK YOU'RE GOING, FAT BOY?" Trevor repeatedly bashes the front windshield. "Y'ALL NOT GOING ANYWHERE!"

The sirens grow louder and nearer.

The once tranquil block suddenly turns into a battle royal arena where the combative crews are putting on a barbaric performance before a frightened, yet captivated audience. And when Kaution bails out of the Suburban and runs for dear life, Vincent comes to the stubborn conclusion that it's about time for him to make a grand exit himself.

So, he takes off running.

His cake-infested shirt flaps in the wind as he runs as fast as his Stacy Adams will allow him. But as swiftly as he is moving, he can't outrun the voices of his partners telling him this was a bad idea from the start. Nor can he distance himself from his own humiliation which led him to this situation in the first place. He allowed his emotions to get the best of him and now his homies are paying the price.

He turns the corner of Cooper Union and keeps it moving towards Astor Place so he can escape into the underground subway station and hop on the 6-train.

He increases his speed.

His heart beats like a drawn-out drum roll as he dodges through and around puzzled pedestrians glancing at his odd appearance, but he doesn't care.

If he can just make it to 59th Street to meet Joy and his other group, everything will be alright. He's *sure* of it. He swings his head around to see if anyone is on his heels.

*DAMN!*

To his disbelieving eyes, Roy rumbles from around the corner and steamrolls towards him like a charging rhinoceros. But he's not alone. The sight of a sprinting Trevor waving his baseball bat over his head has Vincent struggling to keep his stride without tripping over his feet.

He finds himself slowing down a tad.

He quickly changes travel plans.

He spots a taxi sitting on the corner of Astor Place and Third Avenue, twenty feet away. He turns his speed back up a notch.

Ten feet away.

He turns his face to check his followers.

And is met with the meaty part of the bat.

CRACK!!

Vincent is lifted into mid-air and falls face-first onto the hot concrete. Woozy, he tries to get up but can't. Spitting out graveled blood from his busted mouth, he laughs. He laughs so hard that Trevor becomes heated by his outlandish reaction.

"You think this shit is funny?" screams Trevor, standing over Vincent and cocking back his Louisville Slugger. "I'll give you some more shit to laugh about!"

"Fuck you!" Vincent sputters. "You better finish me off while you have the chance because I'ma remember your fucking ass!"

Trevor cocks his bat again. "Boy, I should bust your head wide open—!"

"Don't talk about it—be about it!"

Vincent laughs suicidally through the painful speed knot the bat left on his throbbing head. He chuckles insanely at the hard landing which ripped away some of his cheek. He hollers loudly as police cars circle the corner. Vincent wipes his blood-riddled mouth and shakes his head. For all his illicit accomplishments gained over the years from tampering with identity theft and auto theft, surviving heat from the police, the feds, other competitors, hustlers, and haters in general, the only portion of his street legacy people will now remember is how he and his partners were brought down by a bunch of corny looking mail people. And that's where he loses himself in a maniacal cackle, right before the charging albino mailman—who leaps in the air with his cinder-block fist cocked back in firing position—sends him to the hospital with a final crushing blow to his face.

But the man who was once known to the underworld as Invincible—because of his once perceived immortality in the hustling field—still finds an ounce of strength in his body to talk more hellified shit.

"Y'ALL BETTA KILL ME, MOTHAFUCKAAAAS—"

*BAMMMM!!!!!!!*

# SEVENTY-NINE

## VELOUR

Velour brushes back her naturally black hair while staring at herself in the bathroom mirror. She wraps her hair in one of Joy's silky yellow bandannas and leans closer to the mirror to further inspect her swollen eye.

Twenty-four hours later and the ugly discoloration is still the same. She stares directly at her once flawless face. She turns her head left, then right, and then stares straight ahead. She smiles at herself.

*It's not that bad.*

This may have been the worst punishment she's ever received from her brother, but this incident will fade away, just like all the others. She understands her brother's frustrations. Since she was the bearer of more bad news regarding his crumbling enterprise, she expected to receive some repercussions, and he responded pretty much the way she thought he would. But a positive was born out of that brutal process—Vincent's acceptance of her back into his close-knit world.

Now that is a prize worthy of *two* black eyes!

She turns off the bathroom light and tightens up the belt on Joy's robe before strolling toward the staircase, which leads to the terrace. She reaches the rooftop, walks over, and then leans over the banister to scope out the evening's busy strip. A suit and tie crowd spill out of Café Habana, carrying to-go bags of hearty Cuban cuisine. A flock of pretty ladies scramble into the glossy Intermix boutique to check out the latest fashion trend. Skateboarders scare the bejesus out of people while darting around recklessly in the heart of North Little Italy.

The active scene reminds her of the time when Vincent took her on her first trip overseas to Islington, London, a trendy city whose jazzy nightlife parallels Manhattan's. And the flat her brother owns there has a terrace similar to Joy's which overlooks the pulse of the social life. She can't wait to get back there to enjoy it all.

She checks the time on her Tiffany watch.

It glimmers 7:20 pm.

Hmmm.

She called her brother's cell around three o'clock and he told her he should be back around six. And she still hasn't heard from Joy, who rushed out and stated that she was going to visit her mother in Flatbush before they pull out.

She retrieves her phone and speed-dials Joy. It goes straight to voicemail. "Hey, it's me. Just letting you know that I'm ready to be picked up whenever you get back from visiting your mother." She pauses before resuming. "And, um, when you get a chance, tell my brother that I'm leaving the old Velour behind in New York. The new Velour will be more cooperative and less rebellious. Make sure you tell him that. Bye." She ends the call.

Inhaling and exhaling the warm evening air, Velour soaks in the flourishing scene for the last time before heading back downstairs to the penthouse. She bypasses her packed suitcases to grab the TV remote from the end table. NBC is now sharing breaking news.

*"Earlier today, a bizarre incident occurred downtown Manhattan where a group of postal letter carriers and another group of men—"*

Velour immediately clicks off the TV.

She places the remote back on the entertainment system and turns on the radio. WBLS is playing a Loose Ends song she and Vincent used to sing to one another back in the day when they didn't have anyone but themselves to entertain.

"*...Maaa-maaa/ she always told me/be thankful/for what you got....*"

She falls back on the sofa and plays with the robe's belt as she sings the song to herself.

*Updates about some letter carriers. Hah!*

She doesn't want to see, hear, or think about anything that has to do with the postal system. Those six years of delivering mail all but confirmed to her that nothing about her nature screams blue-collar. She has a jet-setter's mentality with a hustler's heart to match. A winning combination that can't be tamed by anything nine-to-five-ish. She checks her watch again and then takes a deep breath.

*Don't panic, girl, they're on their way.*

She pushes herself from the couch and slips out of the robe to put on her new clothes. A pair of flair-leg pants, a sleeveless blouse, and a pair of open-toe sandals. All in her trademark white color.

As she straps the back of her sandals, Freeman somehow interrupts her thoughts. A touch of anger crawls up her back. She wanted so badly to scratch his eyes out, just to leave a permanent mark on him so he would never be able to forget about what he did to scar her life.

*Bitch-ass snitch.*

She strolls over to the aquarium to feed the fish for the last time, but the thought of Freeman never leaves her mind. Something has been nagging her with the way everything went down that fateful morning at Midway. She knew at some point Dante had to have met up with Freeman and disclosed all her dirty deeds. That's the only way Freeman could've even had an inkling of what she was doing on the low. She would never have confided in him, but she *did* confide in Dante and that's why his wife should be receiving a nice little package addressed especially to her, courtesy of her husband's memory lapse. Oh, how she would just love to be a fly on the wall when Dante's wife plays that DVD!

But Freeman is another issue, altogether.

As she feeds the fish, she distinctly remembers what he said to her before she was kicked out of the post office building.

*"And when I have that talk with Davenport, that's exactly what's gonna happen to you."*

Velour stares at one fish gobbling up all the food from the others.

That's the part that bothers her.

Why would he have said that when the authorities had already terminated her from the postal service? It just doesn't add up.

She concluded that Freeman was acting the entire time and had given Davenport all the information he needed to have the inspectors and detectives come in and serve her that stupid ultimatum. Freeman probably felt sorry for her and didn't want her to go to jail so he asked them to show her mercy but to go after Vincent. That's what her assumption was until she remembers how devastated Davenport looked, sitting behind his desk. Sweaty and in shock, as if her situation was all brand new to him that morning, as well.

She catches herself shaking too much food into the tank. She places the container down.

*Whatever. What's done is done. Time to move on to bigger and better things.*

She checks her watch, and then walks over and plops back down on the sofa.

But her mind continues to run amok.

And it goes back to the video footage about her stealing.

Something about the last part of the video sticks out for reasons she couldn't pinpoint at the time. But now it finally hits her. In the video, she was wearing the team's new softball jersey. She frowns, unsure why that should hold any significance other than it was a recent video clip of her thieving.

She stands and heads for the bedroom. She strolls over to the vanity dresser and samples some of Joy's perfume collection she had left behind. She settles on one that appeals to her and lightly sprays around her neck area and arms. But then she stops spraying altogether.

*Angle shot.*

Now she understands why the softball jersey shot holds meaning. It was a recent aerial shot from above her workstation which stood out from the rest of the footage—

*"Take care, Frank," Cadina said, waving at the painter.*

*The painter stares at her, and then hesitantly smiles. "Have a good afternoon."*

*Velour grins at Cadina. "Okay, I see you..."*

*Cadina shakes her head. "Don't play yourself, alright? He told me his name downstairs."*

Velour stands frozen in one spot.

*Nah, she just met the painter that day, right?*

But there wasn't any new paint up on the ceiling, on the walls nor a whiff of paint smell the following day.

She moves gingerly into the living room and turns off the radio. She sits on the edge of the recliner, sinking deeper into her memory bank.

*Nahhh, she couldn't possibly be a—could she?*

Velour doesn't want to venture down that road, yet her mind continues unraveling disturbing truths. She stands up again and paces the floor. The inspectors told her they monitored her workstation for six months. Cadina started working at the station around late January, early February.

Six months ago.

Velour shakes her head in denial as she paces around the couch like a child playing a solo version of ring-around-the-rosie. She stops instantly. It was something the elder inspector said to her that had her questioning the reason they gave her the ultimatum instead of taking her into custody.

*"This rather unique little package we're offering you is due out of mere sympathy from our inspectors."*

She repeats to herself the last part of that statement.

"*...due out of mere sympathy from our inspectors*."

"She can't be!" Velour yells, but her statement rings hollow.

She falls onto the sofa, covering her face. She refuses to see the forest for the trees. That would have meant her only true friend in Midway was about as phony with their relationship as Velour had been with Freeman. But that's not possible! Everything about Cadina felt so true! Her blunt, but necessary advice. Her humbling persona. Her "around the way" appeal. Her infectious smile. Being around Cadina's very essence convinced Velour that if she was ever to dig deep within her anguish, she would be able to pull out a beautiful side of her that is yearning to be exposed. That's the Cadina she grew to adore! Not the one reality is trying to spoon-feed her!

*"Do yourself a favor and look into that—I'm serious,"* Lexington had said. *"It might be worth your while."*

That pops her head straight up.

Velour zooms in on her leather bag located near the huge potted tree by the window. She pushes herself up and stumbles like a dope fiend across the room to snatch it up so she can locate a certain item inside of it.

The large manila envelope Lexington had given her that dismal morning.

Velour rips open the top and pull out a wad of pictures. Fumbling to turn them upright, she stares at the first photo.

It's a man.

An older, distinguished-looking gentleman wearing glasses and a short, faded haircut.

Puzzled, she quickly flips through the other photos of the same man dressed in a dark suit, in different scenarios. As she studies each picture, the man's face becomes increasingly familiar to her—*Cadina's father?*

The next two photos show the man and Cadina together.

Velour twists her face. *Why would that fool Lexington go out of his way to give me these pics of Cadina with her pops?* She never actually met her father but has seen him now and again, waiting to give Cadina a ride home. *But so what?*

That's when she reads the bottom of the picture and her entire world crashes to the floor.

Deputy Chief Inspector Vernon McThaddeus.

The photo falls from her hand and gently swoops toward the rug.

*He's a fuckin' inspector! But Cadina's last name is Wilson, not McThad—*

That's when she spots Cadina's graduation book peeking out of the same leather bag which now lay next to her feet. She only held onto the book because Cadina had left it at her workstation the past week. She numbly bends down to pick up the book. She flips through the pages in a hurry and finally locates Cadina's choir photo. Her last name was never Wilson at all. Cadina McThaddeus. She immediately flips through the remaining photos from the manila envelope of Cadina and there it was, the icing on the nasty-tasting cake—

*Postal Inspector Cadina McThaddeus.*

In one single motion, Velour launches the book with enough velocity to bust a hole in the living room window. She then stomps the rug in a circular rage. Cadina, of all people, who she considered to be a genuine friend, was indeed an inspector. A sleeper who monitored Velour's every movement within that station for the past six months.

*BITCH, BITCH, BITCH, BITCH, BITCH!*

Betrayal is all she feels. The only person besides her brother that she's felt comfortable with, pulled the rug from beneath her feet; had her fired from her job…almost threw her in jail…*wants* to throw her brother in jail. *She's* the true reason for her brother's downfall! Velour runs over to the busted window to pull out the graduation book. She flips through the pages and finds Cadina's phone bill—which has a home address.

Velour checks her watch. Hesitant, she pulls out a pen and a sheet of paper and scribbles a message to Vincent and Joy.

She grabs her luggage and bolts out of the penthouse. Racing against time, she decides to make a pit stop to purchase something that will send a deadly message to Cadina and her precious daddy, as they have fucked with the wrong family.

Pressing the elevator button, she remembers giving Cadina one last hug from her heart. From the *fuckin'* heart! And what did that imposter have the nerve to say to her on the sly?

*"I'm sorry, too, Velour."*

"You got that right, bitch," Velour mutters, as the elevator doors opened. "You just don't know how sorry you're going to be."

She marches onto the elevator with a heart filled with bad intentions. When it reaches the first floor, she storms from the building. She pulls out her phone and requests an Uber. Minutes later, the driver arrives and pops the back trunk. She throws her luggage into the trunk, and then hops in the back seat, cursing under her breath the entire time.

The African driver turns around and happily asks, "How are we doing today, Ma'am?"

Velour glares at him with her one good eye. "We're making a pit stop to Brooklyn first, then to Queens, so let's get this shit moving–Now!"

*I have a friend to meet.*

Neither one of them had too much to say when they left the Whitestone Multiplex Cinemas. As James exits the Whitestone Bridge, he glances over at Cadina. She quietly stares out the window. She's been in a funk ever since he picked her up from her apartment. Maybe she is still mourning Marc's untimely death. She could also be bothered by the whole Velour ordeal, which he heard about from everybody and their mommas. Lately, it's been hectic at their postal station. Hectic enough to leave a gloomy stain on Cadina, the most optimistic person he knows.

He grabs her hand. She turns around and greets him with a cocked eyebrow.

"What?" James asks, defensively.

"Was that your idea of a surprise, James?" She removes her hand from his and crosses her arms.

"I assume you're referring to the movie we just saw—"

"Yes, I'm talking about the movie you *forced* me to see–"

"But I thought it might boost your spirits up a little, considering the way you've been moping around."

"And you thought *"50 Shades of Black"* was supposed to do the trick?" She swings her head back to the window. "Brother, please."

James stares at her for so long that he almost bypasses her parent's house. "Shit!"

He hit the brakes, shifts in reverse, and then parks in front of the house. He turns the engine off. "You're acting like that's the worst movie we've seen together."

Cadina turns around and glares at him.

"Well, maybe it was, but I had good intentions behind it."

"Next time, *I'll* pick out the movie, okay? I think it's only fair since you're always choosing the flicks I may or may not want to see."

"Alright, let it out."

"Let what out?"

"Whatever it is that's making you talk to me in that smart-ass tone."

"I'm not trying to sound like a smart-ass, James."

"Every word that drops from your lips is filled with sarcasm, girl."

"Then it's not me, it's my father talking."

They stare at each other and then burst into laughter.

"What in the world are you talking about?"

Cadina sighs. "Whenever my father becomes aggravated about something, he usually snaps at the people he loves the most. I guess I take after him in that manner. I'm sorry, Boo."

James takes her hand again. "Talk to me, Babe. What's up?"

"I dunno." Cadina stares out the window again. "I guess it's just the way things have been happening back-to-back-to-back at the station, you know? I can't stop thinking about Marc's death and Lexington being blamed for it. And this whole Velour situation–"

"I'm still trying to wrap my head around that one." James shakes his head. "I mean, who would've thought she'd be that bold to steal people's mail *and* their identities? Just when you think you know a person and I've known Velour for what, five, six years? All that time, smiling in people's faces like everything is cool, yet doing dirt behind our backs. And I heard they let her walk! That was crazy, right?"

"Uh, yeah, r-really crazy," Cadina stutters.

"And sad." James takes a sip of his Mountain Dew before changing subjects. "You know that uptown truck position that was posted the other day? I went ahead and applied for it."

"Really? I didn't know."

"Yeah, it's time to try something different. I've been a letter carrier for a little over ten years and now I want to preserve this body while I'm still young."

Cadina chuckles. "Now you sound like Lex. He said the same thing to me when he had passed that exam."

"Yeah, now look where he's at." James' tone turns solemn. "You know, if Davenport would've let that man go to the academy, none of this nonsense would've happened. Lex wouldn't have been blamed for Marc's death and he definitely wouldn't have tried to knock my head off. Davenport needs to answer to somebody because all of this is his fault."

Cadina nods. She then takes a huge breath. "I—I do have something I need to share with you. It's regarding a rather complex situation I'm involved in."

His shoulders slump. "Now, don't tell me you have a side-dude, Cadina–"

"Noooo, nothing like that."

"You sure?"

"I'm not seeing anyone else, James, nor do I want to see anyone else. Come here."

She grabs him by the head and tongue kisses him.

"Okay, we can scratch that off the list,", he says. "But it's nothing terminal, is it? Wait! Don't tell me you used to be a man? Please, don't let it be that–"

"None of the above, Silly."

James checks his watch and immediately straightens up in his seat. "Oh, shit."

"What's wrong?"

He cranks the truck. "I forgot; I have to drive my mom to work. Can this wait?"

"Uh, yeah, yeah. Do what you have to do. We'll talk about it later tonight."

"You sure? Because it sounds important."

"It can wait."

"Good, because I have some news I want to share with you, as well."

"Really?" She unbuckles her seat belt. "Like what?"

"We'll talk about it later. Now, get out."

She stares at him while opening the door. "You're not trying to be funny, are you?"

He gives her a quick kiss on the lips. "None whatsoever. Love you."

Cadina rolls her eyes in jest and slides out of the truck. "I love you more."

He watches her walk up to her parents' front entrance. She turns around and blows him a kiss, which he grabs out of thin air and gobbles up in his mouth. She smiles beautifully before disappearing into the house.

James' smile vanishes as soon as he pulls off from the curb. When he turns the corner, he lets out a big sigh of disappointment in himself.

*Damn. Blew it again.*

Crossing the Throgs Neck Bridge to return to the Bronx, he analyzes the awkward evening with Cadina. It wasn't so much that he blew the opportunity; the mood just didn't feel right. It wasn't right the entire weekend.

*Nah, I'm just procrastinating.*

Tomorrow, procrastination comes to an end.

When he finally reaches his house, he drags himself into the living room and falls back onto the recliner. He digs into his pocket and pulls out a heart-shaped velvet box. He flips the top open to gaze at the stunning platinum, two-carat princess-cut diamond ring with six baguette diamonds glittering on each side plus a matching platinum band.

Just the sight of the engagement ring alone builds his anxiety.

Janae bounces into the living room and wraps her arms around him from behind. "Oooo, can I see the ring again?"

She doesn't wait for a response as she snatches the box from his hand. She pulls the ring out and holds it high to marvel at. "Beautiful."

"How do you *really* feel about me proposing to Cadina?"

"Dad, I already told you." She slides the ring on her middle finger. "I like Cadina, a lot. She's articulate, she's funny…she can cook better than you. Way better than you. *Way, way* better than you–"

"I get the hint, 'Nae."

"And she makes you happy. So that makes me happy."

"You say that now, but when she becomes your stepmother, you better not give her any back-talk when she tells you to clean up your room or do the dishes."

"Please, she does that now. Where *you* been?"

"Well, I didn't know that. And don't you give me any back-talk, either."

He tickles Janae.

"*OKAY, OKAY!*" she laughs, fighting him off. "I feel you should go for it."

"Thanks for the approval." He kisses her cheek.

Walking into the living room in her floral-blue nursing uniform, Grace digs into her pocketbook and then pauses. "Are you two cackling birds ready to go?"

"Check out Cadina's ring, Ganna!" yells Janae, wiggling her fingers. "It's almost as big as the one Kobe gave his wife!"

Grace drops her purse and covers her mouth. "*Oh, my goodness!*" She takes the ring from her granddaughter and holds it up to her gleaming eyes. "*This is bee-u-tee-ful!* Oh, my goodness. It must've cost you a fortune!"

"You can say that again."

"When are you going to pop the question?"

"He was supposed to do it Friday, but he got cold feet," snickers Janae.

Grace frowns at James. "You were going to propose to her without me knowing? Who raised you, boy?"

"Ma, relax. The only reason I didn't tell you is that I didn't want you thinking I was rushing into this. This is a huge step."

"*Rushing*?" She hands him the ring. "It's about time you put a ring on that lady's finger!"

James smiles.

*This* was the reason he held off proposing to Cadina. He needed confirmation that he was doing the right thing and not making a hasty decision.

Momma Grace was the x-factor.

"So, you're cool with me proposing to Cadina?"

"Child, the moment you introduced me to her, I knew she was going to be my daughter-in-law. It was only a matter of time before you opened your eyes and saw that for yourself."

James hugs his mother. "Thank you for your blessings."

She picks up her pocketbook from the floor. "Where's she now?"

"I dropped her off at her parents' house. Why?"

Grace checks her watch. "Well, that's where we're heading tonight."

"What?"

"It's about time we all get acquainted with one another before you go down on bended knee."

"YES!" rejoices Janae.

"C'mon, Ma," James protests. "You don't have time for all that. You have to be at work soon–"

"Please. I'll call my job right now and let them know I'll be running a little late. This is far too important. You received my blessings and now it's time to get her parents' consent."

"And you're serious, too."

Grace checks her appearance in the wall mirror. "Child, I'm about to be a mother-in-law. That *is* serious business. Let's go!"

"*Daddy's gonna pop the question! Daddy's gonna pop the question*!"

Janae slips on her Nikes and then dances out the front door with her grandmother.

James wipes the dumb look from his face, follows them out the door, and then locks it. He turns his cell phone back on since he'd turned it off before he and Cadina went into the movie theater.

Immediately, nine voicemail messages pop up on the front screen.

Three from Divine and the rest from the crew.

Hmmm. Looks important.

But he'll listen to all the messages later. He has far more important, yet nerve-wracking concerns to deal with.

He slides behind the wheel, backs out of the driveway, and then fumbles to press Cadina's number on speed dial.

"This is crazy, you know that, right?" he says, cutting his eyes at his mother.

*"HERE AND NOOOOOW! I PROMISE TO LOOOOVE FAITHFULLY!"* Grace sings the classic Luther Vandross wedding song with her eyes closed, rocking from side to side. She purposely ignores him.

James turns his attention to the evening traffic as he waits for Cadina to answer his call.

# EIGHTY-ONE

## CADINA

Cadina channel-surfs the living room television and winds up leaving it on the news station. She hears a faint ringing noise and realizes it's her cell phone inside of her purse. She quickly rises from the loveseat and pulls the phone out from her bag, along with her postal inspector's badge.

She smiles upon seeing the number and then presses the talk button. "Hey, Boo."

"Hey," James responds. "What are you doing?"

She flips the badge through her fingers. "Watching TV. Why what's up?"

"Your parents home?"

"Just my father. My mom and my sister went food shopping. Why?"

"HEY, BOO!" Grace and Janae shout.

"Is that Momma Grace and 'Nae?"

"Yes, you're on the truck's speakerphone."

"Hey, y'all!" Cadina responds.

"We'll see you soon, Cadina!" Janae happily yells.

"What 'Nae say?"

"My momma wants to meet your folks before she goes to work tonight."

Her face distorts instantly. "W-What?"

"She feels it's time for her to meet your parents since we're seeing each other."

"Unless y'all have already made plans for this evening, Cadina," Grace asks.

"Uh, no, we don't have any plans, but—"

"Good. We're halfway over the bridge as we speak, so we should be there in no time. See you soon!"

"Alright, bye."

*Click.*

Cadina stares at the wall, stumped.

*Great. Of all nights she wants to get acquainted with somebody.*

Cadina tosses her phone to the side and wrestles with a dilemma that is getting way out of hand. She was so close to revealing her true occupation to James tonight but punked out at the last minute. The agency made it very clear it has zero tolerance for personnel that fails to comply with the guidelines. Her father reinforced the message by verbally etching the rules into her brain. He didn't need to, though.

She made a solid oath not to embarrass her father like she had in the past. But who would've thought she would find her soulmate within the postal system? A person who mirrors her in so many ways, especially with his traditional and moral beliefs regarding the union of man and woman. A man who has been instrumental in making her feel like the ultimate queen. How could she not tell the love of her life that she's been leading a double life, even though it could possibly impact their bond in a major way? The bottom line is that she can't lay claim to this ongoing falsehood any longer. And her father senses this, as well. He hasn't said anything to her yet. However, she has no choice but to bring up this touchy subject as soon as possible, if she plans on being with James for the rest of her life—

*Hey, wait a minute!*

She erases all those thoughts to home in on what actually occurred within the past hour. James says he has '*some news*' he needs to share with her. And now, his mother is coming out of her way from the Bronx to meet her family, and then leave for work after that.

Some news.

Parents meeting each other for the first time.

News.

Meeting.

It's all so apparent to her now.

*Here comes the briiiiiiide! All dressed in whiiiiiiite!*

It takes every morsel of her strength not to blow the roof off the house with a siren-like scream. Instead, she muffles it with both hands and rejoices in a small circle.

"*OhMyGod, OhMyGod! He's gonna do it! OhMyGod! He's gonna—!*"

Within a flash, her celebration becomes short-lived. She's almost forgotten about the critical matter at hand, which will undoubtedly complicate things. She drops back down onto the loveseat, not knowing how to react to everything that's coming her way.

Is James really going to propose to her tonight?

Or is she getting ahead of herself like she usually does?

But what if she's right?

Should she pull him to the side and explain everything before he drops the big question?

DING DONG!

Cadina launches off the loveseat like a space shuttle. She takes a moment to relax her nerves before heading to the door. The bell rings again.

"*YOU GOT THE DOOR?*" her father yells from upstairs. *"I'M WATCHING THE NEWS UPDATE!"*

"I GOT IT!"

Cadina continues to take deep breaths as she shuffles into the foyer area and pauses to check her appearance in the bronze mirror. Satisfied, she turns to the door and switches her fanatic facial expression into a warm, pleasant smile.

"I'M COMING, BOO!"

She opens the door...

# EIGHTY-TWO

## VELOUR

This is such a long shot, but Velour presses the doorbell, anyway. Her betrayer could be anywhere. She could be with James in the Bronx somewhere, having fun and laughing about her downfall. She's willing to bet that even *he* knew about the plot against her the entire time. Yet, he walked around the station, smiling all in her face. *Fake-ass bastard.*

She wishes Cadina was at her apartment so she could accomplish what she has in mind and be on her merry way to London. She checks her watch. 8:10 pm. She rings the doorbell again.

*What the hell are you doing? Hop back into that Uber and get the hell outta here!*

She turns a deaf ear to her pleading conscience. She *can't* leave. Someone must pay, whether it is with Cadina's blood or her father's. Vengeance is all that she seeks, and there is no other way around it.

She reaches for the bell again when she hears footsteps, followed by a familiar voice.

"I'M COMING, BOO!"

Bingo!

*I got your "Boo", Bitch.*

The door swings open and out pops an enthusiastic Cadina, still dressed in her uniform, smiling from ear to ear. It doesn't take long for that smile to slide right off her pretty little face and shatter right onto the doorstep. The new expression she wears contains shock and fear, all wrapped up in one frightening package.

And that's exactly what Velour expected to encounter.

"Hello, Cadina," Velour greets, with a neutral tone.

The betrayer doesn't move or utter a word.

"I know you're not surprised to see me. Are you?"

"No, no, it's not that, um," Cadina quickly peeks back inside her house, and then closes the door halfway on her body. In a hushed tone, she asks, "H-How did you get this address?"

*Bitch, please.*

"You know, it's amazing what you can find once you commit yourself to it."

"Is that right…" Cadina grips the doorknob.

"I'm sure you, of all people, can attest to that…right, Cadina?"

Velour blatantly studies her betrayer's face, which is still trying to process this petrifying moment.

"So, are you going to invite me in or are we just going to continue this awkward conversation on your doorstep?" Velour asks.

"I can't."

"Trust me, it won't take long. I have a prior engagement and as you can see, I have an Uber waiting on me."

Cadina glances over at the driver who stands outside of his blue Toyota Camry, smoking a cigarette. She doesn't budge from the door. "I can't, Velour."

"You can't or you won't, Cadina? Which is it?"

"WHO'S AT THE DOOR, CADINA?" Vernon yells.

Velour attempts to look past Cadina, but she blocks her view. "I see daddy's home. I can't meet your daddy?"

Cadina insists with her eyes. "You gotta go, Velour."

"Daddy's precious little girl–"

"Please, you need to leave, right now."

"Is this how you want it to play out, Cadina? Fine. I'm through talking, anyway."

Velour reaches in her bag, bypasses the 9mm Beretta handgun she acquired from one of her two-bit hustler friends and pulls out Cadina's yearbook. She thrusts it into her betrayer's hand.

"Words of advice, Bitch," Velour grips Cadina's hand and holds onto it. "If you don't want people to know your whereabouts, then I suggest you don't be this sloppy with your profession. Thanks for the second chance in life, Cadina McThaddeus…that's your real name, isn't it?"

A terrified Cadina snatches her hand away from Velour's clutch.

"We *will* continue this conversation at another time, I promise you that."

Velour wants to slap the shit out of her so badly, but instead turns away and marches towards her Uber ride.

*Slam!*

Velour flinches when she hears the door slam shut behind her. The rage flowing through her veins rapidly increases.

*Forget these people! Head back to Manhattan and wait on your brother and—*

Velour shuts down all rational thinking from this point on.

She finishes her staged departure by hopping into the idle Uber. She gives the driver instructions to make a turn on the next corner and park.

The driver follows her orders and parks in front of a hydrant. She gives him two hundred bucks to stay put until she returns. She then rips out of the Camry and marches back down the quiet, dark block toward her betrayer's home, armed and ready to put her purchased item to deadly use—for the sake and honor of her family.

She quickly scans the neighborhood to make sure no one is watching. To her surprise, she spots a window fully opened on the second floor.

*Perfect!*

Now, she must find a way to get up there in a hurry. Without delay, she creeps around the side of the house…

# EIGHTY-THREE

## CADINA

She finds herself hyperventilating, with her back pinned against the front door. The sight of seeing Velour on her parents' doorstep shuts down all her body mechanics.

*How the hell did she know about my parents' address?*

*And how the hell did she find out about me?*

Her mind tries to comprehend what just took place. Velour came here for a reason. And that reason was to expose Cadina's real name and true occupation right in her face. And the way she spoke to her—very condescendingly…very menacingly. She called her a *bitch.* And worse…

…Velour made a threat to her life.

Never in her entire existence has Cadina been threatened, bullied, or even teased.

And when Velour dug into her bag, Cadina thought she was going to pull out something other than her yearbook to get her message across.

Something deadly.

This was new territory for her.

Territory that has her immobilized in fear.

*But how the hell did Velour get her hands on that confidential information? Surely, I didn't mess up!*

Tears drip from her eyes as Vernon rumbles down the staircase with the house phone wedged between his ear and his shoulder.

"Yes. I'm leaving right now," Vernon says through the phone, as he straps on his gun holster. "Make sure you call Inspector Moses and have him contact Border Enforcement, okay? Thanks." He reaches the bottom of the staircase and rushes to the living room to place the phone on the base. "Who was that at the door?"

Cadina forces the name out of her mouth. "V-Velour."

Her response slams the breaks on his momentum.

He whips around to face her. "*Who*?"

"I-It was Velour."

He walks toward Cadina while keenly studying her expression to see if she is telling the truth. "You're kidding me, right? Tell me you're kidding–?"

"I wish I was–"

"HOW THE HELL DOES SHE KNOW ABOUT THIS ADDRESS, CADINA?"

"I-I don't know–"

"DOES SHE KNOW WHO YOU ARE? DID SHE FOLLOW YOU HERE?"

"I-I DON'T KNOW! I'M STILL TRYING TO FIGURE THAT OUT MYSELF!"

"WHERE DID SHE GO?"

"SHE HOPPED IN A BLUE TOYOTA CAMRY AND THEY LEFT!"

"JESUS H. CHRIST!"

Vernon races out the door, through the front gate, and stands in the middle of the street.

She creeps out the door and onto the porch.

They both look up and down the street.

No signs of that car anywhere.

Vernon marches back toward the house and they close the door behind them in the foyer. He places both hands on her shoulders and looks her square in the eyes while controlling his temperament. "I want you to listen to me very carefully; did she do anything or say where she was going?"

"She said she had a prior engagement but didn't give an actual destination."

"What else did she say to you?"

"She said, *'Thanks for the second chance in life, Cadina McThaddeus.'* She made it very clear that she knows who we are–"

"There is no way on earth she would have access to that kind of information without you doing or saying something–"

"You think I would do anything that stupid to jeopardize my own life?"

"You've done stranger things in the past, Cadina–"

"But not something as critical as this! I never gave Velour reason to think I was anything other than a letter carrier, you gotta believe me on that–"

"What else did she say?"

"That was it and then she gave me back my yearbook."

"Where is your yearbook?"

She points to the desk in the foyer.

Vernon snatches the book from the desk and flips through it. An envelope falls to the floor. He picks it up, reads it, and then releases a wave of disappointment. He holds the envelope up for her to view.

It's a Verizon phone bill with her name on it and their residential address.

"You think this might have clued her to our whereabouts, Cadina?"

She buries her face in her hands. "Oh, God, I am so sorry!"

He pulls out his service weapon and checks the magazine. "Do you know who I was on the phone with a minute ago? Agent Whitaker. He called to inform me that they apprehended Vincent and his crew this afternoon."

She lifts her head up, completely surprised. "Really? When did all this happen?"

"This afternoon." He holsters his firearm and then pulls out his mobile phone. "And now we have to apprehend your little friend before she bolts out of town altogether. She's considered dangerous at this point."

"Where did y'all find her brother?"

Vernon turns her way, wearing a grave expression. "You really don't know what happened at your station, do you?"

"No, because I went to the movies with James and then we went to dinner afterward."

She waits for the update with pure anticipation.

"What *happened*?"

DING DONG!

Father and daughter jump as if the doorbell had given them an electrical jolt. Vernon drops the phone and pulls out his Glock and scrambles to the door's peephole.

Cadina creeps to the side of the window. She peeks through the blinds and then releases a huge sigh of relief.

Vernon holsters his gun, but not his annoyance. "You didn't tell me we were having all this company tonight, Cadina."

"I didn't know, either, until they called and told me they were on their way."

"Why are they here?"

"His mother wants to meet you and Mommy."

"For what?"

She twiddles her thumbs but doesn't say anything.

"For *what*, Cadina?"

"I know this is going to sound outlandish to you, but I believe James is going to propose to me tonight."

He squints his eyes at his daughter. "You're right. That does sound outlandish. What would make you think that? Because he's bringing his mother over here–"

"He told me he had something important he wanted to share with me right before he dropped me off here, earlier. Now, all of a sudden, he's brought his whole family here to meet y'all? It's not rocket science, Daddy–"

"And you really believe that?"

The doorbell rings again.

"Yes, I do! That's why we need to tell them the truth about us."

"Now you really have lost your damn mind–"

"I'm tired of lying to him, Daddy." She grips her father by the arms. "Eventually he will find out and I rather he hears it from us instead of someone else down the road. I love this man too much for that to happen, so either we're going to do this together or I will do it myself–it's that simple."

Vernon rubs his face with his hand and then holds his chin. He glares at her. "I've already gambled by honoring your first request to negotiate a deal with Velour. You damn sure better be right about this man's intentions for you." He picks his phone up from the floor and dials a number. "Yeah, it's me. Velour Patterns visited my house ten minutes ago in a blue Toyota Camry. Get some men to the airports, bus, and train terminals...and send a couple of vehicles to my house, just in case she decides to return…yes…I will explain later…"

He walks to the living room.

She quickly checks herself out in the foyer mirror.

Just seeing James with his family at the door alleviated all her present worries.

She takes a moment before turning the doorknob.

# EIGHTY-FOUR

## JAMES

James presses the bell again and then leans in closer to the door.

"Maybe they went to the store," Janae says.

"Maybe. But I could've sworn I heard conversation on the other side of this door."

He glances at his mother. She is touching up her nose in front of a compact mirror. "You put any more powder on that nose, and I will have it dipped in a deep fryer."

"You see this house right here?" Grace points out. "Ashy people don't own houses like these, so I'm going in there correct. Anything between my teeth?"

She exaggerates a smile.

"Ma. Relax."

He rings the doorbell again and then waits. He tries to calm down his jitters. But as the seconds roll by, the jitters only escalate.

The door finally swings open and out floats a glowing Cadina.

"Hey, Baby," she sings, grabbing James for a hug.

"I see the happy side of you has finally showed up," he teases. After a couple of seconds, he tries to let go, but her embrace is unexpectedly strong. "Uh, is everything alright?"

"Yes, now that you're here."

She finally releases him and then greets Grace and Janae with a "*Hey, y'all...*" before showering them with lengthy hugs.

"Come on in, everybody."

She holds the door open for them to enter.

James turns around to say something to Cadina, but winds up watching her scoot all the way down to the front gate. She attentively screens the entire block, as if she is looking for somebody.

She then turns around.

She could be a lamppost the way her face is illuminating the front lawn.

An hour ago, her mood was about as black as the Nikes she's currently sporting. She struts back inside the house and steals another kiss from him as she closes the front door.

"Come, make yourself at home."

She grabs his hand and escorts him into the living room. Once there, he sees his family on one side of the room sitting quietly on the sofa. On the other side of the room is Vernon, dressed in a white-collar dress shirt, dark pants…

…and strapped with a gun underneath his armpit.

*Okayyyy…*

James heads straight to Vernon with his hand extended. "How's it going, Sir?"

Vernon shakes his hand firmly. "It's going. How are things on your end?"

"Can't complain." His eyes bounce from the gun to Vernon's hardened stare. "I see you've met my family."

"Yes, we said our hellos while you two were still outside," Grace replies, admiring the splendid Victorian interior encompassing them. "I must say, Vernon, I'm in awe; you have one beautiful home!"

"Thank you, Grace." Vernon glances at his watch. "I'm sorry if I appear to be a bit caught off-guard. I wasn't expecting company tonight."

James catches Vernon side-eyeing a hesitant Cadina.

He tries to read into that odd exchange.

"And I do apologize for that, Vernon," says Grace. "It was my doing. You see, James has been dating Cadina for some time now, and I wanted to take the time out of my busy schedule to meet the parents of such a beautiful lady."

"Awww, thank you, Ma'am," blushes Cadina .

"I speak the truth, my dear. And I hope we're not intruding in any way, Vernon–"

"I, uh, am in the middle of something–"

"This won't take long at all. Right, James?"

James snaps back into the present. "Uh, yeah, yeah…it won't take long."

"James didn't tell me you were in law enforcement."

Again, James catches Cadina and her father exchanging uncomfortable glances at each other.

Grace points at Vernon's holster. "I, uh, noticed the gun underneath your armpit. You're a detective of some kind?"

The front door bursts open.

Vernon and Cadina jump to their feet and rush toward the foyer.

James notices Vernon's hand moving towards his weapon.

*What the–!*

Entering inside the foyer with groceries in their hands are Lorraine and Camille.

Vernon eases his hand away from his gun as he and Cadina help them with the bags. He leads the way into the living room. "Honey, Camille, I would like for you to meet James' mother, Grace. Grace, this is my wife, Lorraine, and my oldest daughter, Camille."

Grace stands, with her hand reached out. "It's a pleasure meeting the both of you."

Now, James witnesses Vernon, Lorraine, and Camille nervously side-eyeing one another.

*What the hell is going on around here?*

He turns to Grace.

She drops her cheerful demeanor altogether and cuts her eyes at him.

He knows when his mother feels offended.

"Uh, *hello,* everyone!" Lorraine greets with an overblown smile. She smoothed out her gold blouse before shaking Grace's hand. "It's, um, it's nice to finally meet you, Grace."

"I bet it is," Grace replies, in a guarded tone.

"Cadina," Lorraine motions with her head. "…let's take these bags to the kitchen and get our guests something to drink. We have lemonade, iced tea, bottled water—"

"Lemonade, please!" Janae requests.

"I'll take a bottled water," James replies.

"Nothing for me, thank you," Grace adds, with pure skepticism.

"We'll be right back," Vernon says as he and his family shuffle into the kitchen.

James joins his family on the couch.

"Very interesting." Grace glares at the kitchen door before eyeballing him. "Are you *sure* you want to marry into this family?"

"Now, why would you say that, Ma?"

"Don't act like you didn't see the way her mother was looking at me as if I had a booger hanging from my nose–"

"See, now you're overreacting–"

"Really? Why didn't you tell me her father was a detective?"

"I didn't hear him say he *was* a detective–"

"All this time you've been dating Cadina and you don't know what her parents do for a living?"

"I assumed they both were into real estate, that's what her mother does–"

"*OH MY GOD! OOOH, MY GOD! WOOO-HOOO!*"

James and Grace pause their conversation when they hear loud rejoicing coming from the kitchen. The commotion quickly dwindles down to sporadic laughter.

"See! I bet they're talking about us right now!" Grace bitterly declares.

"Ma, stop it."

"Cadina's a beautiful girl and all, but they better not act like she's too good for you or they're going to get a good piece of my mind."

"Just behave yourself. That's all I'm saying."

"I didn't come all the way over here for us to get insulted, that's for sure."

"Ganna…be nice!" Janae warns.

"Hmmph." Grace frowns as she re-adjusts her pocketbook on her lap.

Lorraine and Camille enter the living room with drinks.

James instantly notices a change in their behavior.

They're glowing the way Cadina was outside near the gate.

"Cadina went upstairs to change, she'll be right back," Lorraine announces, as she sashays over toward James to hand him a cold bottled water. "Here you go, James..."

"Thanks."

Vernon enters the living room with his face glued to his phone. He appears to be texting as he walks over to the window.

He seems anxious for some reason as he continuously peeks through the blinds.

*Is he waiting on someone? I thought he wasn't expecting company tonight?*

Lorraine takes a seat and sits her drink on the table. "You know, Grace, I was telling Vernon in the kitchen that had we known earlier about James and Cadina's blossoming relationship, we would've had this get-together months ago–"

"But *I* was aware of their special relationship, Lorraine," Grace counters, leaning in her direction. "And that's why I took the liberty to expedite this much-needed meet-up. So, you can thank me for that."

"And I commend you, wholeheartedly. Cadina told me you bought a home not too long ago. Congratulations!"

A genuine smile finally carves through Grace's ornery disposition. "Well, thank you, Lorraine. But James made that dream a reality for me."

"C'mon, Ma, you know it was a joint effort," James comments.

"I *know* that, James. But can I still acknowledge your efforts?"

James smiles, but his attention, once again, swings back to Vernon, who continues to peek out the window.

"This is so beautiful!" Lorraine claps her hands together. "And as a real estate broker, you know I would love so much to hear about your journey toward ownership!"

Grace bashfully peeks around at everyone. "Ohhh, y'all don't want me to bore you with that story–"

"Oh, we would love for you to share!" Camille turns around to James with a smirk. "We're practically family. Right, James?"

James almost chokes on his water.

He looks up at Lorraine and Camille.

They can no longer conceal their exhilaration.

Even Vernon takes a break from peeking through the blinds to look his way.

*Wait a minute…*

Judging by the way Lorraine and Camille are giggling confirms James' naiveté.

*They know.*

And it doesn't take a genius to name the person who would've shared that news with them.

Cadina.

*No wonder she was beaming like a fog light outside!*

Cadina has taken the surprise right out of his hands and given him something he didn't need—a highly anticipated proposal event.

"I see y'all are persistent around here." Grace sits at the edge of the couch, with her hands ready to illustrate. "Okay, this is how it all happened…"

As she begins her story, Lorraine and Camille listen intently, but their eyes constantly roll over toward him.

Then, they start giggling to themselves again.

James just shakes his head.

*This is embarrassing.*

# EIGHTY-FIVE

## CADINA

Cadina rips off her uniform and rushes into the bathroom for a quick shower. Five minutes later, she wraps herself with a towel and tiptoes into her bedroom. Her heart is filled with excitement, knowing what's about to take place downstairs in the living room.

*James is about to go down on bended knee*!

She feels higher than Method Man and Snoop Dogg at a George Clinton concert. But as she slips on her underwear, the twinkle in her eyes begins to fade.

Her family is about to disclose classified information to the Richards family.

She sits on the bed, feeling a bit worried. She hopes that when they share the complex news with James, his love for her won't diminish. *Naaaaah.* Her daddy will thoroughly explain everything regarding their investigation of Velour. And how during their mission, she just happened to fall in love. There is no plainer or truer explanation than that.

Rejuvenated, she hurries to the closet to pick out an outfit but instinctively turns toward the window.

It's open.

Curious, she walks over and draws the curtains back.

She then frowns.

Clumps of dirt lay all over the windowsill.

Odd.

Very odd.

Cadina sticks her head out the window and into nightfall. She peers down and sees her father's ladder which stands directly underneath the window.

*What the hell?*

Movement in the middle of the street catches her eye.

She turns her head and gasps at the sight of a man running toward the house, waving his arms as if he's about to guide a plane for landing.

But he's waving at *her*!

*PERVERT!*

Cadina slams the window shut, slides the curtains close, and backs away slowly, covering her scantily clad body with her bare arms. Her first thought is to run downstairs and tell her father about the Peeping Tom, but then it occurs to her that she's seen his face before.

*Wasn't that Velour's Uber driver?*

A door creaking from behind alerts Cadina.

She spins around.

And the horrifying sight she sees drains the blood completely from her face.

Raging out of the closet with a swinging fist is Velour, who sends Cadina sprawling to the floor with a brutal jab to the nose. With blood gushing out of her nostrils, Cadina tries to get up, but Velour kicks and stomps on her defenseless body with animalistic fury until she's laid out on the rug.

"*V-Vel—*"

"Don't you call my name, Bitch," Velour seethes.

Cadina coughs violently as the kicking comes to a merciful halt. Blood hazes her vision as she catches a glimpse of Velour snatching a pillow from the bed and then kneeling right next to her head.

"*Nooooo...nooo...*"

Velour uses her knee to press the pillow down on Cadina's face.

"*Mmmmm! Mmmmmmm!*"

"That's right. Bring your daddy up here–he's next."

Cadina hears the frightening sound of a round being chambered inside a gun.

"*MMMMMM! MMMMMMM! MMMMMM!*"

"Hold still, Bitch; this won't take long."

Cadina desperately lunges for Velour's face and digs her thumb deep into her bruised eye.

"*AUGHHH…SHIT—!*"

POOOOOOW!!!!

The shot ricochets off the bedroom wall.

A screaming Cadina flings the pillow across the room, and then struggles to her feet and staggers around, removing hair away from her face to visually locate Velour.

She spots her crouched over, covering her grotesque eye.

"YOU BITCH!" Velour screams as she attempts to raise her gun.

Cadina launches her body into Velour's, causing the gun to fly out of her hand. They land on the floor and roll around until Velour punches her in the face, setting herself free. Both women then land on their feet. Cadina snatches the first thing she can lay her hands on to defend herself.

The steel metal Empire State Building statue.

For a long, harrowing moment, they hesitantly encircle the small area, waiting for the other to make a move. Cadina weakly cocks her blunt weapon, but then stumbles backward when Velour jerks her body in her direction.

Through the ruckus, Cadina manages to hear her family screaming and hollering their way up the staircase.

Crouching in a wrestler's stance, with blood oozing from her eye, Velour threatens, "All I'm saying, Bitch, is that you better not miss—"

"P-Please, V-Velour, y-you don't have to do this!"

Velour makes an attempt for the gun, but Cadina cuts her off with one swing of the statue. To Cadina's surprise, Velour re-routes and torpedoes her body into her, sending them straight to the window.

Struggling to control the velocity of the momentum, Cadina screams, "*NOOOOOOO, VELOURRRR!*" right before the ex-coworkers, ex-friends are sent crashing through the window and into the warm, summer night air, all the way down to an unforgiving fate.

"...And I was really impressed by the way James was able to get the owner to shave twenty percent off the market value!" Grace proudly recalls. "We also hired a building inspector and saved a ton on maintenance costs, so blessings were everywhere, trust me."

"What an awesome story!" Lorraine says, fascinated. "Thank you for sharing, Grace."

"I still get goosebumps when I think about the entire process. So, thanks for listening."

While the women chat, James keeps a close eye on Janae, who entertains herself by gawking over the black figurines and ceramics displayed neatly in the living room.

He then glances at Vernon who remains near the window as if he's on a stakeout.

And Vernon never deviates from his routine.

First, he checks his watch.

After that, he texts someone on his phone.

And then he peeks through the blinds.

Not once has Vernon even tried to join the conversation or have a man-to-man talk with him. His deliberate isolation from everyone is making James feel some type of way.

*Maybe I need to pull him away from that damn window–*

"Grace, James..."

Lorraine stands to her feet.

She smiles but it appears to be apprehensive if anything else.

"I'm going to make a confession; we know why you all are here." Lorraine motions to Vernon to join the gathering. "And we are very excited about what's going to take place in a few minutes. But when Cadina comes back down, we as a family need to discuss a very important matter before James makes his announcement. Is that okay with the both of you?"

"I'm so glad you bought it up, Lorraine," Grace replies, visibly annoyed. "Because, for some reason, and correct me if *I'm* wrong, ever since we've been in this house, we haven't felt particularly welcomed here–"

"I can understand you feeling that way, Grace. But I can assure you that you are very much welcomed here–"

"You say that, yet, your husband has been glued to that window the entire time we've been here. He hasn't even tried to strike up a conversation with James and that to me is very disrespectful–"

"I'm truly sorry for making everyone feel uncomfortable," Vernon injects. "That was never my intention–"

"Oh, so now you can talk!" Grace mocks.

"And this is what we're about to discuss when Cadina returns–"

"We don't have to wait on her, we can talk right now–"

"Ma, let's wait on Cadina so they can share whatever it is they need to share with us–"

"Does this topic you need to share with us have anything to do with that gun you're toting around underneath your armpit?" Grace questions.

Vernon peeks at Lorraine before saying, "In a way, it does, Grace."

"Are you the FBI?"

*Thump...thump...thump...thump....*

"No, I'm not with the FBI."

Grace crosses her arms. "Okay. Then what are you?"

*THUMP...THUMP...THUMP, THUMP, THUMP... THUMP, THUMP!*

Everyone lifts their heads toward the ceiling.

"What in the world is Caddy doing upstairs?" Camille asks.

Vernon walks to the staircase and yells, "Cadina, are you alright up there?"

*POOOOOOOW!!!!*

"Oh, my God!" Lorraine shrieks. "Was that a gunshot?"

A high-pitch scream slices through the house as everyone scrambles around in fear.

"CADINA!!!"

Vernon dashes up the staircase with his gun already out of its holster.

"*MY BABY!*"

Lorraine and Camille bolt upstairs, right on his heels.

James doesn't hesitate as he follows the ladies up the steps.

"JAMES!" screams Grace, holding a terrified Janae. "DON'T GO UP THERE!"

He ignores her plea and makes it to the second floor just in time to witness Vernon aiming his gun and rushing into the room where the commotion is deriving from.

"*NOOOOOOO! VELOURRRR!*" Cadina yells out.

A thunderous crash is heard.

"OHMYGOD, OHMYGOD! NOOOOO!" Vernon bellows.

James slides to a stop.

A frantic Vernon bolts from the room, zooms past James, and heads back downstairs.

Lorraine and Camille rush into the room, but within seconds, a wide-eyed Lorraine backs out of the room and up against the hallway wall to release a sonic cry that rips throughout the already chaotic house.

*"CAAAAAAAAAADDY!"*

Lorraine and Camille haul ass back down the stairs.

James rushes inside the bedroom. He scans the entire area before his eyes fall onto the broken window where fragments of shattered glass continue to drop from the top frame.

"*Hooo, shit!*"

James' turns around and rushes back down the stairs. He blows through the empty living room and pauses on the front doorstep. Fully aware of the curious neighbors, who have now emerged from their homes to find out what's going on, James follows the direction of their gaze and dashes to the other side of the lawn. There, he finds Vernon and another man struggling to dig Cadina out from the adult-sized bushes that square off the front of their home. James rushes over to help the men break branches that entomb her.

*"Cadina, Baby!"* cries Lorraine, holding her mouth as tears glaze her distraught face. She yells at Vernon, *"IS SHE CONSCIOUS? I-IS SHE BREATHING—"*

"*SHE'S ALRIGHT! SHE'S ALRIGHT!*" Vernon confirms, breaking most of the branches required to pull his daughter free.

The three men ease Cadina away from the bushes and lay her down on the grass. Other than minor bruises and scratches, everyone is relieved to see that she didn't suffer anything worse.

Lorraine drops down next to James, horrified at the sight of her daughter's battered face. "*My God...Cadina!*"

Cadina weakly mutters, "*....Am...am...I...alright?*"

Lorraine cuddles her daughter's head. "Yes, you are, Baby, y-you're going to be fine. Don't talk, okay?"

Camille arrives with a blanket to cover up her sister's body. "The ambulance and police should be here soon."

"Where did Vern go?" Lorraine asks.

"He went to check on the condition of the other girl."

"*Girl?* Another *girl* did this to my baby?"

Camille nods. "And she got *exactly* what she deserved, too. Fuckin' bitch."

"I'll be back." James stands up and heads around the other side of the tall bushes. He pushes his way through the growing crowd to see the person who tried to kill his lady. When he reaches the middle of the melee, the ghastly sight he witnesses is way beyond his mortal comprehension.

Lying in the driveway, in her own pool of blood, is a shivering Velour.

Thrusting out of her stomach is a steel metal statue of the Empire State Building.

James feels his legs about to give out from underneath him.

Grace whispers a prayer as she comforts Velour until the medics arrive.

Vernon walks up and hands out towels to Grace. "I think one of you should go inside to console Janae."

James snatches the towels from his hands. "You go, Ma, I got this."

"Okay." Grace struggles to get up. "But isn't this Velour? Your coworker from the station?"

James nods.

"But why would she attack Cadina?"

"I don't know."

"Dear, Lord." She rushes back inside the house.

The growing crowd begins to close in on them.

"LADIES AND GENTLEMEN, THIS IS NOW CONSIDERED A CRIME SCENE," Vernon shouts, while motioning with his hands. "I WILL NEED EVERYBODY TO MOVE BACK—NOW! LET'S GO!"

As the neighbors backpedal to clear the area, Vernon pulls out his cell phone.

James carefully lifts Velour's head to place a towel underneath it. He can't even fathom the reason for her attack on Cadina, but just staring at her deplorable condition is too much for him to grasp.

Velour coughs up blood as she attempts to talk.

"Shhhhh," James advises. "The ambulance is on the way."

She ignores him and manages to form a weak smile. *"J-J-James?"*

"Don't strain yourself, girl, damn."

*"I—I—f-f-fucked uuup...."*

James doesn't know what to say.

He tilts his head to Vernon, who is giving out instructions over his cell phone.

"Yes, this is Deputy Chief Inspector McThaddeus. I need for you to get in touch with Inspector Harris asap and tell him that our primary target has been brought down in front of my house. Yes, my house! Get our units out here immediately. Yes, one of our inspectors is wounded but is in stable condition…EMT has been contacted and their ETA is five minutes. I'll call you back."

Vernon dials another number while walking a few feet away from the scene.

James tries to put together the pieces of Vernon's conversation.

*If he's a Postal Inspector, is Cadina the injured inspector he was referring to?*

Velour grips James' arm, making him jump.

"*Do…mef-fa-favor, J-Jay?*"

James steadies her hand. "Yes…"

"*T-Tell my b-brother I'm s-sorry I let himmm d-down—arghhh… sssshhit—*"

Three ear-splitting fire trucks pull up to the scene first. No sooner than the firefighters bolt out of their trucks, two ambulances arrive and park back-to-back in front of the house. The paramedics rush out of their vehicles, open the back doors to retrieve their gurneys, and push through the scattered onlookers to assist the wounded women.

James releases Velour's hand and moves out of the way.

The police arrive seconds later to investigate the scene, with Vernon's full cooperation.

The first EMT team loaded Cadina into their vehicle. Lorraine and Camille jump in the back, as well, and the ambulance takes off, with a police escort leading the way.

The second EMT team carefully loads Velour onto the gurney, and into the ambulance.

Without giving it a second thought, James catches up to the paramedics and tells them he's Velour's brother. They rush him on board and then close the doors behind him before pulling off.

With sirens blaring, the ambulance barrels down the street, eating every red light they encounter. A paramedic readjusts the oxygen mask on Velour's face, but it becomes increasingly clear that, due to the extensive blood loss, they are losing her, fast. They methodically go through their procedures, exhausting every possibility available en route to the emergency room. It doesn't matter, though. The paramedics put forth their best effort to save her within the short span of time they'd been given.

"I'm sorry, Sir," the lady paramedic gravely replies, as the monitor located behind her flatlines to finalize the outcome.

James stares out the window, maintaining a firm grip on the hand that has waved hello to him every morning at Midway for almost six years. This hand will wave no more at Midway or any other place here on earth.

He lowers his head and cries.

# EIGHTY-SEVEN

## JAMES

James has been circling the Tenth Street block for the past five minutes, in search of a parking space. He tries his luck down Stuyvesant Street. He sees a car leaving. He pulls up to the vacant spot and backs in.

He checks the clock on the dashboard.

6:00 am.

An hour to chill before he clocks in for duty.

He debates whether he should wait until the last minute to head inside or follow his daily regimen of eating his breakfast in the break room, knowing that if he does, he may get confronted with resistance from his fellow coworkers.

*Oh, well.*

He turns the engine off, grabs his shoulder bag and his breakfast, locks his doors via remote, and then trudges down Third Avenue to the station. He raises his head to the overcast sky. At any second, the bottom is going to drop out and the city will be baptized in precipitation.

"*....Tell my brother I'm sorry....*"

He can still hear Velour's frail voice whispering to him; can still feel the strength from her hand slipping away; can still see her body lying lifeless on the gurney, with that steel replica of the Empire State Building wedged deeply into her stomach—

SCREECH!!!!

He unknowingly walks in front of a speeding pick-up truck.

"WATCH WHERE YOU GOING, ASSHOLE!" the driver shouts, as he passes by James.

He shakes it off and continues to Midway Station.

Velour's horrible passing isn't the only reason he's traumatized. Vernon was honorable enough to disclose details that ultimately led to her unfortunate demise. For starters, he revealed that he is a Chief Postal Inspector who'd hired Cadina as an undercover inspector to investigate their station due to numerous complaints about mail tampering and found Velour stealing credit cards and using other people's identities for her own personal gain. Then there was Velour's brother, Vincent, the city's most notorious bootlegger and car thief, who, with his band of hooligans, sent Freeman to the hospital due to a violent beatdown, rendering him unconscious. Vernon went on to state that were it not for the postal crew and the building's tenants showing up when they did, Freeman's situation could've been much worse. Now, Vincent and his goons are locked up, Velour is dead, and Freeman remains in the intensive care unit.

James enters the building and walks up the flight of stairs. He hasn't seen anyone yet, and that's a good thing, for he is quite ticked off. The only other person he's spoken to since Velour's death is Divine. If it wasn't for her, he'd think that he no longer has any postal friends, at all. Virtually every crew member he's tried to contact has given him the cold shoulder. '*I can't talk to you right now, son, I gotta go. Peace.*' Or, '*This you, Jay? Yeah, uh, I heard what happened, but I'll holla at you later, Playboy.*'

He understands their reasons, but they should know him better than what they're assuming.

James makes it to the top of the staircase but stops short upon entering the break room.

Taped to the glass is a Daily News article highlighting the heroics of the postal crew bringing down Vincent and his gang.

But the images underneath the article boil his frustration.

Pictures of him and Cadina, drawn in a caricature style.

Both of their faces are circled in red, with a red line slashed across them.

Written beneath the images is the phrase, 'JUST SAY NO TO INSPECTORS!'

He is already found guilty by association.

*Simple bastards.*

Deep inside the break room, he can hear people conversing; no, more like holding a heated discussion.

He listens closely.

They're talking about him.

*Fuck this shit.*

He snatches the caricature picture of him from the glass and swings the door open.

As soon as he crosses the break room threshold, conversations end like a mic drop.

Almost all the employees are present. Letter carriers. Mail handlers. Window clerks. Truck drivers. Custodians. Some sitting. Others are standing. Some eat their breakfast. Others scroll on their phones.

But the vast majority greet him with contentious glares.

James absorbs the weight of the silent treatment as he marches to the middle of the room.

His crew sits by the window. He reads into each member's demeanor.

Roy seems to be the only one ready to give him the benefit of the doubt.

Both Neville and Shabbazz display baffled expressions.

Lou is another animal, altogether.

He leans back in his seat and studies James through his black-rimmed glasses while stroking his chin. It can go either way with his Latino brethren.

James is about to find out soon enough.

He holds the picture up high for everyone to see.

"Do any of you really believe that after ten years of delivering mail, I've secretly been an inspector?" James asks as he circles around to make eye contact with each of his skeptical peers. "Well, I'm telling all of you right now, I am not, nor have I ever been a postal inspector–"

"But you knew Cadina was," Lou challenges. "Didn't you?"

James tries to keep his emotions in check before answering Lou. "I did not know Cadina was an inspector until the other night–"

"Man, save that shit!" Lou launches out of his seat and points at James. "You've been with that bitch since day one and you're gonna stand there and tell us she didn't share that kind of information with you?"

"Who are you calling a bitch, Lou…"

"*I* called her a bitch! What…you're gonna defend her honor against your own people?"

James takes a couple of steps toward Lou. "You know, I'm getting sick and tired of your ignorant ass trying to start some shit you know nothing about–"

"I'm not the one keeping secrets around here, Papa, that's you!"

"Hey, easy you two," Roy intervenes, stepping in between James and Lou. "Yo, Jay, you can't fault us for wanting to know the truth. People are confused around here…"

"I agree with Lou," shouts a lady window clerk from the back. She stands and directs her attention to James. "You and Cadina have been together for what…almost six months? And I find it very hard to believe you didn't know what she was up to."

"What do you want me to do?" James pleads to everyone. "Bring her here so she can tell y'all the same thing that I'm telling y'all?"

"I already saw Cadina," confesses another lady carrier, rolling her neck and pointing at James. "She tried to sneak up in here to see Davenport without anybody noticing; she ain't slick!"

"Do you want me to get Davenport so we can deal with this out in the open–"

"This ain't about the manager, James, this is about *you* and your dealings with these inspectors! How are we supposed to trust you after what's happened?"

"That's exactly my point!" Lou adds. "And speak for yourself, Roy, I'm not confused, and I'll be damned if I work another day at this station if he or that broad continues to clock in here! You best believe that!"

The crowd murmurs in approval of Lou.

"You know what?" James addresses the entire room. "I'll do all of y'all asses one better."

He rips the picture into shreds, discards the pieces onto the floor, and bolts toward the door.

"See, I told you!" yells the lady carrier. "Leave with your lying ass!"

James spins around to the lady carrier. "I DON'T HAVE TO LIE TO YOU! I DON'T HAVE TO LIE TO ANY OF Y'ALL! BUT DID IT EVER OCCUR TO Y'ALL WHAT VELOUR WAS ALL ABOUT OR WHAT SHE WAS EVEN CAPABLE OF?"

His question hushes the room.

He eyeballs every naysayer before concluding, "I thought so."

As soon as James turns and walks through the door, a big cardboard box narrowly misses the back of his feet. He looks down at the box and popping out from the top is one of the softball jerseys he had bought for the team.

"You can take those back!" Lou roars. "We have no use for them!"

"*Fuck you, Lou!*"

"*Yo, Jay, hold up, man—*"

"*Nah, let his ass go!*"

Slumped on a bench in the women's locker room with her phone stuck to her ear, Divine tries to ignore the ongoing melee inside the break room next door but can't.

"Dee…you still there?" Majestic asks on the other end.

Divine shakes off the distraction to refocus on her conversation with her sister. "I-I'm sorry, Maj, what did you just say?"

"I said Daddy is at the hospital now and I'll be on my way there after I run a few errands."

"Okay."

"How are you holding up?"

Divine's eyes begin to swell. "As best as I can. Any improvement?"

"His condition is still the same. But there is no doubt in my mind he's going to come out of this. I believe it and I know it."

She smiles while wiping away tears. "I claim that, as well."

"I just spoke to Lovelle and she said her and Reverend Newark are bringing some of the church members there to pray over him."

"Yeah, she called me last night and told me the same thing–"

Someone calls her name from behind.

"*Dee…*"

She turns her head.

Her heart drops.

"Uh, Sis, let me call you back." She ends the phone call.

Standing at the far end of the row of lockers is Cadina, in a white camisole top and denim capris. With her ponytail frazzled, small bandages on her bruised face, and swollen eyes, she stands as the sole survivor of that tragic confrontation with Velour.

But Divine only knows her now as an inspector.

Better yet, an imposter.

Cadina takes baby steps toward her.

Divine finds herself slowly picking up a nearby stool as if to use as a weapon against the oncoming imposter.

Cadina stops walking. Tears well in her eyes. "I-I understand."

Cadina holds out what appears to be a blue envelope. She slowly places it on the bench next to her. "I'm so sorry about everything…" She then shoulders her belongings and hurries out of the locker room.

Divine drops the stool on the floor and walks over to the envelope. She opens it and pulls out a get-well card for Freeman and a three-page letter addressed to her. She doesn't read it right away. The card is more than enough to send her sliding down the locker and onto the dusty floor. Sobbing quietly in her hands, she knows that when it comes to forgiveness at this magnitude, she has her work cut out for her.

# EIGHTY-NINE

## TUCKER

Leaning on her parked Lexus near the loading dock, Tucker breaks a two-and-a-half-year-old vow by lighting up a Newport she requested from one of the mail handlers. She takes a pull and expels the smoke from the corner of her mouth like an old pro. Her gaze, and random thoughts, travel past the gloomy skies that fog up the city's tallest buildings.

Ever since she accepted the assistant manager's position, many of her decisions have been questionable, at best. Allowing Freeman to drive when he wasn't fit to. Standing on the sidelines as Davenport was allowed to have his way with Lexington. Failing to stand firm on Marc's health condition, which led to his death. And now the whole Velour, Cadina, Freeman Bermuda Triangle. Situations that could have easily been avoided or handled more appropriately than they had been.

But they weren't.

Now, she stands outside the station nursing on an old habit, all the while questioning her own career path. Does she really want to continue pursuing her dream of becoming a station manager? Does she even have what it takes? She's having a hard enough time filling the assistant manager's role. Tucker takes another long drag and then blows out into the passing wind.

James bursts out the employee's entrance like an angry tornado. With his bag over his shoulder, he avoids making eye contact with her as he pauses to pull out his truck keys.

"Hey!" She takes a final pull before flicking the butt out into the street. "What's wrong?"

He points to the second floor of the building. "Everyone in there has it in their minds that I knew Cadina was an inspector, and I didn't! Do you really expect me to work in that type of atmosphere? Somebody's bound to get hurt and I'ma make damn sure that it isn't me!"

"Look, James, I can't possibly fathom what you and your family's had to go through the past couple of days; it's...it's been terrible everywhere, but as it stands right now, this station is hurting for bodies–"

"You don't even care, do you?"

"I do care, James, but it doesn't negate the fact that we're pulling carriers from other stations because of our current situation."

"The only way I'll go back in there is if Cadina's pops come here himself and clear my name from all of this mess! That's the *only* way!"

"Trust me, it's already in the works."

The employee's entrance swings open.

Cadina rushes outside and then abruptly halts.

She bounces her eyes from Tucker and then to James.

Not one word was passed between the three of them.

Instead, Cadina's eyes express sorrow and guilt.

She hangs her head and scurries down the ramp and into a running black Town car parked across the street.

James watches the vehicle take off before turning back to Tucker.

"It better be, or else I'm putting in a transfer request to get out of this station, immediately."

"But James—"

He marches down the sidewalk at an infuriating pace.

"I probably won't be back today."

Startled, Tucker turns around.

Davenport, in his white dress shirt, black tie and slacks, stands before her, with briefcase in hand.

"Where're you going?" she asks.

He bears a look of defeat. "The Postmaster wants to see me. You know, regarding Lexington's situation."

She nods sympathetically.

"I guess I'll be retiring sooner than I thought, huh?"

Tucker remains silent. His guerrilla tactics have finally come to haunt him. Still, she feels for him, like watching a big brother venture off with his parole officer because of a stupid violation.

Davenport unlocks his Volvo and tosses his briefcase in the backseat. He slides behind the steering wheel and then gives her a long, telling look. The heavy bags under his eyes pretty much symbolize the whole station's mood.

"Oh, that Chief Inspector called," Davenport mentions. "McThaddeus, he said his name was."

She takes a moment for the name to digest. "What did he say?"

"He said he'll be visiting here on Thursday morning to talk to the carriers about the Velour incident."

"Thanks. I'll call you later to update you with everything around here." She points to James, who doesn't break his stride as he turns onto Third Avenue. "As you can see, the day is already starting off with challenges."

"I know." He stares down the block while turning the engine on. "Listen, Denise, next week, the Postmaster will assign another manager here temporarily until they find a permanent manager for this station. Between you and me, I believe she's going to offer you the permanent position, and if she does, I'd advise you to take it. Your leadership style is what's needed around here." He shifts his car into reverse. "They were getting a little tired of mine."

He winks at her as he backs his Volvo into the street and pulls off.

She shakes her head.

*He's about to get the ax, and yet he still finds the time to boss me around.*

She checks her watch and then walks up the ramp. If the station ever needed someone to right the course of this lost vessel, she would have to ante up and *be* that person. She doesn't have the luxury of second-guessing herself from this point on.

It's time to go to work.

Vernon McThaddeus, Deputy Chief Inspector of Eastern Operations for the Postal Inspection Service, puffs on his cherrywood pipe as he overlooks the window view of a foggy Midtown Manhattan from his tenth-floor office. A sudden drizzle peppers the outside windowpane. He takes his glasses off, rubs his restless eyes, and then slides them back on. Cadina called and said she should arrive no later than nine. Said she needed to talk to him about something. He glances at the wall clock. A quarter to ten. His senses tell him it's something he doesn't want to hear, so he's been preparing himself mentally for her arrival.

Inspector Harris enters the office with two coffee mugs and a manila envelope underneath his arm. He hands Vernon his hot java.

"Thanks." Vernon takes a sip.

"Cadina will be placed on administrative leave, as of today," Harris states, slapping the envelope down on Vernon's desk and taking a seat.

Vernon doesn't respond. He sips on his coffee while staring out the window.

"Tomorrow we're scheduled for a meeting with the Chief Postal Inspector and the Postmaster General. They want to review your approach with this assignment."

He finally peels away from the window to take a seat behind his desk. "Let me guess; they want to know why I gave Miss Patterns a proposition and allow her to roam freely around town."

"I believe they want to make it clear that nepotism will not be tolerated within this agency because it has proven to create a boatload of dissension amongst our staff–"

"Do *you* believe I'm showing preference towards my own child?"

Harris squares off into Vernon's eyes. "Would you have given Velour Patterns that same probation offer had the inspector been someone other than Cadina?"

"I did what was necessary to get the overall mission accomplished—to bring down Vincent's entire operation. That was the whole purpose of the joint investigation–"

"And somehow Miss Patterns winds up at your house and almost takes your daughter's life. How did she even have access to your address?"

Vernon sits back in his chair and sighs.

Harris leans forward. "Let's put that to the side for a moment and discuss Cadina's future as an inspector."

"She's earned every right to wear that badge, Bill," he argues, in his daughter's defense. "I wasn't out there holding her hand when she completed basic training, nor was I present when she scored over a ninety-five percent accuracy at the firearms course. So I don't want to hear any more crap about me giving her special treatment–"

"Don't get bullheaded with me, Vernon, you know exactly what I meant." Harris stands and points down on the desk. "I've watched Cadina grow from a teenager into an intelligent young lady, but we still don't know the conversations she had with Velour that could compromise the agency down the road. And to be quite honest, this is not just about Cadina. This is about *you*, trying to relive your career through your youngest child–"

"See, now you're reaching for something that's totally absurd–"

"Am I? Yes, she was in the top rankings at the Academy. Everyone applauded her effort and commitment. But she's doing this for *you*, not for her. And as long as we've known each other, not once have I seen you operate in this manner. Did this somehow become an ego thing with you? You know, becoming the first daddy and daughter team to apprehend criminals within the confines of the postal system?"

Vernon's glare burns a hole through his partner's interrogation.

They hear someone knocking on the door.

"COME IN!" Vernon shouts.

Cadina steps into the office.

Through the small incisions and busted lip, she manages a weary grin.

Harris stands and gives her a warm hug. "How're you feeling?"

"Better, Sir. Thanks for asking."

"That's good, that's good. I'll leave you two alone." Harris grabs his mug, heads for the door, and then turns around. "Vern; we'll talk later." He closes the door behind him.

Cadina throws her bag in one chair and then throws herself in the one beside it.

Vernon walks around his desk to stand in front of his scarred daughter. He gently holds her chin and maneuvers her head from left to right to examine her face.

"How do you *really* feel?" he asks.

"Like crap, but things could've been worse."

"I thought you would've been here earlier."

"I made a detour to the station to clean out my locker."

"I thought I told you I was going to send someone to gather your belongings–"

"I know, I know." She lounges back in the seat and stares at the ceiling. "But I had to give something to a friend."

He places her bag on the floor to sit next to her.

"Next time, listen to me, please? For your own safety?"

She pulls her focus from the ceiling to face him. "I didn't mean to get you into any trouble, Daddy–"

"This is not on you, Babygirl." He holds her hand. "I authorized the plan and we caught the bigger fish. I'm very proud of you."

She reaches for her bag. She unzips it, digs in, and pulls out her badge and holstered firearm. She reaches them out to him. "None of this speaks to me like it does to you."

He stares at the badge and service weapon but doesn't accept them.

It would be too much like accepting failure.

And failure is not an option in his book.

He displays an earnest grin. "How about this; After you complete your therapy sessions, we take a family vacation. A change of scenery would do everyone a world of good. After we return, then you can make a sound decision about your future with the agency–"

"What do you think I've been doing the past couple of days? Twiddling my thumbs? My decision has been made."

She places the badge and holstered firearm on his desk.

He takes a deep breath.

Reaches out to hold her hand again.

And plans his words carefully.

"Look, Cadina, it would be foolish of me to downplay what you experienced the other night. I've never been in a position where I had to defend myself the way you did and I've been in this profession for almost thirty years. Do you know how many times I've thanked God that you're even here to talk about it?" He takes a moment to keep his own emotions at bay. "Now, with that said, it would mean the world to me if you reconsidered. You can have a great future here if you just give it one more chance."

"Velour died because of me, Daddy."

"That's not true, Cadina–"

"If I wasn't so adamant about keeping Velour out of jail, she would still be alive right now. Aside from that, one of my dear friends is in the hospital, because of my actions. The coworkers who *were* my friends, now think I'm full of shit. And the man I love…I can't even look him in the face anymore–"

Listen to me; the last thing you need to do is beat yourself up over this–"

"I messed everything up with everybody," Cadina's voice trembles. "I got you in trouble and the person I thought I was helping, wanted to kill me. *She wanted to kill me, Daddy*! The story of my freakin' life, man."

Cadina pushes herself from the seat and grabs her shoulder bag from the floor. She turns to her father. "Could you do me a favor?"

"What is it?"

"Tell Inspector Harris I said it was an honor working with him and the entire team."

That statement knocked the wind right out of him.

"As much as I don't want to, I will do that for you." He rubs her shoulders. "But what are your plans moving forward?"

"Jesus Christ, Daddy, must we go through this again–"

"The reason I'm asking is that we both know your track record. And the bills don't stop for anyone."

"To be honest? I don't have a clue." She shoulders her bag and turns the doorknob. "But I sure as hell know it can't be this."

She leaves the office.

He runs his fingers through his hair in frustration.

*That went great.*

He retrieves his pipe from the desk, lights it, and puffs away while staring out the window. He struggles to see past the dense fog that blankets Midtown Manhattan, in the same way he struggles to see the hurt and fear his youngest child possesses as he tried his damnest to persuade her to commit to something she has no intentions of doing any longer.

*Has this turned out to be more of an ego thing with you, Vern?*

He scoffs at the echo of his friend's inquiry. Nothing about his character is synonymous with ego-tripping. He just wants what's best for his baby girl.

But as the smoke from his pipe swirls past his hardened grill, he wonders why he's not rejoicing in the fact that his daughter is even alive.

# 2017

# AUTUMN'S DANCE

# NINETY-ONE

## FREEMAN

After flushing the urinal, Freeman pushes up his dress shirt sleeves, squeezes out some liquid soap, and washes his hands thoroughly. He blow-dries them for ten seconds and then returns to the mirror. He adjusts his tie and then leans his face closer to the mirror to inspect his right eye. He closes his right eye to check the vision in his left eye. Perfect as usual. He switches eyes. He does this several times until he's satisfied with the vision in his right eye.

*It's getting there.*

Smiling to himself, Freeman leaves the bathroom.

Midway Postal Station's work floor is busy as usual. Walking toward his section, he buttons his sleeves and greets a couple of truck drivers who roll their loaded dollies toward the elevator lifts. A mail handler informs him that six post-cons of mail are arriving on the floor in a few minutes.

"Thanks for the update," he replies to the mail handler.

He glances over at David Chapman, talking to Section B's supervisor. Chapman, who was recently appointed assistant manager at Midway, waves at him. Freeman waves back and continues moving forward to Section C.

Freeman approaches the podium and grabs two award plaques.

Something tells him to look out the window.

The autumn winds gently blow the reddish leaves from the nearly naked trees without much effort.

He covers his left eye to inspect the sight out of his right eye.

No black spots or shadows in the background, even with the sun shining on his face.

The images he views with his right eye from afar are becoming clearer by the day.

*That's what I'm talking about.*

He makes his way to the middle of the section. He yells out, "SERVICE TALK, LADIES AND GENTLEMEN, LET'S GATHER AROUND!"

"BOOOOOOO!!!!" chimes the letter carriers.

"LET'S GET THIS MEETING OVER WITH SO WE CAN GET BACK TO WORK!"

The carriers grumble as they drag their stools to the front where Freeman is standing. He makes sure everyone is present and accounted for before proceeding.

"Alright, everyone. Today's mail is on its way up to the work floor so I'm not going to take up too much of your time. But I do have a few announcements I want to share with you–"

Letter Carrier Uniqua Hopkins eagerly waves her hand, garnering his attention.

"Yes, Uniqua…"

"I'm ready to receive the award for Employee of the Month. I see the plaques in your hand," she says, enthusiastically.

"And what makes you think you're getting that award?" truck driver Henry Garcia smirks, with a toothpick roaming around in his mouth.

Uniqua rolls her eyes at him. "Please, my work ethic speaks for itself."

"Yeah, and your work ethic says you be milking the clock every day!"

"Oooooooo…." The carriers respond.

She fires back, "I would like to see you deliver my route and be back before nightfall while I drive your truck assignment which, by the way, is a piece of cake. How about that?"

"That ain't happening, Ma!" Henry laughs.

"So be quiet then."

"Hey!" Freeman shouts, getting their attention. "May I have the floor back now?"

"Sorry, Mr. Souls," both Uniqua and Henry reply.

"Thank you." Freeman reads from his clipboard. "Now, this afternoon, I will hand out the instruction manuals for the new scanners we'll be receiving next week, okay? Let's see here, they will be renovating the upstairs break room starting next month, giving y'all a heads up on that…and finally, the moment you all have been waiting for."

Freeman holds up the award plaques.

"In recognition of your outstanding and diligent performances, the Employee of the Month Awards for the month of September goes out to two employees: Uniqua Hopkins–"

"Yes!" rejoices the spunky letter carrier as she launches off her stool to receive the award and a small gift card envelope from Freeman. She hoists the plaque as if she's won the Wimbledon Trophy.

The section applauds.

"And to Henry Lopez."

"What?" a shocked Uniqua yelps.

The section bursts into laughter as the chubby Puerto Rican truck driver struts up to receive his plaque and envelope while teasing Uniqua.

"Hold up, now," she fumes. "Why is *he* getting an award?"

"I don't have to give out any awards," Freeman replies. "I'm doing this out of the kindness of my heart and to acknowledge each employee in their current positions."

She sucks her teeth and then points at her smiling coworker. "Next time, you better not be late with my relay bags, Henry."

"Whenever you see me, I'm always on time, Ma!" laughs Henry.

"Let me snap a pic right quick," Freeman injects while whipping out his phone.

Uniqua and Henry happily pose together with their plaques.

*Click*!

"I want to thank all of you for a great month, it doesn't go unnoticed by any of our staff," Freeman continues. "Oh, and I forgot to mention; WE HAVE VALPAKS ON THE WAY TO THE WORK FLOOR! Have a productive day, folks!"

"AWWWWWWW!" the carriers whine as they break from the meeting.

Freeman returns to the podium where Station Manager Denise Tucker, smartly attired in a navy-blue pants suit, awaits.

He can see in her expression lies a bit of concern.

"I'm not so sure if I'm keen on the idea of adding a monetary component to the plaques," she voices.

"What, the twenty-five-dollar gift cards I gave them? I figured it would really send the message of our appreciation for their hard work."

"But they already get *paid* for their hard work, Freeman."

"I know that, but it's something about seeing the look on their faces when they get that added incentive, especially when it comes from one of us. And I'm hoping the motivation spills over to those carriers who need that extra push, you know?"

Tucker raises an eyebrow. "So, this tells me you're ready for the next step."

He smiles. "Maybe…"

"You better be. The exam is two weeks from now. No turning back."

"You wouldn't let me if I tried."

"You got that right. How's your eye doing these days?"

"Better by the day, thank God."

"That's good to hear. Meeting at two, don't be late."

"I won't."

Tucker spins around and walks boldly down the work floor to check on another section.

Freeman glances around his functioning work section.

As he surveys, he reflects on his past life as well as his current position at Midway Station.

Seasons change.

Nothing stays the same.

Over the past year, he has seen new faces replace those who either moved on physically or transcended spiritually.

Lexington. Marc. Lou. Emmanuel. Shabbazz. James. Velour. Cadina. Davenport.

All gone.

A few he could care less about.

But the majority he will miss dearly from the station.

Nonetheless, life goes on.

And the mail must be delivered.

"Mr. Souls!" Uniqua yells. "We need more rubber bands, please!"

"I'm on it!" he replies.

He watches the young letter carrier as she continues to marvel over the plaque before placing it to the side to resume casing her letters. That alone justifies his intentions of making people feel good about working at the post office.

He makes a call downstairs for more bags of rubber bands.

 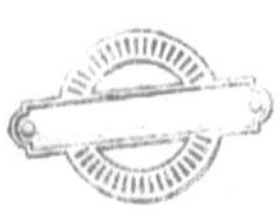 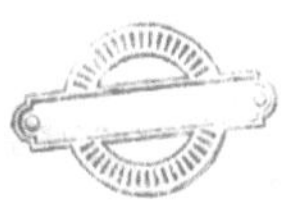

After Freeman signs the supervisor's sheet to end his day, he says his goodbyes to his colleagues and then hustles outside where he is met with unseasonably warm weather for the month of October. He takes off his rust-colored suede jacket and checks his watch.

His phone vibrates in his pocket.

He pulls it out to screen the number.

Lovelle.

A smile jumps to his face.

He quickly swipes to talk. "Hey, Babe…I'm good, I was just about to call you...Yeah, I'm done for the day...You're off, too? Cool."

He happens to look across the street.

A beautiful caramel-skin-toned lady, wearing a vintage mint green tweed blazer and skirt outfit with beige pumps, steps out of a late model BMW X6.

She turns in his direction.

And stands there.

*Is she staring at me?*

*Naaaah.*

He walks toward his Audi A4 while conversing with Lovelle.

"You're on your way here? Cool. Meet me at Yellow Rose; I have a taste for tacos."

Freeman reaches for his car keys but swings his head back across the street.

The lady now stares dead into his eyes.

*Whoa.*

Freeman presses his car remote and opens the back door. "Huh? Oh, yeah, we're still going to Jay's house. See you soon. Love you, too. Bye."

He tosses his briefcase and jacket in the back seat before closing the door. The urge gets the best of him. He glances across the street again.

She flashes a smile.

*Hold up…*

That slim, but curvaceous frame.

The innocent-looking face.

Freeman covers his mouth in total shame.

He guesses his eye isn't doing as great as he thought.

It was the short blond pixie hairstyle that threw him off.

She used to show the world her long, jet-black ponytail—

"CADINA!"

He wastes no time crossing the street to hug a friend whom he hasn't seen or talked to since last year. He sees why he didn't recognize her from the jump, and it isn't just the hair that was misleading. It was her entire elegant ensemble—very refined, superbly cultured. This chic sense of style is something he isn't used to seeing on her. After last year's unforgettable summer, many employees at Midway Station were left wondering just who the real Cadina was. Freeman didn't care back then and doesn't care now. He's just glad to see her—alive.

"Now, this is a nice surprise," he says, as they both release each other. "Man, it's been a minute–"

"I know," she admits. "A little over a year."

He nods. "So…how're you doing? I like your new look; very stylish."

"Why, thank you, Freeman. I, um, I'm doing good. I see you're supervising now."

"Well, I'm currently an acting supervisor, but I take the exam in two weeks."

"I can see you leading the masses. You have a good heart."

"I believe I do, but it's nice to see that someone else recognizes it." His tone becomes a shade curious. "Are you still an inspector–"

"No, not at all. I'm about to open my own restaurant, right on Queens Boulevard."

"Really?"

She pulls out a flyer from her purse and hands it to him.

"*Cravin' Cadina's*. Wow, this is so awesome! Congratulations!"

"Thanks. I guess cooking is my passion, and it also gives me the opportunity to serve the greater good, so I better make the most of it, you know."

"And you will."

"Thanks."

He senses hesitancy on her part, as if she wants to say more, but is committed to keeping the conversation cordial.

"Well, I better get going," she says, sounding less convincing. "I have a meeting with my staff in a couple of hours regarding our grand opening next week and I need to go over my notes, sooo…I'm glad to see that you're doing okay. Take care of yourself, Freeman."

She fumbles with her car keys, causing them to drop.

"Now, let me get this straight," He picks up her keys and hands them to her. "You have a meeting in Queens. Yet, you managed to travel all the way out to Manhattan just to stare at me from across the street without trying to get my attention. That's some stalker-type shit if you ask me."

His joke makes her blush.

"I gotta go, Freeman–"

"You're not getting off that easy. I'm about to grab a bite to eat and you're coming with me."

"But I'm not hungry–"

"So, you will keep me company. Plus, we have a lot of catching up to do, so let's go."

He holds out his arm as if to escort her.

She ponders for a moment before reluctantly grabbing ahold.

That was more like it for him.

The two friends, separated by time and despair, begin their stroll toward Yellow Rose Tex-Mex Restaurant and their journeys back to a painful, yet parallel past.

Soft beams of the afternoon sun pass through the cracked blinds from the window booth Cadina and Freeman share. Sipping her iced water, she watches in silent amusement as he feverishly devours the first of his two loaded tacos.

Freeman licks his fingers and then peeks up at her. "You sure you don't want me to order you anything?"

"I'm good, thanks."

"These Barbacoa tacos right here are the truth! Besides, the only other thing I had today was a cream cheese bagel and that was early this morning, so a brother is starving right about now."

"So, they fired Davenport for abusing Lexington?"

He wipes his hands before opening a towelette. "More like he was forced to retire, and he moved to Greensboro, North Carolina. Anyway, that's what we've heard. But Tucker is our new station manager now."

"Wow. Good for her."

"She wants to change the climate at Midway...create an atmosphere where greater appreciation is shown to the employees. And that's why she recruited me to become a 204B."

"How's that going for you?"

He shrugs. "Some carriers are happy for me while others look at me sideways because I have on a shirt and tie. It is what it is."

"She recruited well. You're one of the good guys."

"Yeah, but it's not without its challenges. For example, this is what happened to me last week..."

Their conversation is swift and enlightening. In addition to learning about Freeman's advancement, she nearly cried happy tears when he announced that Divine and Emmanuel tied the knot earlier in the year and are expecting! She then expressed how shocked she was by the meteoric success of the hip-hop trio, Lou, Shabbazz, and Emmanuel, collectively known as L.S.M., and their string of independent hits topping the Spotify/Billboard charts with a combined total of five hundred million streams.

"We didn't see that coming at all," Freeman says. "Five hundred *million* streams?"

"I bet you can't tell Lou nothing now!"

"We couldn't tell him anything before!"

They holler and make a toast to everyone's golden accomplishments.

The convo gradually turns somber when Velour's name is brought up.

Cadina explains to him how she wound up becoming a postal inspector and gives him startling details about Velour's criminal behavior. Freeman, in return, unveils the suffering he had to endure when his mother passed away and the falling out he had with his fiancée, both of which ignited his alcohol addiction, and ultimately led to the combustible relationship he shared with Velour. Freeman concluded by sharing that he almost lost sight in his right eye, due to a detached retina resulting from the vicious beating he took from Vincent and his henchmen. He never asks about that horrific night at her parent's house, and she is grateful because it still disturbs her to this day. Instead, Freeman brings up another topic, which he knows is the main reason she wanted to visit her old stomping grounds in the first place.

"Why did you never return any of Jay's phone calls?" he asks.

She glances out the sunny window to break away from Freeman's concentrated stare. "I dunno."

"He told me he swung by your apartment a week after the incident, but you'd moved out."

"I relocated for safety reasons."

He gives a quick nod before ripping into his second taco.

She stirs the straw in her glass before halfway explaining, "It was a combination of things, Freeman. The investigation, the therapy sessions, the nightmares of the incident—"

"You know I can attest to all of that. But still, he needed to make sure you were okay–"

"I was *afraid*, okay? I-I just couldn't bear the thought of him acting differently toward me once he discovered my true identity."

"He wouldn't have done that to you."

"I didn't want to give him that chance." She tempers her tone. "You know that night, we were about to reveal everything to James and his family."

"Do you know *why* he brought his family over to your house in the first place?"

Cadina slowly nods. She remembers how nervous James looked when he entered her parents' home, and at the time, she thought it was so cute. A cherished, yet distant memory she still clings on to.

"How's he doing these days?" she asks, rather desperately.

"He misses you if that's what you want to hear. He never says it, but everybody knows it." He peers beyond her shoulder and his eyes sparkle. "Ah, my other guest has finally arrived."

She turns around.

Walking toward their booth is a beautiful dark-skinned woman, dressed in a white cardigan sweater and taupe pinstripe flare-leg pants that cover a pair of brown leather boots.

Cadina follows Freeman's lead as they both stand to greet the oncoming guest.

"Wait a minute." The lady grabs Freeman's face and plants her full lips on his right eye. "Muah. There. Now your eye is healed. Claim it!"

"You crazy," Freeman chuckles, before pointing to Cadina. "Lovelle, this is Cadina. Cadina, this is *my* boo, Lovelle."

Lovelle's sultry eyes light up and her bob hairdo bounces in delight. "Oh my God, so *you're* Cadina! Come here, girl! I've heard so much about you from Divine! It's good to finally meet you!"

Cadina welcomes the embrace. "It's a pleasure to meet you, too."

"So, did you see James yet?"

"Uh, no, not yet."

"I was just about to tell her that James transferred out of Midway and he's now a mail transporter," Freeman states.

"Really?" Cadina's heart flattens.

"Mmm-hmm."

Well, I'ma go use the restroom." Lovelle fumbles in her pocketbook.

"You want me to order you anything?"

"Oooo, yes, the Texas Pink Cake to go, please." She nudges Cadina. "That's a guilty pleasure I can only do once a month–gotta watch this stomach. Be right back!"

Lovelle giggles as she struts to the restroom.

They return to their seats.

"She's beautiful," Cadina notes.

Freeman smiles proudly. "I know."

"When did James leave?"

Freeman flags the waiter and puts in Lovelle's order. "A few weeks ago. You talk about someone happy."

"Does he like his new position?"

He downs his drink, wipes his mouth, and clears his throat before saying, "At six-thirty, everyone will be at James' house to watch our boys who made a guest appearance on the Big Deuce Morning podcast." Freeman leans closer to Cadina. "Now, I know you have your meeting and everything, but you managed to come this far. You need to swing by and ask him that question yourself."

She doesn't say anything.

Lovelle makes her way back to the table with re-applied lipstick and a fabulous smile.

"I know I'm going to see you at James' place later this evening, right?" Lovelle asks.

"I'll try to make it," Cadina responds.

"I hope you do." Freeman pulls his wallet out and hands the waiter two twenties and tells him to keep the change. The waiter says thanks and hands him a to-go bag. Freeman then stands to his feet. "Because James is not the only one who misses you."

Freeman and Lovelle hug Cadina before leaving. She watches them stroll out of the restaurant and down Third Avenue like they were on their very first date.

"Would you care for anything else, Ma'am?"

Cadina snaps out of it to address the waiter. "Uh, no, thanks."

The young waiter quickly attends another table.

Her mind calculates.

She whips out her phone.

The number she dials rings just once before someone answers.

"Hey...do you mind if we postpone the meeting until tomorrow? Something's come up and I need to take care of it asap...cool, tell the others. Thanks. Bye."

She slides the phone back into her purse and stares out the window.

A young letter carrier hurries across the street, with her pushcart leading the way back to Midway.

Her old station.

Sadness consumes her.

When she had James, she wasn't pursuing her passion. Now in full control of her blossoming career, she feels empty without his presence. She misses him. She *loves* him. It's time for her to align the planets in her favor, once and for all.

Cadina pulls out her wallet and places a ten underneath her glass before leaving Yellow Rose.

She has a get-together to attend later.

To claim a lover lost.

# NINETY-THREE

## BIG DEUCE PODCAST

The laughter inside the crowded podcast studio is gut-busting. Big Deuce pulls the mic close to his mouth. "Man, I can't tell you how much I've enjoyed this interview. I'm quite sure the people who joined in took away many jewels from y'all's journey towards superstardom, and more importantly, ownership of your content. Incredible story."

"Thank you for the opportunity," Lou replies. "And we've been following this podcast for many years, so to finally be a guest on it… it's a blessing, man."

"So, you know how this podcast works, I'm assuming?"

Lou, Emmanuel, and Shabbazz chuckle amongst each other.

"Yeah, yeah, we know how y'all do," Shabbazz coolly responds.

"Hey, Jazzy Souffle," Big Deuce calls out.

"Yes, Deuce…", his smiling co-star responds, into her microphone.

"These gentlemen used to work for the post office, so they're known for delivering the mail, right?"

"That's correct."

"But can they deliver a freestyle off the top of the dome for us?"

"Oh, without a doubt," Lou answers, confidently.

"Talk that shit, Papi Lou!" Jazzy cheers.

Big Deuce reads off his pad, "We have Papi Lou, Manny the Great, and Deejay Shabbazz, collectively known as L.S.M., here with us, ladies and gentlemen. Their debut CD, *Deliverance*, drops November second; show your support and go cop the CD, folks. December tenth, they will be the opening act on the Way of the World tour with Common, the Roots, J Cole, Kendrick Lamar..." Big Deuce smiles at them. "Y'all are amongst royalty!"

"We know," Emmanuel adds. "But *they* know what we bring to this concert, too."

"I'm sure they do." Big Deuce points to the deejay in the back. "Yo, DJ Worth, drop the beat on them."

DJ Worth plays the instrumental version of Joe Budden's club banger, *Focus*.

Everyone in the studio nod to the hard boom-bap.

"Ahhh, yeah," Jazzy Souffle chimes, while snapping her fingers.

"Deuce, Jazzy..." Lou adjusts his mic. "I'm gonna start it off with a story."

Big Deuce/Jazzy Souffle both say, "Let's go!"

"EAST NEW YORK – STAND UP!" Lou bobs his head, feeling the beat...

*"A'ight...yo, peep it,*
*It doesn't get any truer than this,*
*My own pops took one look at me and told my moms he was pissed,*
*Those days, I swear to God I don't miss,*
*He said that the day I was born, I was here to exist,*
*I cursed my old man cuz of the crap he brought,*
*The youngest of eight, I was just an afterthought,*
*Tax season I was added as another damn dependent,*
*Never was respected, I quickly became offended,*
*Boriqua pride strong, his persistence became thorough,*
*Like passing down the bodega to older brother Arturo,*

*He didn't think I had it to make it out the borough,*
*Little did he know about the skills inside my verbal,*
*It took many years to get the memory out my system,*
*Four years ago he passed and to this day I still miss him,*
*I took it harder than a mutha, I found myself mopin',*
*Coping with the fact I had to come out with guns smokin',*
*Or should I say Papi Lou came out with guns blazin',*
*Like Luther Vandross said, I started feeling so amazin',*
*Standing on my own two, cuz that's what I'm supposed to,*
*I chose to go Postal, no other job comes close to,*
*After a while, I felt my gift was taken for granted,*
*My peoples couldn't relate, plus wifey couldn't understand it,*
*Until I met up with a youngsta, I'm ten years his senior,*
*But he compliments the complexities of my crazed demeanor."*

DJ Worth blends in the instrumental to Jeru Da Damaga's street anthem, *Come Clean.*

"Uh…uh…uh, yo, check it…" Emmanuel pulls the mic up close.

*"My moms often said I was raised by a village,*
*But remained a young knucklehead straight off the scrimmage,*
*Stealin' was appealin', plus other forms of pillage,*
*The brutal facts of life to paint my tainted image,*
*My moms always prayed I receive the holy blessin's,*
*The prayers never worked, so she boldly caved my chest in,*
*Reckless with my mouth, I had paid her no attention,*
*The yellin' and the stressin' led up to one suggestion,*
*Booted from the nest for all my nonsense,*
*Now the product of the streets was homeless and jobless,*
*Suddenly the village that raised me became distant,*
*They didn't want to risk it by raisin' a total misfit,*
*I had to step back to access this insanity,*
*I felt no kind of love when the family abandoned me,*
*The reflection in the mirror revealed a grim reality,*
*'Get it together or become another young black catastrophe!'*
*Long story short, I did what was expected,*
*In order to be respected, better thoughts were implemented,*

*Resurrected from the ashes, no longer the thoughtless victim,*
*Life as a mailman provided my source of income,*
*In the midst of it all, I had skills yearnin' exposure,*
*To tell the world about a page in my life that needed closure,*
*I hooked up with an elder that shared the same interests,*
*We built on our knowledge and kept it moving with the quickness,*
*His crazy disposition balances out my mild-mannered,*
*But we share a common goal and that's strivin' for higher standards,"*
*(Lou)*
*"Yo, that last statement made, it needs some piggybackin',*
*The status of the street apparatus and what it's lackin',*
*Too many of my peoples walk around with minds feeble,*
*Don't let the streets mislead you or bite the hand that feeds you,"*
*(Emmanuel)*
*"Yo, I feel you on that, Lou, you have to keep it in perspective,*
*I used to be aggressive and stayed hard on the defensive,*
*But God is in my heart and just for the record,*
*I don't have to be a Reverend for my gift to be effective."*
*(Lou)*
*"We manifest success just like my man Kanye,*
*With pockets singin' more high notes than a group led by Wanya,*
*But the end of the road don't apply to major winners,*
*My soul had to outshine the sparkle of my spinners."*
*(Emmanuel)*
*"Speakin' of sparkles, I have one in particular,*
*Divine is all mine, it was best for me to get with her,*
*To avoid the streets extracurricular, I left it lonely,*
*I swear it's nuthin' phony about our mutual matrimony."*
*(Lou)*
*"Yo, to sum it all up, we got more than we could bargain,*
*To lace our peers' ears with our effortless jargon,*
*Our joints are on point, plus we limit the rehearsals,*
*I do the runnin' man because the dance is universal,*
*Blendin' style with some substance without soundin' redundant,*

*The best is yet to come, cuz we flow with abundance."*
*(Lou, Manny, Shabbazz)*
*"Neither rain… snow… sleet or hail,*
*Can stop the LSM, we're not groomed to fail,*
*If you're blind in both eyes, you could read it in Braille,*
*A tale of how we do when we move the mail. Peace!"*

"HOOOOOOOOOO!"

The entire studio erupts in scattered high-fives and applauses.

Big Deuce bounces around in his seat and then glares into the camera. "DID Y'ALL HEAR THAT? THEY DIDN'T COME HERE TO PLAY AROUND! RAPPERS, STEP YOUR GAME UP! THEY STOOD AND DELIVERED!"

"Yo, when Lou said, *'I do the running man because the dance is universal'*, I was done," claps Jazzy Souffle. "Great job, y'all."

"They were going back and forth with it, like old school legends!" marvels Deuce. "And they made references to their old job, showing them some love."

"That's where it all started," Emmanuel adds.

"Shout out to the Postal Service!" Jazzy commends.

"Where my check at?" jokes DJ Worth.

They all laugh.

"But that one line Manny said, hit home for me," Deuce states, in a more serious tone. "He said *'I don't have to be a Reverend for my gift to be effective,'*. Don't let that go over y'all heads, folks."

"They were dropping bars, crazy," echoes DJ Worth.

"Appreciate the love," Lou responds to the podcast family.

"We each have our own unique gift which can positively impact the world. It doesn't matter who you are nor the circumstances, and Lou, Manny, Shabbazz? Y'all are doing just that. Thanks for being a part of the Big Deuce Podcast. Tell the audience where they can reach you on Facebook, Instagram, etc."

"Papi Lou on all social media handles."

"Manny Da Best, the same."

"Deejay Shabbazz the Great, the same as them and you can also check out our new website, www.loumannyshabbazz.com, where you can order some nice merch and we also do giveaways, as well."

"And also, a big shout out to all of our families and friends for all the love and support, I didn't want to forget them," Lou adds.

"And there you have it, folks! It's the Big Deuce Podcast…"

"…with moi, Jazzy Souffle, signing off, peace!"

# NINETY-FOUR

## JAMES

"A-HAAAAA! YEAH, BABY!"

Lou jumps up from his seat, nearly toppling over his food. With a mouth full of ziti, and a pair of smirking eyes that dart a '*How you like me now?*' look at everyone in the room, the lyrical Latino does a two-step dance in celebration of his televised fame.

James laughs as he presses the pause button to stop the podcast.

"C'mon, man," Neville quips, downplaying the moment. "That wasn't a freestyle, y'all wrote that."

"Some of it was written." Lou wipes the crumbs from his black Sean John track outfit. "But the back-and-forth part toward the end? That was just me and Manny flowing from the top–facts. Ask Manny when he gets here."

James places his beer on the table and points at Lou. "What *I* want to know is how in the world did y'all accumulate five hundred *million* streams? I mean, wow…"

"Those are Drake-type numbers," Roy professes, sitting on the floor in his postal uniform. "How is that even possible being that y'all are independent and unknown?"

Lou grins while stuffing more food in his mouth. "Yo, 'Bazz, explain to them how we accomplished that feat."

Lounging back in the recliner, next to his wife Najya, Shabbazz chuckles before sitting upright and clasping his hands. "Jay, it all started with this social network app called TikTok."

"*TikTok*?" James scrunches his face. "I can't even keep up with all these new social media platforms that keep popping up. What is that?"

Janae pulls out her iPhone, scoots over to her father, and opens the app right in front of him. "This is TikTok, Daddy. It basically showcases people creating really cool short videos of themselves."

"Huh?"

"It's the new thing, Jay," Shabbazz continues. "Manny put us on to it and we used TikTok to our advantage by uploading our music and short videos…and it literally started blowing us up–within months! And that was earlier this year, it's crazy."

"Another route we took as an independent entity was that we licensed out our songs, which are registered with ASCAP, through external distribution deals," Lou explains. "These companies put our tracks on some of their compilation albums, which garnered heavy rotation in the States and overseas. So, that's when *everyone* started to take notice of us–through the compilation albums, TikTok…not to mention our strong social media presence, and influencers and–*Boom*!–Five hundred million hits."

"Man," James says, impressed. "I'm proud of y'all, seriously."

"That's what's up." Lou gives James an explosive pound.

Grace and Marisol enter the living room with plates and drinks for everyone. Grace hands a plate and cup to Shabbazz and says, "All this talk about Facebook, Twitter, Tic-tac-toe–"

"It's TikTok, Ganna," shouts Janae.

"*Whatever*." Grace sits down next to James. "I'm just glad you use these platforms to talk about other topics besides women and cars and all that other nonsense–"

"No, Ma'am, we were never about that," Shabbazz laughs.

"I was referring to Lou."

"Why does everybody think I'm the bad apple of the group?" Lou stands to defend himself. "Jay, tell your moms I'm more radio-friendly than she thinks!"

James turns to his mother. "He has changed for the better."

"Ha-Haaa. See? I told ya." Lou sits next to Marisol.

Grace shakes her head. "Honey, how do you put up with him now that he's this big famous artist?"

"*Please.*" Marisol nudges Lou's head. "Nothing's changed. When he gets home, he knows the rules."

"*Oooooooo,*" chants the entire room.

"I guess she told you—*Papa*!"

As the laughter dies down, Roy stands and raises his beer.

Everyone follows his lead, with drinks held in the air.

"Much success to our brothers, Lou, Shabbazz, and Manny, better known as, L…S…M!"

"To L.S.M.!"

Everyone sips to that tribute.

"Manny just texted me, they're almost here," says Lou, as he pockets his phone. "Where's the remote?"

"Papa, sit down and finish your food before it gets cold," Marisol orders.

"I will, once I find the remote. Jay, help me out."

"Here." James tosses the firestick remote to Lou. "I'ma get out of this uniform."

James unbuttons his postal shirt as he climbs the steps by twos. As he reaches the second floor, a flashback invades his memory of the ugly confrontation he had with Lou which could have destroyed a rock-solid friendship that was built throughout their years at Midway.

And he has no one to blame but his ex-girlfriend.

Resentment twists his gut just thinking about the woman who sent him on an astronomical high for six months, only to have him crashing back down to earth like a smoldering meteor.

And he still hasn't heard anything from her since last year.

He rips the shirt from his frame while muttering choice words about his former lover.

# NINETY-FIVE

## CADINA

The picturesque sunset behind the faraway Manhattan skyline doesn't do anything for Cadina's heart-stomping jitters. She checks the clock on the dashboard. 6:15 pm. She's been sitting across from James' house for over half an hour, building up the courage to visit a place she used to call a home away from home, a little more than a year ago.

Her eyes take in all the attractive additions to the exterior of the Richards' home. The hanging potted plants. The green turf stretching from the top of the porch to the bottom of the iron gate. The colorful botanical garden near the driveway. Cadina envisions James laying down the artificial grass while Janae assists her grandmother with the gardening. She wishes she could've been there to help with the beautification.

Her sullen thoughts are distracted by movement on her right.

Freeman rolls past her vehicle and parks the Audi right in front of James' house.

Driving by and parking directly behind the Audi is a burgundy Range Rover Sport.

Freeman and Lovelle hop out of the Audi and head over to the Range Rover. Rushing out from the driver's side, sporting a black and cream sweatsuit and a pair of black Jordans, is Emmanuel, who says something to Freeman before they both scramble around to the passenger side of the SUV. Divine slaps both of their hands away so she can ease out of the truck by herself.

Cadina's eyes moisten at the sight of Divine's pregnant stomach protruding from her black and cream maternity sweatsuit.

Cadina sucks in deep breaths.

*You can do this, you can do this.*

*You must do this.*

She lets out a huge, final breath before grabbing her purse and exiting her vehicle.

Cadina moves timidly across the street.

Her heart drums like a tribal ceremony.

She wonders how her used-to-be close friend is going to react to her presence.

A second later, she receives her answer.

Divine, grabbing a bag from the rear of the truck, happens to swing her head in Cadina's direction.

Immediately, Divine drops her bag.

Cups her mouth.

And waddles across the street with arms outstretched like a panda bear.

Cadina finds herself doing the same thing.

They embrace like long, lost sisters.

"But God, that's all I can say!" Divine sniffles on the side of Cadina's neck. "Freeman told me he hung out with you earlier and I was praying you would swing by. I've missed you so *muuuuuuch*!"

"*I've missed you, too, girl*!" Cadina whimpers, trying not to put pressure on Divine's stomach.

"I'm so, so sorry for acting the way I did in the locker room that day. So much was going on, I just couldn't think straight–"

"Girl, hush." Tears drizzle down her cheek. "There's nothing to forgive. If anything, I'm the one who needs to be apologizing."

"Hey, the letter you wrote was more than enough for me."

She releases Divine and places a hand on her swollen belly. "Look at *you*, Ma! How many months?"

"Six, but Lord knows I'm ready to drop this load right now!"

"The first of many to come," interrupts Emmanuel, who flashes a Kobe Bryant-type grin.

Divine huffs, "Then I guess you'll be carrying the next one yourself."

"I don't think so."

"Come here, you." Cadina motions to Emmanuel for a hug. "Congratulations on your music career, I'm so happy for all of y'all."

"Appreciate you."

"A-hem." Freeman gestures with his hand toward the front gate. "Can we take this conversation inside, please? Manny, escort your fat wife up these steps and into this house."

"We're right behind y'all, now leave me alone." Divine rolls her eyes at her brother before she returns to Cadina. "They act like I can't do anything by myself."

"They mean well."

Divine interlocks her arm around Cadina's and they begin strolling. "So, Freeman says you're about to have a grand opening with your restaurant next week. I know you're excited!"

"Very excited. And nervous. I'm a bunch of emotions right about now."

"I can imagine. But you're built for this and it's going to be a success."

"I receive that."

They walk through the gate.

"Have you spoken to James yet?"

Just the mention of his name releases more butterflies in her stomach. "Not yet. This is kind of a surprise visit."

"Oooooo, I can't wait to see his face when he sees you!" Divine shimmies her shoulders in enthusiasm. "You know he hasn't been the same since you left. He misses you like crazy!"

"Does he really?" Her voice wants to cling to any thread of validity in Divine's statement. "I mean, I've given him every reason in the world to forget about me and move on."

"Girl, ain't nobody forgot about you! You'll see in a minute."

They reach the top of the staircase as Cadina surveys the entire porch. A Spalding basketball lay near two Mongoose bicycles. A newly built wooden porch swing. More potted plants in the corners.

Her head snaps up to the now opened front door. She hears loud talking and laughter from inside. The aroma of pasta fills her nostrils. As she crosses the threshold, she distinguishes each of the voices. Roy, Neville, Shabbazz, and Lou, being the loudest as usual.

Her jitters amplify to Richter scale magnitudes.

Inside the hallway, she spots Momma Grace greeting each guest with a motherly hug. First Lovelle, then Freeman, Emmanuel next, and now Divine.

Her heart pounds through her blouse like a cartoon character from Hanna-Barbera.

Grace hugs Divine carefully. "How is my pregnant baby feeling these days?"

"Hungry," smiles Divine. "You know I'm eating for two now."

"How did the sonogram go?"

"Everything's looking good. But me and Manny both agreed on not knowing the gender until the delivery date, so you can hold off on your next question."

"Y'all just gonna keep everybody in suspense, huh?"

Divine laughs. "Yep! Y'all will be alright."

"H-Hi, Ms. Richards," Cadina stutters.

"Hey, just call me Momma Grace, that's what all my babies call—"

The rest of her greeting gets stuck in her throat.

She cups her mouth and with wide-eyed, jaw-dropping exhilaration, she yells out, "CADINAAAAAAA!!!!"

Grace grabs and hugs her so fast and so tight that it catches her off-guard, but she feels relieved for the moment. She returns the tight hug.

"IT'S SO GOOD TO SEE YOU, CHILD!" Grace rocks her from side to side. "GIRL, I DIDN'T EVEN RECOGNIZE YOU!" She releases her python-like grip to take in Cadina's appearance. "You look *stunning*!"

"Doesn't she?" Divine proudly adds.

Grace pats Cadina's new hairdo. "*This* is you, girl. Not that you didn't look good in your ponytail—awww, you know what I'm trying to say, shoot!"

Cadina delays her response.

Deep inside the living room, she faintly hears Marisol say, "*Ohhhh! Look who's at the door. It's Cadina!*" That's when she hears murmuring from the crew. She tenses back up.

"Come on in and make yourself at home." Grace embraces Cadina's arm and escorts her into the living room. "Janae just went upstairs and James is changing out of his uniform." Grace walks to the foot of the staircase, looks up, and yells, "JAMES! JANAE! WE GOT COMPANY!"

For Cadina, entering inside the house has felt more like walking into a courtroom and taking the stand in front of a set of jurors who've been selected to determine her guilty on all moral accounts.

Every pair of eyes are now centered on her.

Her former peers never stared at her the way they are staring at her now, not even when she first met them at Midway Station.

Too quiet. Too studious. Too spooked.

Her heart quadruples the pounding.

*Damn, girl, maybe this wasn't such a good idea.*

But Marisol and Najya break through that wall of silence by showering Cadina with welcome-back hugs.

"How're you *doing*, Chica?" Marisol asks. "I was wondering if I was ever going to see you again!"

"It's so good to see you again, my sister," Najya smiles, holding onto Cadina's hand.

"It's so good to see you both," Cadina says.

Marisol takes a step back to marvel at Cadina's attire. "I can't understand how a person can get prettier each time I see her."

"Oh, stop it, Mari," Cadina blushes.

"You calling my baby a liar or what?"

Cadina turns around and lets out a huge sigh of relief.

Lou, the soldier of sarcasm, the sultan of swag, the pied piper of popping the most ignorant shit known to mankind, bebops over and drapes Cadina with a heartfelt hug.

"If my baby says you look good, you take that shit and run with it, ya heard?" Lou whispers in her ear.

"I missed you, too, Lou," she says, as her voice trembles in joy.

The rest of the postal crew overwhelm her with the love and support she was hoping to receive from them. This was major. She fights back happy tears.

"CADINAAAAA!"

She looks up the staircase and smiles.

Janae dashes down the steps and leaps into her arms.

The long embrace they share has a beautiful mother/daughter feel to it. She kisses Janae's neck and says, "Missed you, 'Nae. How are you?"

"Fine. I'm glad you're alive. I never had a chance to tell you that."

Janae seemed to have grown a foot taller since the last time she saw her. Or maybe it's the flat-ironed hairstyle that's giving off the mature impression. Either way, just being in Janae's presence melts all her doubts away.

She wipes a runaway tear from Janae's face. "I'm glad to be alive myself."

"Are you here to stay or are you leaving after today?"

She kneels in front of her. "Well, I have to talk with your father first. See what happens after that."

"I hope you stay. I miss your company. It just hasn't been the same…you know?"

Janae says that so matter-of-factly, it stirs up even more emotions inside Cadina. They share another lengthy hug.

"WHAT'S ALL THE RUCKUS DOWN HERE?" James yells, rumbling down the stairs.

She faces in his direction.

A lump of anxiety clogs her throat.

James hops off the bottom step and approaches Freeman with his hand extended. "About time y'all showed–"

His neck makes a snapping sound as he whips around to her.

She slowly releases Janae and rises from her kneeling position.

It couldn't get any quieter inside the Richards household.

They lock eyes for about five seconds, but it felt like infinity to her.

She examines his evolved appearance. His face is a tad fatter than she remembers, but it doesn't take away from his handsomely rugged features. In fact, the slight weight gain he's amassed looks good on him.

She senses the gathering collectively holding their breaths.

Waiting for something to happen.

She decides to break the silence immediately.

But Janae beats her to the punch.

"Daddy, you're not gonna welcome Cadina back home?"

James turns away from her and ignores his daughter's query to shake a startled Emmanuel's hand. "Bruh, you handle yourself quite well on that podcast interview *and* that freestyle–I'm proud of you."

"Uh, thanks." Emmanuel peeks at everyone.

"James…" Grace grabs his attention. "I know you're not trying to be rude to Cadina, are you?"

He sarcastically sighs before marching up to her. In a ho-hum way, he asks, "So…what's up, Cadina? You're doing alright?"

His bland attitude deflates her.

She tries not to show it. "I-I'm doing well."

"You look a little hungry, Cadina," he continues, sounding animatedly robotic. "I'll go make you a plate. Are you cool with that?" He circles around to his gathering and loudly asks, "Is everybody cool with that?"

Janae calls out, "*Daddy…*"

But he bolts into the kitchen.

Cadina stares at the swinging kitchen door to avoid making eye contact with anyone in the room. She halfway expected this cold response from him. But no amount of self-preparation in the world can wither the hurt or the embarrassment she feels at this precise moment.

Grace holds her hand and in a lowered voice, says, "If you want, I can go in there and talk to him–"

"No…no. That's the reason why I'm here."

Grace mulls over Cadina's decision. "Just...just don't let his stubbornness get the best of you, okay?"

Grace pats her hand before letting go.

Cadina turns around.

With a clear path to the kitchen, she exhales and begins walking. She tries to look straight ahead but her attention is drawn to faces along the way. Smiling and encouraging faces like Neville's and Roy's. Lovelle rubs her arm in passing. Nayja squeezes her hand in good spirits. Cadina nods to all in appreciation.

From her peripheral, she catches Lou aiming the firestick at the wall-mounted flat-screen and clicking on a podcast show. Everyone once again makes themselves comfortable in the living room.

Janae runs over and hugs her waist. "Promise me you will stay after y'all talk? Like old times?"

The plea in her voice anchors Cadina.

She rests her chin on top of Janae's head and says, "I'll promise to do my best to stay; would you be okay with that?"

Janae reluctantly nods yes and slowly releases her.

Cadina kisses her forehead.

She then pushes open the kitchen door, hoping to rekindle whatever is left of the relationship that she once shared with her heartbroken soulmate.

# NINETY-SIX

## JAMES

*SLAM!*

After snatching a Corona out of the refrigerator, James swings the door back with so much force that it reopens slightly. He closes the door again, gently this time, before falling back down on a kitchen stool.

Leaning on a counter crowded with aluminum pans, paper plates, plasticware, and condiments, he pops the cap off the bottle and flings it perfectly into the trash can. He takes huge gulps of the brew to settle his biting nerves. A quick breather is needed before he sucks the bottle completely dry. It doesn't work. If anything, the beer only intensifies his flaming emotions. His heart thumps a bass drum pattern like what you hear in house music—loud, heavy, and repetitive.

He wasn't ready for this moment.

He wasn't ready for *her*.

*She has some nerve popping up here, unannounced.*

*Like everything will resume back to normal.*

*She should've called first.*

That way he would've had his thoughts and words together to undermine whatever shit she came here to say to him. He returns to the fridge for another cold one.

Someone enters the kitchen.

A certain someone who used to make his skin tingle just by the sound of her sexy stroll alone. Not anymore. He grabs another Corona and closes the door.

He turns around.

Sitting on his stool is Cadina.

Not the Wilson alter-ego he wanted to marry.

But the McThaddeus character whom he barely knows.

James drags himself to another stool across from her. He pops the cap off the bottle and tosses it to the trash can, missing it completely. He doesn't bother picking it up. Instead, he takes an extremely long swallow of the beer as he thoroughly dissects Cadina's revamped appearance, since everyone in the living room found it in their best interest to gawk over her new look.

He won't give her the satisfaction.

Not when she's had the audacity to chop off the long free-flowing hair he used to enjoy running his fingers through. Not while she sits on the stool with her gorgeously toned legs crossed as if she's ready to take some serious dictation. And especially not when she stares at him with those beautiful, yet somber eyes that are begging for forgiveness. Those same brown eyes exude nervousness, as they should because, at any given moment, the asshole buried within his core is going to explode right out of him.

"It's good to see you, James," Cadina says.

He belches loudly and deliberately.

He then leans forward with a curious glare. "Tell me something; is *Cadina* your real name? Or was it just your last name that was fake about you?"

She was floored by the question.

"It-It was just the last name that was different," she answers, keeping her poise. "Cadina is my real first name."

He leans back on the stool.

Takes another swig.

Eyeballs her every fidgeting movement.

The mood inside the kitchen is embarrassingly uncomfortable.

"What brings you here?" He places the beer on the counter. "Shouldn't you be somewhere with your pops monitoring another post office?"

She grins before responding, "Well, no, because I don't work for my father anymore."

"Why not?"

"I co-own a restaurant now."

He didn't see this coming.

He scoffs, "Really…"

She fumbles inside her purse and pulls out a small stack of flyers. She reaches one flyer toward him.

He doesn't budge.

She slides off the stool, walks up to him, hands him the flyer, and returns to her seat.

"I felt it was time for me to take authority over my own destiny," she explains. "So, I partnered with an investor who's a friend of the family. She drew up a business plan for me and got the funding we needed to get the process started. So, that's what I've been working on for the past year. Grand opening is next week."

He halfway listens as he reads the flyer. "*Cravin' Cadina's*, huh…"

"I felt it was a catchy name. What do you think?"

"Sounds like a title to one of my porno flicks."

He crumbles the flyer and shoots it like a three-pointer, straight into the trash can.

Cadina's face saddens. Her eyes grip the floor. "I know you're disappointed in me—"

"Disappointed? Is that what you think?" Hostility creeps into his tone. "I passed that stage a *long* time ago."

"Believe it or not, I really wanted to call you so I could explain everything that took place during our investigation–"

"Does it really matter now, Cadina? Because it was obvious that I was the least of your concerns before you dropped the disappearing act on me–"

"Can I finish, James?"

"Say what you have to say."

"I was completely shut down by the agency right after the incident. That meant no calling or seeing anybody–including you. But make no mistake; my feelings toward you were very sincere."

"You mean your intentions were sincere."

"It wasn't like that at all, James–"

"For once, Cadina, let's be honest about this! You *used* all of us to get what you needed in order to charge Velour for her criminal activity, didn't you?"

"I was assigned to your station to complete a task, which I did. Who knew I would wind up crossing paths with my soulmate during that time? Believe me, it was very difficult balancing both lives, so I told my father we had to tell you everything about us–"

"And you expect me to believe this now?"

"You can call my father right now and he will tell you the same. We have no reason to lie to you–"

"But you couldn't pick up a phone to let me know you were okay? You let a whole year go by before you felt it was convenient to just drop in to see how everyone is doing?"

"I really wasn't in a good place to talk to anyone last year. So, I had to go away for a while."

"Yeah, well, I wish I had the luxury of going away myself. That way, I wouldn't have had the whole damn station interrogate me about our relationship! I almost had a fight with Lou, defending *your* name, Cadina! I let you get close to my family! Janae kept asking me if you were okay and I didn't have an answer for her! I went out and bought you an engagement ring, not knowing I was about to propose to an imposter playing the role of a soulmate! *That* was the position you put me in–"

"*I…I…I…*that's all I'm hearing, is what I did to you!" She launches to her feet. "You want to throw that in my face? Well, let me clue you in on some reality! Velour deserved every bit of jail time with all the shit she did, but for some reason, I felt sorry for her and begged my father to grant her parole in exchange for her brother's freedom! But she didn't want parole, she wanted revenge! Broke into my parent's house and aimed a *gun* at my head! Have you ever had a gun aimed at your head, James? HAVE YOU?"

He can still hear the violent blast from Velour's gun, exploding through her parents' house. Can still visualize her and Velour laid out on the grass after crashing through the upstairs window. But as horrific as that night was, he continues to see himself as a misguided pawn in their determined quest to bring down a wanted criminal.

So, he glares at her.

Watches the tears form in her eyes.

And remains quiet until she finishes.

"You don't want to experience that, trust me, I know I didn't." She grabs a napkin from the counter and pats her wet eyes. "But that's what I signed up for. Even after therapy, I was an emotional wreck and didn't know what my next move was going to be until the opportunity to co-own a restaurant presented itself. That was my wake-up call."

She moves closer to him.

Gently places her hand on his face.

And stares into his inebriated eyes.

"My love for you is very real, James, but my absence was never about you; I needed time to find the value within myself…and the woman standing before you now has never been clearer about her self-worth."

*Good, she's finished.*

He brushes her hand from his face and thinly seethes, "And you're still a stranger in my eyes, no matter how many ways you try to slice it."

He returns to the fridge for another brew.

"You haven't heard one thing I said." She throws her hands up in total amazement. "After all the hell I went through, you have the nerve to act salty towards me?"

He slams the refrigerator door. "What the hell did you expect when you came here? Huh? Acceptance? Some forgiveness, maybe–"

"I expected a little compassion! But I'm now seeing that's not even in your DNA!"

"I can tell you what else is not in my DNA; your extended visitation here. Have a nice life, Cadina."

He guzzles his brew and points her directly to the kitchen door.

"I can't believe this sh–" She cuts herself off. She snatches the flyers from the counter and stuffs them inside her purse. Her razor-edge glare slashes right into him. "I really expected more from you, James. But now, I'm seeing you for who you really are–"

"Tell your story walking, sweetheart." Beer spits from his mouth. He continues pointing. "Get outta here!"

"You know what? Fuck you, James."

She straps her pocketbook over her shoulder and barges through the kitchen door, hitting an eavesdropping Lou square on the head.

"OUCH!"

"Oh, I'm sorry, Lou!" Cadina sniffles. "Are you okay?"

Quickly standing up and rubbing his head, Lou replies, "Uh, yeah, I'm good, Ma."

James glares through the swinging door as Divine, Lovelle, Marisol, and Najya walk over to console Cadina.

The door slows to a complete stop.

James feels the anger still percolating inside his chest cavity.

His ears latch onto the conversation taking place on the other side of the door.

*"Do you want me to go in there and talk some sense in him?" Divine asks.*

*"It's alright, Dee. I'm okay," replies Cadina. "Look, if any of you happen to be in my neighborhood, please stop by my restaurant and have a meal on me, okay?"*

*"Forget about that, Cadina. Do you want me to talk to that fool in there?"*

*"No, just leave it alone. I'm alright."*

James pops off the stool and stomps his way into the living room.

He scowls at the sight of Cadina handing out flyers to everybody.

He doesn't waste any time snatching the flyers from the ladies' hands.

"C'mon, James, now that's taking it a little too far," Lovelle states.

"Why are you being such a dodo brain?" Divine tries to snatch her flyer back.

James ignores them and hands a surprised Cadina back the flyers. "What you're not gonna do is curse me out in my own house, and then solicit my peoples. Take your mess and continue bouncing up outta here!"

"You know what?" Cadina whispers. "Stick'em in your ass for me, okay, Mr. Porno?"

Cadina slaps the flyers from his hand, causing them to swoop all the way down on the hardwood floor, and then she scampers toward the front entrance.

"Cadina, wait!" yells Divine. She glares back at James. "Why are you acting like this?"

"Mind your business, thank you." James kneels to pick up the flyers.

"Give them to me. I'll give them back to her since you're so adamant about throwing her out." He shoves the flyers in her hands. She shakes her head in shame. "I really thought you were bigger than that, man."

She waddles out the front door.

The ladies peek out the window at Cadina.

"Awww, man, this is bad," Marisol says.

"I know." Lovelle turns to the ladies. "I'm going to talk to her."

"I'm right behind you," Najya says.

All three ladies glare at James as they rush out the front door.

James sees Janae standing by the staircase.

Shaking in anger.

"Go to your room," James firmly orders, pointing upstairs. "Right now."

Janae's face twists in disgust as she squeals to herself and darts up the staircase, passing her grandmother.

"James!" Grace roars. "I want to see you in the kitchen!"

"Oh, shit," utter the men.

"Why?"

"You don't get to ask *me* why! You just *do*! In the kitchen–NOW!"

Acting more like an adolescent, James slams through the kitchen door, with a fed-up Grace right on his heels.

James paces around in frustration before leaning back on the kitchen counter.

Grace says, "I don't know what just happened out there, but I know that wasn't *my* son acting like a complete fool to our guest and upsetting *my* granddaughter–"

"Ma, just because everybody else chose to welcome her back with open arms doesn't mean I have to follow suit–"

"Do you have any idea the courage she had to muster up just to come here and talk to you? And for you to mistreat her the way you did…who made you her judge and jury?"

"I never said I was. You're the one putting words in my mouth."

Freeman quietly slips into the kitchen and takes a seat.

"Freeman, I hope you came in here to talk some sense into your friend's head, because I'm not gonna take too much of his foolishness, not up in this house–"

"He's not gonna say anything I haven't heard already, ain't that right, Free?"

Freeman sips on bottled water but doesn't respond.

"Then maybe you need to stay by yourself, James, because she didn't deserve to be embarrassed like that." Grace calms her breathing before saying, "You owe that woman *and* your daughter an apology–bottom line."

She eyeballs him, shakes her head at Freeman, and storms out the kitchen.

"THANKS FOR LETTING ME KNOW WHOSE SIDE YOU'RE ON, MA!" James roars.

"So, you're gonna wait until your moms leave before you start clapping back at her?"

"I'm not in the mood, Free…"

James yanks the refrigerator door open and grabs a Bud Light Lime. He cops a squat on a stool and pops the top from his beer.

Freeman finishes his water, and then states, "Had I known you were going to flip out on Cadina, I would've never invited her over here."

He looks up at Freeman, mildly surprised. "When did you speak to her?'

"She dropped by the station this afternoon. I thought this would've been the ultimate surprise, but man, I thought wrong."

"I'm surprised you even gave her the time of day, being that she's partly responsible for you winding up in the hospital–"

"C'mon, bruh; like Cadina really knew Vincent was going to stop by my route and whoop my ass. I don't pin that on her, and neither should you."

Freeman slides off the stool and heads for the fridge.

Meanwhile, James turns his bottle upside down, making sure to nurse his ornery mood with the last drops of his brew. Freeman returns with an Aquafina water bottle. He hasn't seen his best friend drink a cold brew or any liquor in quite a while. Not even at social gatherings like this one. Freeman's definitely a changed man–for the better.

"You think I'm being shallow?" James asks.

Freeman takes a swig of water before responding, "Well, I wouldn't say that."

"Then, what would you say..."

"Well, I guess everybody thought you would've been just a *little* more open-minded given the circumstances of everything that happened."

"Look, I know everyone is viewing me as an asshole right now, I get it. But don't confuse it with me being insensitive. I'm glad Cadina survived that attack by Velour. But let's take it way back to the day she arrived at the station. If you were in my shoes, Freeman, with everything that has transpired up to this point, you wouldn't look at Cadina differently than you did before? Keep it real with me…"

"I probably would've had my reservations…"

"Yeah, you and the rest of them cats in the living room would've done the same thing. So why is everybody acting like I'm the one out of pocket?"

"Well, I can tell you firsthand, this doesn't have anything to do with Cadina."

"And it's not about me over exaggerating, either–"

"All of this stems back to LaToya."

"What?"

Freeman leans forward and stares into James' lit eyes. "Jay, this is me you're talking to. Need I remind you, I've been your earpiece during all of the drama LaToya put you through."

"And?"

"You told me right after you broke up with LaToya that you didn't want anything to do with another long-term commitment. You were gonna concentrate on raising Janae and living life–you remember telling me that?"

"Yeah, somewhat."

"And yet, Cadina showed up and threw a monkey wrench all up in your plans. She even had you thinking of marriage! But then the bottom fell out and now you feel like another lady done did you wrong and left you hanging–just like LaToya did. Correct me if I'm wrong."

James chugs on his beer, totally avoiding the question.

"Yes, Cadina was an inspector. Yes, a lot has happened during that time frame, and you can't change any of that–that's the past. We're here now. *All* of us. Now, she took the first step toward making things right. How it plays out, depends solely on you, bruh." Freeman checks his watch. "And on that note, I'm out."

"I'm not chasing you out of here, am I?"

Freeman stands and wipes the wrinkles from his pants. "Remember I told you I'm going with Lovelle to a church meeting at eight? Our Men's Day Anniversary is next month, and my Pastor wants me to direct it this year."

"Oh, yeah, I forgot." James struggles to his feet. "Yo, how's your eye coming along?"

"Clearer by the day. All I can say is God is good, all the time."

"AYO!" Lou barrels his way into the kitchen like a one-man entourage. He overwhelms James and Freeman with half-hug/pounds. "Roy and Neville are coming with us to the studio, so we're outta here. Tell your moms we said thanks for the food."

"No problem."

Lou bounces out of the kitchen, with James and Freeman following suit.

Everybody in the living room is preparing to leave.

"Yo, Jay, you rolling with us to the studio?" Roy asks, zipping up his Giants jacket.

"He's drunk, y'all," Lou reveals to the room. "He's in for the night!"

Roy gives James a hug, and then whispers in his ear, *"You don't wanna end it like that, son. Give her another chance, a'ight?"* Roy gives him a serious nod before heading out of the house.

Neville and Shabbazz fist-bump James, grab their to-go containers and follow Roy.

Lovelle, Marisol, and Najya give him a hug and some advice. His only responses are, "Thanks", and "Get home safe."

Divine places her food container in a plastic bag and then cuts her eyes at James before giving him a half-hearted hug.

"And I love you, too," James says.

"Mmm, hmm. I love you back, but I'm not feeling the way you handled that whole situation with Cadina. You know that, right?"

"Well, I know now."

"You better pray she finds it in her heart to forgive you for what you put her through this afternoon."

"Get home safe, Dee."

Divine shakes her head as she and Emmanuel walk out the front door.

James follows them out onto the porch. He watches the crew load into their vehicles and start their engines. Lou, in his gleaming black Range Rover, leads the way, blasting one of his songs from his megawatt system. The convoy of vehicles snake their way down the one-way street and disappear around the corner.

James returns inside and stumbles to his loveseat.

His head begins a woozy spin-cycle due to having too many beers.

He closes his eyes to replay the rocky scene he created in the kitchen with Cadina.

*Maybe, just maybe, they're right about her intentions.*

James mumbles something under his breath against his own conscience.

He refuses to go down that road.

Getting to know somebody all over again proves to be too much work, time, and energy; none of which he has.

Something tells him to look to the top of the staircase.

Standing on the top step is Janae.

From where he sits, he can clearly see her chest heaving in resentment.

"You chased away Mommy and now you threw Cadina out. Why?"

Her watery-eyed scowl demands an answer.

But his mouth opens and nothing comes out except a beer stench.

"IS THERE ANYBODY OUT HERE GOOD ENOUGH FOR YOU, MR. PERFECT?!?"

She runs back to her room and slams the door with grown-adult force.

*Shit.*

That rhetorical question knifes him in his heart.

James pushes himself from the loveseat and stumbles toward the staircase. The first thing he needs to do is stop by the bathroom and swallow a couple of Motrin to ease his wig-splitting headache. The next stop will be to his daughter's room to explain why he did what he felt was necessary to protect his family from other people's obscure motives and inflated promises. In due time, the *big, bad daddy* label will wear off and he'll go back to being her best friend again.

But why is that hostile emotion he's clinging onto trying its best to cover up his *true* feelings concerning Cadina?

*Damn you, girl!*

# NINETY-SEVEN

## DELIVERANCE

"Thank you so much for coming," Cadina humbly says to the older couple leaving. "I hope you enjoyed everything–"

"Are you kidding me, the food was amazing!" The lady lauds, cutting her off. "Our anniversary is next month, and I won't be surprised if we find ourselves back here, dressed to the nines! Isn't that right, Hubert?"

"Is this your restaurant, young lady?" Hubert asks, in a sturdy voice and with the hard glare of a war veteran.

"Yes, Sir."

"Love the layout. Who taught you how to cook like that, your momma?"

"For the most part, yes."

"She taught you well." He throws on his black U.S. Retired 1st Sergeant Army cap and jacket. "We'll be back and make sure you keep the yams on the menu."

"What are your full names?"

"Hubert and Shirley Washington; and have a bottle of two thousand eight Elyse Winery C'est Si Bon in an ice bucket when we return."

"We don't serve wine at the present moment, Sir–"

"It's for our anniversary–make it happen."

He smiles a perfect set of new teeth and marches in a slow cadence out the entrance, along with his smiling wife.

"Zana?"

The attentive hostess in black reports to Cadina with a pencil and pad. "Ma'am?"

"You see that couple who just left?"

"Yes."

"Their names are Hubert and Shirley Washington. They may be back next month to celebrate their anniversary, and I want to have a surprise for them. Make a note of it."

Zana finishes scribbling on the pad. "Already done!"

"Thanks."

The spirited hostess briskly returns to the front podium and welcomes new customers.

Cadina turns around and quietly basks in her new sanctuary.

A spacious layout that comfortably holds eight square maple wood tables with cushioned seats in the center of the dining room. High-top seating is arranged perfectly near the front window. Four wide booths hug the exposed brick wall in the back for intimate gatherings. Various portraits are placed around the walls, portraying Cadina's early years of developing her culinary craft. Eighties and nineties R&B pour out from surrounding overhead speakers. The overall rustic structure and emerald-green backsplash create an elegant contrast.

Green, white, and silver balloons float everywhere, indicating a Grand Opening.

This is her restaurant.

And the place is packed.

Dazzling in her dark green velvet dress and gold accessories, Cadina makes her way around the tables, chatting, laughing, and thanking everyone for supporting her big day.

Looking out the front window, she spots a female letter carrier parking her pushcart by a tree and rushing into the front entrance.

Cadina motions to the cashier for the to-go bag sitting on the counter.

The cashier hands it to her and she meets the lady carrier at the entrance.

"Here you go, Ma'am," the carrier says, handing her the mail. "Congratulations on your new restaurant."

"Thank you so much and this is for you." She hands the carrier the bag. "On behalf of Cravin' Cadina's, a packed food container, plus dessert. Hope you enjoy it."

The carrier's mouth drops open. "Oh, my goodness, thank you! You must've heard my stomach grumbling from across the street."

"I figured you'd need something hearty after a long day's work."

"Girl, my cart broke down as soon as I stepped out the station and had to go back and look for another cart, which took a half-hour to find, then had to transfer everything into that one and I've been running and gunning ever since." The carrier shakes her head and sighs. "If you only knew what I go through at my job."

Cadina holds back a giggle. "I can't imagine…"

"Anyhoo, thanks again for my dinner and I'll tell my coworkers there's a new restaurant on my route that we have to support. Take care!"

The lady carrier rushes out the door, places her bag inside of her pushcart, and continues with her delivery.

At the same time, a young couple enters the restaurant.

Cadina says, "Welcome to Cravin' Cadina's", hands them menus and they follow Zana to an open table in the back.

She keeps her eyes on the handsome couple.

The young man pulls out the seat for his lady friend.

He takes a seat and they both study their menus while holding hands.

After placing their orders, they lean forward on the table and converse intimately.

They laugh in each other's faces.

Eyes focused solely on one another.

As if nothing else matters in the world.

It reminds her of the time when she and James would go–

She quickly shakes off the recurring memory like it was a cold chill down her back.

Don't want to ruin her day with wishful thoughts of what could have been.

More patrons enter her place of business, and she welcomes them with menus in hand and warmth in her bittersweet smile.

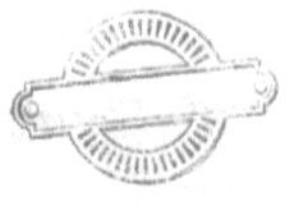 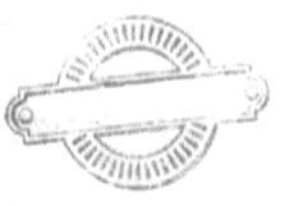 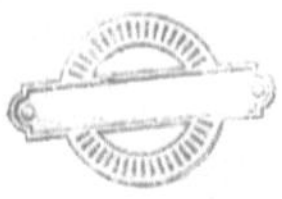

SHE'S TIRED.

But pleased.

Extremely pleased.

The Grand Opening was beyond successful.

It was everything she didn't dream for herself two years ago.

Never thought could happen to her in a lifetime.

And now it has become her reality.

The start of a newfound journey.

Two of her cooks walk out from the back after cleaning up the kitchen.

"We'll see you tomorrow at eleven," shouts Cook Jackson, in a tired but pleased drawl.

She waves at them. "Get home safe. Great job today."

They wave back as they walk out the front entrance.

She pushes herself to her feet, locks the door, and then grabs a broom.

Delroy the busser finishes placing the seats upside down on each table and prepares the mop bucket while she sweeps the floor.

They hear a knock at the door.

It's her sister, Camille.

Cadina unlocks the door to let her in.

Camille shuffles in and plops on one of the high seats by the window. "Girl, I'm so sorry I had to leave right after the ceremony, but I was literally swamped with walk-ins today. So, how was your first day?"

Cadina smiles and says, "Busy."

"Busy is a good thing."

"Busy is a *great* thing."

The sisters slap a high-five.

"I'm so proud of you, girl," Camille says. "Now, where's my plate?"

"It's in the back, along with Moms and Pops. Speaking of Pops, I thought he was catching a ride with you."

"He drove himself here. He's outside talking."

"Oh." Cadina begins sweeping. She then stops and looks at her sister. "Cammy…"

"Whassup?"

"Do you like the name I gave my restaurant?"

"*Cravin' Cadina's*? Love it. Why?"

"It doesn't sound a bit risqué, you know, maybe teetering on the kinky side?"

"Hell, I think it's a *sexy* name for a restaurant! *Cravin' Cadina's*. Like, they just *hunger* for your edibles, baby!"

"But it doesn't sound like someone *might* crave something else besides food to you?"

Her sister laughs while peeking out the window. "Where is all this stemming from? I thought you loved the name?"

Cadina sighs. "I do. I don't know why I'm bugging."

She resumes sweeping and then stops again. "Who is Pop talking to outside?"

Camille smiles devilishly at her. "Look out the window and find out."

"You and your drama, I tell ya…"

Cadina drags herself over to peek out the glass door.

Then it happens.

First, her bottom jaw hits the floor.

Then her heart flutters like a flock of pigeons leaving the coop.

When she tries to speak, she can't, because her vocal cords ball up into a knot.

But her eyes continue to function as she is clearly able to see her father standing on the corner having a discussion with, of all people, James, who listens intently with flowers in his hand.

Camille releases the blinds and says, “Puppy dogs always find their way back. Didn’t I tell you it was gonna happen?”

Cadina turns around and leans her back against the door. She deliriously looks around her restaurant, catches her breath, and then mutters, “The nerve of his stupid ass.”

“I see you have two choices, Sis,” Camille slides off the seat. “Either you let Pops talk his ear off about nothing or you go out there and make that fine brother sweat out an apology for the way he treated you last week. Shouldn’t be a hard decision to make, right?”

Camille giggles to herself as she sashays to the kitchen.

Cadina peeks through the glass door again.

She can’t deny it.

*The brother does look good.*

Dressed in a forest green turtleneck shirt, a camel wool coat, denim pants, and green Timberlands, James is casually on point. They always did have a knack for wearing similar colors on the same day.

That’s before their kindred spirits went their separate ways.

*Or did it?*

“I got it from here, Ma’am,” Delroy offers.

The eager busser takes the broom from her hand and begins sweeping.

She stares through the glass door again.

Her father wraps up his conversation with James and approaches the door.

She lets him in.

Vernon loosens his tie. He then studies her demeanor before asking, “You good?”

She nods. “I packed you and Mom’s food containers in a bag.”

“You had any yams left–”

“I gave you a good helping.”

“Yes!”

He rubs his hands together and heads to the kitchen.

Cadina retrieves her sweater from the back of the counter and steps outside.

The crisp mid-forties temperature has her folding the sweater over her chest as she walks over to James who stands by his SUV.

He holds a gorgeous bouquet of red roses in his hand.

And he looks nervous as hell.

She stares deeply into his eyes.

Into the cornerstone of his soul.

There she finds sorrow.

And compassion.

There she finds James.

The kindred spirit she still loves infinitely.

Not the rude representation of him she encountered at his house last week.

But that rude representative hurt her with lethal words and a spiteful attitude.

Now he comes bearing roses and his tail between his legs.

He quickly breaks away from her stare and lowers his head.

Ashamed.

And he needs to be.

As much as she adores this man, she's going to find solace in giving him a nasty dose of his own insensitive medication.

He clears his throat and says, "Your pops gave me the address to your restaurant–"

"We're closed for the night, James." Her eyes are as dull as her voice. "We open back up at one tomorrow."

"That's not why I'm here."

"So, why are you here? To continue yelling at me like I'm some stray dog?"

James reaches out the roses to her.

She pushes them right back. "Please, James, I don't have any use for them–"

"It's the beginning of an overdue apology, Cadina—"

"Unlike *you*, I'll accept your verbal apology, but that's about it. Now, if you'll excuse me, I have to finish closing up."

Cadina turns around to head back inside.

But he quickly cuts her off.

"What, James?" she hisses, swinging her arm violently to keep him from touching her. "You said what you had to say the other day—now move!"

"And I was way out of line," he says, in a calm manner. "It's just that I didn't think I was going to see you anymore. And when I saw you the other day standing in my living room…I don't know…something came over me where I completely went into defense mode–"

"And I expected you to, James." Her eyes begin to well. "But what I didn't expect was for you to humiliate me in front of your family and friends like I meant absolutely nothing to you! You showed me a side of you that I didn't know existed and it hurt, James…and after everything I went through, too? You *hurt* me, James…"

Now the tears begin to fall.

She wishes she had better control over her emotions.

She uses the sweater to wipe her face and then says, "Look, we've already been down this road before, and I don't feel like crying and being miserable all over again. I love you, James, and I always will, but maybe I did show up at your house with high expectations, and that was my fault. I just have to deal with that, so…have a goodnight, James–"

"I need you to be quiet for a minute."

"For what now?"

"To allow me to finish what I started a year ago."

He tosses the roses to the ground.

He then pulls out a velvet heart-shaped ring box from his pocket.

And drops down on one knee.

"Trust me when I say I've learned a lot about myself this past year." James' eyes begin to water. "What I need in my life, who I can't live without…I know I came off like an asshole last week, but tonight, I'm not about to miss out on this opportunity again."

He lifts the top of the box.

It was like a beam of light radiating from his hand.

The diamond ring sparkles so brilliantly that her heart begins to palpitate.

From the corner of her eye, she sees an audience forming outside the entrance.

Vernon. Camille. Bussers Delroy and Archie.

All of them are waiting for an answer like James.

She looks down at him, from his watery eyes to his groomed mustache, to his full, succulent lips. She wants to kiss them, suck on them; she misses the taste of them.

But she stiffens back up.

"I think you'd better get up before you embarrass yourself," she strongly advises.

"Well, it wouldn't be the first time."

He stays on bended knee, smiling that handsome smile of his.

She can't do this any longer.

As bad as she wants to hold onto her anger, he's making it impossible for her to do so. His sincerity is melting away the last of her defenses. This is her *true* mate talking to her now. Both have had to overcome too many obstacles, individually and collectively. Still, the test of time proves to be no match for what they have for one another.

She tries to suppress a smile, but it comes out anyway.

"Ah, do I see an opening?" he asks.

She turns to her family at the door.

"Don't look at us!" Camille yells out. "He's talking to you!"

She turns back to him. The smile becomes bashful.

He adjusts his knee to the ground and clears his throat. "Okay… so, allow me to reintroduce myself. I, James Richards, proud member of the United States Postal Service, would be honored to have you as my wife…if you don't mind putting up with my foolishness."

"Are you sure about this? You might be proposing to an imposter."

"I think I can trust you."

"You *think* you can trust me now–"

"Give me your hand."

Cadina holds her breath.

Bites down hard on her bottom lip.

Slowly, she extends her trembling hand to James.

Then smiles upward.

Toward the heavens above.

She mouths, "Thank you…", to the Most High.

Feels utopia pouring into her very being…

…as the platinum ring glides smoothly onto her finger.

She raises her hand to gaze at the bedazzling jewel which fits her finger perfectly. She quivers with belated joy.

"Well?" he asks.

"Well, what?"

"Is it a yes or no?"

"SHE SAID YES!!!" screams Camille.

Cadina laughs. "My family said yes!"

"I'm not marrying them!"

She composes herself and announces, "I, Cadina McThaddeus, happily say yes. Yes, yes, yes…"

She kneels in front of her future husband. She holds his face, and they suck on each other's lips and tongue like pieces of mouthwatering fruit. James grabs a hold of her head and forms a kissing trail that starts at her soft lips, then to her cheekbone and to her neck, where she takes in deep breaths of the evening's air. He circles back to her lips as the mixture of her tears and the moisture of his tongue create its own intoxicating mai tai.

"I love you, Mr. Richards."

"I love you back, *future* Mrs. Richards."

She hears a round of applause from the audience at the front entrance.

The men head back into the restaurant.

But Camille, in her high heels rushing over, rejoices loudly as she bears her weight right on top of them.

*"OH, MY GOD! OH, MY GOD!"* Camille yells, in her own set of tears. *"IT'S ABOUT DAMN TIME! I'M SO HAPPY FOR Y'ALL! My chest is gonna explode—I'm so excited!"*

Camille's bosom weighs solidly on Cadina's back, but she doesn't mind. As long as she's in James' arms, nothing else is more peaceful… more sacred.

*"Let me see the ring! Quick, c'mon, you too slow, Sis!"* Camille yanks her sister's hand to inspect the engagement ring. She turns to James with a thumbs up. "You've redeemed yourself, brother-in-law. Big time!"

"Thanks, Sister-in-law. Now can you get off me, please?"

"Oooo, I'm calling Mommy right now and telling her the good news!" Camille lifts herself up. "We've got some serious planning to do, girl! Y'all's wedding is going to be fierce, you hear me?" She cups her mouth, gazes emotionally at the happy couple, and then skips back inside.

They stare at each other for a while.

James wipes her wet face with his hand.

She grabs his hand and kisses each finger on it.

"I missed you so much, James," she whispers.

James kisses her hand. "I felt the same way."

"Are you hungry? I can make you a plate right quick and you can check out my new establishment." She runs her fingers through his hair and whispers, "And then maybe we can go back to my apartment and get re-acquainted…"

He smiles. "That can wait until later. We have somewhere to be."

"Like where?"

"Our boys are performing at Webster Hall in about an hour. The rest of the crew is gonna meet us there."

"Hold up. *They* know I'm coming? What if I had said *no* to you? Then what?"

"Then, I would have dragged your ass along with me. Now, do you need my help with closing?"

"No, we're pretty much done."

He sizes up her desirable appearance. "You're wearing the hell out of that dress."

She fully blushes. "Keep talking like that and we won't be going anywhere near Webster Hall."

He throws his head back in laughter. "Then I'll be quiet. Hurry up."

They share another kiss before she snatches the bouquet of roses from the ground and dances back into the restaurant.

She sees her father woofing down his food at a table.

"You couldn't wait until you got home?" She places the roses in an empty vase.

"I told you I was hungry."

She glides over to her father and extends her hand with the ring on it.

"BAM!" she shouts.

Vernon smirks as he uses a napkin to wipe his mouth. "He showed it to me outside. Looks like it cost him a pretty penny."

"What were y'all two talking about before I stepped outside?"

"Just men-talk, that's all."

"Men-talk, huh..."

"Well, you know I had to threaten him a little..."

"You *what*?"

"I told him if he didn't come here to take you off my hands that he might as well turn around and go back home."

Cadina shakes her head and then hugs her daddy. "Thank you for your blessings."

"He's a good guy."

Camille steps out of the restroom and sings out loud, *"CADINA IS GETTIN' MAAARRIED! CADINA IS GETTIN' MAAARRIED! I'MA HAVE A BRUTHA-IN-LAW, AND SHE'S GONNA SPIT OUT CHILDREN GALORE!"*

"Really, Cammy?"

"Momma said she hates that she missed the proposal and to bring her plate home."

"Alright," says Vernon.

"Archie!" Cadina yells.

The young busser wrings the mop out in the bucket and turns to Cadina. "Yes, Ma'am?"

"Can you be a doll and lock up after y'all finish?"

"We're pretty much done," Archie says, wiping his hands.

"I'll stay with them and get the keys when they leave."

"Thanks, Dad."

"Oooo, I see James wants to make up for lost time, huh," Camille teases.

"No, Crazy. He's taking me to a show tonight."

"I bet he is. Smooches!" Camille waves at everybody as she leaves through the front.

Cadina walks behind the counter, retrieves the restaurant keys, and hands them to Vernon. "Thank you so much. I'll swing by the house to pick them up."

"Where're y'all off to?"

"Webster Hall." She slips her purse over her shoulders. "Our friends are performing there."

"Really? Have I heard of them?"

"They're a rap group."

"Oh." Vernon rolls his eyes. "Then I guess I haven't."

"Bye everybody."

Cadina kisses her father's cheek and then dashes out of the front door.

She spots Camille bear-hugging James and then climbing into her Durango. She blows the horn to say goodbye. Cadina waves at her as she walks toward James, who holds open the door like the true gentleman he is. She slides in, he shuts the door, and then he races around to the driver's side and peels off down the street.

James turns to her and says, "You know, your pops is mad cool."

"What were y'all talking about before I stepped outside?"

"Just men-talk—"

"I'm not trying to hear that! You better tell me."

Merging into the flowing Grand Central Parkway traffic, he says, "I asked him for your hand in marriage."

Her face turns into a tongue-in-cheek grin. "And what did he say?"

"He said, '*Please do. I'm tired of her moping around my house, crying all the time!*' He said that he'd pay me to take you off his hands at this point."

"No he did not!"

"Those were his exact words, I swear! That man is crazy!"

"We all are." She kisses and holds on to his hand. "Over you."

James kisses the back of her hand and then focuses on the road ahead of him.

Cadina sits back and quietly admires her man.

Correction—her *future* husband.

She releases her hand from his and begins to stroke his hair and neck. Never has he looked so confident, so wonderfully debonair, so damn *fine,* to her. Her once dormant hormones now send an immense *ringing* sensation throughout her tingling body…

*RINGGGGG!*

Vernon snatches his cell from his hip, screens the number, and then answers. "Hey, what's up? Yeah, I'm still dressed, why?" His eyes widened. "Okay, yeah, I should be there within the hour...bye."

He places his cell back on his hip.

Delroy and Archie shut the lights off and they all walk out the front entrance.

Archie locks the door behind them, hands the keys to Vernon, and climbs in the car with Delroy.

They drive off.

Vernon pulls out his cell and texts Lorraine.

*Had to return to the office for an emergency meeting. I'll make it quick so I can bring you your food.*

He slides into his Cadillac, starts the engine, and floors it down the street.

Traveling across the Queensboro Bridge, Vernon's thoughts drift back to Cadina. Millions of people walking the earth's surface would've allowed a traumatic experience, such as the one she had to endure, to have eaten them alive. He's proud to say that she was not one of those people. She could've withered away and let the pain haunt her for the rest of her life, but she didn't allow her circumstance to pin her into a dark corner.

Instead, she came out swinging.

It took her a while, but she dug deep within herself to find the strength and commitment to rise above her tormented state. And he is so humbled by it.

He, too, had to re-align his priorities, just as Cadina did.

He got a little too carried away with a personal agenda that almost cost him his daughter's life and if that tragic event couldn't alter his way of thinking, then maybe he wasn't the kind, loving, responsible father he thought of himself as and always inspired to be.

He exits off the interstate and makes his way…

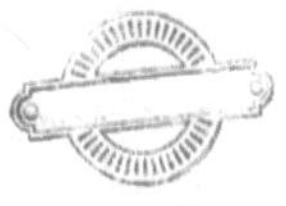 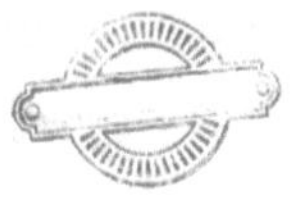 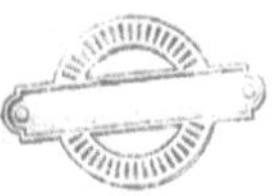

…TO THE FIRST AVAILABLE PARKING SPOT THEY SEE ON ELEVENTH Street.

As they approach Webster Hall, James slips a VIP pass over her neck so they can avoid waiting in a line that's beginning to slither its way toward the corner of Third Avenue. They choose to avoid the packed sidewalk altogether and walk in the street, weaving their way in and out of every double-parked stretched Hummer and limousine town car they see. They finally arrive at the front entrance where security is monitoring the door.

A beefy Italian security guard directs them to wait for a moment.

This provides enough time for Cadina to whip out her compact mirror and check her appearance. Satisfied, she puts her mirror away and gawks at the chattering line behind them. Suddenly, something catches her eye, calls out her name—

*Cadinaaaaa…*

She quickly turns to her left.

It was the building on the corner.

Midway Postal Station.

Tucker's Midway Postal Station.

Standing as bold and illustrious as ever in a quiet shadowy backdrop. That sandstone structure will forever hold a special place in her heart. She stares at the memorable institution with a goose-bumped engendering affinity.

The security guard finally waves them in through the velvet rope.

They hurry through the double entrance doors and walk down the semi-dark grand entrance hall to the room where the concert is being held. Holding hands, they hear and feel the energy pounding on the other side of the door as they draw closer to it. When they enter, they are captivated by the roving, multicolored spotlights that seem to match the intensity of the hard, steady boom-bap that blasts out of the surrounding speakers.

Dedicated fans dance and position their camera phones for the show.

Cadina finds herself getting caught up in the scene's festive hysteria.

James says something to her, but she can barely hear what he's saying due to the loud, vibrating…

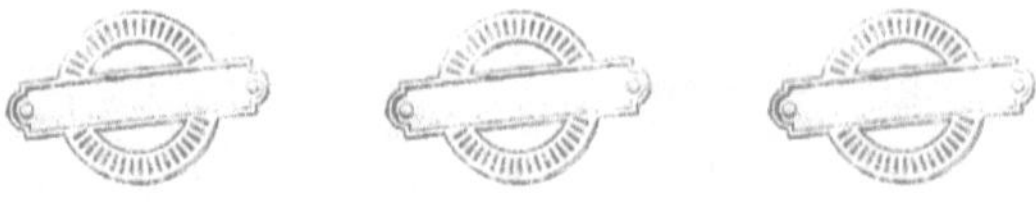

…SILENCE THAT SEEMS TO WALK WITH VERNON ALL THE WAY INTO THE building's elevator.

He presses his floor and then watches the doors close in one smooth motion. As he wipes his glasses with his handkerchief, he reflects on what occurred at the restaurant earlier.

A new member will be added to the family, in the form of a son-in-law.

Cadina knew he would approve of James, and she was right. Humble sincerity is what he sees in the handsome young man whose determination and commitment to raising his daughter *and* taking care of his mother made Vernon envision himself when he was a young man doing the same exact thing. More power to the couple who's destined for a happy ending.

Unfortunately, happy endings don't apply to everybody.

He slips his glasses back on and exits the elevator.

With his Kenneth Coles clicking away on the buffed hallway floor, Vernon purposely morphs his face so it displays the icy-hardened expression usually reserved for individuals he's about to interrogate. And the individual currently waiting in his office is about to feel a bit of his personal wrath. This individual, at one time, shared a short yet warped relationship with Cadina. Vernon learned later it was one fueled by jealousy and rage. And it's a shame because, under any other circumstance, Vernon would've been impressed by this vindictive lad, whose computer-hacking skills were savvy enough to break into the Academy's computer terminals. In fact, he probably would've offered the young man a position within the company, especially since the young man was taken advantage of by his self-serving station manager.

But the young man put his daughter's life in jeopardy and that's where he crossed the line.

Vernon pauses in front of his office door and tugs on his tie one last time.

His face is in full grilling mode.

He clears his throat and opens his office door.

Inside his office are his comrades; Inspector Harris and Inspector Moses, standing next to his computer desk. Standing on the opposite side of the room with their arms folded are Detective Strait and Special Agent Whitaker. Vernon nods to them as an acknowledgment of their success.

They always get their man.

In the middle of the room, shifting nervously in his seat is Lexington VanGuard.

His eyes widened as Vernon enters his office.

Sneaky little fellow.

He tried to flee the Big Apple because he had an inkling the authorities were going to eventually seek him out as a link to the whole Velour/Vincent Patterns scandal. They know Lexington was not involved with that crime family—but they're not going to tell him that, yet.

Vernon strolls over to his desk and plops his worn body in his chair. He opens a drawer to retrieve his favorite pipe, loads it with his favorite tobacco, and lights it. The cherry tobacco burns with the same intensity Vernon's glaring eyes do on the captive individual.

Lexington, now sporting a thick beard, breaks his silence immediately. "S-S-Sir, Mr. Wilson, I-I mean, Mr. McThaddeus—"

Vernon smokes on his pipe which now puffs like the Chattanooga Choo Choo.

"I s-swear to you, sir, I-I didn't know anything about what Velour was doing! She was just a coworker of mine! We had a *working* relationship at the station—that was it! I didn't know her brother, I didn't know anything about this credit card, bootleg ring, I-I didn't know any of that! The only thing I did wrong was digging into your files, that's it! And I'm sorry for doing that because now, as I think of it, I must've served as the link that put your daughter in harm's way and I'm *really* sorry about that! I-I was just a little upset with everybody at the time, that's all. Is Cadina okay?"

They all remain intensely silent.

Lexington isn't saying anything they don't already know. All Vernon wants to know is what on earth possessed him to hack into their computer terminals in the first place.

And he wants to hear an apology, which he's currently receiving a great deal of.

And maybe they will reinstate him back into the postal system.

Maybe.

As for now, Vernon sits back in his chair and puffs away, as the poor lad doubles up on his endless pleading.

*"I'm sooo sorry!"* a now crying Lexington shrieks, with veins popping from his neck. *"I don't wanna go to jail! I didn't know! You must believe me! I swear to you!"* Lexington now sits on the edge of his seat, trembling. *"I didn't know, dammit! I DID NOT KNOW—!"*

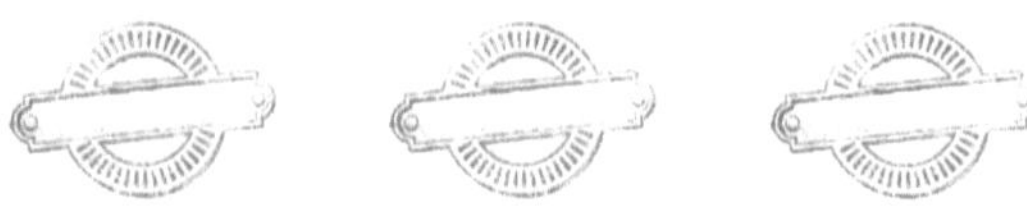

*"I DID NOT KNOW SHABBAZZ COULD DO ALL OF THAT!"* Cadina screams, over the noisy audience and into James' ear.

*"ALL I CAN SAY IS THAT THE BOY IS NICE!"* James screams back.

Cadina, James, and the rest of the enthralled audience marvel over DJ Shabbazz, who puts on a masterful exhibition of turntable wizardry. With high-flying hand speed, the ex-truck driver backspins his way into everyone's hearts with nostalgic underground tunes from the Treacherous Three, The Crash Crew, Super Lover Cee, and Casanova Rud before lowering the volume to yell into the mike:

"EVERYONE GET ON YOUR FEET AND MAKE SOME NOISE FOR YOUR BOY, POPPY LOU, AND HIS PARTNER-IN-RHYME, THE MIGHTY MANNY DEBEST! ALONG WITH

ME, SHABBAZZ DA GREAT, WE ARE COLLECTIVELY KNOWN AS, *L—S—MMMMMMM!!!!!!*

Shabbazz immediately drops his diamond needle on the instrumental version of EPMD's classic jam, *"You Gots to Chill"*.

Strutting out from opposite sides of the curtains, dipped in royal blue DEMOODAY jerseys, Lou and Emmanuel motion for the frenzied audience to put two fingers in the air for peace. The excited fans follow their lead, as camera flashes flicker from every angle of the room like fireflies in the night.

Lou, amped and hyper as ever, stares down the packed arena and paces from side to side. Then he raises his arm in the air and yells out in the microphone, "YOOOO! ALL I WANNA KNOW IS Y'ALL READY TO ROCK WITH LOU AND MANNY? WHASSUP?"

Cadina finds herself screaming, "YEAH!" along with the rest of the electrified audience.

"I THINK Y'ALL SHOULD KNOW THE WORDS TO THIS JOINT RIGHT HERE!" yells Emmanuel, with his arm raised to instruct the audience. "LET ME TEST Y'ALL'S MEMORY FOR A MINUTE: *'WHEN WE ROCK IT TO THE EAST SIDE—'"*

The audience response, "WHEN WE ROCK IT TO THE WEST,

AND WHEN WE ROCK WITH LOU,

YES, THE LYRICAL DUDE,

THEN WE ROCK IT WITH DEBEST!"

"AHHHH, YEAH! Lou screams into the mic. "THEY'RE LIVE WITH IT!"

"I KNOW THAT'S RIGHT!"

Shabbazz immediately switches to the *"Warm it Up, Kane!"* instrumental.

"LET'S KEEP IT FUNKY, THEN! *YO, WE CAME HERE TONIGHT—"*

The audience responds, "TO DOUBLE DA DOSE!"

*"MINUS DA STAGE FRIGHT, CUZ WE—"*

"DOUBLE DA DOSE!"

*"WE STAY FLY AND STAY FRESH, CUZ WE—"*

"DOUBLE DA DOSE!"

*"YOU ASK WHY? CUZ WE'RE BLESSED, HEY! WE—"*

"DOUBLE DA DOSE!"

James tugs Cadina to the front of the stage where the rest of the crew are pumping fists in the air.

James grabs their attention, and the ladies immediately bypass him to greet Cadina.

First, Lovelle, Marisol, and Najya bounce harmoniously with excitement over the sight of her engagement ring.

Then, Divine leans forward in her oversized DEMOODAY jersey to greet Cadina with a ridiculously toothy grin. They embrace and do a circle-dance with Divine shouting, *"I KNEW THIS DAY WAS COMING! THANK YOU, JESUS!"* all in Cadina's ringing ear.

"WHERE'S ROY AND NEVILLE?" yells Cadina.

Divine points to the stage. Cadina howls in laughter.

Standing on opposite sides of the turntables wearing DEMOODAY jerseys are Roy and Neville, in full b-boy mode as they nod their heads to the thunderous beat.

"CHECK THEM OUT; TRYING TO LOOK ALL HARD!" Divine shouts. "KNOWING DOGGONE WELL THEIR BEHINDS GOTTA BE BACK AT WORK MONDAY MORNING!"

Then last, but definitely not least, Freeman scoots over to Cadina.

They hug each other the longest.

The misery they shared from a common denominator earns them that right, and Cadina begins to cry tears of joy.

"WELCOME HOME, GIRL!" shouts Freeman.

"THANKS, FREE!"

They release the embrace and continue to root their people on.

Cadina is proud of them and everyone else that's present tonight. James gives her a quick kiss and then peels off his coat to get comfortable. She does the same thing.

Shabbazz mixes in the instrumental to their debut song, igniting the fans once again.

Cadina smiles and ponders.

This is how it's supposed to be.

Her new and improved life, with her man right beside her.

Now all her stars are aligned.

Universal completion.

Just like she prayed for.

Cadina begins shouting, right along with her affiliates.

Lou, Emmanuel, and Shabbazz simultaneously begin waving their arms from side to side and yell out:

"NOW WAVE YOUR HANDS IN THE AIR!
AND WAVE THEM LIKE YOU JUST DON'T CARE!
AND IF YOU CAME TONIGHT,
CUZ YOUR GAME IS TIGHT,
SOMEBODY SAY, OHHHH, YEAH!"

Audience: "OHHHH, YEAHHH!"

"AWWWW, YEAHHH! WE LIKE THAT!
NOW SOMEBODY…ANYBODY… *EVERYBODY*
SCREEEEAAAAAMMM!"

"AAAAAAAAAAAAAAAAAA!"

*FINI*

# ABOUT THE AUTHOR

**PETER McNEIL**, novelist and filmmaker, was born in Brooklyn, New York and now resides in Charlotte, North Carolina with his wife Pamela and three young adults, Justin, Jordan, and Milahn. His inspiration to narrate compelling stories derived from the socially conscious filmmaker Spike Lee and the legend of horror novels, Stephen King. He formed A Brighter Path Productions to self-publish his novels and finance his film projects. Navigating in the film and literary arena, he felt it was important to take ownership of his content while also conveying universal messages that will have a global impact.

"I take my craft seriously so I can give you the best work possible. I appreciate you taking the time out of your busy schedule to read anything I've created, so honest feedback will allow me to continue to grow as a writer. Stay blessed."

Pete McNeil

# NEW FROM PETER MCNEIL

"A husband, in denial of a porn addiction, must choose between conquering the "urge" within or risk losing his family and ultimately his life."

COMING SOON TO A STREAMING PLATFORM NEAR YOU

www.ingramcontent.com/pod-product-compliance
Lightning Source LLC
Chambersburg PA
CBHW020944310726
48980CB00001B/52

*9780985699079*